## Praise for the Novels of Daniel Silva

### The Confessor

"Accomplished . . . elegantly written . . . a compelling piece of fiction, one that manages to be both superior entertainment and a hard look at serious issues."
—*The Washington Post*

"A shrewd, timely thriller that opens the heart of the Vatican . . . many scenes of thumping action, passionate words, hot pursuit, and cold revenge. . . . It's a different kind of thrill than you might expect from a commercial thriller, but it certainly leaves a tingle." —*Chicago Tribune*

"[Silva] keeps *The Confessor*'s pages turning."
—*The Palm Beach Post*

"Provocative historical revelations will keep readers enthralled." —*Publishers Weekly*

"Silva, who here loads new excitement into the word *thriller*, will touch nerves with this hypothetical exploration of the Church's silence on these topics. The Vatican, Venice, and Munich are perfectly drawn as the settings for these dark acts of ambition, greed, and revenge, as are the characters, who you'd scarcely believe live only on the page." —*Library Journal*

"Another polished and entertaining thriller from the prolific Silva . . . powered by steady pacing, keen detail, and a strong, ironic finish." —*Kirkus Reviews*

## The English Assassin

"An exceptionally readable, sophisticated thriller . . . abundant action. . . . Silva ranks . . . among the best of the younger American spy novelists."
—*The Washington Post*

"[A] swift new spy novel. . . . Silva excitingly delivers his story's twists and turns."        —*The New York Times*

"Good assassin vs. bad assassin. . . . The plot is rich, multilayered, and compelling with issues as timely as the daily headlines and problems as old as humankind. . . . Silva maintains tension and suspense."—*The Denver Post*

"Enthralling . . . a thriller that entertains as well as enlightens."        —*The Orlando Sentinel*

"Breathtakingly orchestrated. Silva makes a stunning contribution to the spy thriller."
—*Booklist* (starred review)

"Thrilling . . . a good cinematic story."
—*St. Louis Post-Dispatch*

"Smooth and compelling."        —*Detroit Free Press*

## Also by Daniel Silva

# DANIEL SILVA

# THE KILL ARTIST

A SIGNET BOOK

SIGNET
Published by New American Library, a division of
Penguin Group (USA) Inc., 375 Hudson Street,
New York, New York 10014, USA
Penguin Group (Canada), 90 Eglinton Avenue East, Suite 700, Toronto,
Ontario, Canada M4P 2Y3 (a division of Pearson Penguin Canada Inc.)
Penguin Books Ltd., 80 Strand, London WC2R 0RL, England
Penguin Ireland, 25 St. Stephen's Green, Dublin 2,
Ireland (a division of Penguin Books Ltd.)
Penguin Group (Australia), 250 Camberwell Road, Camberwell, Victoria
3124, Australia (a division of Pearson Australia Group Pty. Ltd.)
Penguin Books India Pvt. Ltd., 11 Community Centre, Panchsheel Park,
New Delhi - 110 017, India
Penguin Group (NZ), 67 Apollo Drive, Rosedale, North Shore 0632,
New Zealand (a division of Pearson New Zealand Ltd.)
Penguin Books (South Africa) (Pty.) Ltd., 24 Sturdee Avenue,
Rosebank, Johannesburg 2196, South Africa

Penguin Books Ltd., Registered Offices:
80 Strand, London WC2R 0RL, England

Published by Signet, an imprint of New American Library, a division of Penguin
Group (USA) Inc. Published by arrangement with the Ballantine Publishing
Group, a division of Random House, Inc.

First Signet Printing, April 2004
30 29 28 27 26 25 24

*For Jamie, who made this
one possible, and everything else,
for that matter*

*The Lord spoke to Moses, saying, "Send men that they may spy out the land of Canaan, which I give to the children of Israel; of every tribe of their fathers shall you send a man, every one a prince among them."*

—Numbers 13:1–2

*By way of deception, thou shalt do war.*

—Motto of the Mossad

*The Kill Artist* is a work of fiction and should be construed as nothing but. All characters, locales, and incidents portrayed in the novel are products of the author's imagination or have been used fictitiously. Any resemblance to any person, living or dead, is entirely coincidental. However, in order to add verisimilitude to the story and the characters, I have drawn from real episodes in the secret war between Israeli intelligence and the Palestinian guerrillas. For example, the 1988 assassination of PLO commando leader Abu Jihad happened much as it is portrayed, with minor modifications. Francesco Vecellio is a real Italian old master painter—indeed, he was the lesser-known brother of Titian—but *The Adoration of the Shepherds* portrayed in the novel is fictitious. Sadly, the London art gallery portrayed in *The Kill Artist* does not exist and neither does its owner.

# PROLOGUE

The restorer raised his magnifying visor and switched off the bank of fluorescent lights. He waited for his eyes to adjust to the murkiness of evening in the cathedral; then he inspected a tiny portion of the painting just below an arrow wound on the leg of Saint Stephen. Over the centuries the paint had worn completely down to the canvas. The restorer had so carefully repaired the damage that without the use of specialized equipment it was now quite impossible to tell his work from the original, which meant he had done his job very well indeed.

The restorer crouched on the work platform, wiped his brushes and palette, and packed away his paints into a flat rectangular case of polished wood. Nightfall had blackened the soaring stained-glass windows of the cathedral; a blanket of new snow had muffled the usual hum of the Vienna evening rush. So quiet was the Stephansdom that the restorer would scarcely have been surprised to see a medieval sexton scurrying across the nave by torchlight.

He climbed off the high scaffolding with the agility

of a house cat and dropped silently onto the stone floor of the chapel. A knot of tourists had been watching him work for several minutes. As a rule the restorer did not like spectators—indeed, some days he shrouded the platform in a gray tarpaulin. Tonight's crowd dispersed as he pulled on a reefer coat and woolen watch cap. Softly, he bid them *buona sera,* instinctively recording each face in his mind, as permanently as if they were rendered with oil on canvas.

An attractive German girl tried to engage him in conversation. She spoke to him in poor Italian. In rapid, Berlin-accented German—his mother had lived in Charlottenburg before the war—the restorer said he was late for an appointment and could not talk now. German girls made him uneasy. Reflexively his eyes wandered over her—across her large, rounded breasts, up and down her long legs. She mistook his attention for flirting, tilted her head, smiled at him through a lock of flaxen hair, suggested a coffee in the café across the square. The restorer apologized and said he had to leave. "Besides," he said, looking up at the soaring nave, "this is Stephansdom, Fräulein. Not a pickup bar."

A moment later he passed through the entrance of the cathedral and struck out across the Stephansplatz. He was of medium height, well below six feet. His black hair was shot with gray at the temples. His nose was rather long and angular, with sharp edges across the bridge that left the suggestion it had been carved from wood. Full lips, cleft chin, cheekbones broad and square. There was a hint

of the Russian steppes in his eyes—almond shaped, unnaturally green, very quick. His vision was perfect, despite
the demanding nature of his work. He had a confident
walk, not an arrogant swagger or a march but a crisp,
purposeful stride that seemed to propel him effortlessly
across the snowbound square. The box containing his
paints and brushes was under his left arm, resting on the
metal object that he wore, habitually, on his left hip.

He walked along the Rotenturmstrasse, a broad pe-
destrian mall lined with bright shops and cafés, pausing
before shop windows, peering at sparkling Mont Blanc
pens and Rolex watches, even though he had no need
for such things. He stopped at a snow-covered sausage
stand, purchased a *käsewurst*, dropped it into a rubbish
bin a hundred yards away without taking a bite. He entered a telephone booth, slipped a schilling into the coin
slot, punched a random series of numbers on the keypad,
all the while scanning the street and storefronts around
him. A recorded voice informed him that he had made a
dreadful mistake. The restorer replaced the receiver, collected his schilling from the coin tray, kept walking.

His destination was a small Italian restaurant in the
Jewish Quarter. Before the Nazis there had been nearly
two hundred thousand Jews living in Vienna, and Jews
had dominated the city's cultural and commercial life.
Now there were just a few thousand, mainly from the
East, and the so-called Jewish Quarter was a strip of
clothing stores, restaurants, and nightclubs clustered
around the Judenplatz. Among Viennese the district

was known as the Bermuda Triangle, which the restorer found vaguely offensive.

The restorer's wife and son were waiting for him— rear table, facing the door, just as he had taught her. The boy sat next to his mother, sucking strands of buttered spaghetti through rose-colored lips. He watched her for a moment, appraising her beauty the way he might assess a work of art: the technique, the structure, the composition. She had pale olive-toned skin, oval brown eyes, and long black hair, which was drawn back and lying across the front of one shoulder.

He entered the restaurant. He kissed his son on the top of the head, chatted in Italian with the man behind the bar, sat down. His wife poured wine for him.

"Not too much. I have to work tonight."

"The cathedral?"

He pulled down his lips, cocked his head slightly. "Are you packed?" he asked.

She nodded, then looked at the television above the bar. Air-raid sirens over Tel Aviv, another Iraqi Scud missile streaking toward Israel. The citizens of Tel Aviv putting on gas masks and taking shelter. The shot changed: a tongue of fire, falling from the black sky toward the city. The restorer's wife reached across the table and touched his hand.

"I want to go home."

"Soon," the restorer said and poured himself more wine.

*       *       *

She had left the car on the street just outside the restaurant, a dark blue Mercedes sedan, Vienna registration, leased by a small chemical company in Bern. He placed the boy in the backseat, buckled his safety belt, kissed his wife.

"If I'm not there by six o'clock, something has gone wrong. You remember what to do?"

"Go to the airport, give them the password and the clearance number, and they'll take care of us."

"Six o'clock," he repeated. "If I don't walk through the door by six o'clock, go straight to the airport. Leave the car in the parking lot and throw away the keys. Do you understand me?"

She nodded. "Just be home by six."

The restorer closed the door, gave a terse wave through the glass, and started to walk away. In front of him, floating over the rooftops of the old city, was the spire of the cathedral, ablaze with light. One more night, he thought. Then home for a few weeks until the next job.

Behind him he heard the starter of the Mercedes engage, then hesitate, like a record album being played at the wrong speed. The restorer stopped walking and spun around.

"No!" he screamed, but she turned the key again.

# PART ONE

# ACQUISITION

# 1

By coincidence Timothy Peel arrived in the village the same week in July as the stranger. He and his mother moved into a ramshackle cottage at the head of the tidal creek with her latest lover, a struggling playwright named Derek, who drank too much wine and detested children. The stranger arrived two days later, settling into the old foreman's cottage just up the creek from the oyster farm.

Peel had little to do that summer—when Derek and his mother weren't making clamorous love, they were taking inspirational forced marches along the cliffs—so he determined to find out exactly who the stranger was and what he was doing in Cornwall. Peel decided the best way to begin was to watch. Because he was eleven, and the only child of divorced parents, Peel was well schooled in the art of human observation and investigation. Like any good surveillance artist, he required a fixed post. He settled on his bedroom window, which had an un-obstructed view over the creek. In the storage shed he found a pair of ancient Zeiss binoculars, and at the village store he purchased a small notebook and ballpoint pen for recording his watch report.

The first thing Peel noticed was that the stranger liked old objects. His car was a vintage MG roadster. Peel would watch from his window as the man hunched over the motor for hours at a time, his back poking from beneath the bonnet. A man of great concentration, Peel concluded. A man of great mental endurance.

After a month the stranger vanished. A few days passed, then a week, then a fortnight. Peel feared the stranger had spotted him and taken flight. Bored senseless without the routine of watching, Peel got into trouble. He was caught hurling a rock through the window of a tea shop in the village. Derek sentenced him to a week of solitary confinement in his bedroom.

But that evening Peel managed to slip out with his binoculars. He walked along the quay, past the stranger's darkened cottage and the oyster farm, and stood at the point where the creek fed into the Helford River, watching the sailboats coming in with the tide. He spotted a ketch heading in under power. He raised the binoculars to his eyes and studied the figure standing at the wheel.

The stranger had come back to Port Navas.

The ketch was old and badly in need of restoration, and the stranger cared for it with the same devotion he had shown his fickle MG. He toiled for several hours each day: sanding, varnishing, painting, polishing brass, changing lines and canvas. When the weather was warm he would strip to the waist. Peel couldn't help but compare the stranger's body with Derek's. Derek was soft and flabby; the stranger was compact and very hard, the kind of man you would quickly regret picking a fight with. By the end of August his skin had turned nearly as dark as the varnish he was so meticulously applying to the deck of the ketch.

He would disappear aboard the boat for days at a time. Peel had no way to follow him. He could only imagine where the stranger was going. Down the Helford to the sea? Around the Lizard to St. Michael's Mount or Penzance? Maybe around the cape to St. Ives.

Then Peel hit upon another possibility. Cornwall was famous for its pirates; indeed, the region still had its fair share of smugglers. Perhaps the stranger was running the ketch out to sea to meet cargo vessels and ferry contraband to shore.

The next time the stranger returned from one of his voyages, Peel stood a strict watch in his window, hoping to catch him in the act of removing contraband from the boat. But as he leaped from the prow of the ketch onto the quay, he had nothing in his hands but a canvas rucksack and plastic rubbish bag.

The stranger sailed for pleasure, not profit.

Peel took out his notebook and drew a line through the word *smuggler*.

The large parcel arrived the first week of September, a flat wooden crate, nearly as big as a barn door. It came in a van from London, accompanied by an agitated man in pinstripes. The stranger's days immediately assumed a reverse rhythm. At night the top floor of the cottage burned with light—not normal light, Peel observed, but a very clear white light. In the mornings, when Peel left home for school, he would see the stranger heading down the creek in the ketch, or working on his MG, or setting off in a pair of battered hiking boots to pound the footpaths of the Helford Passage. Peel supposed he slept afternoons, though he seemed like a man who could go a long time without rest.

Peel wondered what the stranger was doing all night. Late one evening he decided to have a closer look. He pulled on a sweater and coat and slipped out of the cottage without telling his mother. He stood on the quay, looking up at the stranger's cottage. The windows were open; a sharp odor hung on the air, something between rubbing alcohol and petrol. He could also hear music of some sort—singing, opera perhaps.

He was about to move closer to the house when he felt a heavy hand on his shoulder. He spun around and saw Derek standing over him, hands on his hips, eyes wide with anger. "What in the bloody hell are you doing out here?" Derek said. "Your mother was worried sick!"

"If she was so worried, why did she send you?"

"Answer my question, boy! Why are you standing out here?"

"None of your business!"

In the darkness Peel did not see the blow coming:

open-handed, against the side of his head, hard enough to make his ear ring and bring water instantly to his eyes.

"You're not my father! You've no right!"

"And you're not my son, but as long as you live in my house you'll do as I say."

Peel tried to run, but Derek grabbed him roughly by the collar of his coat and lifted him off the ground.

"Let go!"

"One way or another you're coming home."

Derek took a few steps, then froze. Peel twisted his head around to see what was the matter. It was then that he saw the stranger, standing in the center of the lane, arms crossed in front of his chest, head cocked slightly to one side.

"What do you want?" snapped Derek.

"I heard noises. I thought there might be a problem."

Peel realized this was the first time he had ever heard the stranger speak. His English was perfect, but there was a trace of an accent to it. His diction was like his body: hard, compact, concise, no fat.

"No problem," Derek said. "Just a boy who's someplace he shouldn't be."

"Maybe you should treat him like a boy and not a dog."

"And maybe you should mind your own fucking business."

Derek released Peel and stared hard at the smaller man. For a moment Peel feared Derek was going to try to hit the stranger. He remembered the man's taut, hard muscles, the impression that he was a man who knew how to fight. Derek seemed to sense it too, for he simply took Peel by the elbow and led him back toward the cottage. Along the way Peel glanced over his shoulder and caught sight of the stranger still standing in the lane, arms crossed like a silent sentinel. But by the time Peel returned to his room and peered out his window, the stranger was gone. Only the light remained, clean and searing white.

By the late autumn Peel was frustrated. He had not learned even the most basic facts about the stranger. He still had no name—oh, he had heard a couple of possible names whispered around the village, both vaguely Latin—nor had he discovered the nature of his nocturnal work. He decided a crash operation was in order.

The following morning, when the stranger climbed into his MG and sped toward the center of the village, Peel hurried along the quay and slipped into the cottage through an open garden window.

The first thing he noticed was that the stranger was using the drawing room as a bedroom.

He quickly climbed the stairs. A chill ran over him.

Most of the walls had been knocked down to create a spacious open room. In the center was a large white table. Mounted on the side was a microscope with a long retractable arm. On another table were clear flasks of chemicals, which Peel reckoned were the source of the strange odor, and two strange visors with powerful magnifying glasses built into them. Atop a tall, adjustable stand was a bank of fluorescent lights, the source of the cottage's peculiar glow.

There were other instruments Peel could not identify, but these things were not the source of his alarm. Mounted on a pair of heavy wooden easels were two paintings. One was large, very old-looking, a religious scene of some sort. Parts had flaked away. On the second easel was a painting of an old man, a young woman, and a child. Peel examined the signature in the bottom right-hand corner: *Rembrandt*.

He turned to leave and found himself face-to-face with the stranger.

"What are you doing?"

"I'm s-s-sorry," Peel stammered. "I thought you were here."

"No you didn't. You knew I was away, because you were watching me from your bedroom window when I left. In fact, you've been watching me since the summer."

"I thought you might be a smuggler."

"Whatever gave you that idea?"

"The boat," Peel lied.

The stranger smiled briefly. "Now you know the truth."

"Not really," said Peel.

"I'm an art restorer. Paintings are old objects. Sometimes they need a little fixing up, like a cottage, for example."

"Or a boat," said Peel.

"Exactly. Some paintings, like these, are very valuable."

"More than a sailboat?"

"Much more. But now that you know what's in here, we have a problem."

"I won't tell anyone," Peel pleaded. "Honest."

The stranger ran a hand over his short, brittle hair. "I could use a helper," he said softly. "Someone to keep an eye on the place while I'm away. Would you like a job like that?"

"Yes."

"I'm going sailing. Would you like to join me?"

"Yes."

"Do you need to ask your parents?"

"He's not my father, and my mum won't care."

"You sure about that?"

"Positive."

"What's your name?"

"I'm Peel. What's yours?"

But the stranger just looked around the room to make certain Peel hadn't disturbed any of his things.

# 2

PARIS

The stranger's restless Cornish quarantine might have gone undisturbed if Emily Parker had not met a man called René at a drunken dinner party, which was thrown by a Jordanian student named Leila Khalifa on a wet night in late October. Like the stranger, Emily Parker was living in self-imposed exile: she had moved to Paris after graduation in the hope that it would help mend a broken heart. She possessed none of his physical attributes. Her gait was loose-limbed and chaotic. Her legs were too long, her hips too wide, her breasts too heavy, so that when she moved, each part of her anatomy seemed in conflict with the rest. Her wardrobe varied little: faded jeans, fashionably ripped at the knees, a quilted jacket that made her look rather like a large throw pillow. And then there was the face—the face of a Polish peasant, her mother had always said: rounded cheeks, a thick mouth, a heavy jaw, dull brown eyes set too closely together. "I'm afraid you have your father's face," her mother had said. "Your father's face and your father's fragile heart."

Emily met Leila in mid-October at the Musée de

Montmartre. She was a student at the Sorbonne, a stunningly attractive woman with lustrous black hair and wide brown eyes. She had been raised in Amman, Rome, and London, and spoke a half-dozen languages fluently. She was everything that Emily was not: beautiful, confident, cosmopolitan. Gradually, Emily unburdened all her secrets to Leila: the way her mother had made her feel so terribly ugly; the pain she felt over being abandoned by her fiancé; her deep-rooted fear that no one would ever love her again. Leila promised to fix everything. Leila promised to introduce Emily to a man who would make her forget all about the boy she had foolishly fallen for in college.

It happened at Leila's dinner party. She had invited twenty guests to her cramped little flat in Montparnasse. They ate wherever they could find space: on the couch, on the floor, on the bed. All very Parisian bohemian: roast chicken from the corner rotisserie, a heaping *salade verte,* cheese, and entirely too much inexpensive Bordeaux. There were other students from the Sorbonne: an artist, a young German essayist of note, the son of an Italian count, a pretty Englishman with flowing blond hair called Lord Reggie, and a jazz musician who played the guitar like Al DiMeola. The room sounded like the Tower of Babel. The conversation moved from French to English, then from English to Italian, then from Italian to Spanish. Emily watched Leila moving about the flat, kissing cheeks, lighting cigarettes. She marveled at the ease with which Leila made friends and brought them together.

"He's here, you know, Emily—the man you're going to fall in love with."

*René*. René from the south somewhere, a village Emily had never heard of, somewhere in the hills above Nice. René who had a bit of family money and had never had the time, or the inclination, to work. René who traveled. René who read many books. René who disdained politics—*"Politics is an exercise for the feebleminded, Emily. Politics has nothing to do with real life."* René who had a face you might pass in a crowd and never notice, but if you looked carefully was rather good-looking. René whose eyes were lit by some secret source of heat that Emily could not fathom. René who took her to bed the night of Leila's dinner party and made her feel things she had never thought possible. René who said he wanted to remain in Paris for a few weeks—*"Would it be possible for me to crash at your place, Emily? Leila has no room for me. You know Leila. Too many clothes, too many things. Too many men."* René who had made her happy again. René who was eventually going to break the heart he had healed.

He was already slipping away; she could feel him growing slightly more distant every day. He was spending more time on his own, disappearing for several hours each day, reappearing with no warning. When she asked him where he had been, his answers were vague. She feared he was seeing another woman. A skinny French girl, she imagined. A girl who didn't have to be taught how to make love.

That afternoon Emily wound her way through the narrow streets of Montmartre to the rue Norvins. She stood beneath the crimson awning of a bistro and peered through the window. René was seated at a table near the door. Funny how he always insisted on sitting near the doorway. There was a man with him: dark hair, a few years younger. When Emily entered the bistro, the man stood and quickly walked out. Emily removed her coat and sat down. René poured wine for her.

She asked, "Who was that man?"

"Just someone I used to know."

"What's his name?"

"Jean," he said. "Would you like—"

"Your friend left his backpack."

"It's mine," René said, putting a hand on it.

"Really? I've never seen you carry it before."

"Trust me, Emily. It's mine. Are you hungry?"

*And you're changing the subject again.* She said, "I'm famished, actually. I've been walking around in the cold all afternoon."

"Have you really? Whatever for?"

"Just doing some thinking. Nothing serious."

He removed the backpack from the chair and placed it on the floor at his feet. "What have you been thinking about?"

"Really, René—it was nothing important."

"You used to tell me all your secrets."

"Yes, but you've never really told me yours."

"Are you still upset about this bag?"

"I'm not upset about it. Just curious, that's all."

"All right, if you must know, it's a surprise."

"For who?"

"For you!" He smiled. "I was going to give it to you later."

"You bought me a backpack? How very thoughtful, René. How romantic."

"The surprise is inside the backpack."

"I don't like surprises."

"Why not?"

"Because it's been my experience that the surprise itself never quite lives up to the anticipation of the surprise. I've been let down too many times. I don't want to be let down again."

"Emily, I'll never let you down. I love you too much."

"Oh, René, I wish you hadn't said that."

"It happens to be the truth. Let's eat something, shall we? Then we'll take a walk."

Ambassador Zev Eliyahu stood in the grand center hall of the Musée d'Orsay, using every diplomatic skill he possessed to hide the fact that he was bored to tears. Trim, athletic, deeply tanned in spite of the dreary Parisian fall, he crackled with a brash energy. Gatherings like this annoyed him. Eliyahu had nothing against art; he simply didn't have time for it. He still had the work ethic of a *kibbutznik,* and between ambassadorial postings he had made millions in investment banking.

He had been talked into attending the reception to-night for one reason: it would give him an opportunity to have an *unofficial* moment or two with the French foreign minister. Relations between France and Israel were icy at the moment. The French were angry because a pair of Israeli intelligence officers had been caught trying to recruit an official from the Defense Ministry. The Israelis were angry because the French had recently agreed to sell jet fighters and nuclear reactor technology to one of Israel's Arab enemies. But when Eliyahu approached the French foreign minister for a word, the minister virtually ignored him, then pointedly engaged the Egyptian ambassador in a lively conversation about the Middle East peace process.

Eliyahu was angry—angry and bored silly. He was leaving for Israel the following night. Ostensibly, it was for a meeting at the Foreign Ministry, but he also planned to spend a few days in Eilat on the Red Sea. He was looking forward to the trip. He missed Israel, the cacophony of it, the hustle, the scent of pine and dust on the road to Jerusalem, the winter rains over the Galilee.

A waiter in a white tunic offered him champagne. Eli-yahu shook his head. "Bring me some coffee, please." He looked over the heads of the shimmering crowd for his wife, Hannah, and spotted her standing next to the chargé d'affaires from the embassy, Moshe Savir. Savir was a professional diplomat: supercilious, arrogant, the perfect temperament for the posting in Paris.

The waiter returned, bearing a silver tray with a single cup of black coffee on it.

"Never mind," Eliyahu said, and he sliced his way through the crowd.

Savir asked, "How did it go with the foreign minister?"

"He turned his back on me."

"Bastard."

The ambassador reached out his hand for his wife. "Let's go. I've had enough of this nonsense."

"Don't forget tomorrow morning," Savir said. "Breakfast with the editorial staff of *Le Monde* at eight o'clock."

"I'd rather have a tooth pulled."

"It's important, Zev."

"Don't worry. I'll be my usual charming self."

Savir shook his head. "See you then."

The Pont Alexandre III was Emily's favorite spot in Paris. She loved to stand in the center of the graceful span at night and gaze down the Seine toward Notre-Dame, with the gilded Église du Dôme to her right, floating above Les Invalides, and the Grand Palais on her left.

René took Emily to the bridge after dinner for her surprise. They walked along the parapet, past the ornate lamps and the cherubs and nymphs, until they reached the center of the span. René removed a small rectangular, gift-wrapped box from the backpack and handed it to her.

"For me?"

"Of course it's for you!"

Emily tore away the wrapping paper like a child and opened the leather case. Inside was a bracelet of pearls, diamonds, and emeralds. It must have cost him a small fortune. "René, my God! It's gorgeous!"

"Let me help you put it on."

She put out her arm and pulled up the sleeve of her coat. René slipped the bracelet around her wrist and closed the clasp. Emily held it up in the lamplight. Then she turned around, leaned her back against his chest, and gazed at the river. "I want to die just like this."

But René was no longer listening. His face was expressionless, brown eyes fixed on the Musée d'Orsay.

The waiter with the platter of tandoori chicken had been assigned to watch the ambassador. He removed the cellular phone from the pocket of his tunic and pressed a button that dialed a stored number. Two rings, a man's voice, the drone of Parisian traffic in the background. *"Oui."*

"He's leaving."

*Click.*

Ambassador Eliyahu took Hannah by the hand and led her through the crowd, pausing occasionally to bid good night to one of the other guests. At the entrance of the museum, a pair of bodyguards joined them. They looked like mere boys, but Eliyahu took comfort in the fact that they were trained killers who would do anything to protect his life.

They stepped into the cold night air. The limousine was waiting, engine running. One bodyguard sat in front with the driver; the second joined the ambassador and his wife in back. The car pulled away, turned onto the rue de Bellechasse, then sped along the bank of the Seine.

Eliyahu leaned back and closed his eyes. "Wake me when we get home, Hannah."

"Who was that, René?"

"No one. Wrong number."

Emily closed her eyes again, but a moment later came another sound: two cars colliding on the bridge. A minivan had smashed into the rear end of a Peugeot sedan, the asphalt littered with shattered glass, traffic at a standstill. The drivers jumped out and began screaming at each other in rapid French. Emily could tell they weren't French—Arabs, North Africans perhaps. René snatched up his backpack and walked into the roadway, picking his way through the motionless cars.

"René! What are you doing?"

But he acted as though he hadn't heard her. He kept walking, not toward the wrecked cars but toward a long black limousine caught in the traffic jam. Along the way he unzipped the bag and pulled something out of it: a small submachine gun.

Emily couldn't believe what she was seeing. René, her lover, the man who had slipped into her life and stolen her heart, walking across the Pont Alexandre III with a machine gun in his hand. Then the pieces began falling into place. The nagging suspicion that René was keeping something from her. The long, unexplained absences. The dark-haired stranger at the bistro that afternoon. *Leila?*

The rest of it she saw as slow-moving half images, as though it were taking place beneath murky water. René running across the bridge. René tossing his backpack beneath the limousine. A flash of blinding light, a gust of fiercely hot air. Gunfire, screams. Someone on a motorbike. Black ski mask, two pools of black staring coldly through the eyeholes, damp lips glistening behind the slit for the mouth. A gloved hand nervously revving the throttle. But it was the eyes that captured Emily's attention. They were the most beautiful eyes she had ever seen.

Finally, in the distance, she could hear the two-note song of a Paris police siren. She looked away from the motorcyclist and saw René advancing slowly toward her through the carnage. He expelled the spent magazine from his weapon, casually inserted another, pulled the slide.

Emily backpedaled until she was pressed against the parapet. She turned and looked down at the black river gliding slowly beneath her.

"You're a monster!" she screamed in English, because in her panic her French had abandoned her. "You're a fucking monster! Who the fuck are you?"

"Don't try to get away from me," he said in the same language. "It will only make things worse."

Then he raised his gun and fired several shots into her heart. The force of the bullets drove her over the edge of the parapet. She felt herself falling toward the river. Her hands reached out, and she saw the bracelet on her wrist. The bracelet René, her lover, had given her just moments before. Such a beautiful bracelet. Such a terrible shame.

She collided with the river and slipped below the surface. She opened her mouth, and her lungs filled with frigid water. She could taste her own blood. She saw a flash of brilliant white, heard her mother calling her name. Then there was only darkness. A vast, silent darkness. And the cold.

# 3

## TIBERIAS, ISRAEL

Despite the events in Paris, the stranger might have managed to remain in seclusion but for the resurrection of the legendary spymaster Ari Shamron. It was not necessary to awaken Shamron that night, for he had long ago lost the gift of sleep. Indeed, he was so restless at night that Rami, the young head of his personal security detail, had christened him the Phantom of Tiberias. At first Shamron suspected it was age. He had turned sixty-five recently and for the first time had contemplated the possibility that someday he might actually die. During a grudging annual physical his doctor had had the audacity to suggest—"And this is just a suggestion, Ari, because God knows I'd never try to actually give you an order"—that Shamron reduce his daily intake of caffeine and tobacco: twelve cups of black coffee and sixty strong Turkish cigarettes. Shamron had found these suggestions mildly amusing.

It was only during an uncharacteristic period of introspection, brought on by his forced retirement from the service, that Shamron had settled on the causes of his chronic sleeplessness. He had told so many lies, spun so many deceptions, that sometimes he could no longer tell fact from fiction, truth from untruth. And then there was the killing. He had killed with his own hands, and he had ordered other men, younger men, to kill for him. A life of betrayal and violence had taken its toll. Some men go crazy, some burn out. Ari Shamron had been sentenced to remain forever awake.

Shamron had made an uneasy peace with his affliction, the way some people accommodate madness or terminal disease. He had become a night wanderer, roaming his sandstone-colored villa overlooking the Sea of Galilee, sitting on the terrace when the nights were fine and soft, staring at the lake and the moonlit expanse of the Upper Galilee. Sometimes he would slip down to his studio and engage in his great passion, repairing old radios—the only activity that completely released his mind from thoughts of work.

And sometimes he would wander down to the security gate and pass a few hours sitting in the shack with Rami and the other boys, telling stories over coffee and cigarettes. Rami liked the story of Eichmann's capture the best. Each time a new boy joined the detail, Rami urged Shamron to tell it again, so the new boy would understand that he had been given a great privilege: the privilege of protecting Shamron, the Sabra superman, Israel's avenging angel.

Rami had made him tell the story again that night. As usual it had dredged up many memories, some of them not so pleasant. Shamron had no old radios in which to lose himself, and it was too cold and rainy to sit outside, so he lay in bed, wide-eyed, sorting through new operations, remembering old ones, dissecting opponents for frailty, plotting their destruction. So when the special telephone on his bedside table emitted two sharp rings, Shamron reached out with the relieved air of an old man grateful for company and slowly pulled the receiver to his ear.

Rami stepped outside the guardhouse and watched the old man pounding down the drive. He was bald and thick, with steel-rimmed spectacles. His face was dry and deeply creviced—like the Negev, thought Rami. As usual he wore khaki trousers and an ancient leather bomber jacket with a tear on the right breast, just below the armpit. Within the service there were two theories about the tear. Some believed the jacket had been pierced by a bullet during a reprisal raid into Jordan in the fifties. Others argued that it had been torn by the dying fingers of a terrorist whom Shamron garroted in a Cairo back alley. Shamron always insisted gruffly that the truth was much more prosaic—the jacket had been torn on the corner of a car door—but no one within the service took him seriously.

He walked as if he were anticipating an assault from behind, elbows out, head down. The Shamron shuffle, the walk that said, "Get the fuck out of my way or I'll have your balls for breakfast." Rami felt his pulse quicken at the sight of the old man. If Shamron told him to jump off a cliff, he'd jump. If the old man told him to stop in midair, he'd figure out some way to do it.

As Shamron drew closer, Rami caught sight of his face. The lines around his mouth were a little deeper. He was angry—Rami could see it in his eyes—but there seemed to be a hint of a smile across his arid lips. *What the hell is he smiling about?* Chiefs aren't disturbed after midnight unless it's urgent or very bad news. Then Rami hit upon the reason: the Phantom of Tiberias simply was relieved he had been spared another sleepless night with no enemies to fight.

Forty-five minutes later Shamron's armored Peugeot slipped into the underground garage of a cheerless office block looming over King Saul Boulevard in northern Tel Aviv. He stepped into a private elevator and rode up to his office suite on the top floor. Queen Esther, his long-suffering senior secretary, had left a fresh packet of cigarettes on the desk next to a thermos bottle of coffee. Shamron immediately lit a cigarette and sat down.

His first action after returning to the service had been to remove the pompous Scandinavian furnishings of his predecessor and donate them to a charity for Russian émigrés. Now the office looked like the battlefield headquarters of a fighting general. It stressed mobility and function over style and grace. For his desk Shamron used a large, scarred library table. Along the wall opposite the window was a row of gunmetal file cabinets. On the shelf behind his desk was a thirty-year-old German-made short-wave radio. Shamron had no need for the daily summaries of the Office radio-monitoring department, because he spoke a half-dozen languages fluently and understood a half-dozen more. He could also repair the radio himself when it broke down. In fact, he could fix almost anything electronic. Once his senior staff had arrived for a weekly planning meeting to find Shamron peering into the entrails of Queen Esther's videocassette player.

The only hint of modernity in the office was the row of large television sets opposite his desk. Using his remote controls, he switched them on one by one. He had lost the hearing in one ear, so he turned up the volume quite loud, until it sounded as if three men—a Frenchman, an Englishman, and an American—were having a violent row in his office.

Outside, in the chamber between Esther's office and his own, Shamron's senior staff had gathered like anxious acolytes awaiting an audience with their master. There was the whippetlike Eli from Planning and the Talmudic Mordecai, the service's executive officer. There was Yossi, the genius from the Europe Desk who had read the Greats at Oxford, and Lev, the highly flammable chief of Operations, who filled his precious empty hours by collecting predatory insects. Only Lev seemed to have no physical fear of Shamron. Every few minutes he would thrust his angular head through the doorway and shout, "For God's sake, Ari! When? Sometime tonight, I hope!"

But Shamron was in no particular hurry to see them,

for he was quite certain he knew more about the terrible events that evening in Paris than they ever would.

For one hour Shamron sat in his chair, stone-faced, smoking one cigarette after another, watching CNN International on one television, the BBC on another, French state television on the third. He didn't particularly care what the correspondents had to say—they knew next to nothing at this point, and Shamron knew he could put words in their mouths with one five-minute phone call. He wanted to hear from the witnesses, the people who had seen the assassination with their own eyes. They would tell him what he wanted to know.

A German girl, interviewed on CNN, described the auto accident that preceded the assault: "There were two vehicles, a van of some sort, and a sedan. Maybe it was a Peugeot, but I can't be sure. Traffic on the bridge came to a standstill in a matter of seconds."

Shamron used his remote to mute CNN and turn up the volume on the BBC. A taxi driver from the Ivory Coast described the killer: dark hair, well dressed, good-looking, cool. The killer had been with a girl on the bridge when the accident occurred: "A blond girl, a little heavy, a foreigner, definitely not French." But the taxi driver saw nothing else, because he took cover beneath the dashboard when the bomb went off and didn't look up again until the shooting stopped.

Shamron removed a scuffed leather-bound notebook from his shirt pocket, laid it carefully on the desk, and opened it to a blank page. In his small precise hand he wrote a single word.

*GIRL.*

Shamron's gaze returned to the television. An attractive young Englishwoman called Beatrice was recounting the attack for a BBC correspondent. She described a traffic accident involving a van and a car that brought traffic on the bridge to a standstill, trapping the ambassador's car. She described how the killer walked away from his girlfriend and drew a weapon from his bag. How he then tossed the bag beneath the undercarriage of the limousine and waited for it to detonate before calmly walking forward and killing everyone inside.

Then Beatrice described how the killer walked slowly toward the girl—the girl who seconds before he had been passionately kissing—and fired several bullets into her chest.

Shamron licked the tip of his pencil and below the word *GIRL* he wrote a name:

*TARIQ.*

Shamron picked up his secure telephone and dialed Uzi Navot, the head of his Paris station. "They had someone inside that reception. Someone who alerted the team outside that the ambassador was leaving. They knew his route. They staged an accident to tie up traffic and leave the driver with no way to escape."

Navot agreed. Navot made it a habit to agree with Shamron.

"There's a great deal of very valuable artwork inside that building," Shamron continued. "I would suspect there's a rather sophisticated video surveillance system, wouldn't you, Uzi?"

"Of course, boss."

"Tell our friends in the French service that we'd like to dispatch a team to Paris immediately to monitor the investigation and provide any support they require. And then get your hands on those videotapes and send them to me in the pouch."

"Done."

"What about the bridge? Are there police surveillance cameras covering that bridge? With any luck we may have a recording of the entire attack—and their preparation."

"I'll look into it."

"Anything left of the limousine?"

"Not much. The fuel tank exploded, and the fire consumed just about everything, including the bodies, I'm afraid."

"How did he get away?"

"He hopped on the back of a motorcycle. Gone in a matter of seconds."

"Any sign of him?"

"Nothing, boss."

"Any leads?"

"If there are any, the Paris police aren't sharing them with me."

"What about the other members of the team?"

"Gone too. They were good, boss. Damned good."

"Who's the dead girl?"

"An American."

Shamron closed his eyes and swore softly. The last thing he needed now was the involvement of the Americans. "Have the Americans been told yet?"

"Half the embassy staff is on the bridge now."

"Does this girl have a name?"

"Emily Parker."

"What was she doing in Paris?"

"Apparently she was taking a few months off after graduation."

"How wonderful. Where was she living?"

"Montmartre. A team of French detectives is working the neighborhood: poking around, asking questions, trying to pick up anything they can."

"Have they learned anything interesting?"

"I haven't heard anything else, boss."

"Go to Montmartre in the morning. Have a look around for yourself. Ask a few questions. Quietly, Uzi. Maybe someone in her building or in a local café got a look at lover boy."

"Good idea, boss."

"And do me one other favor. Take the file photographs of Tariq with you."

"You think he was behind this?"

"I prefer to keep my options open at this point."

"Even if they got a look at him, those old photographs won't be any help. He's changed his appearance a hundred times since then."

"Humor me." Shamron jabbed at the winking green light on the telephone and killed the connection.

It was still dark as Shamron's Peugeot limousine sped across the coastal plain and rose into the Judean Mountains toward Jerusalem. Shamron removed his spectacles and rubbed the raw red skin beneath his eyes. It had been six months since he had been pulled from retirement and given a simple mission: bring stability to an intelligence service badly damaged by a series of highly publicized operational blunders and personnel scandals. His job was to rebuild morale. Restore the esprit de corps that had characterized the Office in the old days.

He had managed to stem the bleeding—there had been no more humiliations, like the bungled attempt to assassinate a violent Moslem cleric in Amman that had been orchestrated by his predecessor—but there had been no stunning successes either. Shamron knew better than anyone that the Office had not earned its fearsome reputation by playing it safe. In the old days it had stolen MiGs, planted spies in the palaces of its friends and its enemies, rained terror on those who dared to terrorize the people of Israel. Shamron did not want his legacy to be an Office that no longer made mistakes. He wanted to leave behind an Office that could reach out and strike at will. An Office that could make the other services of the world shake their heads in wonder.

He knew he did not have much time. Not everyone at King Saul Boulevard had celebrated his return. There

were some who believed Shamron's time had come and
gone, that Shamron should have been left in Tiberias
to wrestle with his radios and his conscience while the
torch was passed to the next generation. Certainly a man
like Mordecai deserved to be chief after all those years
slugging it out in the trenches of Operations, Shamron's
detractors had argued. Eli had the makings of a fine chief,
they said. He just needed a bit more seasoning in the
executive suite and he would be ready for the top job.
Even Lev of Operations was thought to be suitable material, though Lev did let his temper get the better of him
now and again, and Lev had made his share of enemies
over the years.

Shamron was stuck with them. Because he was only
a caretaker, he had been given almost no power to make
changes among the senior staff at King Saul Boulevard.
As a result he was surrounded by a pack of predators
who would pounce at the first sign of weakness. And the
volcanic Lev was the most threatening of all, for Lev had
anointed himself Shamron's personal Brutus.

Shamron thought: *Poor little Lev. He has no idea who
he's fucking with.*

"Zev Eliyahu was a personal friend of mine," the prime
minister said as Shamron took his seat. "Who did this to
him?"

He poured coffee and slid the cup across the desk, his
placid brown eyes fixed on Shamron. As usual Shamron
had the feeling he was being contemplated by a sheep.

"I can't say for certain, but I suspect it may have been Tariq."

Just Tariq. No last name. None necessary. His résumé was engraved on Shamron's brain. Tariq al-Hourani, son of a village elder from the Upper Galilee, born and raised in a refugee camp outside Sidon in southern Lebanon, educated in Beirut and Europe. His older brother had been a member of Black September, assassinated by a special unit led by Shamron himself. Tariq had dedicated his life to avenging his brother's death. He joined the PLO in Lebanon, fought in the civil war, then accepted a coveted post in Force 17, Yasir Arafat's personal bodyguard and covert operations unit. During the eighties he had trained extensively behind the Iron Curtain—in East Germany, Romania, and Moscow—and was transferred from Force 17 to the Jihaz el-Razd, the PLO's intelligence and security apparatus. Eventually he led a special unit whose mission was to wage war on the Israeli secret services and diplomatic personnel. In the early nineties he split with Arafat over his decision to enter into negotiations with Israel and formed a small, tightly knit terror organization dedicated to one end: the destruction of Arafat's peace process.

Upon hearing Tariq's name, the prime minister's eyes flashed, then resumed their calm appraisal of Shamron. "What makes you think it was Tariq who did this?"

"Based on the preliminary descriptions, the attack had all the hallmarks of one of his operations. It was meticulously planned and executed." Shamron lit a cigarette and waved away the cloud of smoke. "The killer was calm and utterly ruthless. And there was a girl. It smells of Tariq."

"So you're telling me that you have a *hunch* it was Tariq?"

"It's more than a hunch," Shamron said, pressing on in the face of the prime minister's skepticism. "Recently we received a report that suggested Tariq's organization was about to resume its activities. You may remember that I briefed you personally, Prime Minister."

The prime minister nodded. "I also remember that you discouraged me from giving the report wider circulation. Zev Eliyahu might be alive this morning if we had warned the Foreign Ministry."

Shamron rubbed out his cigarette. "I resent the suggestion that the Office is somehow culpable in the ambassador's death. Zev Eliyahu was a friend of mine as well. *And* a colleague. He worked in the Office for fifteen years, which is why I suspect Tariq targeted him. And I discouraged you from giving the report wider circulation in order to protect the source of that information. Sometimes that's necessary when it comes to vital intelligence, Prime Minister."

"Don't lecture me, Ari. Can you prove it was Tariq?"

"Possibly."

"And if you can? Then what?"

"If I can prove it was Tariq, then I'd like your permission to take him down."

The prime minister smiled. "Take down Tariq? You'll have to find him first. You really think the Office is ready for something like that? We can't afford another situation like Amman—not now, not with the peace process in such a tenuous state."

"The operation in Amman was poorly planned and disastrously executed, in part because of interference and unprecedented pressure from the man who was sitting in this office at the time. If you give me authority to go after Tariq, I assure you it will be a very different kind of operation, with very different results."

"What makes you think you can even *find* Tariq?"

"Because I am better positioned to find him now than ever before."

"Because of this source of yours?"

"Yes."

"Tell me about this source."

Shamron smiled briefly and picked at the thumbnail of his right hand. "It was a case I ran personally before I was told that my services were no longer required at King Saul Boulevard—a long-term penetration case, something that took years to unfold. Now, the source is involved in the planning and logistical side of Tariq's organization."

"Did the source know about Paris in advance?"

"Of course not! If the source had alerted me about Paris, I would have warned everyone necessary, even if it required pulling the source."

"So do it," the prime minister said. "Take Tariq down. Make him pay for Eliyahu and all the others he's killed over the years. Take him down hard, and make certain he never gets up again."

"Are you prepared for the repercussions of an assassination at this time?"

"There won't be any repercussions if it's handled properly."

"The Palestinian Authority and their friends in Washington and Western Europe won't look kindly on an assassination, even if the target is Tariq."

"Then make sure you leave no fingerprints. Make certain your *kidons* don't get caught, like that pair of bumbling amateurs that were sent to Amman. Once I sign the order, the operation is in your hands. You get rid of him any way you see fit—just get rid of him. The people of Israel will never allow me to make peace while Tariq or anyone else is running around killing Jews."

"I'll need the proper documentation to set things in motion."

"You'll have it by the end of the day."

"Thank you, Prime Minister."

"So who do you have in mind for the job?"

"I thought you had no intention of interfering."

"I just want to know who you're assigning the case to. I don't believe that qualifies as interference."

"I was thinking about Allon."

"*Gabriel* Allon? I thought he left the Office after Vienna."

Shamron shrugged; such things did not matter when it came to a man like Gabriel Allon. "It's been a long time since anyone at the Office has handled a case like this. And they've generally fucked them up. But there's one other reason why I want Allon. Tariq operates mainly in Europe. Allon is very experienced on the Continent. He knows how to get things done without making a racket."

"Where is he now?"

"Living somewhere in England last time I heard."

The prime minister smirked. "It'll be easier for you to find Tariq than Gabriel Allon."

"I'll find Allon, and Allon will find Tariq." Shamron pulled his lips into a fatalistic frown. "And then it will be done."

# 4

## SAMOS, GREECE

The ferry from Turkey arrived twelve hours late because of heavy seas in the Straits of Mycale. Tariq had never cared for boats—he hated the feeling of being surrounded by water with no route of escape. He stood at the bow, collar up against the night wind, watching the approach to Samos. In the moonlight he could see the peaks of the island's two distinctive mountains: Mount Ampelos in the foreground and Mount Kerkis in the distance.

In the five days since the Paris assassination, he had worked his way southeast across Europe, changing identities and passports, subtly altering his appearance. Six times he changed automobiles. The last, a dark green Volvo station wagon, he left near the terminal in Kusadasi on the Turkish side of the strait. It had been collected by an agent from his organization.

He had seduced three women during his odyssey: a waitress in Munich, a hairdresser in Bucharest, and a hotel hostess in Sofia. He told each of them a different story. To the German girl he was an Italian fabric salesman on his way to Paris. To the Romanian girl he was an

Egyptian trader hoping to do some business in Ukraine. To the Bulgarian hostess he was a Frenchman with rich parents who traveled and read books about philosophy. He made love to each of them differently. He slapped the German girl and was unconcerned about her satisfaction. He gave the Romanian many orgasms and a gold brace- let. The Bulgarian was a dark-haired girl with olive skin. She reminded him of girls from Palestine. They made love all night, until it was time for her to go back on duty. He was sad when she was gone.

The ferry slipped into the sheltered water of the harbor and tied up. Tariq disembarked and walked to a brightly lit taverna. Parked outside was a dark blue motor scooter with a smashed rearview mirror, just as he had been promised. Inside his coat pocket was the key. He strapped his overnight bag onto the back of the bike and started the engine. A moment later he was speeding along a narrow track toward the mountains.

He was not dressed for a night ride; his thin leather gloves, low-cut loafers, and black jeans were no match for the cold. Still, he opened the throttle and pushed the little bike as hard as it would go up a long hill at the base of Mount Kerkis. He slowed for a switchback, then opened the throttle again and raced through a vineyard spilling down the side of the hill into a little valley. Above the vineyard lay an olive grove and above the olive grove a line of towering cypress trees, silhouettes against a car- pet of wet stars. The tang of cypress was heavy on the air. Somewhere, meat was cooking over a wood fire. The scent reminded him of Lebanon. Good to be out of Paris, he thought. Dull gray Paris of late autumn. Good to be back in the eastern Mediterranean.

The road turned to a pitted track. Tariq eased off the throttle. It was a stupid thing to do, driving so fast on an unfamiliar road, but he had taken to doing needlessly risky things lately. For the first time since leaving Paris, he thought of the American girl. He felt no remorse or guilt. Her death, while unfortunate, was completely necessary.

He opened the throttle again and raced down a gentle slope into a tiny valley. He thought about this need of his, this compulsion to be in the company of a woman during an operation. He supposed it came from growing up in the camps of Sidon. His father had died when Tariq was young, and his older brother, Mahmoud, was murdered by the Jews. Tariq was raised by his mother and his older sister. There was only one room in their hut at the camp, so Tariq and his mother and sister all slept in the same bed—Tariq in the middle, head resting against his mother's bosom, his sister's bony body pressed against his back. Sometimes he would lie awake and listen to the shelling or the rhythmic thump of the Israeli helicopters hovering over the camp. He would think of his father— how he had died of a broken heart with the keys to the family home in the Upper Galilee still in his pocket—and he would think of poor Mahmoud. He hated the Jews with an intensity that made his chest ache. But he never felt fear. Not when he was in his bed, protected by his women.

The whitewashed villa stood atop a rock outcropping on a craggy hillside between the villages of Mesogion and Pirgos. To reach it Tariq had to negotiate a steep path through an old vineyard. The smell of the last harvest hung in the air. He shut down the motor, and the silence rang in his ears. He put the bike on its kickstand, drew his Makarov pistol, and walked through a small garden to the entrance of the villa.

He slid the key into the lock, turned it slowly, testing the chamber for unnatural resistance. Then he opened the door and stepped inside, Makarov drawn. As he closed the door a light came on in the living room, illuminating a slender young man with long hair seated on a rustic couch. Tariq nearly shot him before he saw that the other man's gun was lying on a table in front of him and his hands were raised in a gesture of surrender.

Tariq pointed the Makarov at the young man's face. "Who are you?"

"My name is Achmed. Kemel sent me."

"I nearly killed you. Then I'd never have known why Kemel sent you here."

"You were supposed to come this morning. I had nowhere else to wait."

"The ferry was delayed. You would have known that if you'd bothered to pick up the telephone and place a single call. What does he want?"

"He wants to meet. He says he needs to discuss something with you, and it's too important to do it through the usual methods of communication."

"Kemel knows I don't like face-to-face meetings."

"He's made special arrangements."

"Tell me."

"Would you mind pointing that gun somewhere else?"

"I would, actually. How do I know you were really sent here by Kemel? Maybe your real name is Yitzhak or Jonathan. Maybe you're an Israeli. Maybe you work for the CIA. Maybe Kemel has been compromised, and you've come here to kill me."

The young man sighed heavily and began to speak. "Kemel wants to meet with you three days from now in a first-class compartment of a train between Zürich and Prague. You're to join him there at any point during the journey when you feel it's safe."

"You have a ticket?"

"Yes."

"Give it to me."

Achmed reached into the pocket of his blazer.

Tariq lifted the Makarov. "Slowly."

Achmed removed the ticket, held it up for Tariq to see, and dropped it onto the table. Tariq looked at the ticket briefly, then turned his gaze back on the boy seated in front of him. "How long have you been waiting at the villa?"

"Most of the day."

"*Most* of the day?"

"I went into the village in the afternoon."

"Whatever for?"

"I was hungry and I wanted to have a look around."

"Do you speak Greek?"

"A little."

How perfect, thought Tariq derisively. A young man who speaks a few words of Greek with an Arabic accent had been hanging around the port all afternoon. Tariq imagined a scenario: a busybody Greek shopkeeper gets suspicious about an Arab loitering in the village and calls the police. A policeman comes down to have a look for himself. Maybe he has a friend or a cousin who works in the Greek security service. *Damn!* It was a miracle he hadn't been picked up the moment he stepped off the ferry. He asked, "Where are you planning to spend the night?"

"I thought I might stay here."

"Out of the question. Go to the Taverna Petrino. It's near the harbor. You can get a room there at a reasonable price. In the morning take the first ferry to Turkey."

"Fine."

Achmed leaned forward to pick up the gun. Tariq shot him twice in the top of the head.

Blood spread over the stone floor. Tariq looked at the body and felt nothing more than a vague sense of disappointment. He had been looking forward to a few days of recuperation on the island before the next operation. He was tired, his nerves were frayed, and the headaches were getting worse. Now he would have to be on the move again, all because the goddamned ferry had been held up by high seas and Kemel had sent a bumbling idiot to deliver an important message.

He slipped the Makarov into the waistband of his trousers, picked up the train ticket, and went out.

# 5

## TEL AVIV

Uzi Navot traveled to Tel Aviv the following morning. He came to Shamron's office "black," which meant that neither Lev nor any other member of the senior staff witnessed his arrival. Hanging from the end of his brick-layer's arm was a sleek metal attaché case, the kind carried by businessmen the world over who believe their papers are too valuable to be entrusted to mere leather. Unlike the other passengers aboard the El Al flight from Paris that morning, Navot had not been asked to open the case for inspection. Nor had he been forced to endure the maddening ritualistic interrogation by the suntanned boys and girls from El Al security. Once he was safely in-side Shamron's office, he worked the combination on the attaché case and opened it for the first time since leaving the embassy in Paris. He reached inside and produced a single item: a videotape.

Navot lost count of how many times the old man watched the tape. Twenty times, thirty, maybe even fifty. He smoked so many of his vile Turkish cigarettes that Navot could barely see the screen through the fog. Shamron was entranced. He sat in his chair, arms folded, head tilted back so he could peer through the black-rimmed reading glasses perched at the end of his daggerlike nose. Navot offered the occasional piece of narrative background, but Shamron was listening to his own voices.

"According to museum security, Eliyahu and his party got into the car at ten twenty-seven," Navot said. "As you can see from the time code on the screen, the Arab makes his telephone call at exactly ten twenty-six."

Shamron said nothing, just jabbed at his remote control, rewound the tape, and watched it yet again.

"Look at his hand," Navot said breathlessly. "The number has been stored into the mobile phone. He just hits the keypad a couple of times with his thumb and starts talking."

If Shamron found this scrap of insight interesting or even remotely relevant he gave no sign of it.

"Maybe we could get the records from the telephone company," Navot said, pressing on. "Maybe we could find out the number he dialed. That phone might lead us to Tariq."

Shamron, had he chosen to speak, would have informed young Navot that there were probably a half-dozen operatives between Tariq and the French cellular telephone company. Such an inquiry, while admirable, would surely lead to a dead end.

"Tell me something, Uzi," Shamron said at last. "What kind of food did that boy have on his silver platter?"

"What, boss?"

"The food, the hors d'oeuvres, on his platter. What were they?"

"Chicken, boss."

"What kind of chicken, Uzi?"

"I don't know, boss. Just chicken."

Shamron shook his head in disappointment. "It was tandoori chicken, Uzi. Tandoori chicken, from India."

"Whatever you say, boss."

"Tandoori chicken," Shamron repeated. "That's interesting. You should have known that, Uzi."

Navot signed out an Office car and drove dangerously fast up the coast road to Caesarea. He had just pulled off a very nice piece of work—he had stolen a copy of the videotape from the Musée d'Orsay—but the only thing the old man cared about was the chicken. What difference did it make if it was tandoori chicken or Kentucky Fried Chicken? Maybe Lev was right. Maybe Shamron was past his prime. *To hell with the old man.*

There was a saying inside the Office these days: the further we are from our last disaster, the closer we are to our next. Shamron would step into the shit too. Then they'd shove him out again, this time for good.

But Navot realized he *did* care what the old man thought about him. In fact he cared too much. Like most officers his age, he revered the great Shamron. He'd done a lot of jobs for the old man over the years—dirty jobs no one else wanted. Things that had to be kept secret from

Lev and the others. He'd do almost anything to get back in his good graces.

He entered Caesarea and parked outside an apartment house a few blocks from the sea. He slipped inside the foyer, rode the lift up to the fourth floor. He still had a key but chose to knock instead. He hadn't called to say he was coming. She might have another man there. Bella had many men.

She answered the door dressed in faded jeans and a torn shirt. She had a long body and a beautiful face that seemed perpetually in mourning. She regarded Navot with a look of thinly veiled malice, then stepped aside and allowed him to enter. Her flat had the air of a secondhand bookstore and smelled of incense. She was a writer and a historian, an expert in Arab affairs, a sometime consultant to the Office on Syrian and Iraqi politics. They had been lovers before the Office sent Navot to Europe, and she despised him a little for choosing the field over her. Navot kissed her and pulled her gently toward the bedroom. She resisted, only for a moment.

Afterward, she said, "What are you thinking about?"

"Shamron."

"What now?"

He told her as much as he could, no specifics, just the essence.

"You know how Shamron works," she said. "He beats you down when he wants something. You have one of two choices. You can go back to Paris and forget about it, or you can drive up to Tiberias tonight and see what the old fucker has in mind for you now."

"Maybe I don't want to know."

"Bullshit, Uzi. Of course you want to know. If I told you I never wanted to see you again, you wouldn't give it a second thought. But if the old man looks at you cross-eyed, you fall to pieces."

"You're wrong, Bella."

"About which part?"

"The first. If you told me you never wanted to see me again, I'd quit the Office and beg you to marry me."

She kissed his lips and said, "I never want to see you again."

Navot smiled and closed his eyes.

Bella said, "My God, but you're a horrible liar, Uzi Navot."

"Is there an Indian restaurant in Caesarea?"

"A very good one, actually, not far from here."

"Does it serve tandoori chicken?"

"That's like asking if an Italian restaurant serves spaghetti."

"Get dressed. We're going."

"I'll make something for us here. I don't want to go out."

But Navot was already pulling on his trousers. "Get dressed. I need tandoori chicken."

For the next seventy-two hours Ari Shamron acted like a man who smelled smoke and was frantically looking for fire. The mere rumor of his approach could empty a room as surely as if an antipersonnel grenade had been rolled along the carpet. He prowled the halls of King Saul Boulevard, barging unannounced into meetings, exhorting the staff to look harder, listen more carefully. What was the last confirmed sighting of Tariq? What had happened to the other members of the Paris hit team? Had there been any interesting electronic intercepts? Were they talking to one another? Were they planning to strike again? Shamron had the fever, Lev told Mordecai over a late supper in the canteen. The bloodlust. Best to keep him isolated from the uninfected. Send him into the desert. Let him howl at the moon until it's passed.

The second break in the case came twenty-four hours after Navot delivered the videotape. It was the wispy Shimon of Research who made the discovery. He raced up to Shamron's office in his sweatshirt and bare feet, clutching a file in his gnawed fingertips. "It's Mohammed Azziz, boss. He used to be a member of the Popular Front, but when the Front signed on with the peace process, Azziz joined Tariq's outfit."

"Who's Mohammed Azziz?" asked Shamron, squinting at Shimon curiously through a cloud of smoke.

"The boy from the Musée d'Orsay. I had the technicians in the photo lab digitally enhance the surveillance videotape. Then I ran that through the database. There's no doubt about it. The waiter with the cell phone was Mohammed Azziz."

"You're certain it's Azziz?"

"Positive, boss."

"And you're certain Azziz is now working for Tariq?"

"I'd stake my life on it."

"Choose your words carefully, Shimon."

Shimon left the file on his desk and went out. Shamron now had what he wanted: proof that Tariq's fingerprints were all over the attack in Paris. Later that same evening, a bleary-eyed Yossi appeared at Shamron's door. "I just heard something interesting, boss."

"Speak, Yossi."

"A friend of ours from the Greek service just passed a message to Athens station. A Palestinian named Achmed Natour was murdered a couple of days ago on the Greek island of Samos. Shot through the head twice and left in a villa."

"Who's Achmed Natour?"

"We're not sure. Shimon is having a look around."

"Who owns the villa?"

"That's the most interesting thing, boss. The villa was rented to an Englishman named Patrick Reynolds. The Greek police are trying to find him."

"And?"

"There's no Patrick Reynolds at the London address on the rental agreement. There's no Patrick Reynolds at the London telephone number either. As far as the British and Greek authorities can figure, Patrick Reynolds doesn't exist."

*     *     *

The old man was going away for a while—Rami could sense it.

Shamron's last night was a restless one, even by the lofty standards of the Phantom of Tiberias. He spent a long time pacing the terrace, then killed a few hours tinkering with a vintage Philco radio that had arrived that day from the States. He did not sleep, made no telephone calls, and had just one visitor: a penitent-looking Uzi Navot. He spoke to the old man on the terrace for fifteen minutes, then quickly departed. On the way out his face reminded Rami of the look Shamron had worn the night of the Paris attack: part grim determination, part self-satisfied smirk.

But it was the garment bag that confirmed Rami's worst fears: Italian manufacture, black leather, audacious gold-plated snaps and buckles. It was everything the old man was not. The Phantom could carry his kit in his back pocket and still have room for his billfold. Then there was the name on the tag dangling from the grip: Rudolf Heller, Bern address, Bern telephone number. Shamron was going under.

Rami was distant over breakfast, like the mother who picks a fight with her child the morning of a separation. Instead of sitting with him at the table, he stood at the counter and violently flipped through the sports section of *Maa'riv*.

"Rami, please," said Shamron. "Are you reading it or trying to beat a confession out of it?"

"Let me come with you, boss."

"We're not going to have this conversation again. I know you may find this difficult to believe, but I know how to function in the field. I was a *katsa* long before your parents saw fit to bring you into this world."

"You're not as young as you used to be, boss."

Shamron lowered his newspaper and peered at Rami over his half-moon glasses. "Any time you think you're ready, you may have a go at testing my fitness."

Rami pointed his finger at Shamron like a gun and said, "Bang, bang, you're dead, boss."

But Shamron just smiled and finished his newspaper. Ten minutes later Rami walked him down to the gate and loaded the bag into the car. He stood and watched the car drive away, until all that was left of Ari Shamron was a puff of pink Galilee dust.

# 6

## ZÜRICH

Schloss Pharmaceuticals was the largest drug company in Europe and one of the largest in the world. Its research labs, production plants, and distribution centers were scattered around the globe, but its corporate headquarters occupied a stately gray stone building on Zürich's exclusive Bahnhofstrasse, not far from the shores of the lake. Because it was a Wednesday, the division chiefs and senior vice presidents had assembled in the paneled boardroom on the ninth floor for their weekly meeting. Martin Schloss sat at the head of the table beneath a portrait of his great-grandfather Walther Schloss, the company's founder. An elegant figure, dark suit, neatly trimmed silver hair. At twelve-thirty he looked at his watch and stood up, signaling the meeting had concluded. A few of the executives gathered around him, hoping for one last word with the chief.

Kemel Azouri gathered up his things and slipped out. He was a tall man with a lean, aristocratic build, narrow features, and pale green eyes. He stood out at the Schloss empire, not only because of his appearance but because of his remarkable story. Born in a Palestinian refugee camp in Lebanon, he had studied medicine briefly at Beirut University before coming to Europe in search of work. He was hired by Schloss and given a low-level job in the sales department. He proved so successful that within five years he was placed in charge of the company's Middle East sales division. The job kept him on the road constantly, leaving him no time for a family, or a personal life of any kind. But Kemel was not troubled by the fact that he had never found the time to marry and have children. He had been rewarded in many other ways. A year ago he had been promoted to chief of the company's sales division. Martin Schloss had made him a millionaire. He lived in a grand house overlooking the Limmat River and rode around Zürich in a chauffeured company Mercedes.

He entered his office: a large room, high ceiling, Persian rugs, pale Danish furniture, a magnificent view of the Zürichsee. He sat down at his desk and reviewed his notes of the meeting.

His secretary entered the room. "Good morning, Herr Azouri. I hope your meeting went well."

She spoke to him in German, and he answered flawlessly in the same language. "Very well, Margarite. Any messages?"

"I left them on your desk, Herr Azouri. Your train tickets are there too, along with your hotel information for Prague. You should hurry, though. Your train leaves in half an hour."

He flipped through the pile of telephone messages.

There was nothing that couldn't wait. He pulled on an overcoat, placed a fedora on his head, and tied a silk scarf around his throat. Margarite handed him his briefcase and a small overnight bag.

Kemel said, "I'd like to use the time on the train to catch up on some paperwork."

"I won't bother you unless it's a crisis. Your driver is waiting downstairs."

"Tell him to take the rest of the afternoon off. I'll walk to Hauptbahnhof. I need the exercise."

Snow drifted over the Bahnhofstrasse as Kemel made his way past the glittering shops. He entered a bank and quietly withdrew a large sum of cash from a personal numbered account. Five minutes later he was outside again, money tucked in a hidden compartment of his briefcase.

He entered the Hauptbahnhof and walked across the main hall, pausing to check his tail. Then he walked to a newsstand and bought a stack of papers for the ride. As he gave money to the clerk, he glanced around the terminal to see if anyone was watching him. Nothing.

He walked to the platform. The train was nearly finished boarding. Kemel stepped into the carriage and picked his way along the corridor toward his first-class compartment. It was empty. He hung up his coat and sat down as the train pulled out of the station. He reached into his briefcase and got out his newspapers. He started with the European edition of *The Wall Street Journal*, then the *Financial Times, The Times* of London, and finally *Le Monde*.

Forty-five minutes later the steward brought him coffee. Kemel started working his way through a batch of quarterly sales figures from the South American division—just another successful business executive, too driven to relax even for a moment. Kemel smiled; it was so far from the truth.

For years he had lived a double life, working for Schloss Pharmaceuticals while at the same time serving as an agent of the PLO. His job and respectable front had provided him an airtight cover, allowing him to travel the Middle East and Europe without raising the suspicion of security and intelligence services. The ultimate wolf in sheep's clothing, he moved among the most elite and cultured circles of Europe, worked with the Continent's most powerful business leaders, socialized with the rich and famous. Yet all the while he was working for the PLO—maintaining networks, recruiting agents, planning operations, carrying messages, collecting money from donors across the Middle East. He used the shipping and distribution systems of Schloss to move weaponry and explosives into place for operations. Indeed, it always gave him a rather morbid sense of pleasure to think that packed among life-giving medicines were the instruments of murder and terror.

Now his situation was even more complicated. When Yasir Arafat agreed to renounce violence and enter into negotiations with the Zionists, Kemel became enraged and secretly joined forces with his old comrade Tariq al-Hourani. Kemel served as the chief of operations and planning for Tariq's organization. He saw to the finances, ran the communications networks, secured the weaponry and explosives, and handled operational planning—all from his office in Zürich. They formed a rather unique partnership: Tariq, the ruthless terrorist and cold-blooded killer; Kemel, the refined and respectable front man who provided him the tools of terror.

Kemel closed his sales reports and looked up. *Damn! Where is he?* Perhaps something had gone wrong.

Just then the compartment door opened and a man stepped inside: long blond hair, sunglasses, Yankees baseball hat, rock music blaring from his headphones. Kemel thought: *Christ! Who is this idiot? Now Tariq will never dare to show.*

He said, "I'm sorry, but you're in the wrong compartment. These seats are all taken."

The man lifted one earpiece of his headphones and said, "I can't hear you." He spoke English like an American.

"These seats are taken," Kemel repeated impatiently. "Leave, or I'll call a steward."

But the man just sat down and removed his sunglasses. "Peace be with you, my brother," Tariq said softly in Arabic.

Kemel smiled in spite of himself. "Tariq, you bastard."

\*    \*    \*

"I was worried when Achmed failed to check in after I sent him to Greece," Kemel said. "Then I heard a body had been found in the villa on Samos, and I knew you two must have spoken."

Tariq closed his eyes, tilted his head slightly to one side. "He was sloppy. You should choose your messengers more carefully."

"But did you really have to kill him?"

"You'll find another—better, I hope."

Kemel looked at him carefully for a moment. "How are you feeling, Tariq? You don't—"

"Fine," Tariq said, cutting him off. "How are things proceeding in Amsterdam?"

"Quite nicely, actually. Leila has arrived. She's found you a woman and a place to stay."

Tariq said, "Tell me about her."

"She works in a bar in the red-light district. Lives alone on a houseboat on the Amstel. It's perfect."

"When do I go?"

"About a week."

"I need money."

Kemel reached into his briefcase and handed Tariq the envelope of cash. Tariq slipped it into his coat pocket. Then his pale gray eyes settled on Kemel. As always Kemel had the uncomfortable feeling that Tariq was deciding how best to kill him if he needed to.

"Surely you didn't drag me all the way here to criticize me for killing Achmed and to ask about my health. What else do you have?"

"Some interesting news."

"I'm listening."

"The men from King Saul Boulevard are convinced you were behind the attack in Paris."

"How brilliant of them."

"Ari Shamron wants you dead, and the prime minister has given him the green light."

"Ari Shamron has wanted me dead for years. Why is this so important now?"

"Because he's going to give the job to an old friend of yours."

"Who?"

Kemel smiled and leaned forward.

# 7

## ST. JAMES'S, LONDON

The sometimes-solvent firm of Isherwood Fine Arts resided in a crumbling Victorian warehouse in a quiet backwater of St. James's called Mason's Yard. It was wedged between the offices of a minor shipping company and a pub that always seemed to be filled with pretty office girls who rode motor scooters. The formal sign in the first-floor window stated that the gallery specialized in the works of the old masters, that the owner, Julian Isherwood, was a member in good standing of the Society of London Art Dealers, and that his collection could be seen by appointment only. Galleries in Venice and New York were also promised, though they had closed a long time ago—Isherwood simply hadn't the heart, or the spare cash, to update the sign to reflect the shrinking fortunes of his empire.

Shamron arrived at twelve-thirty. His bomber jacket and khaki trousers had given way to a double-breasted suit, a silk shirt and tie of matching dark blue, and a gray cashmere overcoat. The steel-rimmed goggles had been replaced by fashionable tortoiseshell spectacles. On his wrist was a gold Rolex watch, on the last finger of his right hand a signet ring. The absence of a wedding band bespoke sexual availability. He moved with an easy, cosmopolitan saunter instead of his usual death charge.

Shamron pressed the cracked buzzer next to the ground-floor entrance. A moment later the sultry voice of Heather, Isherwood's latest in a series of young and unhelpful personal assistants, came over the intercom.

"My name is Rudolf Heller," Shamron said in German-accented English. "I'm here to see Mr. Isherwood."

"Do you have an appointment?"

"I'm afraid I don't, but Julian and I are very old friends."

"One moment, please."

A moment turned to two, then three. Finally the automatic door lock snapped back. Shamron went inside and mounted a short flight of groaning stairs. There was a large brown stain in the carpet on the landing. Heather was seated in the anteroom behind an empty desk and a silent telephone. Isherwood's girls all followed a familiar pattern: pretty art school graduates seduced into his service with promises of apprenticeship and adventure. Most quit after a month or two when they became hopelessly bored or when Isherwood couldn't seem to scrape together the cash to pay them.

Heather was flipping through a copy of *Loot*. She smiled and pointed into Isherwood's office with the end of a chewed pink pencil. Isherwood flashed past the open door, all pinstripe and silk, speaking rapid Italian into a cordless telephone.

"Go inside if you dare," said Heather in a lazy Mayfair drawl that secretly set Shamron's teeth on edge. "He'll be off in a minute. Can I get you anything to drink?"

Shamron shook his head and went inside. He sat down and surveyed the room. Bookshelves filled with monographs on artists, cloth-bound ledgers, old catalogs, a pedestal covered in black velvet for showing paintings to prospective buyers. Isherwood was pacing before a window overlooking Mason's Yard. He paused once to glare at Shamron, then again to coax a groaning fax machine into action. Isherwood was in trouble—Shamron could sense it. But then he was always in trouble.

Julian Isherwood was very selective about the paintings he bought and even more selective about whom he sold them to. He slipped into a state of melancholia each time he watched one of his paintings walk out the door. As a result he was an art dealer who did not sell a great deal of art—fifteen pictures in a normal year, twenty in a good one. He had made a fortune in the eighties, when anyone with a few feet of gallery space and half a brain had made money, but now that fortune was gone.

He tossed the telephone onto his chaotic desk. "Whatever it is you want, the answer is no."

"How are you, Julian?"

"Go to hell! Why are you here?"

"Get rid of the girl for a few minutes."

"The answer will still be no, whether the girl's here or not."

"I need Gabriel," Shamron said quietly.

"Well, I need him more, and therefore you can't have him."

"Just tell me where he is. I need to talk to him."

"Sod off!" Isherwood snapped. "Who the hell do you think you are, barging in here like this and giving me orders? Now, if you're interested in purchasing a painting, perhaps I can be of some assistance. If it's not art that brings you here, then Helen will show you the door."

"Her name is Heather."

"Oh, Christ." Isherwood sat down heavily into the chair behind his desk. "Helen was last month's girl. I can't keep them straight anymore."

"Things aren't going well, Julian?"

"Things *haven't* been going well, but all that's about to change, which is why I need you to crawl back under your rock and leave me, and Gabriel, in peace."

"How about lunch?" Shamron suggested. "You can tell me your problems, and perhaps we can come to some mutually beneficial solution."

"You never struck me as someone who was terribly interested in compromise."

"Get your coat."

Shamron had taken the precaution of booking a quiet corner table at Green's restaurant in Duke Street. Isherwood ordered the cold boiled Canadian lobster and the most expensive bottle of Sancerre on the wine list. Shamron's jaw clenched briefly. He was notoriously tightfisted when it came to Office funds, but he needed Isherwood's help. If that required a pricey lunch at Green's, Shamron would tickle his expense account.

In the lexicon of the Office, men like Julian Isherwood were known as the *sayanim*: the helpers. They were the bankers who tipped Shamron whenever certain Arabs made large transactions or who could be called upon in the dead of night when a *katsa* was in trouble and needed money. They were the concierges who opened hotel rooms when Shamron wanted a look inside. They were the car rental clerks who provided Shamron's field agents with clean transport. They were the sympathetic officers in unsympathetic security services. They were the journalists who allowed themselves to be used as conduits for Shamron's lies. No other intelligence service in the world could claim such a legion of committed acolytes. To Ari Shamron they were the secret fruit of the Diaspora.

Julian Isherwood was a special member of the *sayanim*. Shamron had recruited him to service just one very important *katsa*, which was why Shamron always displayed uncharacteristic patience in the face of Isherwood's volatile mood swings.

"Let me tell you why you can't have Gabriel right now," Isherwood began. "Last August a very dirty, very damaged painting appeared in a sale room in Hull— sixteenth-century Italian altarpiece, oil on wood panel, *Adoration of the Shepherds,* artist unknown. That's the most important part of the story, artist *unknown*. Do I have your full attention, *Herr Heller?*"

Shamron nodded and Isherwood sailed on.

"I had a hunch about the picture, so I piled a load of books into my car and ran up to Yorkshire to have a look at it. Based on a brief visual inspection of the work, I was satisfied my hunch was correct. So when this same very dirty, very damaged painting, artist *unknown*, came up for sale at the venerable Christie's auction house, I was able to pick it up for a song."

Isherwood licked his lips and leaned conspiratorially across the table. "I took the painting to Gabriel, and he ran several tests on it for me. X ray, infrared photography, the usual lot. His more careful inspection confirmed my hunch. The very dirty, very damaged work from the sale room in Hull is actually a missing altarpiece from the Church of San Salvatore in Venice, painted by none other than Francesco Vecellio, brother of the great Titian. That's why I need Gabriel, and that's why I'm not going to tell you where he is."

The sommelier appeared. Shamron picked at a loose thread in the tablecloth while Isherwood engaged in the elaborate ritual of inspection, sniffing, sipping, and pondering. After a dramatic moment of uncertainty, he pronounced the wine suitable. He drank a glass very fast, then poured another.

When he resumed, his voice had turned wistful, his eyes damp. "Remember the old days, Ari? I used to have a gallery in New Bond Strasse, right next to Richard Green. I can't afford New Bond Strasse these days. It's all Gucci and Ralph Lauren, Tiffany and Miki-Bloody-Moto. And you know who's taken over my old space?

The putrid Giles Pittaway! He's already got two galleries in Bond Street alone, and he's planning to open two more within the year. Christ, but he's spreading like the Ebola virus—mutating, getting stronger, killing everything decent in his wake."

A chubby art dealer with a pink shirt and a pretty girl on his arm walked past their table. Isherwood paused long enough to say, "Hullo, Oliver," and blow him a kiss.

"This Vecellio is a real coup. I need a coup once every couple of years. The coups are what keep me in business. The coups support all the dead stock and all the small sales that earn me next to nothing." Isherwood paused and took a long drink of wine. "We all need coups now and again, right, Herr *Heller*? I suspect that even someone in your line of work needs a big success every now and again to make up for all the failures. Cheers."

"Cheers," said Shamron, tipping his glass a fraction of an inch.

"Giles Pittaway could've bought the Vecellio, but he passed. He passed because he and his boys didn't bother to do their homework. They couldn't authenticate it. I was the only one who knew what it was, because I was the only one who did my homework. Giles Pittaway wouldn't know a Vecellio from vermicelli. He sells crap. High-gloss crap. Have you seen his stuff? Total crap! Complete and utter greeting card crap!"

Shamron, playing the part of Herr Heller, said it had been some time since he had visited the galleries of the infamous Giles Pittaway.

Isherwood leaned forward across the table, eyes wide, lips damp. "I need this Vecellio cleaned and ready for sale by the spring," he said, sotto voce. "If it's not ready, I'll lose my buyer. Buyers don't grow on trees these days, especially for a Vecellio altarpiece. I can count the number of potential buyers for a piece like this on the fingers of one hand. If my buyer gets cold feet, I may never find another. And if I can't find another, my Vecellio becomes just another piece of dead stock. Burned, as we say in the trade. You burn agents, we burn our paintings. A picture gets snatched up, or it turns to dust in some art dealer's storeroom. And once a painting's been burned it's worthless, just like your agents."

"I understand your dilemma, Julian."

"Do you *really*? There are maybe five people in the world who can restore that Vecellio properly. Gabriel Allon happens to be one of them, and the other four would never lower their standards to work for someone like me."

"Gabriel is a talented man. Unfortunately, I require his talents too, and it's something a bit more important than a five-hundred-year-old painting."

"Oh, no, you don't! The sharks are circling, and my fickle bank is threatening to set me adrift. I'm not going to be able to find a backer quickly enough to save the ship. Giles Pittaway has backers! Lloyd's Bank! When art and high finance start to intermarry, I say it's time to head for the Highlands and build a bloody ark." A pause. "And by the way, *Herr* Heller, few things in this life are more important than good paintings. And I don't care how old they are."

"I should have chosen my words more carefully, Julian."

"If I have to liquidate I'll lose my shirt," Isherwood said. "I'd be lucky to get thirty pence on the pound for what my collection is really worth."

Shamron was unmoved by his pleadings. "Where is he?"

"Why should I tell you?"

"Because I need him, Julian. *We* need him."

"Oh, Christ! Don't pull that shit with me, because it won't work a second time. I've heard all your stories, and I know how they end. And by the way, Gabriel feels the same way. He's through with your lot, too."

"So tell me where he is. What harm would it do?"

"Because I know you too well to trust you. No one in his right mind would trust you."

"You can tell me where he is, or we can find him ourselves. It might take a few days, but we'll find him."

"Suppose I tell you. What are you prepared to offer in return?"

"Maybe I could find a backer to keep you afloat until you sell your Vecellio."

"Reliable backers are as rare as a reliable Vecellio."

"I know someone who's been thinking about getting into the art business. I might be able to speak to him on your behalf."

"What's his name?"

"I'm afraid he would insist on anonymity."

"If Gabriel suspects I told you—"

"He won't suspect a thing."

Isherwood licked his bloodless lips.

# 8

## PORT NAVAS, CORNWALL

The old man came while the stranger was away on his boat. Peel spotted him from his bedroom window as the man tried to guide a big Mercedes along the narrow lane overlooking the quay. He stopped at the foreman's cottage, rang the bell, and knocked on the door. Peel could hear the old man's knuckles striking the wood all the way across the creek: short, brutal blows. He pulled on a sweater and raincoat and dashed out of the cottage. A moment later he was standing behind the man, panting, face hot from exertion.

The old man said, "Who are you?"

An accent, Peel noted—like the stranger's, but heavier.

"I'm Peel. Who are you?"

But the old man ignored this question. "I'm looking for the man who lives in this cottage."

"He's not here now."

"I'm a friend. Do you know where he is?"

Peel said nothing, for the notion of the stranger having a friend who would appear unannounced was ludicrous. The old man looked toward the quay, then his gaze settled once again on Peel. "He's out on his boat, isn't he?"

Peel nodded. Something about the man's eyes made the boy shiver.

The old man looked at the sky: pewter-colored clouds pressing down on the creek, thick and heavy with coming rain. "Rather unpleasant weather for sailing."

"He's very good."

"Yes, he is. When will he be back?"

"He never says. I'll tell him you stopped by."

"Actually, I think I'd like to wait for him." He looked like a man who could wait a long time if he set his mind to it. "Is there someplace to get some coffee around here?"

Peel pointed toward the village.

But the old man didn't go into the village for coffee. In fact he didn't go anywhere. He just climbed into the Mercedes and settled himself behind the wheel like a statue. Peel walked to the point and made a base camp next to the oyster farm, staring down the river toward the sea, waiting for the stranger. By midafternoon there were whitecaps on the river, and a rainstorm was coming up. At four o'clock it was thoroughly dark. Peel was soaked, freezing half to death. He was about to give up his vigil when he spotted a cluster of soft blue running lights floating upriver through the mist. A moment later he heard the rhythmic rattle of an engine:

the stranger's fine wooden ketch, heading for home under power.

Peel switched on his flashlight and signaled the stranger. The ketch made a gentle turn to starboard, headed toward the point, slicing through black water. When the boat was within a few yards of the shore, the stranger shouted, "What's wrong?"

"There's a man waiting for you."

"What does he want?"

"He says he's a friend of yours."

"Did he tell you his name?"

"No."

Peel heard his voice coming back at him from the other side of the creek.

"How did he look?"

"Unhappy."

"Did he have an accent?"

"A bit like yours, only heavier."

"Go home."

But Peel didn't want to leave him alone. "I'll meet you at the quay and help you tie her up."

"Just do as I say," said the stranger, and he vanished below the deck.

Gabriel Allon entered the galley. In the cabinet above the propane stove he found his gun, a Glock 9mm semiautomatic. Gabriel preferred the midsized model, which was slightly less accurate because of the shorter barrel but easier to conceal. He pulled the square, chunky slide, chambering the first round, dropped the gun into the front right-hand pocket of his amber oilskin slicker. Then he doused the running lights and clambered back onto the deck.

He reduced speed as the ketch rounded the point and entered the quiet of the creek. He spotted the large Mercedes parked outside his cottage, heard the door opening and the tinny electronic warning chime. The interior light had been switched off. A professional. He reached into his pocket and wrapped his hand around the Glock, his finger outside the trigger guard.

The intruder crossed the quay and descended a short set of stone steps to the water level. Gabriel would have recognized him anywhere: the bullet head, the weather-beaten jaw, the distinctive march, like a fighter advancing toward the center of the ring. For an instant he considered turning around and heading back downriver into the squall, but instead he released his grip on the Glock and guided the boat toward the quay.

Shamron led himself on a restless tour of Gabriel's studio, pausing in front of the Vecellio. "So this is Isherwood's great coup, the lost Vecellio altarpiece. Imagine, a nice Jewish boy, working on a painting like this. I can't understand why people waste time and money on such things."

"That doesn't surprise me. What did you do to poor Julian to make him betray me?"

"I bought him lunch at Green's. Julian never was the stoic sort."

"What are you doing here?"

But Shamron wasn't ready to show his hand. "You've done very well for yourself," he said. "This cottage must have cost you quite a bit of money."

"I'm one of the most respected art restorers in the world."

"How much is Julian paying you for fixing that Vecellio?"

"That's none of your business."

"You can tell me, or Julian can tell me. I would prefer to hear it from you. It might bear some semblance to the truth."

"One hundred thousand pounds."

"Have you seen any of it yet?"

"We're talking about Julian *Isherwood*. I get paid when he sells the Vecellio, and even then I'll probably be forced to beat it out of him."

"And the Rembrandt?"

"A quick job for Christie's. It doesn't need much work, a clean coat of varnish, maybe a bit of retouching. I haven't finished the assessment yet."

Shamron moved from the Vecellio to the trolley containing Gabriel's pigments and oils. "Which identity are you using these days?"

"Not one of yours, if that's what you're wondering."

"Italian?"

"Yes. And you are?"

"Rudolf Heller."

"Ah, Herr Heller, one of my favorites. I trust business has been good for Herr Heller of late?"

"We have our good days and our bad days."

Gabriel switched on the bank of fluorescent lights and turned the lights on Shamron.

Shamron squinted. "Gabriel, shut that thing off."

"I know you prefer to work in the dark, Herr Heller, but I want to see your face. What do you want?"

"Let's take a drive."

They sped along a narrow road lined with tall hedgerows. Gabriel drove one-handed and very fast. When Shamron asked him to slow down, Gabriel pressed the accelerator even harder. Shamron tried to punish him with smoke, but Gabriel lowered the windows, filling the car with freezing air. Shamron signaled his surrender by tossing his cigarette into the darkness.

"You know about Paris?"

"I saw the television and read the papers."

"They were good, the people who did Paris—better than anything we've seen for a long time. They were good like Black September was good. These were not stone throwers or boys who walk into a market with fifty pounds of Semtex strapped to their bodies. These were professionals, Gabriel."

Gabriel concentrated on his driving and not the drumbeat cadence of Shamron's speech. He didn't like the reaction it had already provoked within him. His pulse had quickened and his palms were damp.

"They had a large team—ten, maybe twelve operatives. They had money, transport, false passports. They planned the hit down to the last detail. The entire thing was over and done in thirty seconds. Within a minute every member of the hit team was off the bridge. They all managed to escape. The French have come up with nothing."

"What does this have to do with me?"

Shamron closed his eyes and recited a verse from Scripture: "And the enemy shall know I am Lord when I can lay down my vengeance upon them."

"Ezekiel," said Gabriel.

"I believe that if someone kills one of my people, I should kill him in return. Do you believe that, Gabriel?"

"I used to believe it."

"Better yet, I believe that if a boy picks up a stone to throw at me, I should shoot him before it ever leaves his hand." Shamron's lighter flared in the dark, making shadows in the fissures of his face. "Maybe I'm just a relic. I remember huddling against my mother's breast while the Arabs burned and looted our settlement. The Arabs killed my father during the general strike in 'thirty-seven. Did I ever tell you that?"

Gabriel kept his eyes fastened on the winding Cornish road and said nothing.

"They killed your father, too. In the Sinai. And your mother, Gabriel? How long did she live after your father's death? Two years? Three?"

Actually it was a little more than a year, thought Gabriel, remembering the day they laid her cancer-ridden body into a hillside overlooking the Jezreel Valley. "What's your point?"

"My point is that revenge is good. Revenge is healthy. Revenge is purifying."

"Revenge only leads to more killing and more revenge. For every terrorist we kill, there's another boy waiting to step forward and pick up the stone or the gun. They're like sharks' teeth: break one and another will rise in its place."

"So we should do nothing? Is that what you mean to say, Gabriel? We should stand aside and wring our hands while these bastards kill our people?"

"You know that's not what I'm saying."

Shamron fell silent as the Mercedes flashed through a darkened village.

"It's not my idea, you know. It's the prime minister's. He wants his peace with the Palestinians, but he can't make peace if the extremists are throwing tomatoes onto the stage from the balcony."

"Since when did you become such a peacenik, Ari?"

"My own opinions are irrelevant. I am merely a secret servant who does what he is told."

"Bullshit."

"All right, if you want my opinion, I believe we will be no more secure after a peace deal than before it. If you want my opinion, I believe the fire in the Palestinian heart will never be extinguished until the Jews are driven into the sea. And I'll tell you one other thing, Gabriel. I would much rather do battle with a sworn enemy than with an enemy who finds expediency in posing as a friend."

Shamron rubbed the spot on the bridge of his nose where his elegant tortoiseshell glasses were pinching him. He had aged; Gabriel could see it at the edges of his eyes when he removed the little spectacles. Even the great Shamron was not immune to the ravages of time.

"You know what happened in Amman?" Shamron asked.

"I read about it in the newspapers. I also know what happened in Switzerland."

"Ah, Switzerland," Shamron said mildly, as if Switzerland were an unfortunate romance he would rather forget. "A simple operation, right? Bug the flat of a high-level Islamic extremist. Nothing to it. In the old days we could do something like this with our eyes closed. Place the device and get out before anyone realizes we've been there. But these idiots forget that the Swiss are the most vigilant people on earth. One old lady makes a telephone call, and the entire team is in the hands of the Swiss police."

"How unfortunate."

"And I'm on the next plane to Zürich begging our Swiss brethren not to make it public."

"I would have enjoyed watching that."

Shamron emitted a few grunts of laughter. Gabriel realized that in an odd way he had missed the old man. How long had it been since they had seen each other? *Eight years? No, nearly nine.* Shamron had come to Vienna after the bombing to help clean up the mess and make certain the real reason for Gabriel's presence in the city remained secret. Gabriel saw Shamron once more after that: when he returned to Tel Aviv to tell him he wanted out.

"I'm not sure where it went wrong," Shamron said. "Everyone thinks now that peace is at hand there are no more threats to our survival. They don't understand that peace will only make the fanatics more desperate. They don't understand that we will need to spy on our new Arab friends just as hard as when they were openly committed to our destruction."

"A spy's work is never done."

"But these days all the smart boys do their compulsory service in the IDF and then run like hell. They want to make money and talk on their cell phones from the cafés of Ben Yehuda Street. We used to get only the best. Like you, Gabriel. Now we get the ones who are too stupid or lazy to make it in the real world."

"Change your recruiting tactics."

"I have, but I need someone now. Someone who can run an operation in Europe without permission from the host government and without it ending up on the front page of *The Sunday Times*. I need you, Gabriel. I need a prince. I need you to do for the Office what you are doing to that Vecellio. Our service has been damaged. I need you to help me restore it."

"Five hundred years of dirt and neglect I can fix. Ten years of institutional incompetence is another matter entirely. Find someone else to find your terrorists and fix your Office. I'm already under contract."

Shamron removed his glasses, breathed on the lenses, polished them with his scarf. "It was Tariq, by the way," he said, inspecting the glasses in the weak dashboard light. "Did I mention that, Gabriel? It was Tariq who killed the ambassador and his wife in Paris. It was Tariq who made the Seine run red with the blood of my people. Tariq—your old friend."

Gabriel slammed on the brakes, and Shamron's spectacles careened against the windshield.

Gabriel drove through Lizard Town, then raced across a stark plain of windblown grass down to the sea. He pulled into a car park near the lighthouse and killed the engine. The car shuddered in the wind. He led Shamron along a darkened footpath down to the cliffs. The crashing of the waves filled the air. A seabird screamed at them. When the foghorn in the lighthouse groaned, Shamron spun around and braced himself as if he were preparing for a silent kill.

Lights burned in the little café on the edge of the cliffs. The staff was trying to close up, but Gabriel charmed them out of a couple of omelets and a pot of tea. Shamron, acting the role of Herr Heller, used a damp paper napkin to dab the dust of the footpath from his costly suede loafers. The girl who served them wore so many earrings and bracelets she sounded like a wind chime when she moved. There was something of Leah in her—Gabriel could see it; Shamron could see it too.

"Why do you think it was Tariq?"

"Did you hear about the girl? The American girl? The one he used for cover and then murdered in cold blood? Tariq always liked women. Too bad they all ended up the same way."

"That's all you have? A dead American girl?"

Shamron told him about the videotape, about the waiter who made a mysterious telephone call a minute before the ambassador and his wife stepped into the car. "His name is Mohammed Azziz. He told the catering company he was an Algerian. He's not a waiter, and he's not Algerian. He's been a member of Tariq's organization for ten years. He's played a supporting role in several of Tariq's operations."

Shamron fell silent as the girl with the bracelets came to their table and added hot water to their teapot.

When she was gone he asked, "Do you have a girl?" He knew no boundaries when it came to asking personal questions. No corner of a man's life, friend or enemy, was off limits.

Gabriel shook his head and busied himself with the tea—milk on the bottom, tea on top, English style. Shamron dumped three packets of sugar into his cup, stirred violently, and pressed on with his inquiries. "No little loves? No loose women that you lure onto your boat for a pleasure cruise?"

"No women on the boat. Just Peel."

"Ah, yes, Peel. Your watcher."

"My watcher."

"May I ask why not?"

"No, you may not."

Shamron frowned. He was accustomed to unimpeded access into Gabriel's personal life.

"What about this girl?" Shamron cocked his head in the direction of the waitress. "She can't take her eyes off of you. She doesn't interest you in any way?"

"She's a child," said Gabriel.

"You're a child."

"I'm closing in on fifty now."

"You look forty."

"That's because I don't work for you anymore."

Shamron dabbed omelet from his lips. "Maybe you won't take another woman because you're afraid Tariq will try to kill her too."

Gabriel looked up as if he had heard a gunshot.

"Maybe if you help me take down Tariq, you can forgive yourself for what happened in Vienna. I know you blame yourself, Gabriel. If it wasn't for Tunis, Leah and Dani would never have been in Vienna."

"Shut up—"

"Maybe if you help me take down Tariq, you can finally let go of Leah and get on with your life."

Gabriel stood up, tossed a crumpled ten-pound note onto the table, and went out. Shamron smiled apologetically at the girl and followed softly after him.

At the base of the cliff, on the little gray-sand beach at Polpeor Cove, stood the ruins of a lifeguard station slip. A bright wet moon shone through the broken clouds, and the sea held the reflection of light. Gabriel thrust his hands into the pockets of his jacket, thinking of Vienna. The afternoon before the bombing. The last time he had made love to Leah. *The last time he had made love to anyone*. . . . Leah had insisted on keeping the blinds of their bedroom window open, even though it overlooked the courtyard of the apartment house and Gabriel was convinced the neighbors were watching them. Leah hoped they were. She found perverse justice in the idea of Jews—even secret Jews living as an Italian art restorer and his Swiss girlfriend—seeking pleasure in a city where they had suffered so much persecution. Gabriel remembered the damp heat of Leah's body, the taste of salt on her skin. Afterward they had slept. When he awakened he found her sitting on the edge of the bed, watching him. "I want this to be your last job. I can't take this anymore. I want you to leave the Office and do something normal. We can stay in Europe and you can work only as a restorer. Promise me, Gabriel."

Shamron joined him on the beach.

Gabriel looked up. "Why did you go back to the Office? Why couldn't you stay in Tiberias and live life? Why did you go running back when they called?"

"Too much unfinished business. I've never known anyone who left the secret world with all his affairs in order. We all leave behind bits of loose thread. Old operations, old enemies. They pull at you, like memories of old lovers. I also couldn't bear to watch the Alsatian and Lev destroying my service any longer."

"Why did you keep Lev?"

"Because I was forced to keep Lev. Lev made it clear to the prime minister that he would not go quietly if I tried to push him out. The last thing the prime minister wanted was a paralyzed Operations division. He got weak knees and made Lev untouchable."

"He's a snake."

"The prime minister?"

"Lev."

"A venomous snake, however, who needs to be handled carefully. When the Alsatian resigned, Lev believed he was next in the line of succession. Lev is no longer a young man. He can feel the keys to the throne room slipping through his fingers. If I come and go quickly, Lev may still get his chance. If I serve out my full term, if I linger and take a long time to die, then perhaps the prime minister will choose a younger prince as my successor. Needless to say, I do not count Lev as one of my supporters at King Saul Boulevard."

"He never liked me."

"That's because he was envious of you. Envious of your professional accomplishments. Envious of your talent. Envious of the fact you earned three times as much in your cover job as Lev earned on his Office salary. My God, he was even envious of Leah. You're everything Lev wanted to see in himself, and he hated you for it."

"He wanted to be part of the Black September team."

"Lev is brilliant, but he was never field material. Lev is a headquarters man."

"Does he know you're here?"

"He knows nothing," Shamron said coldly. "And if you decide to come back, he'll know nothing about that either. I'll handle you personally, just like the old days."

"Killing Tariq isn't going to bring back Dani. Or Leah. Haven't you learned anything? While we were busy killing the members of Black September, we didn't notice that the Egyptians and the Syrians were preparing to drive us into the sea. And they nearly succeeded. We killed thirteen members of Black September, and it didn't bring back one of the boys they slaughtered in Munich."

"Yes, but it felt good."

Gabriel closed his eyes: an apartment block in Rome's Piazza Annabaliano, a darkened stairwell, a painfully thin Palestinian translator named Wadal Abdel Zwaiter. Black September's chief of operations in Italy. He remembered the sound of a neighbor practicing piano—a rather tedious piece he didn't recognize—and the sickening thud of the bullets tearing through tissue and cracking bone. One of Gabriel's shots missed Zwaiter's body and shattered a bottle of fig wine that he had purchased moments earlier. For some reason Gabriel always thought of the wine, dark, purple and brown, flowing over the stone floor, mingling with the blood of the dying man.

He opened his eyes, and Rome was gone. "It feels

good for a while," he said. "But then you start to think you're as bad as the people you're killing."

"War always takes a toll on the soldiers."

"When you look into a man's eyes while pouring lead into his body, it feels more like murder than war."

"It's not murder, Gabriel. It was never *murder*."

"What makes you think I can find Tariq?"

"Because I've found someone who works for him. Someone I believe will lead us to Tariq."

"Where is he?"

"Here in England."

"Where?"

"London, which presents me with a problem. Under our agreements with British intelligence, we're obligated to inform them when we are operating on their soil. I would prefer not to live up to that agreement, because the British will inform their friends at Langley, and Langley will pressure us to knock it off for the sake of the peace process."

"You *do* have a problem."

"Which is why I need you. I need someone who can run an operation in England without arousing suspicion among the natives. Someone who can run a simple surveillance operation without fucking it up."

"I watch him, and he leads me to Tariq?"

"Sounds simple, doesn't it?"

"It's never that simple, Ari. Especially when you're involved."

*    *    *

Gabriel slipped into the cottage and tossed his jacket onto the cot in the sitting room. Immediately he felt the Vecellio pulling at him. It was always this way. He never left the house without first spending one more moment before his work, never returned home without going directly to his studio to gaze at the painting. It was the first thing he saw each afternoon when he awoke, the last thing he saw each morning before he went to sleep. It was something like obsession, but Gabriel believed only an obsessive could be a good restorer. *Or a good assassin, for that matter.*

He climbed the stairs to his studio, switched on the fluorescent lamp, gazed at the painting. God, how long had he been at it already? Six months? Seven? Vecellio had probably completed the altarpiece in a matter of weeks. It would take Gabriel ten times that long to repair it.

He thought of everything he had done so far. Two weeks studying Vecellio himself. Life, influences, techniques. A month analyzing *The Adoration of the Shepherds* with several pieces of high-tech equipment: the Wild microscope to view the surface, X-ray photography to peer below the surface, ultraviolet light to expose previous retouching. After the assessment, four months removing the dirty, yellowed varnish. It was not like stripping a coffee table; it was tedious, time-consuming work. Gabriel first had to create the perfect solvent, one that would dissolve the varnish but leave the paint intact. He would dip a homemade cotton swab into the solvent and then twirl it over the surface of the painting until it became soiled with dirty varnish. Then make another swab and start all over again. *Dip . . . twirl . . . discard. Dip . . . twirl . . . discard.* Like swabbing the deck of a battleship with a toothbrush. On a good day he could remove a few square inches of dirty varnish.

Now he had begun the final phase of the job: retouching those portions of the altarpiece damaged or destroyed over the centuries. It was mind-bending, meticulous work, requiring him to spend several hours each night with his face pressed against the painting, magnifying glasses over his eyes. His goal was to make the retouching invisible to the naked eye. The brush strokes, colors, and texture all had to match the original. If the surrounding paint was cracked, Gabriel painted false cracks into his retouching. If the artist had created a unique shade of lapis lazuli blue, Gabriel might spend several hours mixing pigment on his palette trying to duplicate it. His mission was to come and go without being seen. To leave the painting as he had found it, but restored to its original glory, cleansed of impurity.

He needed sleep, but he needed time with the Vecellio more. Shamron had wakened his emotions, sharpened his senses. He knew it would be good for his work. He switched on the stereo, waited for the music to begin, then slipped his Binomags on his head and picked up his palette as the first notes of *La Bohème* washed over him. He placed a small amount of Mowolith 20 on the palette, added a bit of dry pigment, thinned down the mixture with arcosolve until the consistency felt right. A portion of the Virgin's cheek had flaked away. Gabriel had been struggling to repair the damage for more than a week. He touched his brush to the paint, lowered the magnifying visor on the Binomags, and gently tapped the tip of the brush against the surface of the painting, carefully imitating Vecellio's brush strokes. Soon he was completely lost in the work and the Puccini.

After two hours Gabriel had retouched an area about half the size of the button on his shirt. He lifted the visor on the Binomags and rubbed his eyes. He prepared more paint on his palette and started in again.

After another hour Shamron intruded on his thoughts.

*It was Tariq who killed the ambassador and his wife in Paris.*

If it wasn't for the old man, Gabriel would never have become an art restorer. Shamron had wanted an airtight cover, something that would allow Gabriel to live and travel legitimately in Europe. Gabriel had been a gifted painter—he had studied art at a prestigious institute in Tel Aviv and had spent a year studying in Paris—so Shamron sent him to Venice to study restoration. When he had finished his apprenticeship, Shamron had recruited Julian Isherwood to find him work. If Shamron needed to send Gabriel to Geneva, Isherwood used his connections to find Gabriel a painting to restore. Most of the work was for private collections, but sometimes he did work for small museums and for other dealers. Gabriel was so talented he quickly became one of the most sought-after art restorers in the world.

At 2:00 A.M. the Virgin's face blurred before Gabriel's eyes. His neck felt as though it were on fire. He pushed back the visor, scraped the paint from his palette, put away his things. Then he went downstairs and fell into his bed, still clothed, and tried to sleep. It was no good. Shamron was back in his head.

*It was Tariq who made the Seine run red with the blood of my people.*

Gabriel opened his eyes. Slowly, bit by bit, layer by layer, it all came back, as though it were depicted in some obscene fresco painted on the ceiling of his cottage: the day Shamron recruited him, his training at the Academy, the Black September operation, Tunis, *Vienna.* . . . He could almost hear the crazy Hebrew-based lexicon of the place: *kidon, katsa, sayan, bodel, bat leveyha.*

*We all leave behind bits of loose thread. Old operations, old enemies. They pull at you, like memories of old lovers.*

*Damn you, Shamron,* thought Gabriel. *Find someone else.*

At dawn he swung his feet to the floor, climbed out of bed, and stood in front of the window. The sky was low and dark and filled with swirling rain. Beyond the quay, in the choppy water off the stern of the ketch, a flotilla of seagulls quarreled noisily. Gabriel went into the kitchen and fixed coffee.

Shamron had left behind a file: ordinary manila folder, no label, a Rorschach-test coffee stain on the back cover next to a cometlike smear of cigarette ash. Gabriel opened it slowly, as if he feared it might explode, and gently lifted it to his nose—the file room at Research, yes, that was it. Attached to the inside of the front cover was a list of every officer who had ever checked out the file. They were all Office pseudonyms and meant nothing to him—except for the last name: Rom, the internal code name for the chief of the service. He turned the first page and looked at the name of the subject, then flipped through a series of grainy surveillance photographs.

He read it once quickly, then poured himself more coffee and read it again more slowly. He had the strange sensation of walking through the rooms of his childhood—everything was familiar but slightly different, a bit smaller than he remembered, a bit shabbier perhaps. As always he was struck by the similarities between the craft of restoration and the craft of killing. The methodology was precisely the same: study the target, become like him, do the job, slip away without a trace. He might have been reading a scholarly piece on Francesco Vecellio instead of an Office case file on a terrorist named Yusef al-Tawfiki.

*Maybe if you help me take down Tariq, you can finally let go of Leah and get on with your life.*

When he had finished it a second time, he opened the cabinet below the sink and removed a stainless steel case. Inside was a gun: a Beretta .22-caliber semiautomatic, specially fitted with a competition-length barrel. The Office weapon of choice for assassinations—quiet, rapid, reliable. Gabriel pressed the release and thumbed the eight cartridges into the magazine. The rounds contained a light power loading, which made the Beretta fire extremely quietly. When Gabriel had killed the Black September operative in Rome, the neighbors mistook the lethal shots for firecrackers. He rammed the magazine into the grip and pulled the slide, chambering the first round. He had fine-tuned the spring in the blowback mechanism to compensate for the light power in the cartridges. He raised the weapon and peered through the sights. An image appeared before his eyes: pale olive skin, soft brown eyes, cropped black hair.

*It was Tariq who made the Seine run red with the blood of my people. Tariq—your old friend.*

Gabriel lowered the gun, closed the file, pressed the heels of his hands against his eyes. He had made himself a promise after the disaster in Vienna. He would leave the Office for good: no return engagements, no trips down memory lane, no contact with headquarters, period. He would restore his paintings and match wits with the sea and try to forget that Vienna ever happened. He had seen too many old-timers get pulled in whenever the Office had a lousy job and no one to do it—too many men who could never quite leave the secret world behind.

But what if it were true? What if the boy could actually lead him to Tariq?

*Maybe if you help me take down Tariq, you can forgive yourself for what happened in Vienna.*

By instinct he drifted upstairs to his studio and stood before the Vecellio, inspecting that evening's work. He approved. At least something good had come of Shamron's visit. He felt a pang of regret. If he went to work for Shamron, he would have to leave the Vecellio behind. He would be a stranger to the painting when he got back. It would be like starting over. *And the Rembrandt?* The Rembrandt he would return to Christie's, with his deepest professional apologies. But not the Vecellio. He had invested too much time—put too much of himself into it—to let anyone else touch it now. It was *his* painting. Julian would just have to wait.

He slipped downstairs, extinguished the gas fire, packed away his Beretta, slipped Shamron's file into a drawer. As he stepped outside, a gust of wet wind rocked him onto his heels. The air was oppressively cold, the rain on his face like pellets. He felt as though he were being pulled from a warm, safe place. The halyards snapped against the mast of his ketch. The gulls lifted from the surface of the river, screamed in unison, turned toward the sea, white wings beating against the gray of the clouds. Gabriel pulled his hood over his head and started walking.

Outside the village store was a public telephone. Gabriel dialed the number for the Savoy Hotel and asked to be connected to the room of Rudolf Heller. He always pictured Shamron in portrait over the telephone: the creviced face, the leather hands, the afflicted expression, a patch of bare canvas over the spot where his heart might be. When Shamron answered, the two men exchanged pleasantries in German for a moment, then switched to

English. Gabriel always assumed telephone lines were monitored, so when he spoke to Shamron about the operation, he used a crude code. "A project like this will require a large amount of capital. I'll need money for personnel, transportation, office space, apartment rentals, petty cash for unexpected expenses."

"I assure you, capital will not be a problem."

Gabriel raised the issue of Lev and how to keep the operation secret from him. "But if memory serves, the bank where you have obtained financing for such ventures in the past is now under the control of your competitors. If you approach the bank for financing now, you run the risk of alerting the competition to our intentions."

"Actually, I have another source of capital that will permit me to raise the money for the project without the knowledge of the competition."

"If I accept your proposal, I would demand complete authority to run the venture as I see fit. Keeping the project secret from the competition will require the use of independent contractors and other freelance personnel. These people cost money. I will require the independent authority to spend money and use resources as I deem necessary."

"You have it, though overall operational control of the venture will remain with me in Geneva."

"Agreed. Then there is the matter of my own compensation."

"I'm afraid you are in a position to name your own price."

"One hundred and fifty thousand pounds. If the job lasts longer than six months, I will be paid an additional one hundred thousand pounds."

"Done. So, do we have an agreement?"

"I'll let you know by the end of the day."

But it was Peel, not Shamron, who received the news first.

Late that afternoon Peel heard noises on the quay. He raised his head from his schoolwork and peered out the window. There, in the dying twilight, he saw the stranger on the deck of his ketch, dressed in his yellow oilskin and a black woolen watch cap pulled so low that Peel could barely see his eyes. He was putting the ketch in mothballs: taking down sails, removing aerials, locking hatch covers. There was a look of grim determination on his face that Peel had never seen before. He considered running down to see if there was something wrong, but the stranger's demeanor suggested he was in no mood for visitors.

After an hour the stranger disappeared into the cottage. Peel returned to his schoolwork, only to be interrupted again a few minutes later, this time by the sound of the stranger's MG starting up. Peel rushed to the window in time to see the car rolling slowly up the lane, rain drifting through the beams of the headlights. He lifted his hand, more a gesture of surrender than a wave. For a moment he thought the stranger didn't see him. Then the headlights flashed once and the little MG vanished.

Peel waited in the window until the sound of the motor died away. A tear spilled down his cheek. He punched it away. Big boys don't cry, he told himself. The stranger would never cry for me. I won't cry for him. Downstairs his mother and Derek were quarreling again. Peel climbed into bed and pulled his pillow around his ears.

# 9

## HOLBORN, LONDON

Looking Glass Communications, a multibillion-dollar international publishing conglomerate, was headquartered in a modern office building overlooking New Square. It was owned by a six-foot-eight-inch, three-hundred-pound tyrant named Benjamin Stone. From his luxuriously appointed penthouse atop the headquarters, Stone ruled an empire of companies stretching from the Middle East to the United States. He owned dozens of newspapers and magazines as well as a controlling stake in the venerable New York publishing house Horton & McLawson. But the jewel in Stone's crown was the tabloid *Daily Sentinel,* Britain's third-largest-selling national newspaper. Among the journalists of Fleet Street, the *Daily Sentinel* was known as the *Daily Stone,* because it was not unusual for the paper to publish two stories in a single day about Stone's business and philanthropic activities.

What his competitors did not know was that Stone, a Hungarian Jew by birth, was also Ari Shamron's most valuable *sayan.* When Shamron needed to insert a *katsa* into a hostile country on short notice, he could turn to

Stone and the *Daily Sentinel* for cover. When a disgruntled former *katsa* tried to peddle a tell-all book about the Office, Shamron turned to Stone and his New York publishing house to knock it down. When Shamron wanted to plant a story in the Western press, he simply had to pick up a telephone and whisper into Benjamin Stone's ear.

But Stone's most valuable contribution to the Office was money. Among the senior staff at King Saul Boulevard, his charitable instincts had earned him the nickname Hadassah. Indeed, money looted from the pension funds of Stone's companies had been used to bankroll Office operations for years. Whenever Shamron needed funds, Stone moved money through a series of dummy corporations and shell companies into one of Shamron's operational accounts in Geneva.

Stone greeted Shamron that evening in the garish entrance hall. "Fuck's sake!" he roared in his trademark baritone bellow. "Rudolf, my *love*! Didn't realize you were in town. Why didn't you tell me you were coming? I would have arranged something suitable. A banquet. A human sacrifice." Stone laid his huge paw on Shamron's shoulder. "Treasonous bastard! You're lucky I'm here. *Marvelous!* Sensational! Come. Sit. Eat. *Drink*."

Stone pulled Shamron into the sitting room. Everything was oversized, to accommodate Stone's mass: deep chairs and couches of hand-tooled leather, a thick red carpet, large ottomans, and broad, low tables covered with fresh flowers and expensive trinkets given to him by other rich men. Stone forced Shamron into a chair as if he were about to interrogate him. He strode to the window, pressed a button, and the heavy curtains drew back. A window washer was working on the other side of the glass. Stone rapped his fat knuckle against the glass and gave the window washer a karate chop of a wave.

"I am the lord and master of all you see, Herr Heller," Stone announced, admiring his view. "This man washes my window every day. Can't stand a dirty window. Can you? If I ordered him to jump he'd do it and thank me for the suggestion later. Wouldn't do it out of loyalty. Or respect. Or *love*. He'd do it because he'd be afraid not to. Fear is the only emotion that really matters."

The window washer finished quickly and rappelled down the building. Stone lumbered across the room and opened the refrigerator behind the bar. He pulled out two bottles of champagne—he never opened just one—and slammed the door shut again as though he were kneeing a competitor in the balls. He tried to open one of the bottles, but his thick fingers were ill designed for the task of peeling foil and twisting bits of wire. Finally he threw back his head and roared, "Angelina!"

A terrified Portuguese maid entered the room, her eyes slightly averted.

"Take these," Stone commanded, holding the bottles by the necks as though he were strangling them. "Remove the corks, bury them in ice. Bring food, Angelina. Mounds of food. Caviar, smoked salmon, and don't forget strawberries. Big fucking strawberries. Big as a teenage girl's titties."

Stone fell into the corner of a couch and put his feet up on an ottoman. He removed his tie, twirled it into a ball, and tossed it over his shoulder onto the floor. He wore a striped shirt, handmade from Egyptian cotton, and maroon suspenders. The gold cuff links were nearly as big as the face on his solid gold wristwatch. Angelina came back into the room, deposited the tray of food, and fled. Stone poured champagne into flutes the size of beer glasses. He grasped a plum-sized strawberry, dipped it into the wine, and devoured it. He seemed to swallow it whole. Shamron suddenly felt like Alice. Everything was too big: the glasses, the strawberries, the slabs of smoked salmon, the giant-screen television silently playing an American financial news network, Stone and his ludicrous voice.

"May we drop the pretenses, Herr Heller?"

Shamron nodded. A technician from the Office's London station had swept the apartment earlier that evening and found no listening devices.

"Ari, my friend!"

Stone plunged a toast point into a bowl of caviar. Shamron watched as three hundred dollars' worth of beluga vanished down Stone's gullet. For twenty minutes he treated Shamron to tales of his business ventures, his charitable activities, his most recent meeting with the Prince of Wales, his active and diverse sex life. He paused only once to scream for Angelina to bring another vat of caviar. Shamron sat with his legs crossed, watching the bubbles rise in his champagne. Occasionally he murmured, "How interesting," or "That's fascinating."

"How are your children?" Stone blurted, unexpectedly changing course. Shamron had a son serving in the IDF in the security zone of southern Lebanon and a daughter who had moved to New Zealand, gone native, and never returned his calls.

"Fine," said Shamron. "And you? How are the boys?"

"I had to fire Christopher last week."

"So I heard."

"My competitors had great fun at my expense, but I thought it showed courage. Every Looking Glass employee, no matter how far down the food chain, now knows I'm a tough bastard—but fair."

"It was a bit harsh for coming five minutes late to a meeting."

"The principle, Ari. The principle. You should use some of my techniques in your shop."

"And Jonathan?"

"Gone to work for the competition. Told him to forget about his inheritance. Said he'd forgotten about it long ago."

Shamron shook his head at the strange ways of children.

"So what brings you to my doorstep, Ari Shamron? Certainly not food. You've not touched the caviar. *Or* the champagne. Don't just sit there. Speak, Ari."

"I need money."

"Can see that, can't I? Not a complete idiot, after all.

Practically have your cap in hand. What's it for? Share, Ari. Entitled to it after everything I've done for you."

"It concerns the incident in Paris," Shamron said. "I'm afraid that's all I can say."

"Come on, Ari. You can do better than that. Give me something I can hang my hat on."

"I need it to catch the terrorists who did it."

"Now that's more like it. How much this time?"

"Half million."

"What flavor?"

"Dollars."

"Down payment or payment in full?"

"Actually, I may need a line of credit, depending on how long the search for these boys lasts."

"I think I can manage that. How would you like it delivered?"

"There's a small shipping company based in Nassau called Carlton Limited. Its largest container vessel is in dry dock undergoing repairs. Unfortunately, the repairs are taking longer and costing much more than the owners of Carlton Limited projected. They need an infusion of cash quickly, or the ship may go down and take Carlton with it."

"I see."

Shamron rattled off the number of an account in the Bahamas, which Stone jotted down on a notepad with a gold pen.

"I can have a half million in the account by morning."

"Thank you."

"What else?"

"I need you to make another investment."

"Another shipping company?"

"Actually, in an art dealership here in London."

"Art! No, thank you, Ari."

"I'm asking you as a favor."

Stone let out a long sigh. Shamron could smell the caviar and champagne on his breath. "I'm listening."

"I need you to make a bridge loan to a firm called Isherwood Fine Arts."

"Isherwood!"

Shamron nodded.

"*Julian* Isherwood? *Julie* Isherwood? I have made my share of questionable investments, Ari, but lending money to Julie Isherwood is tantamount to setting it on fire. Won't do it. Sorry, can't help."

"I'm asking you as a personal favor."

"And I'm *telling* you that I won't do it. Julie can sink or swim on his own." Stone made another of his sudden course changes. "I didn't know Julie was part of the brotherhood."

"I didn't say that he was."

"Doesn't matter, because I'm not going to give him any of my money. I've made my decision. End of discussion."

"That's disappointing."

"Don't threaten me, Ari Shamron. How dare you, after everything I've done for you? The Office wouldn't have a pot to piss in if it weren't for me. I've lost track of how many millions I've given you."

"You've been very generous, Benjamin."

"Generous! *Christ!* I've single-handedly kept you afloat. But in case you haven't noticed, things aren't going well at Looking Glass these days. I have creditors peering into every orifice. I have banks demanding their money before they'll give me any more. Looking Glass is shipping water, love. And if Looking Glass goes down, you lose your unlimited supply of money."

"I'm aware of your current difficulties," Shamron said. "But I also know Looking Glass will emerge from this crisis stronger than ever."

"Do you? Do you really? *Shit!* And what gives you that idea?"

"My complete confidence in you."

"Don't fox with me, Ari. I've given freely for many years and asked for nothing in return. But now I need your help. I need you to lean on your friends in the City to loosen the grip on their money. I need you to convince my Israeli investors that it might be best for all concerned if they forgive a substantial portion of my debt."

"I'll see what I can do."

"And there's one other thing. I print your black propaganda whenever you ask. Why don't you toss me a real story every once in a while? Something with a little sizzle. Something that will sell newspapers. Show the money boys that Looking Glass is still a force to be reckoned with."

"I'll try to come up with something."

"You *will* come up with something." Stone shoved another fistful of caviar into his mouth. "Together we can move mountains, Ari. But if Looking Glass goes down, things could get quite nasty indeed."

The following morning Shamron and Gabriel met in Hampstead Heath. They walked along a footpath bordered by two rows of dripping beech trees. Shamron waited for a pair of joggers to pass before speaking. "You have your money—five hundred thousand American. Usual account in Geneva."

"And if I need more?"

"Then I'll get you more. But the well is not bottomless. You were always careful about money. I hope nothing will change now that you have no reason to fear the accountants of King Saul Boulevard."

"I'll spend only what I need."

Shamron changed the subject to communication. Because Lev controlled London Station, its staff and facilities were strictly off-limits to Gabriel. There were three London *bodelim* who were loyal to Shamron and could be counted on to do favors for Gabriel without telling the station chief. Shamron recited a series of telephone numbers. Gabriel committed them to memory. It was as if they were back at the Academy, playing silly memory games and awareness drills, like counting the steps on a flight of stairs, or recording the contents of a man's closet, or the registration numbers of a dozen parked cars, with one brief glance.

Shamron moved on. The London Station secure cable could not be used for electronic communication because all transmissions would have to be cleared by the station chief. The London Station pouch could not be used for the same reason. In a pinch Gabriel could insert a field report into the diplomatic pouch addressed to Amos Argov. A friend in the Foreign Ministry would forward it to Shamron at King Saul Boulevard. But he should not abuse the privilege. Gabriel was also forbidden to use London safe flats, because London Station administered them and Lev kept careful track of their use.

Shamron rattled off a telephone number in Oslo that was routed through to his home in Tiberias. Gabriel was to treat the line as though it were insecure.

"If a face-to-face meeting is required, Paris will be the venue," Shamron said. "We'll use the sites from the Black September operation, for old times' sake. Same sequence, same fallbacks, same body talk. Do you remember the Paris sites?"

"We'll always have Paris."

"Any questions?"

Gabriel shook his head.

"Is there anything else I can do for you?"

"You may leave the United Kingdom as quickly as possible," Gabriel said.

Then he turned and walked quickly away.

# 10

## ST. JAMES'S, LONDON

"Listen, Julie," said Oliver Dimbleby, leaning his thick head over the table and lowering his voice. "I know you're in trouble. The whole *street* knows you're in trouble. There're no secrets down here, petal."

Oliver Dimbleby was a pink man in a pink shirt who always seemed unduly pleased with himself. His hair was curly and sandy, with tiny horns over his ears. Isherwood and Dimbleby were as close as two competitors could be in the London art trade, which meant that Isherwood despised him only a little.

"You've lost your backing," Dimbleby said. "You can't *give* a painting away. You even lost this month's girl, two weeks ahead of schedule. Oh, *hell,* what was this one's name?"

"Heather."

"Ah, yes, Heather. A shame to lose one like that, wasn't it? I would have enjoyed getting to know *Heather* a bit better. She came to me before she went to Giles Pittaway. Lovely girl, but I told her I wouldn't poach in a friend's forest. Sent her packing. Unfortunately, she walked to New Bond Strasse and straight into the arms of the devil."

"So I'm in trouble," said Isherwood, trying to change the subject. "What's your point?"

"It's Pittaway, isn't it? Killing all of us, what?" There was a bit of the Estuary in Dimbleby's accent, and it had thickened with the two bottles of Burgundy they'd consumed over lunch at Wilton's. "Allow me to let you in on a little secret, old love. We're all in the same boat. There are no buyers and no good pictures to sell even if there were. It's all modern and the Impressionists, and nobody can afford to deal van Goghs and Monets except the big boys. I had a pop star come into my gallery the other day. Wanted something for his bedroom to pull together his duvet cover and Santa Fe carpet. I sent him to Selfridges. He didn't see the humor in that, thick bastard. Father warned me to stay out of this business. Sometimes, I wish to Christ I'd listened to the old bugger. Giles Pittaway has sucked all the air out of the market. And with such crap. *Jesus!* But it's crap, isn't it, Julie?"

"Beyond crap, Oliver," Isherwood agreed, and poured some more of the wine.

"I wandered past one of his galleries last week. Looked in the window. There was a very glossy, very shiny piece of shit by that French flower painter from Colmar. Oh, shit, what's his name, Julie?"

"Are you referring to Jean-Georges Hirn?"

"Ah, yes, that's it! Jean-Georges Hirn. Bouquet of roses, narcissi, hyacinth, nasturtium, morning glory, and other flowers. I call it chocolate box. Know what I mean, Julie?"

Isherwood nodded slowly and sipped his wine. Dimbleby took a deep breath and plunged on. "That very same night Roddy and I had dinner at the Mirabelle. You know how dinners with Roddy can be. Needless to say, when the two of us left the restaurant at midnight, we were flying very high indeed. Feeling absolutely no pain. *Numb.* Roddy and I wandered the streets for a while. He's getting divorced, Roddy. Wife's finally had enough of his antics. In any case, we soon found ourselves standing in front of the very same gallery owned by the venerable Giles Pittaway, in front of the very same piece of shit by Jean-Georges Hirn, bouquet of roses, narcissi, hyacinth, nasturtium, morning glory, and other flowers."

"I'm not sure I want to hear the rest," Isherwood moaned.

"Oh, but you do, petal." Dimbleby leaned forward even closer and moistened his thin lips with his agile little tongue. "Roddy went crazy. Made one of his speeches. He was so loud they probably heard him in St. John's Wood. Said Pittaway was the devil. Said his ascendancy was a sign the apocalypse was near. Marvelous stuff, really. I just stood on the pavement and applauded and tossed in a 'hear, hear' every now and again for good measure."

Dimbleby drew even closer and lowered his voice to an excited whisper. "When he's finished with the sermon, he starts beating his briefcase against the glass. You know that hideous metal creature he insists on carrying. After a couple of throws, the window shatters and the alarm starts to sound."

"Oliver! Tell me this is just another one of your stories! My God!"

"Truth, Julie. Unvarnished truth. Not telling tall tales. I grabbed Roddy by the collar and we started to run like hell. Roddy was so pissed he can't remember a thing."

Isherwood was getting a headache from the wine. "Is there a point to this wretched story, Oliver?"

"My point is that you're not alone. We're all hurting. Giles Pittaway has us all by the balls, and he's squeezing harder than ever. Mine are turning blue, for Christ's sake."

"You're surviving, Oliver. And you're getting fatter. You're going to need a bigger gallery soon."

"Oh, doing quite nicely, thank you very much. But I could be doing better. And so could you, Julie. No criticism intended, but you could move a few more pictures than you're moving."

"Things are going to turn around. I just need to hold on by my fingernails for a few weeks, and then I'll be fine. What I *need* is a new girl."

"I can get you a girl."

"Not that kind of girl. I need a girl who can answer the phone, a girl who knows something about art."

"The girl I was thinking about is very good on the phone and is a real work of art. And you're not pinning your hopes on that piece you bought at Christie's last summer?"

"Oliver, how did you—"

"Like I said, petal. There are no secrets down here."

"Oliver, if there is a point to this conversation, please *do* come to it soon."

"My *point* is that we need to band together. We need to form an alliance if we're to survive. We're never going to defeat the dreaded Giles Pittaway, but if we create a mutual defense pact perhaps we can live side by side in peace."

"You're babbling, Oliver. Try talking straight for once in your life, for God's sake. I'm not one of your girlfriends."

"All right, straight talk. I'm thinking about a partnership."

"A partnership? What kind of partnership?"

"You want it straight?"

"Yes, of course."

"The kind of partnership where I buy you out."

"Oliver!"

"You've a nice gallery."

"Oliver!"

"You've nice paintings down there in your vault."

"*Oliver!*"

"You've even managed to retain something of a reputation. I would like to inspect your inventory and come to a fair price. Enough money for you to clear away your debt. Then I'd like to burn all your dead stock, get something for it, and start over. You can work for me. I'll pay you a generous salary, plus commission. You can do quite nicely, Julie."

"Work for you? Are you completely insane? Oliver, how dare you?"

"Don't get your back up. Don't get your pride up. It's business, not personal. You're drowning, Julian. I'm throwing you a lifeline. Don't be a fool. Take the bloody thing."

But Isherwood was getting to his feet and digging through his pockets for money.

"Julian, please. Keep your money. It's my party. Don't behave like this."

"Piss off!" Isherwood hurled a pair of twenty-pound notes toward Dimbleby's pink face. "How dare you, Oliver! Really!"

He stormed out of the restaurant and walked back to the gallery. So, the jackals of St. James's were circling, and fat Oliver Dimbleby wanted the biggest piece of the carcass for himself. *Buy me out, Oliver! Imagine the nerve! Imagine me working for that tubby little misogynist!* He had half a mind to call Giles Pittaway and tell him the story about the broken window.

As Isherwood marched across Mason's Yard, he vowed not to surrender without a fight. But in order to fight he needed a clean Vecellio, and for that he needed Gabriel. He had to find him before he fell under Shamron's spell and was gone forever. He walked up the stairs and let himself into the gallery. It was terribly depressing to be alone. He was used to seeing a pretty girl behind the desk when he came back to work after lunch. He sat down at his desk, found Gabriel's number in his telephone book, dialed the number, let it ring a dozen times, slammed down the receiver. *Maybe he's just gone to the village. Or maybe he's out on that bloody boat of his.*

*Or maybe Shamron has already got to him.*

"Shit!" he said softly.

He left the gallery, flagged down a taxi on Piccadilly, rode up to Great Russell Street. He paid off the cab a few blocks from the British Museum and stepped through the doorway of the L. Cornellissen & Son art supplies shop. He felt strangely calm as he stood on the scuffed wooden floor, surrounded by the varnished shelves filled with paints, palettes, paper, canvases, brushes, and charcoal pencils.

A flaxen angel called Penelope smiled at him over the counter.

"Hullo, Pen."

"Julian, *super*," she breathed. "How are you? God, but you look all in."

"Lunch with Oliver Dimbleby." No other explanation was necessary. "Listen, I was wondering if you've seen our friend. He's not answering his phone, and I'm starting to think he's wandered off the edge of a cliff down there in Cornwall."

"Unfortunately, I haven't been fortunate enough to lay eyes on that lovely man in quite some time."

"Anyone else in the shop heard from him?"

"Hold on. I'll check."

Penelope asked Margaret, and Margaret asked Sherman, and Sherman asked Tricia, and on it went until a disembodied male voice from deep in the shop—the acrylic paint and pencil section judging by the sound of it—announced solemnly, "I spoke to him just this morning."

"Mind telling me what he wanted?" said Isherwood to the ceiling.

"To cancel his monthly shipment of supplies."

"How many *monthly* shipments exactly?"

"*Every* monthly until further notice."

"Did he say why?"

"Does he ever, darling?"

Next morning Isherwood canceled his appointments for the rest of the week and hired a car. For five hours he sped along the motorways. Westward to Bristol. Southward along the Channel. Then the long haul down through Devon and Cornwall. Weather as volatile as Isherwood's mood, marbles of rain one moment, weak white winter sun the next. The wind was constant, though. So much wind Isherwood had trouble keeping the little Ford Escort attached to the road. He ate lunch while he drove and stopped only three times—once for petrol, once for a piss, and a third time on Dartmoor when his car struck a seabird. He picked up the corpse, using an empty plastic sandwich bag to protect his fingers, and said a brief Jewish prayer for the dead before ceremoniously tossing the bird into the heather.

He arrived at Gabriel's cottage shortly before three o'clock. Gabriel's boat was covered in a tarpaulin. He crossed the lane and rang the bell. He rang it a second time, then hammered on the door, then tried the latch. Locked.

He peered through the paned glass into a spotless kitchen. Gabriel was never one for food—throw him a scrap of bread and a few grains of rice and he could walk another fifty miles—but even by Gabriel's standards the kitchen was exceptionally clean and free of supplies. He was gone, Isherwood concluded. Gone for a very long time.

He entered the back garden and walked along the edge of the cottage, trying each of the windows on the off chance that Gabriel had forgotten to lock one. Not Gabriel's style.

He retraced his steps and stood on the quay again. Gunpowder clouds were rolling up the river from the sea. A fat ball of rain struck him in the center of the forehead and rolled down the bridge of his nose beneath his glasses. He removed them and the river scene blurred. He dug a handkerchief from his pocket, wiped his face, and put the glasses back on.

When his surroundings came back into focus, he discovered a young boy standing a few feet away. He seemed to have come out of nowhere, like a cat stalking prey. Isherwood had never had children and was terrible at placing ages. He guessed that the pinched-faced lad was eleven or twelve.

The boy said, "Why are you sneaking around that cottage?"

"I'm not sneaking, and who the bloody hell are you?"

"I'm Peel. Who are you?"

"I'm a friend of the man who lives there. My name is Julian."

Isherwood held out his hand, but the boy just stood there, body rigid and coiled.

"He never mentioned he had a friend named Julian."

"He doesn't mention a lot of things."

"What do you want?"

"To talk to him."

"He's away."

"I can see that. Do you know where he is?"

"He didn't say."

"Know when he'll be back?"

"Didn't say."

The rain started to come down harder. The boy remained still. Isherwood held a hand over his head and turned to look at the cottage. "Do you know what he does for a living?" Isherwood asked.

Peel nodded.

"Does anyone else in the village?"

Peel shook his head.

"He works for me," Isherwood said, as if he were confessing some misdeed. "I own the painting he's restoring."

"The Rembrandt or the Vecellio?"

Isherwood smiled and said, "The Vecellio, my dear fellow."

"It's beautiful."

"Indeed, it is."

They stood side by side for a moment, oblivious of the rain. Isherwood saw something of himself in Gabriel's miniature sentinel. Another Gabriel refugee, another piece of wreckage adrift in Gabriel's wake. Another damaged soul in need of restoration by Gabriel's skilled hands.

"Who took him?" Isherwood finally asked.

"The bald man who walked like a soldier. Do you know him?"

"Unfortunately, I do." Isherwood smiled at Peel. "Are you hungry?"

Peel nodded.

"Is there someplace in the village to get some tea and sweets?"

"And a pastie," Peel said. "Do you like sausage pasties?"

"Can't say I've ever tried one, but there's no time like the present. Should you ask your parents for permission first?"

Peel shook his head. "He's not my dad, and my mum won't care."

Ari Shamron arrived at Lod Airport in Tel Aviv late the following evening. Rami was waiting at the gate. He shepherded Shamron through the arrivals area into a secure room reserved for Office personnel and special guests. Shamron stripped off his European business suit and pulled on his khakis and bomber jacket.

"The prime minister wants to see you tonight, boss."

Shamron thought: *So much for keeping his nose out of the operation.*

They rode into the hills toward Jerusalem. Shamron passed the time by leafing through a stack of paperwork that had piled up in his brief absence.

As usual there was a crisis in the prime minister's diverse coalition. To reach his office Shamron first had to negotiate a smoky corridor filled with feuding politicians.

The prime minister listened raptly as Shamron brought him up-to-date. He was by nature a schemer. He had begun his career in the cutthroat atmosphere of academia, then moved to the hornets' nest at the Foreign Ministry. By the time he entered the political arena, he was well versed in the black arts of bureaucratic treachery. His meteoric rise through the party ranks was attributed to his powerful intellect and his willingness to resort to subterfuge, misdirection, and outright blackmail to get what he wanted. In Shamron he saw a kindred spirit—a man who would stop at nothing if he believed his cause was right.

"There's only one problem," Shamron said.

The prime minister glanced at the ceiling impatiently. He was fond of saying, "Bring me solutions, not problems." Shamron had an innate distrust of men who lived by catchy maxims.

"Benjamin Stone."

"What now?"

"His business is in terrible shape. He's robbing Peter to pay Paul, and Peter's friends are getting upset about it."

"Will it affect us?"

"If he goes under quietly, we'll just miss his money. But if he goes under in a messy way, he could make things uncomfortable for us. I'm afraid he knows too much."

"Benjamin Stone never does anything quietly."

"Point taken."

"What about those lovely home movies you made of him last year at the King David?"

"It seemed like a good idea at the time, but Stone has developed a rather high threshold for public embarrassment. I'm not sure he's going to be terribly upset if the world sees him utilizing the services of an Israeli prostitute."

"The politicians outside my door are my problem," the prime minister said. "But I'm afraid that Benjamin Stone is yours. Deal with him as you see fit."

# PART TWO

# ASSESSMENT

# 11

*Before the war Maurice Halévy was one of the most promi-
nent lawyers in Marseilles. He and his wife, Rachel, had
lived in a stately old house on the rue Sylvabelle in the Beaux
Quartiers, where most of the city's successful assimilated Jews
had settled. They were proud to be French; they considered
themselves French first and Jews second. Indeed, Maurice
Halévy was so assimilated that he rarely bothered to go to
synagogue. But when the Germans invaded, the Halévys'
idyllic life in Marseilles came to an abrupt end. In October
1940 the collaborationist Vichy government handed down
the* statut des Juifs, *the anti-Jewish edicts that reduced Jews
to second-class citizens in Vichy France. Maurice Halévy
was stripped of the right to practice law. He was required to
register with the police, and later he and his wife were forced
to wear the Star of David on their clothing.*

*The situation worsened in 1942, when the German
army moved into Vichy France after the Allied invasion of
North Africa. French Resistance forces carried out a series
of deadly attacks on German forces. The German security
police, with the help of Vichy French authorities, responded
with brutal reprisal killings. Maurice Halévy could ig-
nore the threat no longer. Rachel had become pregnant.*

*The thought of trying to care for a newborn in the chaos of Marseilles was too much to bear. He decided to leave the city for the countryside. He used his dwindling savings to rent a cottage in the hills outside Aix-en-Provence. In January, Rachel gave birth to a son, Isaac.*

*A week later the Germans and French police began rounding up the Jews. It took them a month to find Maurice and Rachel Halévy. A pair of German SS officers appeared at the cottage on a February evening, accompanied by a local gendarme. They gave the Halévys twenty minutes to pack a bag weighing no more than sixty pounds. While the Germans and the gendarme waited in the dining room, the woman from the next cottage appeared at the door.*

*"My name is Anne-Marie Delacroix," she said. "The Halévys were looking after my son while I went to the market."*

*The gendarme studied his papers. According to the documents, only two Jews lived in the cottage. He called for the Halévys and said, "This woman says the boy belongs to her. Is this the truth?"*

*"Of course it is," Maurice Halévy said, squeezing Rachel's arm before she could utter a sound. "We were just watching the boy for the afternoon." The gendarme looked at Maurice Halévy incredulously, then consulted the registration documents a second time. "Take the child and leave," he snapped to the woman. "I have a good mind to take you into custody myself for entrusting a French child to the care of these dirty Jews."*

*Two months later Maurice and Rachel Halévy were murdered at Sobibor.*

*After the liberation, Anne-Marie Delacroix took Isaac to a synagogue in Marseilles and told the rabbi what had happened that night in Aix-en-Provence. The rabbi offered her the choice of placing the child for adoption by a Jewish family or raising him herself. She took the boy back to Aix and raised him as a Jew alongside her own Catholic children. In 1965 Isaac Halévy married a girl from Nîmes named Deborah and settled in Marseilles in his father's old house on the rue Sylvabelle. Three years later they had their first and only child: a girl they named Sarah.*

PARIS

Michel Duval was the hottest fashion photographer in Paris. The designers and the magazine editors adored him because his pictures radiated an eye-grabbing aura of dangerous sexuality. Jacqueline Delacroix thought he was a pig. She knew he achieved his unique look by abusing his models. She wasn't looking forward to working with him.

She stepped out of a taxi and entered the apartment building on the rue St-Jacques where Michel kept his studio. Upstairs a small crowd was waiting: makeup artist, hairdresser, stylist, a representative from Givenchy. Michel stood atop a ladder, adjusting lights: good-looking, shoulder-length blond hair, feline features. He wore black leather trousers, low-slung around narrow hips, and a loose pullover. He winked at Jacqueline as she came in. She smiled and said, "Nice to see you, Michel."

"We'll have a good shoot today, yes? I can feel it."

"I hope so."

She entered a changing room, undressed, and studied her appearance in the mirror with professional dispassion. Physically she was a stunning woman: tall, graceful arms and legs, elegant waist, pale olive skin. Her breasts were aesthetically perfect: firm, rounded, neither too small nor abnormally large. The photographers had always loved her breasts. Most models detested lingerie work, but it never bothered Jacqueline. She'd always had more offers for work than she could fit into her schedule.

Her gaze moved from her body to her face. She had curly raven hair that fell about her shoulders, dark eyes, a long, slender nose. Her cheekbones were wide and even, her jawline angular, her lips full. She was proud of the fact that her face had never been altered by a surgeon's scalpel. She leaned forward, probed at the skin around her eyes. She didn't like what she saw. It wasn't a line, really—something more subtle and insidious. The intangible sign of aging. She no longer had the eyes of a child. She had the eyes of a thirty-three-year-old woman.

*You're still beautiful, but face facts, Jacqueline. You're getting old.*

She pulled on a white robe, went into the next room, and sat down. The makeup artist began applying a base to her cheek. Jacqueline watched in the mirror as her face was slowly transformed into that of someone she didn't quite recognize. She wondered what her grandfather would think if he could see this.

*He'd probably be ashamed. . . .*

When the makeup artist and hairstylist finished, Jacqueline looked at herself in the mirror. Had it not been for the courage of those three remarkable people—her grandparents and Anne-Marie Delacroix—she would not be here today.

*And look at what you've become—an exquisite clothes hanger.*

She stood up, walked back to the changing room. The dress, a black strapless evening gown, waited for her. She removed her robe, stepped into the gown, and pulled it up over her bare breasts. Then she glanced at herself in the mirror. Devastating.

A knock at the door. "Michel is ready for you, Miss Delacroix."

"Tell Michel I'll be out in a moment."

*Miss Delacroix . . .*

Even after all these years she was still not used to it: Jacqueline Delacroix. Her agent, Marcel Lambert, was the one who had changed her name—*"Sarah Halévy sounds too . . . well . . . you know what I mean,* mon chou. *Don't make me say it out loud. So vulgar, but such is the way of the world."* Sometimes the sound of her French name made her skin crawl. When she learned what had happened to her grandparents in the war, she had burned with hatred and suspicion of all French people. Whenever she saw an old man, she would wonder what he had done during the war. Had he been a guard at Gurs or Les Milles or one of the other detention camps? Had he been a gendarme who helped the Germans round up her family? Had he been a bureaucrat who stamped and processed the paperwork of death? Or had he simply stood by in silence and done nothing? Secretly it gave her intense delight that she was deceiving the fashion world. Imagine their reaction if they found out the lanky, raven-haired beauty from Marseilles was in fact a Provençal Jew whose grandparents had been gassed at Sobibor. In a way being a model, the very image of French beauty, was her revenge.

She took one last look at herself, lowering her chin toward her chest, parting her lips slightly, bringing fire to her coal black eyes.

Now she was ready.

They worked for thirty minutes without stopping. Jacqueline adopted several poses. She sprawled across a simple wooden chair. She sat on the floor, leaning back on her hands, with her head tilted upward and her eyes closed. She stood with her hands on her hips and her eyes boring through the lens of Michel's camera. Michel seemed to like what he was seeing. They were in sync. Every few minutes he would pause for a few seconds to change his film, then quickly resume shooting. Jacqueline had been in the business long enough to know when a shoot was working.

So she was surprised when he suddenly stepped from

behind the camera and ran a hand through his hair. He was frowning. "Clear the studio, please. I need some privacy."

Jacqueline thought: *Oh, Christ. Here we go.*

Michel said, "What the hell's wrong with you?"

"Nothing's wrong with me!"

"Nothing? You're flat, Jacqueline. The pictures are flat. I might as well be taking pictures of a mannequin wearing the dress. I can't afford to give Givenchy a set of flat prints. And from what I hear on the street, you can't afford it either."

"What's that supposed to mean?"

"It means you're getting old, darling. It means that no one's quite sure whether you have what it takes anymore."

"Just get back behind the camera, and I'll show you I have what it takes."

"I've seen enough. It's just not there today."

"Bullshit!"

"You want me to get you a drink? Maybe a glass of wine will help loosen you up."

"I don't need a drink."

"How about some coke?"

"You know I don't do that anymore."

"Well, I do."

"Some things never change."

Michel produced a small bag of cocaine from his shirt pocket. Jacqueline sat down in the prop chair while he prepared two lines on a glass-topped table. He snorted one, then offered her the rolled-up hundred-franc note. "Feel like being a bad girl today?"

"All yours, Michel. Not interested."

He leaned over and snorted the second line. Then he wiped the glass with his finger and spread the residue over his gums. "If you're not going to have a drink or do a line, maybe we need to think of some other way to light a fire in you."

"Like what?" she said, but she knew what Michel had on his mind.

He stood behind her, placed his hands lightly on her bare shoulders. "Maybe you need to be thinking about getting fucked." His hands moved from her shoulders, and he stroked the skin just above her breasts. "Maybe we can do something to make the idea a little more realistic in your imagination."

He pressed his pelvis against her back, so that she could feel his erection beneath his leather trousers.

She drew away.

"I'm just trying to help, Jacqueline. I want to make sure these pictures come out well. I don't want to see your career crash and burn. My motives are purely selfless."

"I never knew you were such a philanthropist, Michel."

He laughed. "Come with me. I want to show you something." He took her by the hand and pulled her off the set. They walked down a hallway and entered a room furnished with nothing but a large bed. Michel pulled off his shirt and began unbuttoning his trousers.

Jacqueline said, "What do you think you're doing?"

"You want good pictures, I want good pictures. Let's get in the right frame of mind. Take off the dress so it doesn't get ruined."

"Go fuck yourself, Michel. I'm leaving."

"Come on, Jacqueline. Stop fooling around and get into bed."

"No!"

"What's the big deal? You slept with Robert Leboucher, so he would give you that swimwear shoot in Mustique."

"How did you know that?"

"Because he told me."

"You're a bastard, and so is he! I'm not some seventeen-year-old who's going to spread her legs for you because she wants good pictures from the great Michel Duval."

"If you walk out of here, your career is over."

"I don't give a shit."

He pointed at his erection. "What am I supposed to do about this?"

Marcel Lambert lived a short distance away, on the rue de Tournon, in the Luxembourg Quarter. Jacqueline needed time to herself, so she walked, taking her time in the narrow side streets of the Latin Quarter. Darkness falling, lights coming on in the bistros and the cafés, the smell of cigarettes and frying garlic on the chill air.

She crossed into the Luxembourg Quarter. How

quickly it had come to this, she thought—Michel Duval, trying to threaten her into a quickie between takes. A few years ago he wouldn't have considered it. But not now. Now she was vulnerable, and Marcel had decided to test her.

Sometimes she was sorry she ever got into this business. She had planned to be a ballet dancer—had studied at the most prestigious academy in Marseilles—but at sixteen she was spotted by a talent scout from a Paris modeling agency, who gave her name to Marcel Lambert. Marcel scheduled a test shoot, let her move into his flat, taught her how to move and act like a model instead of a ballerina. The photographs from the test shoot were stunning. She had dominated the camera, radiated a playful sexuality. Marcel quietly put the pictures into circulation around Paris: no name, nothing about the girl, just the pictures and his card. The reaction was instantaneous. His telephone didn't stop ringing for a week. Photographers were clamoring to work with her. Designers wanted to sign her up for their fall shows. Word of the photographs leaked from Paris to Milan and from Milan to New York. The entire fashion world wanted to know the name of this mysterious raven-haired French beauty.

*Jacqueline Delacroix.*

How different things were now. The quality work had started to slow down when she turned twenty-six, but now that she was thirty-three the good jobs had dried up. She still got some runway work in Paris and Milan in the fall, but only with lower-level designers. She still landed the occasional lingerie ad—"There's nothing wrong with your tits, darling," Marcel liked to say—but he had been forced to hire her out for different types of shoots. She had just finished a shoot for a German brewery in which she posed as the attractive wife of a successful middle-aged man.

Marcel had warned it would happen this way. He had told her to save her money, to prepare herself for a life after modeling. Jacqueline had never bothered—she'd assumed the money would pour in forever. Sometimes she tried to remember where all of it had gone. The clothes. The crash pads in Paris and New York. The extravagant vacations with the other girls in the Caribbean or the South Pacific. The ton of cocaine she had sucked up her nose before getting straight.

Michel Duval had been right about one thing: she *had* slept with a man to get a job, an editor from French *Vogue* named Robert Leboucher. It was a high-profile job that she needed desperately—a swimsuit and summer-wear shoot in Mustique. It could change everything for her—give her enough money to get back on stable ground financially, show everyone in the industry that she still had what it took for the hot jobs. At least for one more year, two at the most. *Then what?*

She walked into Marcel's building, entered the lift, rode up to his flat. When she knocked on the door, it flew back. Marcel stood there, wide-eyed, mouth open. "Jacqueline, my pet! Please tell me it's not true. Tell me you didn't kick Michel Duval in the balls! Tell me he made up the entire thing!"

"Actually, Marcel, I kicked him in the cock."

He threw back his head and laughed loudly. "I'm certain you're the first woman who's ever done that. Serves the bastard right. He almost ruined Claudette. You remember what he did to her? Poor little thing. So beautiful, so much talent."

He pulled his lips downward, emitted a Gallic snort of disapproval, took her by the hand, and pulled her inside. A moment later they were drinking wine on the couch in his sitting room, the hum of evening traffic drifting through the open windows. Marcel lit her cigarette and deftly waved out the match. He wore tight-fitting faded blue jeans, black loafers, and a gray turtleneck sweater. His thinning gray hair was cropped very short. He'd had another face-lift recently; his blue eyes seemed unnaturally large and bulging, as if he were constantly surprised. She thought about those days so long ago, when Marcel had brought her to this flat and prepared her for her life ahead. She'd always felt safe in this place.

"So what kind of stunt did Michel pull now?"

Jacqueline described the shoot, holding nothing back. There were few secrets between them. When she finished Marcel said, "You probably shouldn't have kicked him. He's threatening to sue."

"Let him try. Every girl he's coerced into having sex will testify at his trial. It'll destroy him."

"Robert Leboucher called me a few minutes before you arrived. He's trying to back out of Mustique. He says he can't work with a woman who kicks photographers."

"Word travels fast in this business."

"It always has. I think I can talk some sense into Robert." Marcel hesitated, then added, "That is, if you want me to."

"Of course I want you to."

"Are you sure, Jacqueline? Are you sure you still have what it takes for this kind of work?"

She took a long drink of the wine, leaned her head against Marcel's shoulder. "Actually, I'm not quite sure I do."

"Do me a favor, sweetheart. Go to your house in the south for a few days. Or take one of those long trips like you used to take. You know—the ones you were always so mysterious about. Get some rest. Clear your head. Do some serious thinking. I'll try to talk some sense into Robert. But you have to decide whether this is really what you want."

She closed her eyes. Perhaps it was time to get out while she still had some shred of dignity. "You're right," she said. "I could use a few days in the countryside. But I want you to call that fucking Robert Leboucher right now and tell him that you expect him to keep his word about the shoot in Mustique."

"And what if I can't make him change his mind?"

"Tell him I'll kick him in the cock too."

Marcel smiled. "Jacqueline, darling, I've always liked your style."

# 12

Fiona Barrows looked a great deal like the block of flats she managed in Sussex Gardens: broad and squat with a bright coat of paint that could not conceal the fact she was aging and not terribly gracefully. The short walk from the lift to the entrance of the vacant flat left her slightly out of breath. She shoved the key into the lock with her plump hand, pushed open the door with a little grunt. "Here we are," she sang.

She led him on a brief tour: a sitting room furnished with well-worn couches and chairs, two identical bedrooms with double beds and matching bedside tables, a small dining room with a modern table of tinted gray glass, a cramped galley kitchen with a two-burner stove and a microwave oven.

He walked back into the sitting room, stood in the window, opened the blinds. Across the road was another block of flats.

"If you want my opinion, you couldn't ask for a better location in London for the price," Fiona Barrows said.

"Oxford Street is very close, and of course Hyde Park is just around the corner. Do you have children?"

"No, I don't," Gabriel said absently, still looking at the block of flats across the street.

"What kind of work do you do, if you don't mind me asking?"

"I'm an art restorer."

"You mean you spruce up old paintings?"

"Something like that."

"You do the frames as well? I have an old frame in my flat that needs patching up."

"Just the paintings, I'm afraid."

She looked at him as he stood in the window, gazing into space. A handsome man, she thought. Nice hands. Good hands were sexy in a man. Imagine, an *art* restorer, right here in the building. It would be nice to have a touch of class around for a change. Oh, that she were still single—single, twenty years younger, twenty pounds lighter. He was a cautious fellow; she could see that. A man who never made a move without thinking through every angle. He would probably want to see a dozen more flats before making up his mind. "So, what do you think?"

"It's perfect," he said to the window.

"When would you like it?"

Gabriel closed the blind. "Right now."

For two days Gabriel watched him.

On the first day he saw him just once—when he rose

shortly after noon and appeared briefly in the window wearing only a pair of black underpants. He had dark, curly hair, angular cheekbones, and full lips. His body was lean and lightly muscled. Gabriel pulled open Shamron's file and compared the face in the window with the photograph clipped to the manila cover.

Same man.

Gabriel could feel an operational coldness spreading over him as he studied the figure in the window. Suddenly everything seemed brighter and sharper in contrast. Noises seemed louder and more distinct—a car door closing, lovers quarreling in the next flat, a telephone ringing unanswered, his teakettle screaming in the kitchen. One by one he tuned out these intrusions and focused all his attention on the man in the window across the street.

Yusef al-Tawfiki, part-time Palestinian nationalist poet, part-time student at University College London, part-time waiter at a Lebanese restaurant called the Kebab Factory on the Edgware Road, full-time action agent for Tariq's secret army.

A hand appeared on Yusef's abdomen: pale skin, luminous against his dark complexion. A woman's hand. Gabriel saw a flash of short blond hair. Then Yusef vanished behind the curtains.

The girl left an hour later. Before climbing into the taxi, she looked up toward the flat to see if her lover was watching. The window was empty and the curtains drawn. She closed the door, a little harder than necessary, and the taxi drove away.

Gabriel made his first operational assessment: Yusef didn't treat his women well.

The next day Gabriel decided to mount a loose physical surveillance.

Yusef left the flat at midday. He wore a white shirt, black trousers, and a black leather jacket. As he stepped onto the pavement, he paused to light a cigarette and scan the parked cars for any sign of surveillance. He waved out the match and started walking toward the Edgware Road. After about a hundred yards he stopped suddenly, turned around, and walked back to the entrance of the block of flats.

Standard countersurveillance move, thought Gabriel. He's a professional.

Five minutes later Yusef was back outside and walking in the direction of the Edgware Road. Gabriel went into the bathroom, rubbed styling oil into his short hair, and slipped on a pair of red-tinted spectacles. Then he pulled on his coat and went out.

Across the street from the Kebab Factory was a small Italian restaurant. Gabriel went inside and sat down at a table next to the window. He remembered the lectures at the Academy. If you're watching a target from a café, don't do things that make you look like you're watching a target from a café, such as sitting alone for hours pretending to read a newspaper. Too obvious.

Gabriel transformed himself. He became Cedric, a

writer for an upstart Paris cultural magazine. He spoke English with a nearly impenetrable French accent. He claimed to be working on a story about why London was so exciting these days and Paris so dreary. He smoked Gitane cigarettes and drank a great deal of wine. He carried on a tiresome conversation with a pair of Swedish girls at the next table. He invited one of them to his hotel room. When she refused he asked the other. When she refused he asked them both. He spilled a glass of Chianti. The manager, Signor Andriotti, appeared at the table and warned Cedric to keep quiet or he would have to leave.

Yet all the while Gabriel was watching Yusef across the street. He watched him while he skillfully handled the lunch crowd. Watched him when he left the restaurant briefly and walked up the road to a newsstand that stocked Arabic-language newspapers. Watched while a pretty dark-haired girl jotted her telephone number on the back of a napkin and slipped it into his shirt pocket for safekeeping. Watched while he carried on a long conversation with a vigilant-looking Arab. In fact, at the moment Gabriel was spilling his Chianti, he was memorizing the make and registration number of the Arab's Nissan car. And while he was fending off the exasperated Signor Andriotti, he was watching Yusef talking on the telephone. *Who was he talking to?* A woman? A cousin in Ramallah? His control officer?

After an hour Gabriel decided it was no longer wise to remain in the café. He paid his check, left a generous tip, and apologized for his boorish behavior. Signor Andriotti guided him to the door and cast him gently out to sea.

That evening Gabriel sat in the chair next to his window, waiting for Yusef to return home. The street shone with the night rain. A motorcycle sped past, boy driving, girl on the back, pleading with him to slow down. Probably nothing, but he made a note of it in his logbook, along with the time: eleven-fifteen.

He had a headache from the wine. Already the flat was beginning to depress him. How many nights had he spent like this? Sitting in a sterile Office safe flat or a shabby rented room, watching, waiting. He craved something beautiful, so he slipped a compact disc of *La Bohème* into the portable stereo at his feet and lowered the volume to a whisper. Intelligence work is patience, Shamron always said. Intelligence work is tedium.

He got up, went into the kitchen, took aspirin for his headache. Next door a mother and a daughter began to quarrel in Lebanese-accented Arabic. A glass shattered, then another, a door slamming, running outside in the corridor.

Gabriel sat down again and closed his eyes, and after a moment he was back in North Africa, twelve years earlier.

*The rubber dinghies came ashore with the gentle surf at Rouad. Gabriel climbed out into warm shin-deep water and pulled the dinghy onto the sand. The team of Sayaret commandos followed him across the beach, weapons at their sides. Somewhere a dog was barking. The scent of woodsmoke and grilling meat hung on the air. The girl waited behind the wheel of the Volkswagen minibus. Four of the commandos climbed into the Volkswagen with Gabriel. The rest slipped into a pair of Peugeot station wagons parked behind the minibus. A few seconds later the engines started in unison, and they sped off through the cool April evening.*

*Gabriel wore a lip microphone connected to a small transmitter in his jacket pocket. The radio broadcast over a secure wavelength to a specially equipped Boeing 707 flying just off the Tunisian coastline in a civilian air corridor, masquerading as an El Al charter. If anything went wrong, they could abort the mission within seconds.*

*"Mother has arrived safely," Gabriel murmured. He released the talk button and heard the words "Proceed to Mother's house."*

*Gabriel held his Beretta between his knees during the drive, smoked for his nerves. The girl kept both hands on the wheel, eyes fixed on the darkened streets. She was tall, taller than Leah, with black eyes and a mane of dark hair held in place by a simple silver clasp at the nape of her neck. She knew the route as well as Gabriel. When Shamron dispatched Gabriel to Tunis to study the target, the girl had gone with him and posed as his wife. Gabriel reached out and gently squeezed her shoulder as she drove. Her muscles were rigid. "Relax," he said softly, and she smiled briefly and let out a long breath. "You're doing fine."*

*They entered Sidi Boussaid, a wealthy Tunis suburb not*

*far from the sea, and parked outside the villa. The Peugeots
pulled in behind them. The girl killed the engine. Twelve-
fifteen. Exactly on schedule.*

*Gabriel knew the villa as well as he knew his own home.
He had studied it and photographed it from every conceiv-
able vantage point during the surveillance operation. They
had built a perfect duplicate in the Negev, where he and
the rest of the team rehearsed the assault countless times.
During the final session they had managed to carry out the
mission in twenty-two seconds.*

*"We've arrived at Mother's house," Gabriel murmured
over the radio.*

*"Pay Mother a visit."*

*Gabriel turned and said, "Go."*

*He opened the door of the minibus and crossed the street,
walking swiftly, not running. He could hear the quiet
footfalls of the Sayaret team behind him. Gabriel drew several even breaths to try to slow his heart rate. The villa be-
longed to Khalil el-Wazir, better known as Abu Jihad, the
PLO's chief of operations and Yasir Arafat's most trusted
lieutenant.*

*Just outside the villa, Abu Jihad's driver was sleeping
behind the wheel of a Mercedes, a gift from Arafat. Gabriel
shoved the end of a silenced Beretta into the driver's ear,
pulled the trigger, kept walking.*

*At the entrance of the villa, Gabriel stepped aside as a
pair of Sayaret men attached a special silent plastique to
the heavy door. The explosive detonated, emitting less sound
than a handclap, and the door blew open. Gabriel led the*

*team into the entrance hall, the Beretta in his outstretched hands.*

*A Tunisian security guard appeared. As he reached for his weapon, Gabriel shot him several times through the chest.*

*Gabriel stood over the dying man and said, "Tell me where he is, and I won't shoot you in the eye."*

*But the security guard just grimaced in pain and said nothing.*

*Gabriel shot him twice in the face.*

*He mounted the stairs, ramming a fresh clip into his Beretta as he moved, and headed toward the study where Abu Jihad spent most nights working. He burst through the door and found the Palestinian seated in front of a television set, watching news footage of the* intifada, *which he was helping to direct from Tunis. Abu Jihad reached for a pistol. Gabriel charged forward as he fired, just as Shamron had trained him to do. Two of the shots struck Abu Jihad in the chest. Gabriel stood over him, pressed the gun against his temple, and fired two more times. The body convulsed in a death spasm.*

*Gabriel darted from the room. In the hallway was Abu Jihad's wife, clutching their small son in her arms, and his teenage daughter. She closed her eyes and held the boy more tightly, waiting for Gabriel to shoot her.*

*"Go back to your room!" he shouted in Arabic. Then he turned to the daughter. "Go and take care of your mother."*

*Gabriel dashed from the house, followed by the entire*

*Sayaret team. They piled into the minibus and the Peugeots
and sped away. They drove through Sidi Boussaid back to
Rouad, where they abandoned the vehicles at the beach and
boarded the dinghies. A moment later they were speeding
over the black surface of the Mediterranean toward the
lights of a waiting Israeli patrol boat.*

*"Thirteen seconds, Gabriel! You did it in thirteen
seconds!"*

*It was the girl. She reached out to touch him, but he
recoiled from her. He watched the lights of the ship drawing
closer. He looked up into the ink-black sky, searching for the
command plane, but saw only a fingernail moon and a
spray of stars. Then he saw the faces of Abu Jihad's wife and
children, staring at him with hatred burning in their eyes.*

*He tossed the Beretta into the sea and began to shake.*

The fight next door had gone quiet. Gabriel wanted to
think about something besides Tunis, so he imagined sailing his ketch down the Helford Passage to the sea. Then
he thought of the Vecellio, stripped of dirty varnish, the
damage of the centuries laid bare. He thought of Peel,
and for the first time that day he thought of Dani. He
remembered pulling what remained of his body from the
flaming wreckage of the car in Vienna, checking to see
if somehow he had survived, thanking God that he had
died quickly and not lingered with one arm and one leg
and half a face.

He stood up and paced the room, trying to make the
image go away, and for some reason found himself think-

ing of Peel's mother. Several times during his stay in Port Navas he'd found himself fantasizing about her. It began the same way each time. He would bump into her in the village, and she would volunteer that Derek was out for a long walk on the Lizard trying to repair the second act. "He'll be gone for hours," she would say. "Would you like to come over for tea?" He would say yes, but instead of serving tea she would take him upstairs to Derek's bed and allow him to pour nine years of self-imposed abstinence into her supple body. Afterward she would lie with her head on his stomach, damp hair spread across his chest. "You're not really an art restorer, are you?" she would say in his fantasy. And Gabriel would tell her the truth. "I kill people for the government of Israel. I killed Abu Jihad in front of his wife and children. I killed three people in thirteen seconds that night. The prime minister gave me a medal for it. I used to have a wife and a son, but a terrorist put a bomb under their car because I had an affair with my *bat leveyha* in Tunis." And Peel's mother would run screaming from the cottage, body wrapped in a white bedsheet, the bedsheet stained with the blood of Leah.

He returned to his chair and waited for Yusef. The face of Peel's mother had been replaced by the face of Vecellio's Virgin Mary. To help fill the empty hours, Gabriel dipped an imaginary brush into imaginary pigment and tenderly healed her wounded cheek.

\*     \*     \*

Yusef came home at 3:00 A.M. A girl was with him, the girl who had given him her telephone number that afternoon at the restaurant. Gabriel watched them disappear through the front entrance. Upstairs in the flat the lights flared briefly before Yusef made his nightly appearance in the window. Gabriel bid him good night as he disappeared behind the curtain. Then he fell onto the couch and closed his eyes. Today he had watched. Tomorrow he would begin to listen.

# 13

## AMSTERDAM

Three hours later a slender young woman named Inge van der Hoff stepped out of a bar in the red-light district and walked quickly along a narrow alley. Black leather skirt, black leggings, black leather jacket, boots clattering over the bricks of the alley. The streets of the Old Side were still dark, a light mist falling. She lifted her face skyward. The mist tasted of salt, smelled of the North Sea. She passed two men, a drunk and a hash dealer, lowered her head, kept moving. Her boss didn't like her walking home in the morning, but after a long night of serving drinks and fending off the advances of drunken customers, it always felt good to be alone for a few minutes.

Suddenly she felt very tired. She needed to crash. She thought: *What I really need is a fix. I hope Leila scored tonight.*

*Leila.* . . . She loved the sound of her name. Loved everything about her. They had met two weeks earlier at the bar. Leila had come for three consecutive nights, each time alone. She would stay for an hour, have a shot of *jenever*, a Grolsch, a few hits of hash, listen to the music.

Each time Inge went to her table she could feel the girl's eyes on her. Inge had to admit that she liked it. She was a stunningly attractive woman, with lustrous black hair and wide brown eyes. Finally, on the third night, Inge introduced herself and they began to talk. Leila said that her father was a businessman and that she had lived all over the world. She said she was taking a year off from her studies in Paris, just traveling and living life. She said Amsterdam enchanted her. The picturesque canals. The gabled houses, the museums, and the parks. She wanted to stay for a few months, get to know the place.

"Where are you staying?" Inge had asked.

"In a youth hostel in south Amsterdam. It's horrible. Where do you live?"

"A houseboat on the Amstel."

"A houseboat! How wonderful."

"It's my brother's, but he's in Rotterdam for a few months working on a big construction project."

"Are you offering to let me crash on your houseboat for a few days?"

"I'm offering to let you stay as long as you want. I don't like coming home to an empty place."

Dawn was breaking over the river, first lights burning in the houseboats lining the embankment. Inge walked a short distance along the quay, then stepped onto the deck of her boat. The curtains were drawn over the windows. She crossed the deck and entered the salon. She expected to find Leila in bed asleep, but instead she was standing at the stove making coffee. On the floor next to her was a suitcase. Inge closed the door, trying to hide her disappointment.

"I called my brother in Paris last night while you were at work," Leila said. "My father is very ill. I have to go home right away to be with my mother. I'm sorry, Inge."

"How long will you be gone?"

"A week, two at the most."

"Are you coming back?"

"Of course I'm coming back!" She kissed Inge's cheek and handed her a cup of coffee. "My flight leaves in two hours. Sit down. I need to talk to you about something."

They sat in the salon. Leila said, "A friend of mine is coming to Amsterdam tomorrow. His name is Paul. He's French. I was wondering if he could stay here for a few days until he finds his own place."

"Leila, I don't—"

"He's a good man, Inge. He won't try anything with you, if that's what you're worried about."

"I know how to take care of myself."

"So you'll let Paul stay here for a few days?"

"How many days is a few days?"

"A week, maybe."

"And what do I get in return?"

Leila reached into her pocket, pulled out a small bag of white powder, and held it in front of her between her thumb and forefinger.

Inge reached out and snatched it from her. "Leila, you're an angel!"

"I know."

Inge went into her bedroom and pulled open the top drawer of her dresser. Inside was her kit: pack of syringes, candle, spoon, length of rubber to tie around her arm. She cooked the drug while Leila packed the last of her things. Then she loaded the drug into the syringe and carefully slipped the needle into a vein in her left arm.

An instant later her body was overcome by an intensely pleasant sensation of numbness. And the last thing she remembered before slipping into unconsciousness was the sight of Leila, her beautiful lover, slipping out the door and floating across the deck of the houseboat.

# 14

Randall Karp, formerly of the Office of Technical Services, Langley, Virginia, lately of the dubiously named Clarendon International Security, Mayfair, London, arrived at Gabriel's flat in Sussex Gardens in the still moments just before dawn. He wore a fleece pullover against the morning cold, pale blue jeans, and suede sandals with the thick woolen socks of an outdoorsman. From the end of each spiderlike arm hung a canvas duffel bag, one containing his kit, the other the tools of his trade. He set down his bags in the living room with an air of quiet complacency and appraised his surroundings.

"I like what you've done with the place, Gabe." He spoke with a flat Southern California accent and, since Gabriel had seen him last, had grown a ponytail to compensate for his rapidly encroaching baldness. "It even has the right smell. What is it? Curry? Cigarettes? A bit of spoiled milk? I think I'm going to like it here."

"I'm so pleased."

Karp moved to the window. "So, where's our boy?"

"Third floor, directly above the entrance. White curtains."

"Who is he?"

"He's a Palestinian who wishes to harm my country."

"I could have figured that out myself. Can you elaborate? Hamas? Hezbollah? Islamic Jihad?"

But Gabriel said nothing, and Karp knew better than to press. Karp was a consummate audio tech, and techs were used to working with only half the picture. He had achieved legendary status within the Western intelligence community by successfully monitoring a meeting between a Russian and an agent in Prague by attaching a bug to the collar of the Russian's dog. Gabriel had met him in Cyprus during a joint American-Israeli surveillance of a Libyan agent. After the operation, at Shamron's suggestion, Gabriel hired a yacht and took Karp for a sail around the island. Karp's seamanship was as good as his surveillance work, and during their three-day cruise they built a professional and personal bond.

"Why me, Gabe?" said Karp. "Your boys have the best toys in the business. Beautiful stuff. Why do you need an outsider like me to do a simple job like this?"

"Because our boys haven't been able to do a job like this lately without getting their fingers burned."

"So I've read. I'd rather not end up in jail, Gabe, if you get my drift."

"No one's going to jail, Randy."

Karp turned and gazed out the window. "What about

the boy across the street? Is he going to jail, or do you have other plans for him?"

"What are you asking?"

"I'm asking if this one's going to end up in an alley filled with twenty-two-caliber bullet holes. People have a funny way of ending up dead whenever you come around."

"It's a straight surveillance job. I want to know who he's talking to, what he's saying. The usual."

Karp folded his arms and studied the angles. "Is he a pro?"

"He seems to be good. Very disciplined on the street."

"I could try a windowpane pickoff, but if he's a pro he'll take countermeasures and make life miserable for us. Besides, the laser is not very discriminating. It reads the vibrations of the glass and converts them into sound. Traffic makes the glass vibrate, the wind, the neighbors, his CD player. It's not the best way to do it."

"What do you want to do?"

"I could get his telephone from the subscriber inter-face box."

"The subscriber interface?"

Karp raised his hand and pointed toward the block of flats. "That metal box on the wall just to the left of the entrance. That's where the British Telecom lines enter the building. From there, the lines branch out to the individual subscribers. I can put a rather simple r/f bug on his line right there. It would transmit an analog signal, and we could listen to his phone conversations from here with an ordinary FM radio."

"I need room coverage, too."

"If you want good room coverage, you're going to have to get inside his flat."

"So we'll get inside his flat."

"That's how people end up in jail, Gabe."

"No one's going to jail."

"Does our boy have a computer?"

"I assume so. He's a part-time student."

"I could Tempest him."

"Forgive me, Randy, but I've been out of the game for a few years."

"It's a system that was developed by a Dutch scientist called Van Eyck. The computer communicates with the monitor by transmitting signals over the cable. Those signals have frequency and can be captured by a properly tuned receiver. If he's doing business on the computer, we can watch him from here. It will be like standing over his shoulder while he works."

"Do it," Gabriel said. "I want his work phone, too."

"Where does he work?"

"A restaurant on the Edgware Road."

"An r/f bug will never be able to transmit from the Edgware Road to here. The path loss is too great. I'll need to set up a repeater—a relay point between the restaurant and here to boost the signal."

"What do you need?"

"A vehicle of some sort."

"Will a car do?"

"A car will be fine."

"I'll get you one today."

"Clean?"

"Clean."

"Are you going to get it from one of your little helpers?"

"Don't worry about how I get it."

"Just don't steal it, please. I don't want to be driving hot wheels."

At that moment Yusef appeared in the window and engaged in his morning inspection of the street below.

"So that's our boy?" Karp asked.

"That's him."

"Tell me something, Gabe. Exactly *how* are you planning on getting inside his flat?"

Gabriel looked at Karp and smiled. "He likes girls."

At two o'clock the following morning Gabriel and Karp slipped into the alley behind the Kebab Factory. To reach the subscriber interface box, Karp had to balance himself atop a large rolling rubbish bin filled with rotting garbage. He picked the lock, pulled open the little door, and for two minutes worked silently by the thin beam of a penlight held between his front teeth.

Gabriel stood guard below, his attention focused on the entrance of the alley. "How much longer?" he murmured.

"One minute if you shut up. Two if you insist on talking to me."

Gabriel looked down again and spotted two men in leather jackets walking toward him. One picked up a bottle and shattered it against a wall. His friend nearly fell over with laughter.

Gabriel moved a few feet away from Karp, leaned against a wall, and pretended to be sick. The two men approached him. The larger of the two grabbed his shoulder. He had a raised white scar along his right cheek and stank of beer and whiskey. The other grinned stupidly. He was thin and had shaved his head. His pale skin glowed in the dim light of the alley.

"Please, I don't want any trouble," Gabriel said in French-accented English. "I'm just sick. Too much to drink, you know?"

"A bloody Frog," sang the bald one. "And he looks queer, too."

"Please, I don't want trouble," Gabriel repeated.

He reached into his pocket, removed several crumpled twenty-pound notes, and held them out. "Here, take my money. Just leave me alone."

But the big man with the scar slapped the money from Gabriel's hand. Then he drew back his fist and threw a wild roundhouse punch toward Gabriel's head.

Ten minutes later they were back in the flat. Karp was seated in front of his equipment at the dining room table. He picked up a cell phone and dialed the restaurant. While the line was ringing he set down the phone and turned up the volume on his receiver. He could hear a recorded message saying the Kebab Factory was closed and would not reopen until eleven-thirty the following day. He dialed the number a second time, and once again he could hear the message over the receiver. The bug and the repeater were working perfectly.

As he put away his tools, he thought about Gabriel's contribution to that evening's work. It had lasted precisely three seconds by Karp's calculation. He saw none of it—his attention had remained fixed on his work—but he had heard the whole thing. There had been four sharp blows. The last was the most vicious. Karp had definitely heard bone shattering. He had looked down only after he finished the installation and closed the box. He would never forget the sight: Gabriel Allon, bending over each of his victims, tenderly checking each throat for a pulse, making certain he hadn't killed them.

Next morning Gabriel went out to buy the paper. He walked through a light drizzle to the Edgware Road and purchased a copy of *The Times* from a newsstand. He tucked the paper into his jacket and walked across the street to a small market. There he bought glue, scissors, and a second copy of *The Times*.

Karp was still sleeping when Gabriel returned to the flat. He sat at the table with two sheets of plain paper in front of him. At the top of one page he wrote the security clearance—top secret—and the recipient—Rom, the code name for the chief.

For fifteen minutes Gabriel wrote, right hand scratching rhythmically across the page, left pressed to his temple. His prose was terse and economical, the way Shamron liked it.

When he was finished he took one copy of *The Times*, turned it to page eight, and carefully cut out a large advertisement for a chain of men's clothing stores. He threw away the remainder of the paper, then took the second copy and opened it to the same page. He placed his report over the advertisement, then glued the cutout over the report. He folded the newspaper and slipped it into the side flap of a black overnight travel bag. Then he pulled on a coat, shouldered the bag, and went out.

He walked to Marble Arch and entered the Underground. He purchased a ticket from the automated machine and before passing through the turnstiles made a brief telephone call. Fifteen minutes later he arrived at Waterloo.

Shamron's *bodel* was waiting in a café in the Eurostar ticket terminal, holding a plastic shopping bag bearing the name of an American cigarette. Gabriel sat at the next table, drinking tea and reading the newspaper. When he finished his tea he stood and walked away, leaving the newspaper behind. The *bodel* slipped it into the shopping bag and headed in the opposite direction.

Gabriel waited in the terminal for his train to be called. Ten minutes later he boarded the Eurostar for Paris.

# 15

## AMSTERDAM

The elegant canal house stood on the Herengracht in the Golden Curve of Amsterdam's Central Canal Ring. It was tall and wide, with large windows overlooking the canal and a soaring gable. The owner, David Morgenthau, was the multimillionaire chairman of Optique, one of the world's largest makers of designer eyeglasses. He was also a passionate Zionist. Over the years he had given millions of dollars to Israeli charities and invested millions more in Israeli businesses. An American of Dutch-Jewish descent, Morgenthau had served on the boards of several New York Jewish organizations and was regarded as a hawk when it came to matters of Israeli security. He and his wife, Cynthia, a renowned New York interior designer, visited their home in Amsterdam like clockwork twice each year—once in the summer, on the way to their villa outside Cannes, and once again in the winter for the holidays.

Tariq sat in a café on the opposite side of the canal, drinking warm sweet tea. He knew other things about David Morgenthau—things that did not appear in the society pages or the world's business journals. He knew that Morgenthau was a personal friend of the Israeli prime minister, that he had performed certain favors for Ari Shamron, and that he had once served as a secret conduit between the Israeli government and the PLO. For all those reasons, Tariq was going to kill him.

Leila had prepared a detailed surveillance report during her stay in Amsterdam. David and Cynthia Morgenthau left the house each morning to visit museums or go ice-skating in the countryside. During the day the only person who remained in the house was a maid, a young Dutch girl.

*This is going to be too easy.*

A chauffeured Mercedes braked to a halt outside the house. Tariq looked at his watch: 4:00 P.M., right on schedule. A tall, gray-haired man climbed out. He wore a thick sweater and heavy corduroy trousers and was carrying two pairs of ice skates. A moment later an attractive woman emerged, dressed in black stretch leggings and a pullover. As they entered the house the Mercedes drove off.

Tariq left a few guilders on the table and went out.

Snow drifted over the Herengracht as he made his way slowly toward the houseboat on the Amstel. A pair of cyclists glided silently past, leaving ribbons of black in the fresh snow. Evening in a foreign city always made him melancholy. Lights coming on, offices letting out, bars and cafés slowly filling. Through the broad windows of the canal houses he could see parents coming home to children, husbands coming home to wives, lovers re-uniting, warm lights burning. *Life,* he thought. Someone else's life, someone else's homeland.

He thought about what Kemel had told him during their meeting on the train. Tariq's old nemesis, Gabriel Allon, had been brought back to help Ari Shamron find him. The news did not concern him. Indeed, he welcomed it. It would make the next few weeks even sweeter. Imagine, destroying their so-called peace process and settling his score with Gabriel Allon all at the same time. . . .

Killing Allon would not be easy, but as Tariq drifted along the banks of the Herengracht he knew he already held a distinct advantage over his opponent. The simple fact that he knew Allon was out there searching for him gave Tariq the upper hand. The hunter must come to the prey to make the kill. If Tariq played the game well, he could draw Allon into a trap. *And then I'll kill him, the way he killed Mahmoud.*

Intelligence services have two basic ways of trying to catch a terrorist. They can use their superior technology to intercept the terrorist's communications, or they can penetrate his organization by inserting a spy or convincing an existing operative to switch sides. Tariq and Kemel were careful about the way they communicated. They avoided telephones and the Internet whenever possible and used couriers instead. *Like the idiot Kemel sent to Samos!* No, they would not be able to track him by intercepting his communications, so they would have to try to penetrate his group. It was difficult for an intelligence agency to penetrate any terrorist group, but it would be even harder to get inside Tariq's. His organization was small, tightly knit, and highly mobile. They were committed to the struggle, highly trained, and intensely loyal. None of his agents would ever betray him to the Jews.

Tariq could use this to his advantage. He had instructed Kemel to contact every agent and give a simple instruction. If any of them noticed anything out of the ordinary—such as surveillance or an approach by a stranger—they were to report it immediately. If Tariq could determine that Israeli intelligence was involved, he would immediately be transformed from the hunted to the hunter.

He thought of an operation he had conducted while he was still with Jihaz el-Razd, the PLO intelligence arm. He had identified an Office agent working with diplomatic cover from the Israeli embassy in Madrid. The officer had managed to recruit several spies within the PLO, and Tariq decided it was time to pay him back. He sent a Palestinian to Madrid posing as a defector. The Palestinian met with the Israeli officer inside the embassy and promised to turn over sensitive intelligence about PLO leaders and their personal habits. At first the Israeli balked. Tariq had anticipated this, so he had given his agent several pieces of true, relatively harmless intelligence—all things the Israelis already knew. The Israeli believed he was now dealing with a genuine defector and agreed to meet with the Palestinian a second time, at a café a week later. But this time Tariq went to Madrid. He walked into the café at the appointed time, shot the officer twice in the face, and calmly walked out.

He came to the river and walked along the embankment a short distance until he arrived at the girl's houseboat. It was a depressing place—dirty, filled with drug and sexual paraphernalia—but a perfect spot to hide while he planned the attack. He crossed the deck and entered the cabin. The skylights were covered with the new snow, the salon very cold. Tariq switched on a lamp, then turned on the little electric space heater. In the bedroom he could hear the girl stirring beneath her blankets. She was a pathetic wretch, not like the girl he had stayed with in Paris. No one would miss this one when she was gone.

She rolled over and gazed at him through the strands of her stringy blond hair. "Where have you been? I was worried about you."

"I was just out walking. I love walking in this city, especially when it's snowing."

"What time is it?"

"Four-thirty. Shouldn't you be getting out of bed?"

"I don't have to leave for another hour."

Tariq made her a mug of Nescafé and carried it into the bedroom. Inge rolled over and leaned on her elbow. The blanket slipped down her body, exposing her breasts. Tariq handed her the coffee and looked away. The girl drank the coffee, her eyes looking at him over the rim of the mug. She asked, "Something wrong?"

"No, nothing."

"Why did you look away from me?"

She sat up and pushed away the blankets. He wanted to say no, but he feared she might be suspicious of a Frenchman who resisted the advances of an attractive young woman. So he stood at the edge of the bed and allowed her to undress him. And few moments later, as he exploded inside her, he was thinking not of the girl but of how he was going to finally kill Gabriel Allon.

He lay in bed for a long time after she had left, listening to the sounds of the boats moving on the river. The headache came an hour later. They were coming more frequently now—three, sometimes four a week. The doctor had warned it would happen that way. The pain slowly intensified until he was nearly blinded by it. He placed a cool, damp towel on his face. No painkillers. They dulled his senses, made him sleep too heavily, and gave him the sensation of tumbling backward through an abyss. So he lay alone in the Dutch girl's bed, on a houseboat in the Amstel River, feeling as though someone were pouring molten lead into his skull through his eye sockets.

# 16

VALBONNE, PROVENCE

The morning was clear and chilly, sunlight streaming over the hillsides. Jacqueline pulled on a pair of full-length riding chamois and a woolen jersey and tucked her long hair beneath a dark blue helmet. She slipped on a pair of wraparound sunglasses and studied her appearance in the mirror. She looked like a very handsome man, which was her intention. She stretched on the floor of her bedroom, then walked downstairs to the entrance hall, where her Bianchi racing bike leaned against the wall. She pushed the bike out the front door and wheeled it across the gravel drive. A moment later she was gliding through the cold shadows down the long gentle hill toward the village.

She slipped through Valbonne and made the long, steady climb toward Opio, cold air burning her cheeks. She pedaled slowly and evenly for the first few miles while her muscles warmed. Then she switched gears and increased the cadence of her pedaling. Soon she was flying along the narrow road, head down, legs pumping like pistons. The smell of lavender hung on the air. Beside her a grove of olive trees spilled down a terraced hillside. She emerged from the shadows of the olive trees onto a flat plain of warm sunlight. After a moment she could feel the first sweat beneath her jersey.

At the halfway point she checked her split: only thirty seconds off her best time. Not bad for a chilly December morning. She circled a traffic roundabout, switched gears, and started up a long, steep hill. After a few moments her breath was hoarse and ragged and her legs burning—*too many goddamned cigarettes!*—but she forced herself to remain seated and pound up the long hill. She thought of Michel Duval: *Pig!* One hundred yards from the crest she rose from the saddle, angrily driving her feet down into the toe straps, shouting at herself to keep going and not give in to the pain. She was rewarded with a long descent. She could have coasted but took a quick drink and sprinted down the hill instead. As she entered Valbonne again, she looked at her watch. A new personal best by fifteen seconds. *Thank you, Michel Duval.*

She climbed out of the saddle and pushed her bike through the quiet streets of the ancient town. At the central square she propped the bike against a pillar, purchased a newspaper, and treated herself to a warm croissant and a large bowl of steaming café au lait. When she finished she collected her bike and pushed it along a shadowed street.

At the end of a terrace of cottages overlooking the town parking lot was a commercial building. A sign hung in the window: the entire ground floor was available. It had been vacant for months. Jacqueline cupped her hands around her eyes and peered through the dirty glass: a large, open room, wood floors, high ceiling. Perfect for a dance studio. She had a fantasy. She would quit modeling and open a ballet school in Valbonne. It would cater to the local girls most of the year, but in August, when the tourists streamed into Valbonne for their summer holidays, she would open the school to visitors. She would teach for a few hours a day, ride her bike through the hills, drink coffee, and read in the café on the square. Shed her name and her image. Become Sarah Halévy again—Sarah Halévy, the Jewish girl from Marseilles. But to open the school she needed money, and to get money she had to keep modeling. She had to go back to Paris and put up with men like Michel Duval a little while longer. Then she would be free.

She mounted her bike and rode slowly home. It was a rather small villa, the color of sandstone with a red-tile roof, hidden from view by a row of towering cypress trees. In the large terraced garden overlooking the valley, rosemary and lavender grew wild among the olive and drooping pepper trees. At the base of the garden was a rectangular swimming pool.

Jacqueline let herself inside, propped the bike in the entrance hall, and went into the kitchen. The red light on her answering machine was winking. She pressed the playback button and made coffee while she listened to the messages.

Yvonne had called to invite her to a party at the home of a millionaire Spanish tennis player in Monte Carlo.

Michel Duval had called to apologize for his behavior at the shoot the other day. The bruise was healing nicely. Marcel had called to say that he had spoken to Robert. The shoot in Mustique was back on. "You leave in three weeks, angel, so get off the cheese and pasta and get your beautiful ass in shape."

She thought of her bicycle ride and smiled. Her face might have looked thirty-three, but her body had never looked better.

"Oh, by the way, a fellow called Jean-Claude came by the office. Said he wanted to talk to you personally about a job."

Jacqueline set down the coffeepot and looked at the machine.

"I told him you were in the south. He said he was on his way there and that he would look you up when he arrived. Don't be angry with me, angel. He seemed like a nice guy. Good-looking, too. I was insanely jealous. Love you. Ciao."

She pressed the rewind button and listened to the message again to make certain she had heard it right.

"Oh, by the way, a fellow called Jean-Claude came by the office. Said he wanted to talk to you personally about a job."

She pressed the erase button, hand trembling, heart beating against her ribs.

Jacqueline sat outside on the sunlit terrace, thinking about the night she was recruited by Ari Shamron. She had used some of her money from modeling to buy her parents a retirement present: a small beachfront apartment in Herzliya. She visited them in Israel whenever she could get away for a few days. She fell completely in love with the country. It was the only place she felt truly free and safe. More than anything else she loved the fact that she did not have to conceal her being Jewish.

One evening in a jazz café in Tel Aviv an older man appeared at her table. Bald, rather ugly, steel-rimmed glasses, khaki trousers, a bomber jacket with a tear on the right breast.

"Hello, Sarah," he said, smiling confidently. "May I join you?"

She looked up, startled. "How did you know my name is Sarah?"

"Actually, I know a great deal about you. I'm a big fan."

"Who are you?"

"My name is Ari. I work for an organization loosely connected to the Ministry of Defense called the Institute for Coordination. We just call it the Office."

"Well, I'm certainly glad we cleared that up."

He threw his head back and laughed. "We'd like to talk to you about a job. Do you mind if I call you Sarah? I have trouble thinking of you as Jacqueline."

"My parents are the only ones who call me Sarah anymore."

"No old friends?"

"I have only new friends," she said, her voice tinged

with sadness. "At least people who *claim* to be my friends. All my old friends from Marseilles dropped away after I became a model. They thought I'd changed because of my work."

"But you have changed, haven't you, Sarah?"

"Yes, I suppose I have." Then she thought: *Why am I telling this to a man I just met? I wonder if he gets under everyone's skin so quickly.*

"And it isn't just a job, is it, Sarah? It's a way of life. You hang out with fashion designers and famous photographers. You go to glitzy parties and exclusive restaurants with actors and rock stars and millionaire playboys. Like that Italian count you had an affair with in Milan, the one that made the newspapers. Surely you're not the same little girl from Marseilles. The little Jewish girl whose grandparents were murdered by the Nazis at Sobibor."

"You *do* know a great deal about me." She looked at him carefully. She was used to being surrounded by attractive, polished people, and here she was now in the company of this rather ugly man with steel glasses and a tear in his jacket. There was something of the primitive in him—the rough-hewn Sabra that she had always heard about. He was the kind of man who didn't know how to tie a bow tie and didn't care. She found him utterly charming. But more than anything she was intrigued by him.

"As a Jew from Marseilles, you know that our people have many enemies. Many people would like to destroy us, tear down everything we have built in this land." As he spoke his hands carved the air. "Over the years Israel has fought many wars with her enemies. At this moment there is no fighting, but Israel is still engaged in another war, a secret war. This war is ceaseless. It will never end. Because of your passport and, quite frankly, your appearance, you could be a great deal of help to us."

"Are you asking me to become a spy?"

He laughed. "I'm afraid it's nothing quite so dramatic as that."

"What do you want me to do?"

"I want you to become a *bat leveyha*."

"I'm sorry, but I don't speak Hebrew."

"*Bat leveyha* is the term we use for a female assistant agent. As a *bat leveyha*, you may be called on to perform a number of functions for the Office. Sometimes you might be asked to pose as the wife or girlfriend of one of our male officers. Sometimes you might be asked to obtain a vital piece of information that a woman like you might get more readily than a male officer."

He stopped talking for a moment and took his time lighting his next cigarette. "And sometimes we may ask you to perform another kind of assignment. An assignment that some women find too unpleasant to even consider."

"For example?"

"We might ask you to seduce a man—one of our enemies, for instance—in order to place him in a compromising situation."

"There are lots of beautiful women in Israel. Why on earth would you need me?"

"Because you're *not* an Israeli. Because you have a legitimate French passport and a legitimate job."

"That *legitimate* job, as you call it, pays me a great deal. I'm not prepared to throw it away."

"If you decide to work for us, I'll see that your assignments are brief and that you are compensated for lost wages." He smiled affectionately. "Although I don't think I can afford your usual fee of three thousand dollars an hour."

"Five thousand," she said, smiling.

"My congratulations."

"I have to think about it."

"I understand, but as you consider my offer, keep one thing in mind. If there had been an Israel during the Second World War, Maurice and Rachel Halévy might still be alive. It's my job to ensure the survival of the State so that the next time some madman decides to turn our people into soap, they'll have a place to take refuge. I hope you'll help me."

He gave her a card with a telephone number and told her to call him with a decision the following afternoon. Then he shook her hand and walked away. It was the hardest hand she had ever felt.

There had never been a question in her mind what her answer would be. By any objective standard she lived an exciting and glamorous life, but it seemed dull and meaningless compared with what Ari Shamron was offering. The tedious shoots, the pawing agents, the whining photographers—suddenly it all seemed even more plastic and pretentious.

She returned to Europe for the fall fashion season—she had commitments in Paris, Milan, and Rome—and in November, when things quieted down, she told Marcel Lambert she was burned out and needed a break. Marcel cleared her calendar, kissed her cheek, and told her to get as far away from Paris as possible. That night she went to the El Al counter at Charles de Gaulle, picked up the first-class ticket Shamron had left for her, and boarded a flight for Tel Aviv.

He was waiting when she arrived at Ben-Gurion Airport. He escorted her to a special holding room inside the terminal. Everything was designed to convey to her that she was now one of the elite. That she was walking through a secret door and her life would never be the same again. From the airport he whisked her through the streets of Tel Aviv to a luxurious safe flat in the Opera Tower with a large terrace overlooking the Promenade and Ge'ula Beach. "This will be your home for the next few weeks. I hope you find it to your liking."

"It's absolutely beautiful."

"Tonight you rest. Tomorrow the real work begins."

The next morning she went to the Academy and endured a crash course in Office tradecraft and doctrine. He lectured her on the basics of impersonal communication. He trained her to use a Beretta and to cut strategic slits in her clothing so she could grab it in a hurry. He taught her how to pick locks and how to make imprints of keys using a special device. He taught her how to detect and shake surveillance. Each afternoon she spent two hours with a man named Oded, who taught her rudimentary Arabic.

But most of the time at the Academy was spent developing her memory and awareness. He placed her alone in a room and flashed dozens of names on a projection screen, forcing her to memorize as many as possible. He took her into a small apartment, allowed her to look at the room for a matter of seconds, then pulled her out and made her describe it in detail. He took her to lunch at the canteen and asked her to describe the steward who had just served them. Jacqueline confessed she had no idea. "You must be aware of your surroundings all the time," he said. "You must assume that the waiter is a potential enemy. You must be scanning, watching, and surveying constantly. And yet you must appear as though you are doing nothing of the sort."

Her training did not stop at sundown. Each evening Shamron would appear at the Opera Tower and take her into the streets of Tel Aviv for more. He took her to a lawyer's office, told her to break in and steal a specific set of files. He took her to a street filled with fashionable boutiques and told her to steal something.

"You're joking."

"What if you are on the run in a foreign country? What if you have no money and no way to make contact with us? The police are looking for you and you need a change of clothing quickly."

"I'm not exactly built for shoplifting."

"Make yourself inconspicuous."

She entered a boutique and spent ten minutes trying on clothing. When she returned to the lobby she had bought nothing, but inside her handbag was a sexy black cocktail dress.

Shamron said, "Now I want you to find a place to change and discard your other clothing. Then meet me outside at the ice cream stand on the promenade."

It was a warm evening for early November, and there were many people out strolling and taking in the air. They walked arm in arm along the waterfront, like a rich old man and his mistress, Jacqueline playfully licking an ice cream cone.

"You're being followed by three people," Shamron said. "Meet me in the bar of that restaurant in half an hour and tell me who they are. And keep in mind that I'm going to send a *kidon* to kill them, so don't make a mistake."

Jacqueline engaged in a standard countersurveillance routine, just as Shamron had taught her. Then she went to the bar and found him seated alone at a corner table.

"Black leather jacket, blue jeans with a Yale sweatshirt, blond girl with a rose tattooed on her shoulder blade."

"Wrong, wrong, wrong. You just condemned three innocent tourists to death. Let's try it again."

They took a taxi a short distance to Rothschild Boulevard, a broad promenade lined with trees, benches, kiosks, and fashionable cafés.

"Once again, three people are following you. Meet me at Café Tamar in thirty minutes."

"Where's Café Tamar?"

But Shamron turned and melted into the flow of pedestrians. Half an hour later, having located the chic Café Tamar on Sheinkin Street, she joined him once again.

"The girl with the dog, the boy with the headphones and the Springsteen shirt, the kid from the kibbutz with the Uzi."

Shamron smiled. "Very good. Just one more test tonight. See that man sitting alone over there?"

Jacqueline nodded.

"Strike up a conversation with him, learn everything you can, and then entice him back to your flat. When you get to the lobby, find some way of unsnarling yourself from the situation without making a scene."

Shamron got up and walked away. Jacqueline made eye contact with the man, and after a few minutes he joined her. He said his name was Mark, that he was from Boston and worked for a computer firm doing business in Israel. They talked for an hour and began to flirt. But when she invited him back to her apartment, he confessed that he was married.

"Too bad," she said. "We could have had a very nice time."

He quickly changed his mind. Jacqueline excused herself to use the bathroom, went to a public telephone instead. She dialed the front desk at the Opera Tower and left a message for herself. Then she went back to the table and said, "Let's go."

They walked to her flat. Before going upstairs she checked with the front desk. "Your sister called from Herzliya," the clerk said. "She tried your apartment, but there was no answer, so she called here and left a message."

"What is it?"

"Your father has had a heart attack."

"Oh, my God!"

"They've taken him to the hospital. She says he's going to be all right, but she wants you to come right away."

Jacqueline turned to the American. "I'm so sorry, but I have to go."

The American kissed her cheek and walked away, crestfallen. Shamron, who was watching the entire scene from across the lobby, came forward, grinning like a schoolboy. "That was pure poetry. Sarah Halévy, you're a natural."

Her first assignment didn't require her to leave Paris. The Office was trying to recruit an Iraqi nuclear weapons scientist who lived in Paris and worked with Iraq's French suppliers. Shamron decided to set a "honey trap" and gave the job to Jacqueline. She met the Iraqi in a bar, seduced him, and began spending the night at his apartment. He fell head over heels in love. Jacqueline told her lover that if he wanted to continue seeing her, he would have to meet with a friend of hers who had a business proposition. The friend turned out to be Ari Shamron, the proposition simple: work for us or we will tell your wife and Saddam's security thugs you've been fucking an Israeli agent. The Iraqi agreed to work for Shamron.

Jacqueline had been given her first taste of intelligence work. She found it exhilarating. She had played a small role in an operation that had dealt a blow to Iraq's nuclear ambitions. She had helped protect the State of Israel from an enemy that would do anything to destroy it. And in a small way she had avenged the deaths of her grandparents.

She had to wait another year for her next assignment: seducing and blackmailing a Syrian intelligence officer in London. It was another stunning success. Nine months later she was sent to Cyprus to seduce a German chemical company executive who was selling his wares to Libya. This time there was a twist. Shamron wanted her to drug the German and photograph the documents in his briefcase while he was unconscious. Once again she pulled off the job without a hitch.

After the operation Shamron flew her to Tel Aviv, presented her with a secret citation, told her she was finished. It didn't take long for things to circulate through the intelligence underground. Her next target might suspect that the pretty French model was more than she appeared to be. And she might very well end up dead.

She begged him for one more job. Shamron reluctantly agreed.

Three months later he sent her to Tunis.

\*       \*       \*

Jacqueline had thought it was strange that Shamron instructed her to meet Gabriel Allon in a church in Turin. She found him standing atop a platform, restoring a fresco depicting the Ascension. She worked with good-looking men every day in her overt life, but there was something about Gabriel that took her breath away. It was the intense concentration in his eyes. Jacqueline wanted him to look at her the way he was looking at the fresco. She decided she was going to make love to this man before the operation was over.

They traveled to Tunis the following morning and checked into a hotel on the beach. For the first few days he left her alone while he worked. He would return to the hotel each evening. They would have dinner, stroll the souk or the corniche along the beach, then go back to their room. They would talk like lovers in case the room was bugged. He slept in his clothing, stayed rigorously on his side of the bed, a wall of Plexiglas separating them.

On the fourth day he took her with him while he worked. He showed her the beach where the commandos would come ashore and the villa owned by the target. Her passion for him deepened. Here was a man who had devoted his life to defending Israel from its enemies. She felt insignificant and frivolous by comparison. She also found that she couldn't take her eyes off him. She wanted to run her hands through his short hair, touch his face and his body. As they lay in bed together that night, she rolled on top of him without warning and kissed his lips, but he pushed her away and made a Bedouin's camp bed for himself on the floor.

Jacqueline thought: *My God, I've made a complete fool of myself.*

Five minutes later he came back to the bed and sat down by her side. Then he leaned forward and whispered into her ear: "I want to make love to you too, but I can't. I'm married."

"I don't care."

"When the operation is over, you'll never see me again."

"I know."

He was just as she imagined: skilled and artful, meticulous and gentle. In his hands she felt like one of his paintings. She could almost feel his eyes touching her. She felt a stupid pride that she had been able to break through his walls of self-control and seduce him. She wanted the operation to go on forever. It couldn't, of course, and the night they left Tunis was the saddest of her life.

After Tunis she threw herself into her modeling. She told Marcel to accept every offer that came in. She worked nonstop for six months, pushing herself to the point of exhaustion. She even tried dating other men. None of it worked. She thought about Gabriel and Tunis constantly. For the first time in her life she felt obsession, yet she was absolutely helpless to do anything about it. At her wits' end, she went to Shamron and asked him to put her in touch with Gabriel. He refused. She began to have a terrible fantasy about the death of Gabriel's wife. And when Shamron told her what had happened in Vienna, she felt unbearable guilt.

She had not seen or spoken to Gabriel since that night in Tunis. She couldn't imagine why he would want to see her now. But one hour later, as she watched his car pulling into her drive, she felt a smile spreading across her face. She thought: *Thank God you're here, Gabriel, because I can use a little restoration myself.*

# 17

## TEL AVIV

The CIA's executive director, Adrian Carter, was a man who was easily underestimated. It was a trait he had used to great effect during his long career. He was short and thin as a marathoner. His sparse hair and rimless spectacles gave him a slightly clinical air, his trousers and blazer looked like they'd been slept in. He seemed out of place in the cold, modern conference room at King Saul Boulevard, as if he had wandered into the building by mistake. But Ari Shamron had worked with Carter when he was the head of the CIA's Counterterrorism Center. He knew Carter was a seasoned operative—a man who spoke six languages fluently and could melt into the back alleys of Warsaw or Beirut with equal ease. He also knew that his talents in the field were matched only by his skills in the bureaucratic trenches. A worthy opponent indeed.

"Any breaks in the Paris investigation?" Carter asked.

Shamron shook his head slowly. "I'm afraid not."

"Nothing at all, Ari? I find that difficult to believe."

"The moment we hear anything you'll be the first to

know. And what about you? Any interesting intercepts you'd care to share? Any friendly Arab services tell you anything they'd be reluctant to share with the Zionist entity?"

Carter had just completed a two-week regional tour, conferring with intelligence chiefs from the Persian Gulf to North Africa. King Saul Boulevard was his last stop. "Nothing, I'm afraid," he said. "But we've heard a few whispers from some of our other sources."

Shamron raised an eyebrow. "Oh, really?"

"They tell us that the word on the street is that Tariq was behind the attack in Paris."

"Tariq has been quiet for some time. Why would he pull something like Paris now?"

"Because he's desperate," Carter said. "Because the two sides are getting closer to a deal, and Tariq would like nothing better than to spoil the party. And because Tariq sees himself as a man of history, and history is about to pass him by."

"It's an interesting theory, but we've seen no evidence to suggest Tariq was involved."

"If you did receive such evidence, you'd share it with us, of course."

"Of course."

"I don't need to remind you that an American citizen was murdered along with your ambassador. The president has made a promise to the American people that her killer will be brought to justice. I plan to help him keep that promise."

"You can count on the support of this service," Shamron said piously.

"If it *was* Tariq, we'd like to find him and bring him to the United States for trial. But we won't be able to do that if he turns up dead someplace, filled with twenty-two-caliber bullet holes."

"Adrian, what are you trying to say to me?"

"What I'm saying is that the man in the big white house on Pennsylvania Avenue wants the situation handled in a civilized fashion. If it turns out Tariq was the one who killed Emily Parker in Paris, he wants him tried in an American courtroom. No eye-for-an-eye bullshit on this one, Ari. No back-alley execution."

"We obviously have a difference of opinion about how best to deal with a man like Tariq."

"The president also believes a reprisal killing at this time might not be in the best interests of the peace process. He believes that if you were to respond with an assassination, you'd be playing into the hands of those who wish to bring it down."

"And what would the president have us do when terrorists murder our diplomats in cold blood?"

"Show some fucking restraint! In our humble opinion it might be wiser for you to lean on the ropes for a couple of rounds and absorb a few blows to the body if you have to. Give the negotiators room to maneuver. If the radicals hit after you have a deal in place, then by all means hit back. But don't make matters worse now by seeking revenge."

Shamron leaned forward and rubbed his hands together. "I can assure you, Adrian, that neither the Office nor any other branch of the Israeli security services is planning any operation against any member of any Arab terror group—including Tariq."

"I admire your prudence and courage. So will the president."

"And I respect you for your bluntness."

"I'd like to offer a friendly piece of advice if I may."

"Please," said Shamron.

"Israel has entered into agreements with several Western intelligence services pledging it would not conduct operations on the soil of those countries without first notifying the host intelligence service. I can assure you, the Agency and its friends will react harshly if those agreements are breached."

"That sounds more like a warning than a word of advice between friends."

Carter smiled and sipped his coffee.

The prime minister was working through a stack of papers at his desk when Shamron entered the room. Shamron sat down and quickly briefed him on his meeting with the man from the CIA. "I know Adrian Carter too well," Shamron said. "He's a good poker player. He knows more than he's saying. He's telling me to back off or there's going to be trouble."

"Or he suspects something but doesn't have enough

to come straight out with it," the prime minister said. "You have to decide which is the case."

"I need to know if you still want me to carry out the operation under these new circumstances."

The prime minister finally looked up from his paperwork. "And I need to know whether you can carry out the operation without the CIA finding out about it."

"I can."

"Then do it, and don't fuck it up."

# 18

VALBONNE, PROVENCE

The afternoon had turned colder. Jacqueline made sand-
wiches while Gabriel stacked olive wood in the fireplace
and set it alight with newspaper. He was squatting on his
haunches, watching the thin flames lick the wood. Every
few seconds he would reach into the fire and make some
minor adjustment in the disposition of the kindling or the
attitude of one of the larger pieces of wood. He seemed
capable of holding the hot wood for a long time without
discomfort. Finally he stood upright and patted his hands
together to remove the remnants of wood dust and soot.
*He moves with such ease,* Jacqueline thought—a dancer
lifting from a deep knee bend. He seemed somehow
younger. Less gray in his hair, eyes clearer and brighter.

She placed the food on a tray and carried it into the
living room. For years she had imagined a scene like this.
In a sense she had made this room for Gabriel, decorated
it in a way she imagined he might like—the stone floor,
the rustic rugs, the comfortable furnishings.

She placed the tray on a coffee table and sat down
on the couch. Gabriel sat next to her and spooned sugar

into his coffee. *Yes, this is how it would be if we had ended up together.* A simple meal, a drive into the mountains, a stroll through an ancient hill town. Perhaps down to the coast to wander the Old Port of Cannes or take in a film at the cinema. Then home to make love in the firelight. *Stop it, Jacqueline.*

Gabriel said, "I'm working for the Office again, and I need your help."

So, it was just business after all. Gabriel had been pulled back in, and he needed her for a job. He was going to pretend the past had never happened. Perhaps it was easier that way.

"Ari told me you'd left the Office."

"He asked me to come back for one job. You know how Shamron can be when he wants something."

"I remember," Jacqueline said. "Listen, Gabriel, I don't know quite how to say this, so I'll just say it. I'm very sorry about what happened in Vienna."

He looked away, his eyes cold and expressionless. Clearly, Leah was off-limits. Jacqueline had seen a photograph of her once. Gabriel's wife looked just the way she had imagined—a dark-haired Sabra, brimming with the kind of fire and confidence that Jacqueline had longed to possess when she was a Jew growing up in France. The fact that he had chosen a woman like Leah had only made Jacqueline love Gabriel more.

He abruptly changed the subject. "I assume you heard about the attack on our ambassador in Paris?"

"Of course. It was terrible."

"Shamron is convinced Tariq was behind the attack."

"And he wants you to find him?"

Gabriel nodded.

"Why you, Gabriel? You've been out of the game so long. Why not use one of his other *katsas*?"

"In case you haven't noticed, the Office has had more disasters than successes lately."

"Tariq has managed to stay one step ahead of the Office for years. How are you supposed to find him now?"

"Shamron has identified one of his agents in London. I've put a tap on his telephone at work, but I need to bug his flat so I can find out who he's talking to and what he's saying. If we're lucky, we might be able to learn where Tariq is planning to strike next."

"Why do you need me?"

"I need you to help me get inside his flat."

"Why do you need my help? You know how to pick a lock and plant a bug."

"That's just the point. I don't want to have to pick his lock. Break-ins are risky. If he figures out someone has been in his flat, then we lose the advantage. I want you to get inside his flat for me, make a copy of his keys, and check out what kind of telephone he has so I can produce a duplicate."

"And how am I supposed to get inside his flat?" She knew the answer, of course. She just wanted to hear him say it.

Gabriel stood up and added another piece of wood to the fire. "Yusef likes women. He enjoys the London nightlife. I want you to meet him in a bar or a disco and make friends with him. I want you to encourage him to invite you back to his flat."

"Sorry, Gabriel. I'm not interested. Let Ari give you one of his new girls."

He turned and looked at her.

She thought, *He's surprised I said no to him. He didn't expect that.*

"I'm offering you a chance to help me track down Tariq al-Hourani before he kills any more Jews and does any more damage to the peace process."

"And I'm telling you that I've done my bit. Let another girl have a turn."

He sat down again.

"I understand why Shamron would want to pull you back in," Jacqueline said. "You're the best at what you do. But I don't understand why you need me."

"Because you're good too," he said. Then he added, "And because I can trust you."

She thought: *What are you trying to tell me, Gabriel Allon?* She said, "I have to go to the Caribbean for a shoot in three weeks."

"I'll only need you for a few days."

"I'm not going to do this for nothing."

"I want you, and I won't settle for anyone else," Gabriel said. "Therefore, you are in a position to name your price."

She looked toward the ceiling, calculating how much she would need. Rent, renovations, advertising . . .

"Fifty thousand."

"Francs?"

"Don't be ridiculous, Gabriel. Dollars."

He pulled his face into a frown. Jacqueline crossed her arms defiantly. "Fifty thousand, or you can call Shamron and ask him for a new girl."

"Fifty thousand," he said.

Jacqueline smiled.

Jacqueline telephoned Marcel Lambert in Paris and told him to cancel all her shoots for the next two weeks.

"Jacqueline, have you lost your mind? You can't be serious. A woman in your tenuous position does not go around making matters worse by canceling shoots. That's how one earns a reputation in this business."

"Marcel, I've been in this business for seventeen years, and I've never had a reputation for blowing off shoots. Something's come up, and I need to go away for a few days."

"That's what you expect me to tell the people who've been good enough to hire you? 'Something's come up.' Come on, darling. You'll have to do much better than that."

"Tell them I've come down with something."

"Any suggestions?"

"Leprosy," she said.

"Oh, yes, marvelous." His voice turned suddenly serious. "Tell me something, Jacqueline. You're not in any sort of trouble, are you? You know you can trust me.

I've been there from the beginning, remember. I know all your secrets."

"And don't forget that I know all yours, Marcel Lambert. And no, I'm not in any sort of trouble. There's just something I need to take care of, and it won't wait."

"You're not sick, are you, Jacqueline?"

"I'm in perfect health."

"It's not the coke again, is it?" Marcel whispered.

"Marcel!"

"Surgery? An eye job?"

"Fuck you."

"A man. Is it a man? Has someone finally managed to put a dent in that iron heart of yours?"

"I'm hanging up now, Marcel. I'll call you in a few days."

"So I'm right! It is a man!"

"You're the only man for me, Marcel."

"I wish it were so."

*"À tout à l'heure."*

*"Ciao."*

They set out in the late afternoon and followed the winding highway north into the mountains. Breakaway clouds hovered over the ravines. As they rose higher into the hills, fat balls of rain pounded the windshield of Gabriel's rented Peugeot. Jacqueline reclined her seat and watched tributaries of rainwater racing over the moon roof, but already her mind was focused on London and the target. She lit a cigarette and said, "Tell me about him."

"No," he said. "I don't want anything in your head that might place you in a compromising situation."

"You came for me because I know what I'm doing, Gabriel. Tell me something about him."

"His name is Yusef. He grew up in Beirut."

"Where in Beirut?"

"Shatila."

"Jesus," she said, closing her eyes.

"His parents were refugees in 'forty-eight. They used to live in the Arab village of Lydda, but during the war they fled across the border to Lebanon. They stayed in the south for a while, then moved to Beirut in search of work and settled in the Shatila camp."

"How did he end up in London?"

"An uncle brought him to England. He made sure Yusef was educated and learned to speak perfect English and French. He became a political radical. He felt Arafat and the PLO had surrendered. He supported the Palestinian leaders who wanted to continue the war until Israel was erased from the map. He came to the attention of Tariq's organization. He's been an active member for several years."

"Sounds charming."

"He is, actually."

"Any hobbies?"

"He likes Palestinian poetry and European women. And he helps Tariq kill Israelis."

Gabriel turned off the motorway and followed a small road east into the mountains. They passed through a sleeping village and turned onto a rutted mud track lined with bare, dripping plane trees. He followed the track until he spotted a broken wooden gate leading to a patch of cleared land. He stopped the car, climbed out, pushed the gate open wide enough to accommodate the Peugeot. He drove into the clearing and shut off the engine, leaving the headlights on. He reached into Jacqueline's handbag and took out her Beretta and spare clip. Then he grabbed one of her glossy fashion magazines and ripped off the front and back covers.

"Get out."

"It's raining."

"Too bad."

Gabriel climbed out and walked a few yards across the sodden earth toward a tree where the tattered remains of a No Trespassing sign hung from a bent, rusting nail. He shoved the magazine cover over the head of the nail and walked back toward the car. Jacqueline was silhouetted against the yellow headlights, hood up against the rain, arms folded. It was quiet except for the ticking of the Peugeot's radiator and the distant barking of a farm dog. Gabriel removed the clip from the Beretta, checked to make certain the chamber was empty, then handed the gun and ammunition to Jacqueline.

"I want to know if you can still handle one of these."

"But I know the girl on that cover."

"Shoot her in the face."

Jacqueline shoved the clip into the butt of the Beretta,

tapped the base of the grip against the heel of her palm to make certain it was firmly in place. She stepped forward, raised the gun, bent her knees slightly, turned her body a few degrees to reduce her target profile for the imaginary enemy. She fired without hesitation, rhythmically and steadily, until the clip was empty.

Gabriel, listening to the popping of the little handgun, was suddenly back in the stairwell of the apartment house in Rome. Jacqueline lowered the Beretta, removed the clip, and inspected the chamber to make certain it was empty. She tossed the gun to Gabriel and said, "Let's see you try it now."

Gabriel just slipped the Beretta into his coat pocket and walked over to the tree to examine her results. Only one shot had missed; the hits were grouped tightly in the upper right. He ripped down the front cover, hung the back cover in its place, gave the Beretta back to Jacqueline. "Do it again, but this time, move forward while you're firing."

She rammed the second clip into the Beretta, pulled the slide, and advanced on the target, firing as she went. The last shot was from almost point-blank range. She pulled down the target, turned, and held it up so that the headlamps shone through the bullet holes in the paper. Each shot had found the mark. She walked back to Gabriel and gave him the Beretta and the magazine cover.

He said, "Pick up your brass."

While Jacqueline gathered the spent cartridges, he quickly disassembled the Beretta. He removed the tire iron from the trunk and pounded the gun components until they were inoperable. They got back into the Peugeot, and Gabriel left the way he had come. Along the way he hurled the magazine covers and the broken bits of the Beretta into the darkness. After they had passed through the village, he opened the window once more and scattered the cartridges.

Jacqueline lit another cigarette. "How did I do?"

"You passed."

# 19

## AMSTERDAM

Tariq spent the afternoon running errands. He walked from the houseboat to Centraalstation, where he purchased a first-class ticket for the evening train to Antwerp. From the train station he walked to the red-light district, wandering the labyrinth of narrow alleys, past the sex shops and brothels and dreary bars, until a drug dealer pulled him aside and offered him heroin. Tariq haggled over the price, then asked for enough for three people to trip. Tariq gave him the money, slipped the drugs into his pocket, walked away.

In Dam Square, he hopped onto a streetcar and rode south through the city to the Bloemenmarkt, a floating outdoor flower market on the Singel canal. He went to the largest stall and asked the florist for an elaborate bouquet of traditional Dutch flowers. When the florist asked how much he was willing to spend, Tariq assured him money was no object. The florist smiled and told him to come back in twenty minutes.

Tariq wandered through the market, past tulips and irises, lilies and sunflowers exploding with color, until he came upon a man painting. Short-cropped black hair, pale skin, and ice-blue eyes. His work depicted the Bloemenmarkt, framed by the canal and a terrace of gabled houses. It was dreamlike, an eruption of liquid color and light.

Tariq paused for a moment and watched him work. "Do you speak French?"

*"Oui,"* said the painter without looking up from his canvas.

"I admire your work."

The painter smiled and said, "And I admire yours."

Tariq nodded and walked away, wondering what in the hell the crazy painter was talking about.

He collected the flowers and returned to the houseboat. The girl was asleep. Tariq knelt beside her bed and gently shook her shoulder. She opened her eyes and looked at him as though he were mad. She closed her eyes. "What time is it?"

"Time for work."

"Come to bed."

"Actually, I might have something you'll enjoy more."

She opened her eyes and saw the flowers. She smiled. "For me? What's the occasion?"

"Just my way of thanking you for being such a gracious host."

"I like you better than flowers. Take off your clothes and come to bed."

"I have something else."

He held up the bags of white powder.

Inge quickly pulled on some clothes while Tariq went into the galley. He dug a spoon from the drawer and lit a candle. He heated the drug over the flame, but instead of diluting one bag of heroin into the mixture, he used all three. When he finished, he drew the liquid into a syringe and carried it back into the forward cabin.

Inge was sitting on the edge of the bed. She had tied a length of rubber above her elbow and was probing the bruises along the inside of her forearm, looking for a suitable vein.

"That one looks like it will do," Tariq said, handing her the syringe. She held it in the palm of her hand and calmly inserted the needle into her arm. Tariq looked away as she drew back the plunger with the tip of her thumb and the liquid heroin clouded with her blood. Then she pressed the plunger and loosened the elastic, sending the drug coursing through her body.

She looked up suddenly, eyes wide. "Hey, Paul, *man* . . . what's going—"

She fell backward onto the bed, body shuddering with violent convulsions, the empty needle dangling from her arm. Tariq walked calmly to the galley and made coffee while he waited for the girl to finish dying.

Five minutes later, as he was packing his things into a small overnight bag, he felt the boat rock sharply. He looked up, stunned. Someone was on the deck! Within seconds the door opened and a large, powerfully built man entered the salon. He had blond hair and studs in both ears. Tariq thought he bore a vague resemblance to Inge. Instinctively he felt for his Makarov pistol, which was tucked inside his trousers at the small of his back.

The man looked at Tariq. "Who are you?"

"I'm a friend of Inge's. I've been staying here for a few days." He spoke calmly, trying to gather his thoughts. The suddenness of the man's appearance had thrown him completely off guard. Five minutes ago he had quietly dispensed with the girl. Now he was confronted with someone who could wreck everything. Then he thought: *If I'm truly Inge's friend, I have nothing to fear.* He forced himself to smile and hold out his hand. "My name is Paul."

The intruder ignored Tariq's hand. "I'm Maarten, Inge's brother. Where is she?"

Tariq motioned toward the bedroom. "You know how Inge can be. Still sleeping." He realized he had left the door open. "Let me close her door so we don't wake her. I've just made coffee. Would you like a cup?"

But Maarten walked past him and entered Inge's room. Tariq thought, *Damn it!* He was shocked at how quickly things had spun out of control. He realized he had about five seconds to decide how he was going to kill him.

The easiest thing to do, of course, was to shoot him. But that would have consequences. Murder by handgun was almost unheard of in the Netherlands. A dead girl with a syringe sticking from her arm was one thing. But two dead bodies—one of them filled with 9mm rounds—was quite another. There would be a major investigation. The police would question the occupants of the surrounding houseboats. Someone might remember his face. They would give a description to the police, the police would give a description to Interpol, Interpol would give a description to the Jews. Every policeman and security official in western Europe would be looking for him. Shooting Maarten would be quick, but it would cost him in the long run.

He looked over his shoulder into the kitchen. He remembered that in the drawer next to the propane stove was a large knife. If he killed Inge's brother with a knife it might look like a crime of passion or an ordinary street crime. But Tariq found the idea of killing someone with a knife utterly repulsive. And there was another, more serious problem. There was a good chance he might not kill him with the first blow. The illness had already begun to take a toll on him. He had lost strength and stamina. The last thing he wanted to do was find himself in a life-or-death struggle with a bigger, stronger opponent. He saw his dreams—of destroying the peace process and finally evening the score with Gabriel Allon—evaporating, all because Inge's big brother had come home at an inopportune moment. Leila should have chosen more carefully.

Tariq heard Maarten scream. He decided to shoot him.

He drew the Makarov from his waistband. He realized

the gun had no silencer attached to it. *Where is it?* In the pocket of his coat, and the coat was on the chair in the salon. *Shit! How could I have become so complacent?*

Maarten charged out of the bedroom, face ashen. "She's dead!"

"What are you talking about?" Tariq asked, doing his best to stall.

"She's dead! That's what I'm talking about! She overdosed!"

"Drugs?"

Tariq inched closer to his jacket. If he could pull the silencer from the pocket and screw it into the barrel, then he could at least kill him quietly. . . .

"She has a needle hanging from her arm. Her body is still warm. She probably shot up only a few minutes ago. Did you give her the fucking drugs, man?"

"I don't know anything about drugs." Tariq realized that he sounded too calm for the situation. He had tried to appear unfazed by Maarten's arrival, and now he seemed too casual about his little sister's death. Maarten clearly didn't believe him. He screamed in rage and charged across the salon, arms raised, fists clenched.

Tariq gave up on trying to get the silencer. He gripped the Makarov, pulled the slide, leveled it at Maarten's face, shot him through the eye.

Tariq worked quickly. He had managed to kill Maarten with a single shot, but he had to assume that someone on one of the neighboring houseboats or along the embankment had heard the pop. The police might be on their way right now. He slipped the Makarov back into his waistband, then grabbed his suitcase, the flowers, and the spent cartridge, and stepped out of the salon onto the aft deck. Dusk had fallen; snow was drifting over the Amstel. The dark would help him. He looked down and noticed he was leaving footprints on the deck. He dragged his feet as he walked, obscuring the impressions, and leaped onto the embankment.

He walked quickly but calmly. In a darkened spot along the embankment he dropped his suitcase into the river. The splash was nearly inaudible. Even if the police discovered the bag, there was nothing in it that could be traced to him. He would purchase a change of clothing and a new case when he arrived in Antwerp. Then he thought: *If* I arrive in Antwerp.

He followed the Herengracht westward across the city. For a moment he considered aborting the attack, going directly to Centraalstation, and fleeing the country. The Morgenthaus were soft targets and of minimal political value. Kemel had selected them because killing them would be easy and because it would allow Tariq to keep up the pressure on the peace process. But now the risk of capture had increased dramatically because of the fiasco on the boat. Perhaps it was best to forget the whole thing.

Ahead of him a pair of seabirds lifted from the surface of the canal and broke into flight, their cries echoing off the facades of the canal houses, and for a moment Tariq was a boy of eight again, running barefoot through the camp at Sidon.

The letter arrived in the late afternoon. It was addressed to Tariq's mother and father. It said that Mahmoud al-Hourani had been killed in Cologne because he was a terrorist—that if Tariq, the youngest child of the al-Hourani family, became a terrorist, he would be killed too. Tariq's father told him to run up to the PLO office and ask if the letter spoke the truth. Tariq found a PLO officer and showed it to him. The PLO man read it once, handed it back to Tariq, ordered him to go home and tell his father that it was true. Tariq ran through the squalid camp toward his home, tears blurring his vision. He worshiped Mahmoud. He couldn't imagine living without him.

By the time he arrived home, word of the letter had spread throughout the camp—other families had received similar letters over the years. Women gathered outside Tariq's home. The sound of their wailing and the fluttering of their tongues rose over the camp with the smoke from the evening fires. Tariq thought it sounded like birds from the marshes. He found his father and told him that the letter was true—Mahmoud was dead. His father tossed the letter into the fire. Tariq would never forget the pain on his father's face, the unspeakable shame that he had been told of the death of his eldest son by the very men who had killed him.

No, Tariq thought now as he walked along the Herengracht. He would not call off the attack and run because he was afraid of being arrested. He had come too far. He had too little time left.

Tariq arrived at the house. He climbed the front steps, reached out, and pressed the bell. A moment later the door was opened by a young girl in a maid's uniform.

He held out the flower arrangement and said in Dutch, "A gift for the Morgenthaus."

"Oh, how lovely."

"It's quite heavy. Shall I bring it inside for you?"

*"Dank u."*

The girl stepped aside so Tariq could pass. She closed the door to keep out the cold and waited with one hand on the latch for Tariq to place the box on a table in the entrance hall and leave. He set down the package and drew the Makarov while turning around. This time the silencer was screwed into place.

The girl opened her mouth to scream. Tariq shot her twice in the throat.

He dragged the body out of the entrance hall and used a towel from the bathroom to wipe up the trail of blood. Then he sat in the darkened dining room and waited for David and Cynthia Morgenthau to come home.

# 20

## PARIS

Shamron summoned Gabriel to the Tuileries Gardens the following morning for a crash meeting. Gabriel found him seated on a bench next to a gravel footpath, surrounded by a gang of pigeons. He wore a slate-gray silk scarf around his neck with the ends tucked neatly beneath the lapels of his black overcoat so that his bald head seemed to be mounted atop a pedestal. He stood up, removed a black leather glove from his right hand, and stuck it out like a trench knife. Gabriel found his palm unusually warm and damp. Shamron blew into the throat of the glove and quickly put it back on. He was not accustomed to cold climates, and Paris in winter depressed him.

They walked quickly, not like two men talking in a park but like two men going somewhere in a hurry—along the footpaths of the Tuileries, across the windswept Place de la Concorde. Dead leaves rattled at their feet as they marched along the tree-lined sidewalk next to the Champs-Élysées.

"We received a report this morning from a *sayan* in the

Dutch security service," Shamron said. "It was Tariq who killed David Morgenthau and his wife in Amsterdam."

"How can they be so certain?"

"*They're* not certain, but I am. The Amsterdam police discovered a dead girl on a houseboat in the Amstel. She had overdosed on heroin. Her brother was dead too."

"Heroin?"

"A single bullet through the eye."

"What happened?"

"According to the girl's neighbors, an Arab woman moved into the houseboat a couple of weeks ago. She left a couple of days ago and a man took her place. A Frenchman who called himself Paul."

"So Tariq sent an agent to Amsterdam ahead of time to secure safe lodging and a girl for cover."

"And when he was finished with her, he fed her enough heroin to kill a camel. The police say the girl had a history of drug use and prostitution. Obviously, he thought he could make it look like an accidental overdose."

"How did the brother end up dead?"

"The houseboat is registered in his name. According to the police, he's been working in Rotterdam on a construction project. Maybe he appeared on the scene unannounced while Tariq was killing his sister."

"Makes sense."

"Actually, there's evidence to support that theory. A couple of the neighbors heard the gunshot. If Tariq had been *planning* to kill the brother, he would have used a quieter method of execution. Maybe he was surprised."

"Have they compared the slug from the brother with the slugs taken from the Morgenthaus and the maid?"

"It's a perfect match. Same gun killed all four people."

A young Swedish couple was posing for a photograph. Gabriel and Shamron turned abruptly and walked the other way.

Gabriel said, "Any other news?"

"I want you to watch your step in London. A man from Langley paid a courtesy call on me last week. The Americans have been told by their sources that Tariq was involved in Paris. They want him arrested and prosecuted in the United States."

"The last thing we need now is to be tripping over the CIA."

"It gets worse, I'm afraid. The man from Langley also dropped a not-so-subtle warning about the pitfalls of operating in certain countries without permission."

"Do they know anything?"

"I doubt it, but I wouldn't rule it out completely."

"I was hoping that my return to the Office wouldn't land me in a British jail."

"It won't as long as you stay disciplined."

"Thanks for the vote of confidence."

"Did you find her?" Shamron asked, changing the subject.

Gabriel nodded.

"And she's willing to do it?"

"It took me a while to convince her, but she agreed."

"Why are all my children so reluctant to come home again? Was I such an errant father?"

"Just an overly demanding one."

Gabriel stopped in front of a café on the Champs-Élysées. Jacqueline was seated in the window, wearing large sunglasses and reading a magazine. She glanced up as they approached, then turned her gaze to her magazine once more.

Shamron said, "It's nice to see you two working together again. Just don't break her heart this time. She's a good girl."

"I know."

"You'll need a cover job for her in London. I know someone who's looking for a secretary."

"I'm one step ahead of you."

Shamron smiled and walked away. He melted into the crowds along the Champs-Élysées and a moment later was gone.

Julian Isherwood made his way across the wet bricks of Mason's Yard. It was three-thirty, and he was just returning to the gallery from lunch. He was drunk. He hadn't noticed that he was drunk until he stepped out the door of Green's and took a few deep breaths of the freezing, damp air. The oxygen had resuscitated his brain, and his brain had alerted his body that once again he had poured too much wine into it. His lunch mate had been the tubby Oliver Dimbleby, and once again the topic of conversation had been Oliver's proposal to buy out Isherwood Fine

Arts. This time Isherwood had managed to maintain his composure and discuss the situation somewhat rationally— though not without the assistance of two bottles of superb Sancerre. When one is discussing the dismemberment of one's business—one's very soul, he thought—one is allowed to dull the pain with good French wine.

He pulled his coat up around his ears. A blast of wet wind poured through the passageway from Duke Street. Isherwood found himself caught in a whirlpool of dead leaves and wet rubbish. He stumbled forward a few steps, hands shielding his face, until the maelstrom spun itself out. *For Christ's sake!* Dreadful climate. Positively Siberian. He considered slipping into the pub for something to warm his bones but thought better of it. He'd done enough damage for one afternoon.

He used his key to unlock the door on the ground floor, slowly climbed the stairs, thinking he really should do something about the carpet. On the landing was the entrance to a small travel agency. The walls were hung with posters of fiercely tanned amazons frolicking half naked in the sun. *Perhaps this is the best thing for me,* he thought, staring at a topless girl lying facedown in perfect white sand. *Perhaps I should get out while I still have a few decent years left in me. Flee London, go someplace warm, lick my wounds.*

He shoved the key into the lock, pushed back the door, removed his coat, and hung it on the hook in the anteroom. Then he stepped into his office and flipped the light switch.

"Hello, Julian."

Isherwood spun around and found himself face-to-face with Gabriel Allon. "You! How the bloody hell did you get in here?"

"Do you really want to know?"

"I suppose not," said Isherwood. "What in God's name are you doing here? And where have you been?"

"I need a favor."

"*You* need a favor! *You* need a favor—from *me*! You ran out on me in the middle of a job. You left my Vecellio in a Cornish cottage with no security."

"Sometimes the best place to hide a priceless Vecellio is the last place anyone would think to look for it. If I had wanted to help myself to the contents of your vault downstairs, I could have done it quite easily."

"That's because you're a freak of nature!"

"There's no need to get personal, Julian."

"Oh, really. How's this for personal?" He picked up a coffee mug from his desk and threw it directly at Gabriel's head.

Gabriel could see that Isherwood had been drinking, so he pulled him back outside to sober him. They circled the footpaths of Green Park until Isherwood grew tired and settled himself on a bench. Gabriel sat next to him and waited for a couple to pass by before he started to speak again.

"Can she type?" Isherwood said. "Does she know how to answer the telephone? How to take a message?"

"I don't think she's done an honest day's work her entire life."

"Oh, how perfect. Absolutely stupendous."

"She's a smart girl. I'm sure she'll be able to help out around the office."

"That's comforting. Am I allowed to ask *why* I'm supposed to hire this woman?"

"Julian, please."

"*Julian*, please. *Julian*, mind your own business. *Julian*, shut up and do as we tell you. It's always the same with you people. And all the while my business is going straight to hell. Oliver's made me an offer. I'm going to take him up on it."

"Oliver doesn't seem like your type."

"Beggars can't be choosers. I wouldn't be in this position if you hadn't run out on me."

"I didn't run out on you."

"What do you call it, Gabriel?"

"It's just something I need to do. It's just like the old days."

"In the old days that was part of the arrangement going in. But these aren't the old days. This is business— straight fucking business, Gabriel—and you've given me the right royal shaft. What am I supposed to do about the Vecellio while you're playing games with Ari?"

"Wait for me," Gabriel said. "This will be over soon, and I'll work day and night on it until it's finished."

"I don't want a crash job. I brought it to you because I knew you would take your time and do it right. If I wanted a crash job, I could have hired a hack to do it for a third of what I'm paying you."

"Give me some time. Keep your buyer at bay, and whatever you do, don't sell out to Oliver Dimbleby. You'll never forgive yourself."

Isherwood looked at his watch and stood up. "I have an appointment. Someone who actually wants to buy a picture." He turned and started to walk away; then he stopped and said, "By the way, you left a brokenhearted little boy behind in Cornwall."

"Peel," Gabriel said distantly.

"It's funny, Gabriel, but I never had you figured for the type that would hurt a child. Tell your girl to be at the gallery at nine o'clock tomorrow morning. And tell her not to be late."

"She'll be there."

"What am I to call this *secretary* you're sending me?"

"You may call her Dominique."

"Good-looking?" Isherwood said, regaining a bit of his old humor.

"Not bad."

# 21

## MAIDA VALE, LONDON

Gabriel carried the suitcases in while Jacqueline surveyed her new home, a cramped bed-sit flat with a single window overlooking an inner courtyard. A foldout couch, a club chair of cracked leather, a small writing desk. Next to the window was a flaking radiator and next to the radiator a door leading to a kitchen scarcely larger than the galley on Gabriel's ketch. Jacqueline went into the kitchen and began opening and closing cabinets, sadly, as if each was more repulsive than the last.

"I had the *bodel* do a bit of shopping for you."

"Couldn't you have found something a little bit nicer?"

"Dominique Bonard is a girl from Paris who came to London in search of work. I didn't think a three-bedroom maisonette in Mayfair was appropriate."

"Is that where you're staying?"

"Not exactly."

"Stay for a few minutes. I find the thought of being alone here depressing."

"A few."

She filled the kettle with water, placed it on the stove, and switched on the burner. Gabriel found tea bags and a box of shelf milk. She prepared two mugs of tea and carried them into the sitting room. Gabriel was on the couch. Jacqueline removed her shoes and sat across from him, knees beneath her chin. "When do we start?"

"Tomorrow night. If that doesn't work, we'll try the next night."

She lit a cigarette, threw back her head, blew smoke at the ceiling. Then she looked at Gabriel and narrowed her eyes. "Do you remember that night in Tunis?"

"Which night?"

"The night of the operation."

"Of course I remember it."

"I remember it as though it were yesterday." She closed her eyes. "I especially remember the trip across the water back to the boat. I was so excited I couldn't feel my body. I was flying. We had actually done it. We had walked right into that bastard's house in the middle of a PLO compound and taken him out. I wanted to scream with joy. But I'll never forget the look on your face. You were haunted. It was as if the dead men were sitting next to you in the boat."

"Very few people understand what it's like to shoot a man at close range. Even fewer know what it's like to place a gun against the side of his head and pull the trigger. Killing on the secret battlefield is different from killing a man on the Golan or Sinai, even when it's a murderous bastard like Abu Jihad."

"I understand that now. I felt like such a fool when we got back to Tel Aviv. I acted like you had just scored the winning goal, and all the while you were dying inside. I hope you can forgive me."

"You don't need to apologize."

"But what I don't understand is how Shamron enticed you back after all these years."

"It has nothing to do with Shamron. It's about Tariq."

"What about Tariq?"

Gabriel sat silently for a moment, then stood and walked to the window. In the courtyard a trio of boys kicked a ball in amber lamplight, old newspaper floating above them in the wet wind like cinder.

"Tariq's older brother, Mahmoud, was a member of Black September. Ari Shamron tracked him to Cologne, and he sent me to finish him off. I slipped into his flat while he was sleeping and pointed a gun at his face. Then I woke him up so that he wouldn't die a peaceful death. I shot him in both eyes. Seventeen years later Tariq took his revenge by blowing up my wife and son right before my eyes."

Jacqueline covered her mouth with her hands. Gabriel was still staring out the window, but she could tell it was Vienna that he saw now and not the boys playing in the courtyard.

"For a long time I thought Tariq had made a mistake," Gabriel said. "But he never makes mistakes like that. He's careful, deliberate. He's the perfect predator.

He went after my family for a reason. He went after them to punish me for killing his brother. He knew it would be worse than death." He turned to face her. "From one professional to another, it was an exquisite piece of work."

"And now you're going to kill him in return?"

He looked away and said nothing.

"I always blamed myself for what happened in Vienna," Jacqueline said. "If we hadn't—"

"It wasn't your fault," Gabriel said, cutting her off. "It was my fault, not yours. I should have known better. I behaved foolishly. But it's over now."

The coldness of his voice felt like a knife in her chest. She took a long time crushing out her cigarette, then looked up at him. "Why did you tell Leah about us?"

He stood in the window for a moment, saying nothing. Jacqueline feared she had taken it too far. She tried to think of some way to defuse the situation and change the subject, but she desperately wanted to know the answer. If Gabriel hadn't confessed the affair, Leah and Dani would never have been with him on assignment in Vienna.

"I told her because I didn't want to lie to her. My entire life was a lie. Shamron had convinced me I was perfect, but I wasn't perfect. For the first time in my life I had behaved with a bit of human frailty and weakness. I suppose I needed to share it with her. I suppose I needed someone to forgive me."

He picked up his coat. His face was twisted. He was

angry, not with her but with himself. "You have a long day ahead of you tomorrow." His voice was all business now. "Get settled and try to get some rest. Julian's expecting you at nine o'clock."

And then he went out.

For a few minutes she was distracted by the ritual of unpacking. Then the pain crept up on her, like the delayed sting of a slap. She collapsed onto the couch and began to cry. She lit another cigarette and looked around at the dreary little flat. *What in the hell am I doing here?* She had agreed to come back for one reason—because she thought she could make Gabriel love her—but he had dismissed their affair in Tunis as a moment of weakness. Still, why had he come back after all these years to kill Tariq? Was it simply revenge? An eye for an eye? No, she thought— Gabriel's motives ran far deeper and were more complex than pure revenge. Perhaps he *needed* to kill Tariq in order to forgive himself for what happened to Leah and finally move on with his life. *But will he ever be able to forgive me?* Perhaps the only way to earn his forgiveness was to help him kill Tariq. *And the only way I can help him kill Tariq is to make another man fall for me and take him to bed.* She closed her eyes and thought of Yusef al-Tawfiki.

Gabriel had left his car on the Ashworth Road. He made a show of dropping his keys on the curb and groping in the darkness as if he were trying to find them. In reality he was searching the undercarriage of the car, looking for something that shouldn't be there—a mass, a loose wire. The car looked clean, so he climbed in, started the motor, drove in circles for a half hour through Maida Vale and Notting Hill, making certain he was not being followed.

He was annoyed with himself. He had been taught— first by his father, then by Ari Shamron—that men who could not keep secrets were weak and inferior. His father had survived Auschwitz but refused ever to speak of it. He struck Gabriel only once—when Gabriel demanded that his father tell him what had happened at the camp. If it hadn't been for the numbers tattooed on his right forearm, Gabriel might never have known that his father had suffered.

Indeed, Israel was a place filled with damaged people— mothers who buried sons killed in wars, children who buried siblings killed by terrorists. After Vienna, Gabriel leaned on the lessons of his father: sometimes people die too soon. Mourn for them in private. Don't wear your suffering on your sleeve like the Arabs. And when you're finished mourning, get back on your feet and get on with life.

It was the last part—getting on with life—that had given Gabriel the most trouble. He blamed himself for what had happened in Vienna, not only because of his affair with Jacqueline but because of the way he had killed Tariq's brother. He had wanted the satisfaction of knowing that Mahmoud was aware of his death—that he had been terrified at the moment Gabriel's Beretta quietly dispatched the first scorching bullet into his brain. Shamron had told him to terrorize the terrorists—to think like them and behave like them. Gabriel believed he had been punished for allowing himself to become like his enemy.

He had punished himself in return. One by one he had closed the doors and barred the windows that had once given him access to life's pleasures. He drifted through time and space the way he imagined a damned spirit might visit the place where he had lived: able to see loved ones and possessions but unable to communicate or taste or touch or feel. He experienced beauty only in art and only by repairing damage inflicted by uncaring owners and by the corrosive passage of time. Shamron had made him the destroyer. Gabriel had turned himself back into the healer. Unfortunately, he was not capable of healing himself.

So why tell his secrets to Jacqueline? Why answer her damned questions? The simple answer was he wanted to. He had felt it the moment he walked into her villa in Valbonne, a prosaic need to share secrets and reveal past pain and disappointment. But there was something more important: he didn't have to explain himself to her. He thought of his silly fantasy about Peel's mother, how it had ended when he had told her the truth about himself. The scenario reflected one of Gabriel's deep-seated fears—the dread of telling another woman he was a professional killer. Jacqueline already knew his secrets.

Maybe Jacqueline had been right about one thing, he

thought—maybe he should have asked Shamron for another girl. Jacqueline was his *bat leveyha*, and tomorrow he was going to send her into the bed of another man.

He parked around the corner from his flat and walked quickly along the pavement toward the entrance of the block. He looked up toward his window and murmured, "Good evening, Mr. Karp." And he pictured Karp, peering through the sight of his parabolic microphone, saying, "Welcome home, Gabe. Long time, no hear from."

# 22

## MAIDA VALE, LONDON

Jacqueline felt a peculiar exhilaration the following morning as she walked along Elgin Avenue toward the Maida Vale tube station. She had lived a life of hedonistic excess—too much money, too many men, fine things taken for granted. It felt reassuring to be doing something so ordinary as taking the Underground to work, even if it was only a cover job.

She bought a copy of *The Times* from the newsstand on the street, then entered the station and followed the stairs down to the ticket lobby. The previous evening she had studied street maps and memorized the Underground lines. They had such curious names: Jubilee, Circle, District, Victoria. To get to the gallery in St. James's, she would take the Bakerloo Line from Maida Vale to Piccadilly Circus. She purchased a ticket from an automated dispenser, then passed through the turnstile and headed down the escalator to the platform. So far, so good, she thought. Just another working girl in London.

Her notion of relaxing for a few minutes with the newspaper dissolved when the train arrived at the station.

The carriages were hopelessly crowded, the passengers crushed against the glass. Jacqueline, who was always protective of her personal space, considered waiting to see if the next train was any better. She looked at her watch, saw she had no time to waste. When the doors opened, only a handful of people got off. There seemed to be no place for her to stand. *What would a Londoner do?* Push her way in. She held her handbag across her breasts and stepped aboard.

The train lurched forward. The man next to her was breathing last night's beer into her face. She stretched her long frame, tilted her head back, closed her eyes, found a draft of fresh air leaking through the crack in the doors.

A few moments later the train arrived at Piccadilly Circus. Outside, the mist had turned to light rain. Jacqueline pulled an umbrella from her handbag. She walked quickly, keeping pace with the office workers around her, making subtle alterations in course to avoid oncoming traffic.

Turning into Duke Street, she glanced over her shoulder. Walking a few feet behind her, wearing black jeans and a leather jacket, was Gabriel. She moved south along Duke Street until she arrived at the entrance of Mason's Yard.

Gabriel bumped her elbow as he passed. "You're clean. Give my love to Julian."

The gallery was exactly as Gabriel had described it: wedged between the shipping company office and the pub. Next to the door was a panel, and on the panel were two buttons and two corresponding names: LOCUS TRAVEL and ISHER OO FINE AR S. She pressed the button, waited, pressed it again, waited, glanced at her watch, pressed it again. Nothing.

She crossed Mason's Yard, entered Duke Street, and found a little café where she could wait. She ordered coffee and settled in the window with her *Times*. Fifteen minutes later, at precisely nine-twenty, she spotted a stylishly clothed gray-haired man rushing along Duke Street as though he were running late for his own funeral. He ducked through the passageway and disappeared into Mason's Yard. Isherwood, she thought. Had to be.

She pushed her newspaper into her handbag and slipped out of the café after him. She followed him across Mason's Yard toward the gallery. As he was unlocking the door she called out, "Mr. Isherwood, is that you? I've been waiting for you."

Isherwood turned around. His mouth fell open slightly as she approached.

"I'm Dominique Bonard. I believe you were expecting me this morning."

Isherwood cleared his throat several times rapidly and seemed to have trouble remembering which key opened the office. "Yes, well, delighted, really," he stammered. "Awfully sorry, bloody tube, you know."

"Let me take your briefcase. Maybe that will help."

"Yes, well, you're *French*," he said, as if he thought this might be a revelation to her. "I have fluent Italian, but I'm afraid my French is rather atrocious."

"I'm sure we'll get along just fine in English."

"Yes, quite."

Finally, he managed to unlock the door. He held it open rather too gallantly and gestured for her to lead the way up the stairs. On the landing, Isherwood paused in front of the travel agency and studied the girl in one of the posters. He turned and glanced at Jacqueline, then stared at the girl in the photograph once more. "You know, Dominique, she could be your twin sister."

Jacqueline smiled and said, "Don't be silly."

Isherwood opened the gallery and showed Jacqueline to her desk.

"There's a man called Oliver Dimbleby coming later this morning. He looks rather like an English sausage in a Savile Row suit. Buzz him up when he arrives. Until then, let me show you round the rest of the gallery."

He handed her a pair of keys on a blue elastic band. "These are for you. Whenever one of us leaves the gallery, the doors are to be armed. The disarm code is five-seven-six-four-nine-seven-three-two-six. Get that?"

Jacqueline nodded. Isherwood looked at her incredulously, and she repeated the sequence of numbers briskly and without error. Isherwood was clearly impressed.

They entered a small lift, barely large enough to accommodate two passengers. Isherwood inserted his key into the security lock, turned it, and pressed the button marked *B*. The lift groaned and shuddered, then traveled slowly down the shaft, coming to rest with a gentle bump. The doors opened, and they entered a cool, dark room.

"This is the tomb," he said, switching on the lights. It was a cramped cellar filled with canvases, some framed, some unframed and resting in slots built into the walls. "This is my stockroom. Hundreds of works, many of them valuable, many more that have little or no worth on the open market and are therefore accumulating dust in this room."

He led her back into the lift, and this time they rode up. The doors opened onto a large, high-ceilinged room. Gray morning light trickled through a circular glass dome in the roof. Jacqueline cautiously walked forward a few paces. Isherwood threw a switch, illuminating the room.

It was as if she had stepped into a museum. The walls were cream-colored and pristine, the hardwood floor burnished to a high gloss. In the center of the floor was a low bench covered in soft velvet the color of claret. On the walls were towering canvases lit by focused halogen lamps mounted in the ceiling. Rain pattered softly on the domed skylight. Jacqueline sat down on the bench. There was a Venus by Luini and a Nativity by del Vaga; a Baptism of Christ by Bordone and a stunning landscape by Claude.

"It's breathtaking," she said. "I feel like I'm in the Louvre. You must come up here often."

"When I need to think. Feel free to come up anytime you like. Bring your lunch."

"I will. Thank you for showing it to me."

"If you're going to work here, I suppose you should know your way round the place."

They took the lift to the main level. Jacqueline sat at her new desk, pulled open the drawers, rummaged through the paper clips and pens, experimented with the copy machine.

Isherwood said, "You *do* know how to use those things, don't you?"

"I'm sure I'll get the hang of it."

"Oh, good Lord," he murmured.

Oliver Dimbleby arrived promptly at eleven o'clock. Jacqueline inspected him through the security camera— he *did* look rather like a sausage in a Savile Row suit—and buzzed him up. When he caught sight of her, he pulled in his stomach and smiled affectionately. "So, you're Julian's new girl," he said, shaking her hand. "I'm Oliver Dimbleby. *Very* pleased to meet you. *Very* pleased, in*deed*."

"Come, Oliver," Isherwood called from the inner office. "Here, boy. Let go of her hand and get in here. We haven't got all day."

Oliver reluctantly relinquished her hand and stepped into Isherwood's office. "Tell me, Julie, my love. If I actually buy this place, does that angel in there convey?"

"Oh, *do* shut up, Oliver." Isherwood closed the door.

Jacqueline went back to her office and tried to figure out how to use the fax machine.

*     *     *

The telephone call arrived at the Kebab Factory at 4:00 P.M. Gabriel waited three minutes and twenty seconds for Yusef to come to the phone—he knew the precise amount of time it took because later he felt compelled to measure it with a stopwatch. During Yusef's absence he was treated to the sounds of the kitchen help chattering in Lebanese Arabic and Mohammed, the afternoon manager, screaming at a busboy to clear table seventeen. When Yusef finally came to the phone, he seemed slightly out of breath. Their entire conversation lasted thirty-seven seconds. When it was done Gabriel rewound the tape and listened to it so many times Karp begged him to stop.

"Trust me, Gabe, there's nothing sinister going on. It's two guys talking about getting a drink and maybe finding a girl and getting laid. You remember getting laid, don't you?"

But Gabriel was initiating the next phase of the operation—he was sending Jacqueline into hostile territory—and he wanted to be certain he wasn't sending her into a trap. So he listened again:

*"We still on for tonight?"*

*"Absolutely. Where?"*

*"All Bar One, Leicester Square, nine o'clock."*

*"I'll be there."*

STOP. REWIND. PLAY.

*"We still on for tonight?"*

*"Absolutely. Where?"*

*"All Bar One, Leicester Square, nine o'clock."*

"*I'll be there.*"

STOP. REWIND. PLAY.

"*All Bar One, Leicester Square, nine o'clock.*"

STOP. PLAY.

"*I'll be there.*"

Gabriel picked up the telephone and punched in the number for Isherwood Fine Arts.

# 23

## LEICESTER SQUARE, LONDON

All Bar One stood on the southwest corner of Leicester Square. It had two floors and large windows, so that Gabriel, seated outside on a cold wooden bench, could see the action inside as though it were a play on a multilevel stage. Crowds of tourists and filmgoers streamed past him. The street performers were out too. On one side of the square a German sang Jimi Hendrix through a crackling microphone, accompanied by an amplified acoustic guitar. On the other a group of Peruvians played the music of the mountains to a disconsolate-looking gang of urban punks with purple hair. A few feet from the entrance of the bar a human statue stood frozen atop a pedestal, face painted the color of titanium, eyeing Gabriel malevolently.

Yusef arrived five minutes later, accompanied by a trim, sandy-haired man. They negotiated the short line at the door by bribing the muscled ape who was standing guard. A moment later they appeared in the window on the second level. Yusef said hello to a lanky blonde. Gabriel removed a mobile phone from his coat pocket, dialed a number, murmured a few words, then pressed the END button.

Jacqueline, when she arrived five minutes later, wore the same clothes she had worn to Isherwood's gallery that morning, but she had let down her long hair. She presented herself to the doorman and inquired about the wait. The doorman promptly stepped aside, much to the annoyance of the other patrons gathered outside. As Jacqueline disappeared into the bar, Gabriel heard someone mutter, "French bitch."

She went upstairs, bought herself a glass of wine, and sat down in the window a few feet from Yusef and his friend. Yusef was still talking to the blonde, but after a few moments Gabriel could see his eyes wandering to the tall, dark-haired girl seated to his right.

Twenty minutes later, neither Gabriel nor the statue had moved, but Yusef had disengaged himself from the blonde and was sitting next to Jacqueline. She was feeding on him with her eyes, as though whatever he was saying was the most fascinating thing she had heard in years.

Gabriel stared at the statue, and the statue stared back.

At midnight they left the bar and walked across the square through a swirling wind. Jacqueline shivered and folded her arms beneath her breasts. Yusef put an arm around her waist and pulled her against him. She could feel the wine. She had found that judicious use of alcohol helped in situations like these. She had drunk just enough to lose any inhibitions about sleeping with a complete stranger—inhibitions that might betray her—but not enough to dull her senses or instincts of self-preservation.

They climbed into a taxi on the Charing Cross Road.

Jacqueline said, "Where do you live?" She knew the answer, but Dominique Bonard did not.

"I have a flat in Bayswater. Sussex Gardens. Shall we go there?"

She nodded. They rode up the Charing Cross Road, past darkened shops, then west along Oxford Street toward Marble Arch and the Park. Sometimes they would pass a lighted shop or slip beneath a street lamp and she would see his face for an instant, like a photograph flashed on a screen and then taken away. She studied him in profile. The hinge of his jaw was a perfect right angle, his nose long and slender with crisp lines along the bridge, his lips full. Long eyelashes, wide eyebrows. He had shaved carefully. He wore no cologne.

Based on what Gabriel had told her, she had expected Yusef to be cocky and overly confident. But instead he displayed a pleasant, somewhat shy intelligence. She thought about the German chemical executive she had seduced in Cyprus. He was bald and had foul breath. Over dinner he had told her how much he hated Jews. Later, in bed, he had asked her to do things that made her feel sick.

They headed up the Edgware Road and turned into

Sussex Gardens. She wanted to look up and find the flat where Gabriel had established his listening post. She forced herself to look at Yusef instead. She traced her finger along his jaw. "You're quite beautiful, you know."

He smiled. She thought: *He's used to compliments from women.*

The taxi arrived in front of his building. It was a charmless place, a flat-fronted postwar block house with an air of institutional decay. He helped her out of the taxi, paid off the driver, led her up a short flight of steps to the front entrance. He walked on the balls of his feet—like Gabriel, she thought—as if he were perpetually prepared to lunge or pounce. She wondered if Gabriel was watching them.

He removed his keys, singled out one for the front door—Yale model, she noted—and inserted it into the chamber. He led her across a small lobby of checkered linoleum, then up a dimly lit flight of stairs. She wondered how he would make his move. Would he open a bottle of wine, play soft music, or light candles? Or would he be straightforward and businesslike? If they talked she might learn something about him that could be helpful to Gabriel. She decided she would try to stretch the seduction a little longer.

At the door of his flat he used a second Yale to unlock the dead bolt, then an old-fashioned skeleton for the latch. *Three locks, three separate keys. No problem.*

They entered the flat. The room was in darkness. Yusef closed the door. Then he kissed her for the first time.

Jacqueline said, "I've wanted you to do that all night. You have beautiful lips."

"I've wanted to do other things all night." He kissed her again. "Can I get you something to drink?"

"A glass of wine would be nice if you have any."

"I think so. Let me check."

He switched on a light, a cheap standing lamp with the beam focused on the ceiling, and left his keys on a small table next to the door. Jacqueline placed her handbag beside them. Shamron's training took over. She quickly surveyed the room. It was the flat of an intellectual revolutionary, a sparse, utilitarian base camp. Three cheap Oriental carpets covered the linoleum floor. The coffee table was a large, square piece of pressboard propped on four gray cinder blocks surrounded by a foursome of mismatched chairs. In the center of the table was an ashtray the size of a dinner plate containing several brands of cigarette butts. A few were smudged with lipstick, two different shades. Around the ashtray were a half-dozen small cups, stained, like Rorschach test patterns, with Turkish coffee grounds.

She turned her attention to the walls. There were posters of Bob Marley and Che Guevara, another of Tommie Smith and John Carlos raising their gloved fists at the Mexico City Olympics in 1968. There was a black, green, and red Palestinian flag and a print of a painting depicting a village girl being bathed by other women on the night before her wedding. She recognized the painting as one of Ibrahim Ghannan's. Everywhere there

were books, some stacked, some in piles, as if they were
awaiting gasoline and a match—volumes of Middle East
history, histories of the Middle East wars, biographies of
Arafat, Sadat, Ben-Gurion, Rabin.

"You read a great deal," Jacqueline said.

"It's an addiction of mine."

"Where are you from, if you don't mind my asking?"

"Palestine."

He came into the room from the kitchen and handed
her a glass of red wine. Then he held out his hand. "Come
with me."

Gabriel stood in his window. Karp's laser microphone
picked up snatches of their conversation, but it was like
listening to a vinyl record album that skipped. When they
moved to the bedroom to make love, Gabriel said, "Shut
it off."

"But, Gabe, it's just getting to the good part."

"I said, shut it off."

Karp lowered the microphone and switched off the
power. "I'm hungry. I'm going for a walk."

"Go."

"You all right, Gabe?"

"I'm fine."

"You sure about that?"

"Go."

One hour later Yusef climbed out of bed, walked to the
window, and opened the curtains. The yellow street lamp

had turned his olive skin the color of old newsprint. Jacqueline lay on her stomach. She placed her chin atop her hands and looked at him, eyes following the line from his square shoulders to his lean, muscular waist. She wondered if Gabriel was looking at him too.

Yusef was watching the street—looking into parked cars, scanning the building opposite. He turned his body slightly, and she could see a wide, flat scar on his back, running between his right shoulder blade and the center of his ridged spine. She had felt it when they were making love. It was hard and coarse, like sandpaper. Like the skin of a shark.

He had been a gentle lover, meticulous in his attempts to give her pleasure. When he was inside her, she had closed her eyes and imagined it was Gabriel, and when she felt the scar between his shoulder blades she imagined it was Gabriel's scar, a relic from one of his secret missions, and she wished that she could pass her hand over it and make it go away.

"What are you looking at?" she asked.

Yusef turned around and folded his arms across his chest.

"Have you ever slept with an Arab before, Dominique?"

She thought: *And you're changing the subject.* She said, "You're my first. I may have to do it again sometime."

"Not while you're sleeping with me."

"Are we sleeping together now?"

"That's up to you."

"All right, we are now officially sleeping together." She rolled onto her back, looked at the light from the street falling across her body, imagined it was Gabriel's gaze. "Do you think we should get to know each other a little better, now that we're officially sleeping together?"

He smiled and said, "What do you want to know?"

"I want to know what happened to your back."

He turned and looked out the window.

She studied the digital alarm clock on the bedside table.

"There are some things about my past that you might find unpleasant," he said.

"Bad things you've done?"

"No, Dominique. Bad things that were done to me."

"How did you get that scar on your back?"

He turned and looked at her. "I grew up in a refugee camp in Lebanon—the Shatila camp in south Beirut. Perhaps you've heard of Shatila, Dominique."

"Of course I've heard of Shatila."

"The PLO had offices in the Shatila camp, so when the Israelis invaded Lebanon in 'eighty-two, they shelled the camp day and night. A missile fired by an Israeli fighter jet hit the building where our family lived. The building collapsed on top of me, and a chunk of concrete tore away the skin of my back."

"Why were you in Lebanon?"

"Because that's where my family ended up after they

were driven from their ancestral homes in Palestine by the Jews."

Jacqueline looked at the ceiling.

Yusef said, "Why do you look away from me when I tell you that?"

"I met some Israelis once in a nightclub in Paris. They were debating this issue with a group of French students. They said that the Jews didn't have to expel the Arabs from Palestine because the Arabs left on their own."

Yusef laughed and shook his head. "I'm afraid you have fallen for the great Zionist myth, Dominique. The myth that the Palestinians would voluntarily trade the land where they had lived for centuries for exile and refugee camps. The myth that the Arab governments told the Palestinians to leave."

"It's not true?"

"Does it sound as though it could be true?"

"Not really."

"Then trust your instincts, Dominique. If it doesn't sound plausible, it probably isn't. Do you want to know the truth about what the Jews did to my people? Do you want to know why my family ended up in a refugee camp in Beirut?"

"I want to know about you."

"I'm a Palestinian. It's impossible to separate me from the history of my people."

"Tell me," she said.

"By the way, which nightclub in Paris?"

"What?"

"The nightclub where you met the Israelis. Which one was it?"

"I can't remember. It was so long ago."

"Try to remember, please. It's important."

"We call it *al-Nakba*. The Catastrophe."

He had pulled on a pair of loose-fitting cotton pajama bottoms and a London University sweatshirt, as if suddenly self-conscious about his nakedness. He gave Jacqueline a blue dress shirt. It was unspoken, but the implication was clear: one mustn't discuss something as sacred as *al-Nakba* in a state of postcoital undress. Jacqueline sat in the middle of the bed, her long legs crossed before her, while Yusef paced.

"When the United Nations presented the plan to partition Palestine into two states, the Jews realized they had a serious problem. The Zionists had come to Palestine to build a *Jewish* state, but nearly half of the people in the new partition state were to be Arabs. The Jews accepted the partition plan, knowing full well that it would be unacceptable to the Arabs. And why should the Arabs accept it? The Jews owned seven percent of Palestine, but they were being handed fifty percent of the country, including the most fertile land along the coastal plain and the Upper Galilee. Are you listening, Dominique?"

"I'm listening."

"The Jews devised a plan to remove the Arabs from the land designated for the Jewish state. They even had a name for it: Plan Dalet. And they put it into effect the moment the Arabs attacked. Their plan was to expel the Arabs, to drive them out, as Ben-Gurion put it. To cleanse Jewish Palestine of Arabs. Yes, *cleanse*. I don't use that word lightly, Dominique. It's not my word. It's the very word the Zionists used to describe their plan to expel my people from Palestine."

"It sounds as though they behaved like the Serbs."

"They did. Have you ever heard of a place called Deir Yassin?"

"No," she said.

"Your view of the conflict in the Middle East has been shaped by the Zionists, so it's hardly surprising to me that you have never heard of Deir Yassin."

"Tell me about Deir Yassin."

"It was an Arab village outside Jerusalem on the road to the coast and Tel Aviv. It isn't there anymore. There's a Jewish town where Deir Yassin used to be. It's called Kfar Sha'ul."

Yusef closed his eyes for a moment, as if the next part was too painful even to speak about. When he resumed he spoke with the flat calm of a survivor recounting the last mundane events of a loved one's life.

"The village elders had reached an accommodation with the Zionists, so the four hundred Arabs who lived in Deir Yassin felt they were safe. They had been promised by the Zionists that the village would not be attacked. But at four o'clock one April morning, the members of the Irgun and the Stern Gang came to Deir Yassin. By noon, two thirds of the villagers had been slaughtered.

The Jews rounded up the men and the boys, stood them against a wall, and started shooting. They went house to house and murdered the women and the children. They dynamited the homes. They shot a woman who was nine months pregnant, then they cut open her womb and ripped out the child. A woman rushed forward to try to save the baby's life. A Jew shot the woman and killed her."

"I don't believe things like that happened in Palestine."

"Of course they did, Dominique. After the massacre word spread through the Arab villages like wildfire. The Jews took full advantage of the situation. They mounted loudspeakers on trucks and broadcast warnings. They told the Arabs to get out, or there would be another Deir Yassin. They concocted stories about outbreaks of typhus and cholera. They made clandestine radio broadcasts in Arabic, masquerading as Arab leaders, and urged the Palestinians to take flight to avoid a bloodbath. This is the real reason the Palestinians left."

"I had no idea," she said.

"My own family came from the village of Lydda. Lydda, like Deir Yassin, no longer exists. It is now Lod. It's where the Zionists put their fucking airport. After a battle with the Arab defenders, the Jews entered Lydda. There was complete panic. Two hundred fifty Arab villagers were killed in the crossfire. After the town was captured, the commanders asked Ben-Gurion what should be done with the Arabs. He said, 'Drive them

out!' The actual expulsion orders were signed by Yitzhak Rabin. My family was given ten minutes to pack a
few belongings, as much as they could carry in a single
bag, and told to get out. They started walking. The Jews
laughed at them. Spat at them. That's the truth about
what happened in Palestine. That's who I am. That's
why I hate them."

Jacqueline, however, was thinking not of the Arabs
of Lydda but of the Jews of Marseilles—of Maurice and
Rachel Halévy and the night the Vichy gendarmes came
for them.

"You're shaking," he said.

"Your story upset me. Come back to bed. I want to
hold you."

He crawled back into bed, spread his body gently over
hers, and kissed her mouth. "End of lecture," he said.
"We'll resume tomorrow, if you're interested."

"I'm interested—very interested, in fact."

"Do you believe the things I've told you, or do you
think I'm just another fanatical Arab who wants to see the
Jews driven into the sea?"

"I believe you, Yusef."

"Do you like poetry?"

"I love poetry."

"Poetry is very important to the Palestinian people.
Our poetry allows us to express our suffering. It gives us
the courage to face our past. A poet named Mu'in Basisu
is one of my favorites."

He kissed her again and began to recite:

*And after the flood none was left of this people*
*This land, but a rope and a pole*
*None but bare bodies floating on mires*
*Leavings of kin and child*
*None but swelled bodies*
*Their numbers unknown*
*Here wreckage, here death, here drowned in deep*
*waters*
*Scraps of bread loaf still clasped in my hand.*

She said, "It's beautiful."

"It sounds better in Arabic." He paused for a moment, then said, "Do you speak any Arabic, Dominique?"

"Of course not. Why do you ask?"

"I was just wondering."

In the morning Yusef brought her coffee in bed. Jacqueline sat up and drank it very quickly. She needed the jolt of caffeine to help her think. She hadn't slept. Several times she had considered slipping out of bed, but Yusef was a restless sleeper and she feared he might awaken. If he discovered her making imprints of his keys with a special device disguised as a mascara case, there would be no way to explain. He would assume she was an Israeli agent. He might very well kill her. It would be better to leave his flat without the imprints than to be caught. She wanted to do it right—for Gabriel's sake and her own.

She looked at her watch. It was nearly nine o'clock.

"I'm sorry I let you sleep so long," Yusef said.

"That's all right. I was tired."

"It was a good tired, yes?"

She kissed him and said, "It was a *very* good tired."

"Call your boss and tell him you're going to take the day off and make love to a Palestinian named Yusef al-Tawfiki."

"I don't think he'll see the humor in that."

"This man has never wanted to spend the day making love to a woman?"

"I'm not sure, actually."

"I'm going to take a shower. You're welcome to join me."

"I'll never get to work that way."

"That was my intention."

"Get in the shower. Is there any more coffee?"

"In the kitchen."

Yusef stepped into the bathroom and closed the door halfway. Jacqueline lay in bed until she heard him step into the shower; then she slipped from beneath the blankets and padded into the kitchen. She poured herself a cup of coffee and walked into the sitting room. She placed the coffee on the table next to Yusef's keys and sat down. The shower was still running.

She reached into her bag and withdrew her mascara case. She popped it open and glanced inside. It was filled with a soft ceramic material. All she had to do was place a key against the material and squeeze the lid closed. The ersatz case would produce a perfect imprint.

Her hands were trembling. She picked up the keys carefully, to prevent them from making any sound, and singled out the first: the Yale model he had used for the street entrance. She placed it inside the case, closed the lid, and squeezed. She opened the case and removed the key. The imprint was flawless. She repeated the process two more times, once with the second Yale key, then with the skeleton. She had three perfect imprints.

She closed the lid, placed the keys exactly where Yusef had left them, then returned the mascara case to her purse.

"What are you doing there?"

She looked up, startled, and quickly regained her composure. Yusef was standing in the center of the floor, his wet body wrapped in a beige bath towel. How long had he been standing there? How much had he seen? *Damn it, Jacqueline! Why weren't you watching the door!*

She said, "I'm looking for my cigarettes. Have you seen them?"

He pointed toward the bedroom. "You left them in there."

"Oh, yes. God, sometimes I think I'm losing my mind."

"That's all you were doing? Just looking for cigarettes?"

"What else would I be doing?" She spread her arms to indicate the spartan squalor of his sitting room. "You think I'm trying to make off with your valuables?"

She stood and picked up her handbag. "Are you finished in the bathroom?"

"Yes, but why are you bringing your purse to the bathroom?"

She thought: *He suspects something.* Suddenly she wanted to get out of the flat as quickly as possible. Then she thought: *I should be offended by questions like that.*

"I think I may be getting my period," she said icily. "I don't think I like the way you're acting. Is this the way all Arab men treat their lovers the morning after?"

She brushed past him and entered the bedroom. She was surprised at how convincing she had managed to sound. Her hands were shaking as she collected her clothing and entered the bathroom. She ran water in the sink while she dressed. Then she opened the door and went out. Yusef was in the sitting room. He wore faded jeans, a sweater, loafers with no socks.

He said, "I'll call you a cab."

"Don't bother. I'll find my own way home."

"Let me walk you down."

"I'll see myself out, thank you."

"What's wrong with you? Why are you acting this way?"

"Because I don't like the way you were talking to me. I had a nice time, until now. Maybe I'll see you around sometime."

She opened the door and stepped into the hallway. Yusef followed her. She walked quickly down the stairs, then across the lobby.

At the front entrance he grabbed her arm. "I'm sorry, Dominique. I'm just a little paranoid sometimes. You'd be paranoid too if you'd lived my life. I didn't mean anything by it. How can I make it up to you?"

She managed to smile, even though her heart was pounding against the inside of her ribs. She had no idea what to do. She had the imprints, but there was a chance that he had seen her making them—or at least that he suspected she had done *something*. If she were guilty, the natural impulse would be to reject his invitation. She decided to accept his offer. If Gabriel believed it was a mistake, she could make up an excuse to cancel it.

She said, "You may take me out for a proper dinner."

"What time?"

"Meet me at the gallery at six-thirty."

"Perfect."

"And don't be late. I can't stand men who are late."

Then she kissed him and went out.

# 24

## MAIDA VALE, LONDON

When Jacqueline arrived back at her flat, Gabriel was seated on the couch drinking coffee. "How did it go?"

"It was lovely. Bring me some of that coffee, will you?"

She went into the bathroom, closed the door, and began filling the tub. Then she stripped off her clothing and slipped beneath the warm water. A moment later Gabriel knocked on the door.

"Come in."

He came into the room. He seemed surprised that she was already in the bath. He looked away, searching for a spot to place the coffee. "How do you feel?" he said, eyes averted.

"How do you feel after you kill someone?"

"I always feel dirty."

Jacqueline scooped up a handful of water and let it run over her face.

Gabriel said, "I need to ask you some questions."

"I'm ready when you are."

"It can wait until you're dressed."

"We've lived together as man and wife, Gabriel. We've even *behaved* like man and wife."

"That was different."

"Why was it different?"

"Because it was a necessary part of the operation."

"Sleeping in the same bed, or making love to each other?"

"Jacqueline, please."

"Maybe you won't look at me because I just slept with Yusef."

Gabriel glared at her and went out. Jacqueline permitted herself a brief smile, then slipped below the water.


"The phone is made by British Telecom."

She was sitting in the cracked club chair, her body covered in a thick white robe. She rattled off the name and model number as she worked a towel through her damp hair.

"There's no telephone in the bedroom, but he does have a clock radio."

"What kind?"

"A Sony." She gave him the model number.

"Let's go back to the telephone for a moment," Gabriel said. "Any distinguishing marks? Any price tags or stickers with telephone numbers on them? Anything that would give us a problem?"

"He fancies himself a poet and a historian. He writes all the time. It looks as though he dials the telephone with the tip of a pen. The keypad is covered with marks."

"What color ink?"

"Blue and red."

"What kind of pen?"

"What do you mean? The kind of pen you write with."

Gabriel sighed and looked wearily at the ceiling. "Is it a ballpoint pen? Is it a fountain pen? Perhaps a felt-tipped pen?"

"Felt-tipped, I believe."

"You believe?"

"Felt-tipped. I'm sure of it."

"Very good," he said as though he were speaking to a child. "Now, is it fine point, medium, or bold?"

She slowly raised the long, slender middle finger of her right hand and waved it at Gabriel.

"I'll take that to mean bold point. What about the keys?"

She hunted through her handbag, tossed him the silver mascara case. Gabriel thumbed the release, lifted the lid, looked at the imprints.

She said, "We may have a problem."

Gabriel closed the lid and looked up.

Jacqueline said, "I think he may have seen me with his keys."

"Tell me about it."

She recounted the entire chain of events for him, then added cautiously, "He wants to see me again."

"When?"

"Tonight at six-thirty. He's meeting me at the gallery."

"Did you accept?"

"Yes, but I can—"

"No," Gabriel said, interrupting her. "That's perfect. I want you to meet him and keep him entertained long enough for me to get inside his flat and plant the bugs."

"Then what?"

"Then it will be done."

Gabriel left the building through a back service door. He slipped across the courtyard, scaled a cinder-block wall, and leaped into an alleyway strewn with beer cans and bits of broken glass. Then he walked to the Maida Vale Underground station. He felt unsettled. He didn't like the fact that Yuṣef had asked to see Jacqueline a second time.

He rode the Underground to Covent Garden. The *bodel* was waiting in line for coffee at the market. It was the same boy who had taken Gabriel's field report at Waterloo Station. A black, soft-sided leather briefcase hung on his back from a shoulder strap, a side pocket facing out. Gabriel had placed the silver case containing the imprints of Yusef's keys in a brown envelope—standard size, plain, no markings. He sat at a table drinking tea, eyes working methodically over the crowd.

The *bodel* bought coffee, started to walk away. Gabriel got up and followed him, slicing through the crowded market, until he was directly behind him. Gabriel bumped the *bodel* as he was taking the first sip of coffee, spilling some of it down the front of his jacket. He apologized and walked away, the plain brown envelope now residing safely in the outside pocket of the *bodel*'s briefcase.

Gabriel wound his way through St. Giles, across New Oxford Street, then up Tottenham Court Road, where there were several shops specializing in electronic goods. Ten minutes later, after visiting two of the shops, he was back in a taxi heading across London to the listening post in Sussex Gardens. On the seat next to him was a bag containing four items: a Sony clock radio, a British Telecom phone, and two felt-tipped pens, one red, one blue, both bold.

Karp sat at the dining room table, studying the exposed internal components of the clock radio and telephone through a lighted magnifying glass. As Gabriel watched Karp work, he thought about his studio in Cornwall and imagined he was peering through his Wild microscope at the surface of the Vecellio.

Karp said, "We call it a hot mike. Your outfit calls it a glass if I'm not mistaken."

"You're correct as usual."

"It's a wonderful little piece of equipment, coverage of his flat and his telephone with the same device. Two for the price of one, you might say. And you never have to worry about replacing the battery because the transmitter draws its power from the telephone."

Karp paused for a moment to concentrate on his

work. "Once these go in, the monitoring operation is basically on autopilot. The tape decks are voice-activated. They'll roll only if there's something coming from the source. If you need to leave the flat for any reason, you can check the tapes when you come back. My work is basically finished."

"I'll miss you, Randy."

"Gabe, I'm touched."

"I know."

"That was a nice piece of work, sending in the girl like that. Break-ins can get messy. Always better to get the keys and phone before you go in for the plant."

Karp placed the cover back on the telephone, handed it to Gabriel. "Your turn."

Gabriel the restorer picked up his pens and began making marks on the keypad.

Kemel Azouri had been at Schloss headquarters in Zürich earlier that morning, meeting with his sales staff, when he received a text message over his pager: Mr. Taylor wished to speak to him about a problem with last Thursday's shipment. Kemel cut short his meeting, took a taxi to the Gare du Nord, and boarded the next Eurostar train to London. The timing of the message intrigued him. Mr. Taylor was the code name for an agent in London. "A problem with the shipment" was a code phrase for urgent. Use of the word Thursday meant the agent wished to meet on Cheyne Walk at four-fifteen. Kemel strode through the arrival hall at Waterloo and climbed into a taxi at the stand. A moment later he was speeding across Westminster Bridge.

He told the driver to drop him at Royal Hospital Chelsea. He walked along the river through the gathering darkness and waited at the foot of Battersea Bridge.

He checked his watch: four-twelve.

He lit a cigarette and waited.

Three minutes later, at precisely four-fifteen, a handsome young man in a black leather jacket appeared at his side.

"Mr. Taylor, I presume."

"Let's take a walk."


"I'm sorry to drag you all the way to London, Kemel, but you wanted to know about every potential approach."

"What was her name?"

"She called herself Dominique Bonard."

"French?"

"Claims to be."

"You suspect she's lying."

"I'm not sure. I can't be certain, but it's possible she was going through my things this morning."

"Have you been followed recently?"

"Not that I'm aware of."

"Where's she from?"

"She says she's from Paris."

"What's she doing in London?"

"She works at an art gallery."

"Which one?"

"A place called Isherwood Fine Arts in St. James's."

"Where do you stand with this woman?"

"I'm supposed to see her again in two hours."

"By all means, keep your date with her. In fact I'd like the two of you to develop a very close relationship. Do you think you're up to the job?"

"I'll manage."

"I'll be in touch."

# 25

## ST. JAMES'S, LONDON

The security buzzer groaned early that evening while Julian Isherwood was working his way through a stack of bills and sipping a good whiskey. He remained at his desk—after all, it was the girl's job to answer the door—but when the buzzer howled a second time he looked up. "Dominique, there's someone at the door. Would you mind? *Dominique?*"

Then he remembered he had sent her down to the storeroom to return a batch of paintings. He stood, walked wearily into the anteroom, peered into the security monitor. Standing outside was a young man. Mediterranean of some sort, good-looking. He pressed the button on the intercom. "Sorry, closed. As you can see we show by appointment only. Why don't you ring in the morning? My secretary will be happy to set aside some time for you."

"Actually, I'm here to see your secretary. My name is Yusef."

Jacqueline stepped out of the lift and came into the anteroom.

Isherwood said, "There's a fellow named Yusef downstairs. Says he's here to see you."

Jacqueline looked into the monitor.

Isherwood said, "Do you know him?"

She pressed the buzzer that released the door lock. "Yes, I know him."

"Who is he?"

"A friend. A *good* friend."

Isherwood's jaw fell, and his eyes opened wide.

Jacqueline said, "If you're going to be uncomfortable, perhaps you should leave."

"Yes, I think that's wise." He walked back into his office and put on his jacket. When he returned to the anteroom, the Arab was kissing Jacqueline on the cheek. She said, "Yusef, I'd like you to meet Mr. Isherwood. He's the owner of the gallery."

"Pleasure to meet you, Yusef. I'd love to stay and chat, but I'm afraid I'm running late for an appointment. So if you'll excuse me, I really have to be going."

"Do you mind if I show Yusef around the gallery?"

"Of course not. Delighted. Be sure to lock up, Dominique, darling. Thank you. See you in the morning. Pleasure meeting you, Yusef. Cheers."

Isherwood clambered down the stairs and hurried across Mason's Yard to the sanctuary of the bar at Green's. He ordered a whiskey and drank it very fast, all the while wondering whether it was truly possible that Gabriel's girl had just brought a terrorist into his gallery.

\*       \*       \*

Gabriel sat on a bench on Victoria Embankment, watching the gray river moving sluggishly beneath Blackfriars Bridge, holding a copy of the *Daily Telegraph*. On page thirteen, hidden behind an advertisement, was a coded field report for Shamron. The *bodel* appeared ten minutes later. He walked past Gabriel and headed up the steps toward the Temple Underground station. He wore a hat, which meant he was not being followed and it was safe to proceed. Gabriel followed him into the station, then down the escalator to the platform. When the train arrived, the two men entered the same crowded carriage. They were forced to stand side by side, which made the exchange—Yusef's keys for the newspaper containing Gabriel's field report—quite impossible to detect. Gabriel got off at Paddington Station and headed back to the listening post.

Jacqueline said, "There's something I want to show you." She led Yusef into the lift, and they rode up in silence. When the door opened, she took his hand and guided him into the center of the darkened gallery. She said, "Close your eyes."

"I don't like games like these."

"Close your eyes." Then she added playfully, "I promise to make it worth your while."

He closed his eyes. Jacqueline walked across the room to the lighting control panel and placed her hand on the main dimmer switch. "Now, open them."

She brought the lights up slowly. Yusef's mouth fell

slightly open as he surveyed the surrounding paintings. "It's beautiful."

"It's my favorite place in the world."

Yusef took a few steps forward and stood before one of the paintings. "My God, is that really a Claude?"

"Yes, it is. In fact, that's one of his first river scenes. It's very valuable. Look at the way he depicted the sun. Claude was one of the first artists to actually use the sun as the source of light for an entire composition."

"Claude was born in France, but he lived almost his entire life in Venice, if I'm not mistaken."

"Actually, you are mistaken. Claude lived and worked in Rome, in a small flat on the Via Margutta near the Piazza di Spagna. He became the most sought-after land-scape painter in all of Italy."

Yusef turned away from the painting and looked at her. "You know a great deal about painting."

"Actually, I know very little, but I work in an art gallery."

Yusef asked, "How long have you been working here?"

"About five months."

"*About* five months? What does that mean exactly? Does that mean four months or six months?"

"It means nearly five months. And why do you want to know? Why is this important to you?"

"Dominique, if this relationship is to continue, there must be complete honesty between us."

"Relationship? I thought we were only sleeping together."

"Maybe there can be more between us, but only if there are no lies. No secrets."

"Complete honesty? Are you sure about that? Can there ever be complete honesty between two people? Would that be healthy? Isn't it best to keep some things secret? Have you told me all your secrets, Yusef?"

He ignored this question.

"Tell me, Dominique," he said. "Are you in love with another man?"

"No, I am not in love with another man."

"Are you telling me the truth?"

"Of course I am."

"I don't think so."

"Why do you say that?"

"Because of the way you made love to me last night."

"You've made love to many women? You're an expert in these matters?"

He pulled his lips into a modest smile.

Jacqueline said, "What is it about the way that I make love to you that has convinced you I am in love with another man?"

"You closed your eyes while I was inside you. You closed your eyes as if you didn't want to look at me. You closed your eyes as if you were thinking about someone else."

"And if I were to admit to you that I was in love with another man? How would you feel about this? Would it change anything between us?"

"It might make me care even more for you."

"I like to close my eyes when I make love, Yusef. It doesn't mean anything."

"Are you keeping any secrets from me?"

"None of any consequence." She smiled. "Are you going to take me to dinner?"

"Actually, I had a better idea. Let's go back to my flat. I'll make dinner for us."

Jacqueline felt a stab of panic. He seemed to sense her unease because he tilted his head and asked, "Is something wrong, Dominique?"

"No, nothing," she said, managing a weak smile. "Dinner at your place sounds wonderful."

Gabriel crossed the street, a nylon rucksack over his shoulder. Inside were the duplicate telephone and clock radio. He looked up toward the listening post. Karp had switched on the light, a signal meaning it was safe to proceed. They planned to do all their communication with light signals, though Gabriel carried a cell phone in case of an emergency.

He walked up the steps of Yusef's building and removed the set of duplicate keys from his pocket. He selected the key for the front door, slipped it into the chamber, turned. It stuck. Gabriel swore softly beneath his breath. He jiggled it back and forth, tried again. This time the lock opened.

Once inside he walked across the lobby without hesitation. It was a doctrine that had been pounded into him by Shamron during the Black September operation: hit hard and fast, don't worry about making a bit of noise, get away quickly. After his first job, the assassination of the Black September chief in Rome, Gabriel was flying to Geneva within an hour of the killing. He hoped this operation would go as smoothly.

He mounted the stairs and climbed quickly toward the second floor. Descending toward him were a group of young Indians: two boys, a pretty girl. As they passed him on the first-floor landing, Gabriel turned his face and pretended to be working the zipper on the rucksack. As the Indians continued down the stairs, he risked a glance over his shoulder. None of them looked back. He waited on the second-floor landing a moment and listened as they crossed the lobby and headed out the front entrance. Then he walked to Yusef's flat: number 27.

This time the keys worked perfectly on the first try, and within seconds Gabriel was inside the flat. He closed the door and left the lights off. He reached into the rucksack and removed a small flashlight. He switched it on and quickly played the beam around the floor next to the door, looking for a telltale—a scrap of paper or any other innocent-looking small object that would alert Yusef that the flat had been entered. He saw nothing.

He turned and shone the light quickly around the room. He resisted the impulse to search Yusef's flat. He had watched him from a distance for several days, developed a natural curiosity about the man. Was he neat and orderly, or a slob? What kind of food did he eat? Did he have debts? Did he use drugs? Did he wear strange underwear? Gabriel wanted to search his drawers and read his private papers. He wanted to look at his clothing and his bathroom. He wanted to see anything that might complete the picture—any clue that might help him better understand how Yusef fit into Tariq's organization. But now was not the time for that kind of search. Too risky, the odds of detection too great.

The beam of the flashlight settled on Yusef's telephone. Gabriel crossed the room, knelt beside it. He removed the duplicate from the rucksack and quickly compared it with the original. Perfect match. Jacqueline had done her job well. He pulled the wire from Yusef's phone and exchanged it for the duplicate. The cord connecting the handset to the base on Yusef's telephone was worn and stretched, the cord on the duplicate brand-new, so Gabriel quickly switched the cords.

He glanced out the window toward the listening post. Karp's signal light was still burning. It was safe to continue. He shoved Yusef's phone into the rucksack as he moved from the sitting room into the bedroom.

As he passed the bed, he had a disturbing image of Jacqueline's naked body writhing in rumpled sheets. He wondered whether his curiosity about Yusef was purely professional. Had it become personal as well? Did he now consider the Palestinian something of a rival?

He realized he had been staring at the empty bed for several seconds. *What in the hell has got into you?*

He turned around, focused his attention on the clock

radio. Before unplugging it, he checked the settings. The alarm was programmed to go off at 8:00 A.M. He turned on the radio: BBC Radio Five, volume low.

He shut off the radio, pulled the power cord out of the wall.

At that instant his cell phone rang.

He stood and looked out the window. The signal light was out.

He had been so unnerved by the image of Jacqueline on the bed that he had forgotten to keep an eye on the listening post. He answered the phone before it could ring a second time.

Karp said, "Get the fuck out of there! We have company."

Gabriel crossed the room toward the window and looked out.

Jacqueline and Yusef were getting out of a taxi. *What happened to dinner?*

He turned around. Now he had a serious problem. He had unplugged Yusef's clock radio. He had to plug it back in and reprogram it before leaving. Otherwise Yusef would suspect someone had been in the flat.

He calculated how long it would take them to come upstairs. A few seconds to open the front entrance . . . a few more seconds to cross the lobby . . . about forty-five seconds to climb the stairs and walk down the hallway to the door. He had nearly a minute.

He decided to do it.

He took the duplicate clock radio from the rucksack

and plugged it in. The red display lights flashed *12:00* . . . *12:00* . . . *12:00*. . . . He almost had to laugh at the absurdity of the situation. The future of the operation depended on whether he could set an alarm clock quickly enough to avoid being caught. Ari Shamron had persuaded him to come back and help restore the glory of the Office, but now it was going to be just another fiasco!

He began pressing the hour-setting button. The numbers advanced, but his fingers were trembling from the adrenaline, and he mistakenly set it for nine o'clock instead of eight. *Shit!* He had to go through the entire twenty-four-hour cycle again. The second time he got it right. He set the current time, then switched on the radio, tuned it to Radio Five, and adjusted the volume.

He had no idea how long it had taken.

He snatched up the rucksack, killed the flashlight, moved from the bedroom to the front door. As he walked he pulled his Beretta from the waistband of his trousers and slipped it into the front pocket of his coat.

He paused at the front door and pressed his ear against it. The corridor was quiet. He had to try to get out. There was no place in the flat where he could hide and reasonably expect to slip out again. He pulled open the door and stepped into the corridor.

He could hear footfalls in the stairwell.

He placed his hand around the grip of the Beretta and started walking.

\*    \*    \*

In the taxi Jacqueline had forced herself to calm down. Her job had been to keep Yusef away from the flat, but if she had objected to his idea of eating dinner at home, he might have become suspicious. The chances of Gabriel being in the flat the moment they returned were next to nothing. The entire job would take only minutes. The odds were good that he had already planted the bugs and was gone. There was another, more reassuring possibility: Gabriel had expected Yusef to meet her at the gallery at six-thirty and then take her to dinner. Perhaps he hadn't even entered the flat yet. He would notice that they had returned early, and he would call it off and try another time.

They crossed the lobby, started up the stairs. A man passed them on the second-floor landing: Gabriel, head down, rucksack over his shoulder.

Jacqueline flinched involuntarily. She regained her composure, but not before Yusef noticed that she was rattled. He stopped and watched Gabriel walking down the stairs, then looked at Jacqueline. He took her by the arm and led her to the door. When they entered the flat, he looked around the room quickly, then walked to the window and watched Gabriel walking away through the darkness.

# 26

## LISBON

A dense Atlantic fog rolled up the Rio Tejo as Kemel picked his way through the teeming streets of the Bairro Alto. Early evening, workers streaming home from jobs, bars and cafés filling up, Lisboans lining the counters of the *cervejarias* for an evening meal. Kemel crossed a small square: old men drinking red wine in the chill night air; *varinas,* the fishwives, washing sea bass in their big baskets. He negotiated a narrow alley lined with vendors selling cheap clothing and trinkets. A blind beggar asked him for money. Kemel dropped a few escudos in the black wooden box around his neck. A gypsy offered to tell his fortune. Kemel politely declined and kept walking. The Bairro Alto reminded him of Beirut in the old days—Beirut and the refugee camps, he thought. By comparison, Zürich seemed cold and sterile. No wonder Tariq liked Lisbon so much.

He entered a crowded *fado* house and sat down. A waiter placed a green-tinted bottle of house wine in front of him along with a glass. He lit a cigarette, poured himself a glass of the wine. Ordinary, no complexity, but surprisingly satisfying.

A moment later the same waiter went to the front of the cramped room and stood next to a pair of guitarists. When the guitarists strummed the first dark chords of the piece, the waiter closed his eyes and began to sing. Kemel couldn't understand the words but soon found himself swept away by the haunting melody.

In the middle of the piece, a man sat down next to Kemel. Thick woolen sweater, shabby reefer coat, kerchief knotted at his throat, unshaven. Looked like a dockworker from the waterfront. He leaned over, muttered a few words to Kemel in Portuguese. Kemel shrugged his shoulders. "I'm afraid I don't speak the language."

He turned his attention back to the singer. The piece was reaching its emotional climax, but, in the tradition of *fado*, the singer remained ramrod straight, as though he were standing at attention.

The dockworker tapped Kemel's elbow and spoke Portuguese to him a second time. This time Kemel simply shook his head and kept his eyes on the singer.

Then the dockworker leaned over and said in Arabic: "I asked you whether you liked *fado* music."

Kemel turned and looked carefully at the man seated next to him.

Tariq said, "Let's go somewhere quiet where we can talk."

They walked from the Bairro Alto to the Alfama, a warren of narrow alleys and stone steps winding among whitewashed houses. Kemel was always amazed at Tariq's uncanny ability to blend into his surroundings. Walking the steep hills seemed to tire him. Kemel wondered how much longer he could go on.

Tariq said, "You never answered my question."

"Which question was that?"

"Do you like *fado* music?"

"I suppose it's an acquired taste." He smiled and added, "Like Lisbon itself. For some reason it reminds me of home."

"*Fado* is a music devoted to suffering and pain. That's why it reminds you of home."

"I suppose you're right."

They passed an old woman sweeping the front step of her home.

Tariq said, "Tell me about London."

"It looks as though Allon has made his first move."

"That didn't take long. What happened?"

Kemel told him about Yusef and the girl from the art gallery. "Yusef noticed a strange man in his block of flats last night. He thinks the man may have been an Israeli. He thinks he may have planted a bug in his flat."

Kemel could see that Tariq was already calculating the possibilities. "Is this agent of yours a man who can be trusted with an important assignment?"

"He's a very intelligent young man. And very loyal. I knew his father. He was killed by the Israelis in 'eighty-two."

"Has he looked for the bug?"

"I told him not to."

"Good," Tariq said. "Leave it in place. We can use it to our advantage. What about this girl? Is she still in the picture?"

"I've instructed Yusef to continue seeing her."

"What's she like?"

"Apparently quite attractive."

"Do you have the resources in London to follow her?"

"Absolutely."

"Do it. And get me a photograph of her."

"You have an idea?"

They passed through a small square, then started up a long, steep hill. By the time they had reached the top, Tariq had explained the entire thing.

"It's brilliant," Kemel said. "But it has one flaw."

"What's that?"

"You won't survive it."

Tariq smiled sadly and said, "That's the best news I've heard in a very long time."

He turned and walked away. A moment later he had vanished into the fog. Kemel shivered. He turned up the collar of his coat and walked back to the Bairro Alto to listen to *fado*.

# 27

The operation settled into a comfortable if rather dull routine. Gabriel spent endless stretches of time with nothing to do but listen to the trivial details of Yusef's life, which played out on his monitors like a dreadful radio drama. Yusef chatting on the telephone. Yusef arguing politics over cigarettes and Turkish coffee with his Palestinian friends. Yusef telling a heartbroken girl he could no longer see her because he was seriously involved with another. Gabriel found his life moving to the rhythm of Yusef's. He ate when Yusef ate, slept when Yusef slept, and when Yusef made love to Jacqueline, Gabriel made love to her too.

But after ten days, Gabriel's bugs had picked up nothing of value. There were several possible explanations. Perhaps Shamron had simply made a mistake. Perhaps Yusef really was just a waiter and a student. Perhaps he *was* an agent but was inactive. Or perhaps he was an active agent but was talking with his comrades through other means: signal sights and other forms of impersonal communication. To detect that, Gabriel would have to mount a full-scale round-the-clock surveillance operation. It would require multiple teams, at least a dozen officers—safe flats, vehicles, radios. . . . An operation like that would be difficult to conceal from MI5, the British security service.

But there was one other possibility that troubled Gabriel most: the possibility that the operation was already blown. Perhaps his surveillance had turned up nothing because Yusef already suspected he was being watched. Perhaps he suspected that his flat was bugged and his telephones tapped. And perhaps he suspected that the beautiful French girl from the art gallery was actually an Israeli agent.

Gabriel decided it was time for another face-to-face meeting with Shamron in Paris.

He met Shamron the following morning in a tea shop on the rue Mouffetard. Shamron paid his tab, and they walked slowly up the hill through the markets and street vendors. "I want to pull her out," Gabriel said.

Shamron paused at a fruit stand, picked up an orange, studied it for a moment before placing it gently back in the bin. Then he said, "Tell me you didn't bring me all the way to Paris for this insanity."

"Something doesn't feel right. I want her out before it's too late."

"She's not blown, and the answer is still no." Shamron looked at Gabriel carefully and added, "Why is your face fallen, Gabriel? Are you listening to the tapes before you send them to me?"

"Of course I am."

"Can't you hear what's going on? The endless lectures on the suffering of the Palestinians? The ruthlessness of the Israelis? The recitation of Palestinian poetry? All the old folklore about how beautiful life was in Palestine before the Jews?"

"What's your point?"

"Either the boy is in love, or he has something else on his mind."

"It's the second possibility that concerns me."

"Has it ever occurred to you that maybe Yusef thinks of her as more than just a pretty girl? Has it ever occurred to you that he thinks of her as an impressionable girl who might be useful to Tariq and his organization?"

"It *has,* but she's not prepared for that kind of operation. And frankly, neither are we."

"So you want to fold up your tent and go home?"

"No, I just want to pull Jacqueline out."

"And then what happens? Yusef gets nervous. Yusef gets suspicious and tears apart his flat. If he's disciplined, he throws out every electrical appliance in the place. And your microphones go with them."

"If we handle her departure skillfully, he'll never suspect a thing. Besides, when I hired her, I promised her a short-term job. You know she has other commitments."

"None more important than this. Pay her wages, full price. She stays, Gabriel. End of discussion."

"If she stays, I go."

"Then go!" Shamron snapped. "Go back to Cornwall

and bury your head in your Vecellio. I'll send in someone to take over for you."

"You know I'm not going to leave her in your hands."

Shamron quickly moved for appeasement. "You've been working around the clock for a long time. You don't look so good. I haven't forgotten what it's like. Forget about Yusef for a few hours. He's not going anywhere. Take a drive. Do something to clear your head. I need you at your best."

On the train back to London, Gabriel entered the lavatory and locked the door. He stood for a long time in front of the mirror. There were new lines around his eyes, a sudden tightness at the corners of his mouth, a knife edge to his cheekbones. Beneath his eyes were dark circles, like smudges of charcoal.

*I haven't forgotten what it's like.*

The Black September operation . . . They had all come down with something: heart problems, high blood pressure, skin rashes, chronic colds. The assassins suffered the worst. After the first job in Rome, Gabriel found it impossible to sleep. Every time he closed his eyes he heard bullets tearing through flesh and shattering bone, saw fig wine mingling with blood on a marble floor. Shamron found a doctor in Paris, a *sayan,* who gave Gabriel a bottle of powerful tranquilizers. Within a few weeks he was addicted to them.

The pills and the stress made Gabriel look shockingly older. His skin hardened, the corners of his mouth turned down, his eyes turned the color of ash. His black hair went gray at the temples. He was twenty-two at the time but looked at least forty. When he went home, Leah barely recognized him. When they made love she said it was like sleeping with another man—not an older version of Gabriel but a complete stranger.

He splashed cold water on his face, scrubbed vigorously with a paper towel, then studied his reflection once more. He contemplated the chain of events—the bizarre roulette wheel of fate—that had led him to this place. Had there been no Hitler, no Holocaust, his parents would have remained in Europe instead of fleeing to a dusty agricultural settlement in the Jezreel Valley. Before the war his father had been an essayist and historian in Munich, his mother a gifted painter in Prague, and neither had adjusted well to the collectivism of the settlement or the Zionist zeal for manual labor. They had treated Gabriel more as a miniature adult than a boy with needs different from their own. He was expected to entertain and look after himself. His earliest childhood memory was of their small two-room house on the settlement: his father reading in his chair, his mother at her easel, Gabriel on the floor between them, building cities with crude blocks.

His parents detested Hebrew, so when they were alone they used the languages they had spoken in Europe: German, French, Czech, Russian, Yiddish. Gabriel absorbed them all. To his European languages he added Hebrew and Arabic. From his father he also took a flawless memory, from his mother unshakable patience and attention to detail. Their disdain for the collective had bred in him arrogance and a lone wolf attitude. Their secular agnosticism had encumbered him with no sense of Jewish morality or ethics. He preferred hiking to football, reading to agriculture. He had an almost pathological fear of getting his hands dirty. He had many secrets. One of his teachers described him as "cold, selfish, unfeeling, and altogether brilliant." When Ari Shamron went looking for soldiers in the new secret war against Arab terror in Europe, he came upon the boy from the Jezreel Valley who, like his namesake, the Archangel Gabriel, had an unusual gift for languages and the patience of Solomon. Shamron found one other valuable personality trait: the emotional coldness of a killer.

Gabriel left the lavatory and went back to his seat. Beyond his window was East London: rows of crumbling Victorian warehouses, all shattered windows and broken brick. He closed his eyes. Something else had made them all sick during the Black September operation: fear. The longer they remained in the field, the higher the risk of exposure—not only to the intelligence services of Europe but to the terrorists themselves. That point was driven home in the middle of the operation, when Black September murdered a *katsa* in Madrid. Suddenly every member of the team knew that he too was vulnerable. And it taught Gabriel the most valuable lesson of his career: when agents are operating far from home, in hostile territory, hunters can easily become the hunted.

The train pulled into Waterloo. Gabriel strode across the platform, sliced his way through the crowded arrivals hall. He had left his car in an underground car park. He dropped his keys, engaged in his ritualistic inspection, then climbed inside and drove to Surrey.

There was no sign at the gate. Gabriel had always wanted a place with no sign. Beyond the wall was a well-tended lawn with evenly spaced trees. At the end of a meandering drive stood a rambling redbrick Victorian mansion. He lowered the car window and pressed the button of the intercom. The lens of a security camera stared down at him like a gargoyle. Gabriel instinctively turned his face away from the camera and pretended to fish something from the glove compartment.

"May I help you?" Female voice, Middle European accent.

"I'm here to see Miss Martinson. Dr. Avery is expecting me."

He raised the window, waited for the automatic security gate to roll aside; then he entered the grounds and headed slowly up the drive. Late afternoon, cold and gray, light wind chasing through the trees. As he drew closer to the house, he began to see a few of the patients. A woman sitting on a bench, dressed in her Sunday best, staring blankly into space. A man in an oilskin and Wellington boots strolling on the arm of a towering Jamaican orderly.

Avery was waiting in the entrance hall. He wore expensive corduroy trousers, the color of rust and neatly pressed, and a gray cashmere pullover sweater that looked more suited to the golf links than a psychiatric hospital. He shook Gabriel's hand with a cold formality, as though Gabriel were the representative of an occupying power, then led him down a long carpeted hallway.

"She's been speaking quite a bit more this month," Avery said. "We've actually had a meaningful conversation on a couple of occasions."

Gabriel managed a tense smile. In all these years she had never spoken to him. "And her physical health?" he asked.

"No change, really. She's as fit as can be expected."

Avery used a magnetic card to pass through a secure door. On the other side was another hall, terra-cotta tiling instead of carpet. Avery discussed her medication as they walked. He had increased the dosage of one drug, reduced another, taken her off a third altogether. There was a new drug, an experimental, that was showing some promising results in patients suffering from a similar combination of acute post-traumatic stress syndrome and psychotic depression.

"If you think it will help."

"We'll never know unless we try."

Clinical psychiatry, Gabriel thought, was rather like intelligence work.

The terra-cotta hall ended in a small room. It was filled with gardening tools—pruning shears, hand shovels, trowels—and bags of flower seed and fertilizer. At the other end of the cutting room was a pair of double doors with circular portholes.

"She's in her usual place. She's expecting you. Please don't keep her long. I should think a half hour would be appropriate. I'll come for you when it's time."

A solarium, oppressively hot and moist. Leah in the corner, seated in a straight-backed garden chair of wrought iron, young potted roses at her feet. She wore white. The white rollneck sweater Gabriel had given her for her last birthday. The white trousers he had bought for her during a summer holiday in Crete. Gabriel tried to remember the year but couldn't. There seemed to be only Leah before Vienna and Leah after Vienna. She sat with a schoolgirl's primness, looking away across the expanse of the lawn. Her hair had been cut institutionally short. Her feet were bare.

She turned her head as Gabriel stepped forward. For the first time he could see the swath of scarring on the right side of her face. As always it made him feel violently cold. Then he saw her hands, or what was left of her hands. The hard white scar tissue reminded him of the exposed canvas of a damaged painting. He wished he could simply mix a bit of pigment on his palette and put her back to normal.

He kissed her forehead, smelled her hair for the familiar traces of lavender and lemon, but instead there was only the oppressive moisture of the solarium and the stench of plants in an enclosed space. Avery had left a second chair, which Gabriel pulled a few inches closer. Leah flinched as the wrought-iron legs scraped over the floor. He murmured an apology and sat down. Leah looked away.

It was always like this. It wasn't Leah sitting next to him, only a monument to Leah. A gravestone. He used to try to talk to her, but now he was content to just sit in her presence. He followed her gaze across the misty landscape and wondered what she was looking at. There were days, according to Avery, when she just sat and re-lived it over and over again in excruciatingly vivid detail, unable, or unwilling, to make it stop. Gabriel couldn't imagine her suffering. He had been permitted to carry on with some semblance of his life, but Leah had been stripped of everything—her child, her body, her sanity. Everything but her memory. Gabriel feared that her grip on life, however tenuous, was somehow linked to his con-tinued fidelity. If he allowed himself to fall in love with someone else, Leah would die.

After forty-five minutes he stood and pulled on his jacket; then he crouched at her feet with his hands resting on her knees. She looked over his head for a few seconds before lowering her eyes and meeting his gaze. "I have to go," he said. Leah made no movement.

He was about to stand when suddenly she reached out and touched the side of his face. Gabriel tried not to recoil at the sensation of the scar tissue sliding along the skin at the corner of his eye. She smiled sadly and low-ered her hand. She placed it in her lap, covered it with the other, resumed the frozen pose Gabriel had found her in.

He stood and walked away. Avery was waiting for him outside. He walked Gabriel to his car. Gabriel sat behind the wheel for a long time before starting the engine, thinking about her hand on his face. So unlike Leah, touching him like that. What did she see there? The strain of the operation? Or the shadow of Jacqueline Delacroix?

# 28

Tariq appeared in the doorway of the *fado* house. Once again he was dressed like a dockworker. Ghostly pale, hand trembling as he lit his cigarette. He crossed the room and sat down next to Kemel. "What brings you back to Lisbon?"

"It turns out we have a rather serious bottleneck in our Iberian distribution chain. I may be forced to spend a great deal of time in Lisbon over the next few days."

"That's all?"

"And this." Kemel laid a large color photograph on the table. "Meet Dominique Bonard."

Tariq picked up the photograph, studied it carefully. "Come with me," he said calmly. "I want to show you something that I think you'll find interesting."

Tariq's flat was high in the Alfama. Two rooms, sagging wooden floors, a tiny veranda overlooking a quiet courtyard. He fixed tea Arab style, strong and sweet, and they sat near the open door of the veranda, rain smacking on the stones of the courtyard.

Tariq said, "Do you remember how we found Allon in Vienna?"

"It was a long time ago. You'll have to refresh my memory."

"My brother was in bed when he was killed. He had a girl with him—a German student, a radical. She wrote a letter to my parents a few weeks after Mahmoud was killed and told them how it happened. She said she would never forget the face of the assassin as long as she lived. My father took the letter to the PLO security officer in the camp. The security officer turned it over to PLO intelligence."

"This all sounds vaguely familiar," Kemel said.

"After Abu Jihad was murdered in Tunis, PLO security conducted an investigation. They worked from a simple premise. The killer seemed to know the villa well, inside and out. Therefore he must have spent time around the villa conducting surveillance and planning the attack."

"A brilliant piece of detective work," Kemel said sarcastically. "If PLO security had been doing their job right to begin with, Abu Jihad would still be alive."

Tariq went into the bedroom, returned a moment later holding a large manila envelope. "They began reviewing all the videotape from the surveillance cameras and found several shots of a small, dark-haired man." Tariq opened the envelope and handed Kemel several grainy prints. "Over the years PLO intelligence had kept track of the German girl. They showed her these photographs. She said it was the same man who had killed Mahmoud. No doubt about it. So we started looking for him."

"And you found him in Vienna?"

"That's right."

Kemel held out the photographs to Tariq. "What does this have to do with Dominique Bonard?"

"It goes back to the investigation of the Tunis affair. PLO security wanted to find out where the assassin had stayed in Tunis while he was planning the attack. They knew from past experience that Israeli agents tend to pose as Europeans during jobs like this. They assumed that a man posing as a European had probably stayed in a hotel. They started calling on their spies and informants. They showed the photographs of the assassin to a concierge at one of the beachfront hotels. The concierge said the man had stayed in the hotel with his French girlfriend. PLO security went back to the tapes and began looking for a girl. They found one and showed her to the concierge."

"Same girl?"

"Same girl."

Then Tariq reached into the envelope and removed one more surveillance photograph: this one of a beautiful dark-haired girl. He handed it to Kemel, who compared it with the photograph of the woman in London.

"I could be mistaken," Tariq said. "But it looks to me like Yusef's new girlfriend has worked with Gabriel Allon before."

*    *    *

They reviewed the plan one last time as they walked through the twisting alleys of the Alfama.

"The prime minister and Arafat leave for the United States in five days," Kemel said. "They're going to Washington first for a meeting at the White House, then it's off to New York for the signing ceremony at the United Nations. Everything is in place in New York."

"Now I just need a traveling companion," Tariq said. "I think I'd like a beautiful French woman—the type of woman who would look good on the arm of a successful entrepreneur."

"I think I know where I can find a woman like that."

"Imagine, killing the peace process and Gabriel Allon in one final moment of glory. We're going to shake the world, Kemel. And then I'm going to leave it."

"Are you sure you want to go through with this?"

"You're not concerned about my safety at this point?"

"Of course I am."

"Why? You know what's happening to me."

"Actually, I try not to think about it."

At the bottom of the hill they came to a taxi stand. Tariq kissed Kemel's cheeks, then gripped his shoulders. "No tears, my brother. I've been fighting for a long time. I'm tired. It's best this way."

Kemel released his grip and opened the door to the waiting taxi.

Tariq said, "He should have killed the girl."

Kemel turned around. "What?"

"Allon should have killed the German girl who was with my brother. It would all have ended there."

"I suppose you're right."

"It was a stupid mistake," Tariq said. "I wouldn't have made a mistake like that."

Then he turned and walked slowly up the hill into the Alfama.

# 29

## ST. JAMES'S, LONDON

When the security buzzer sounded, Jacqueline turned and peered into the monitor: a bicycle courier. She looked at her watch: six-fifteen. She pressed the buzzer to let him in, then walked from her desk into the hallway to sign for the package. A large manila envelope. She went back to her office, sat down at the desk, sliced open the envelope with the tip of her forefinger. Inside was a single piece of executive-sized letter paper, light gray in color, folded crisply in half. The letterhead bore the name Randolph Stewart, private art dealer. She read the handwritten note: *Just back from Paris. . . . Very good trip. . . . No problems with the acquisition. . . . Continue with sale as planned.* She placed the letter in Isherwood's shredder and watched it turn to paper linguine.

She stood up, pulled on her coat, then walked into Isherwood's office. He was hunched over a ledger book, chewing on the end of a pencil. He looked up as she entered the room and gave her a weak smile. "Leaving so soon, my love?"

"I'm afraid I must."

"I shall count the hours until I see you again."

"And I shall do the same."

As she walked out she realized that she would miss Isherwood when it was all over. He was a decent man. She wondered how he had become entangled with the likes of Ari Shamron and Gabriel. She hurried across Mason's Yard through windblown rain, then walked up Duke Street toward Piccadilly, thinking about the letter. It depressed her. She could picture the rest of the evening. She would meet Yusef at his flat. They would go to dinner, then return to his flat and make love. Then two hours of Middle East history. The injustices heaped upon the defenseless Palestinians. The crimes of the Jews. The inequity of the two-state solution on the negotiating table. It was getting harder and harder for her to pretend that she was enjoying herself.

Gabriel had promised her a short assignment: seduce him, get into his flat, get his keys and his telephone, and get out again. She had not signed up for a long-term romance. She found the idea of sleeping with Yusef again repulsive. But there was something else. She had agreed to come to London because she thought working with Gabriel would rekindle their romance. If anything it had driven them farther apart. She rarely saw him—he communicated through letters—and the few times they had been together he had been cold and distant. She had been a fool to think things could ever be the way they had been in Tunis.

She entered the Piccadilly Underground station

and walked to the crowded platform. She thought of her villa; of cycling through the sun-drenched hillsides around Valbonne. For a moment she imagined Gabriel riding next to her, his legs pumping rhythmically. Then she felt silly for allowing herself to think about such things. When the train came, she squeezed her way into the packed carriage and clung to a metal handhold. As the car lurched forward, she decided this would be the last night. In the morning, she would tell Gabriel she wanted out.

Gabriel paced the carpet of the listening post, casually dribbling a lime-green tennis ball in his stocking feet. It was shortly before midnight. Jacqueline and Yusef had just finished making love. He listened to their mutual declarations of physical pleasure. He listened to Yusef using the toilet. He listened to Jacqueline padding into the kitchen for something to drink. He heard her ask Yusef where he had hidden her cigarettes.

Gabriel lay on the couch and tossed the ball toward the ceiling while he waited for Yusef to begin tonight's seminar. He wondered what the topic would be. What was it last night?—the myth that only the Jews made the desert bloom. No, that was the night before. Last night had been the betrayal of the Palestinians by the rest of the Arab world. He switched off the lamp and continued tossing the ball and catching it in the dark to test his reflexes and sensory perception.

A door opening, the snap of a light switch.

Yusef said somberly: "We need to talk. I misled you about something. I need to tell you the truth now."

Gabriel snatched the tennis ball out of the darkness and held it very still in the palm of his hand. He thought of Leah, the night she used those same words before telling him that she had retaliated for his infidelity by taking lovers of her own.

Jacqueline said lightheartedly, "Sounds awfully serious."

Gabriel sent the ball floating upward through the darkness with a subtle flick of his wrist.

"It's about the scar on my back."

Gabriel got to his feet and switched on the lamp. Then he checked his tape decks to make certain they were recording properly.

Jacqueline said, "What about the scar on your back?"

"How it got there."

Yusef sat down on the end of the bed. "I lied to you about how I got the scar. I need to tell you the truth now."

He took a deep breath, let the air out slowly, began speaking, slowly and softly.

"Our family stayed in Shatila after the PLO was driven out of Lebanon. Maybe you remember that day, Dominique; the day Arafat and his guerrillas pulled out while the Israelis and the Americans waved good-bye to them from the waterfront. With the PLO gone we had no protection. Lebanon was in shambles. Christians, Sunnis, Shiites, the Druse—everyone was fighting everyone else, and the Palestinians were caught in the middle of it. We lived in fear that something terrible might happen. Do you remember now?"

"I was young, but I think I remember."

"The situation was a powder keg. It would take just one spark to set off a holocaust. That spark turned out to be the assassination of Bashir Gemayel. He was the leader of Lebanon's Maronite Christians and the president-elect of the country. He was killed in a car bomb explosion at the headquarters of the Christian Phalange party.

"That night half of Beirut was screaming for vengeance, while the other half was cowering in fear. No one was sure who had planted the bomb. It could have been anyone, but the Phalangists were convinced the Palestinians were to blame. They loathed us. The Christians never wanted us in Lebanon, and now that the PLO was gone, they wanted to eliminate the Palestinian *problem* from Lebanon once and for all. Before his death Gemayel had said it very clearly: 'There is one people too many: the Palestinian people.'

"After the assassination the Israelis moved into West Beirut and took up positions overlooking Sabra and Shatila. They wanted to cleanse the camps of the remaining PLO fighters, and in order to prevent Israeli casualties they sent in the Phalange militiamen to do the job for them. Everyone knew what would happen once the militiamen were let loose on the camps. Gemayel was dead, and we were the ones who were going to pay the price.

It would be a bloodbath, but the Israeli army let them in anyway.

"The Israelis let the first Phalangists into Shatila at sunset, one hundred and fifty of them. They had guns, of course, but most of them had knives and axes as well. The slaughter lasted forty-eight hours. The lucky ones were shot. Those who weren't so lucky died more gruesome deaths. They chopped people to bits. They disemboweled people and left them to die. They skinned people alive. They gouged out eyes and left people to wander the carnage blindly until they were shot. They tied people to trucks and dragged them through the streets until they were dead.

"Children weren't spared. A child could grow up to be a terrorist, according to the Phalangists, so they killed all the children. Women weren't spared, because a woman could give birth to a terrorist. They made a point of ritualistically slicing off the breasts of the Palestinian women. Breasts give milk. Breasts nourish a people that the Phalangists wanted to exterminate. All through the night they broke into homes and slaughtered everyone inside. When darkness fell, the Israelis lit up the sky with flares so the Phalangists could go about their work more easily."

Jacqueline made a steeple of her fingers and pressed them against her lips. Yusef continued with his account.

"The Israelis knew exactly what was going on. Their headquarters were located just two hundred yards from the edge of Shatila. From the rooftop they could see directly into the camp. They could overhear the Phalangists talking on their radios. But they didn't lift a finger to stop it. And why did they stand by and do nothing? Because it was exactly what they wanted to happen.

"I was just seven at the time. My father was dead. He was killed that summer when the Israelis shelled the camps during the Battle of Beirut. I lived in Shatila with my mother and my sister. She was just a year and a half old at the time. We hid beneath our bed, listening to the screaming and the gunfire, watching the shadows of the flares dancing on the walls. We prayed that the Phalangists would somehow miss our house. Sometimes we could hear them outside our window. They were laughing. They were slaughtering everyone in sight, but they were laughing. My mother covered our mouths whenever they came near to keep us quiet. She nearly smothered my sister.

"Finally they broke down our door. I wriggled out of my mother's grasp and went to them. They asked where my family was, and I told them everyone was dead. They laughed and told me that I would soon be with them. One of the Phalangists had a knife. He grabbed me by the hair and dragged me outside. He stripped off my shirt and sliced away the skin on the center of my back. Then they tied me to a truck and dragged me through the streets. At some point I went unconscious, but before I blacked out I remember the Phalangists shooting at me. They were using me for target practice.

"Somehow, I survived. Maybe they thought I was

dead, I don't know. When I regained consciousness the rope they had used for the dragging was still wrapped around my right ankle. I crawled beneath a pile of rubble and waited. I stayed there for a day and a half. Finally, the massacre was over, and the Phalangists withdrew from the camps. I came out of my hiding place and found my way back to our family's house. I found my mother's body in our bed. She was naked, and she had been raped. Her breasts had been sliced off. I looked for my sister. I found her on the kitchen table. They had cut her into pieces and laid her out in a circle with her head in the center."

Jacqueline tumbled out of bed, crawled into the bathroom, and was violently sick. Yusef knelt beside her and placed a hand on her back as her body wretched.

When she finished he said, "You ask me why I hate the Israelis so much. I hate them because they sent the Phalangists to massacre us. I hate them because they stood by and did nothing while Christians, their great friends in Lebanon, raped and killed my mother and chopped my sister to bits and laid her body out in a circle. Now you know why I'm a rejectionist when it comes to this so-called peace process. How can I trust these people?"

"I understand."

"Do you *really* understand, Dominique? Is it possible?"

"I suppose not."

"Now, I've been completely honest with you about everything. Is there anything you wish to tell me about yourself? Any secrets you've been keeping from me?"

"Nothing of any consequence."

"You're telling me the truth, Dominique?"

"Yes."

The call came at four-fifteen that morning. It woke Yusef, though not Gabriel. He had been sitting up all morning, listening to Yusef's account of Sabra and Shatila over and over again. It rang just once. Yusef, his voice heavy with sleep, said, "Hello."

"Lancaster Gate, tomorrow, two o'clock."

*Click.*

Jacqueline said, "What was that?"

"A wrong number. Go back to sleep."

Maida Vale in the morning. A gang of schoolboys teasing a pretty girl. Jacqueline imagined they were Phalangist militiamen armed with knives and axes. A lorry roared past, belching diesel fumes. Jacqueline saw a man tied to the bumper being dragged to death. Her block of flats loomed in front of her. She looked up and imagined Israeli soldiers standing on the roof, watching the slaughter below through binoculars, firing flares so the killers could better see their victims. She entered the building, climbed the stairs, and slipped into the flat. Gabriel was sitting on the couch.

"Why didn't you tell me?"

"Tell you what?"

"Why didn't you tell me he had survived Shatila? Why didn't you tell me his family had been butchered like that?"

"What difference would it have made?"

"I just wish I had known!" She lit a cigarette and inhaled deeply. "Is it true? Are the things he told me true?"

"Which part?"

"All of it, Gabriel! Don't play fucking games with me."

"Yes, it's true! His family died at Shatila. He's suffered. So what? We've all suffered. It doesn't give him the right to murder innocent people because history didn't go his way!"

"*He* was an innocent, Gabriel! He was just a boy!"

"We're in the middle of an operation, Jacqueline. Now is not the time for a debate on moral equivalence and the ethics of counterterrorism."

"I apologize for permitting the question of morality to enter my thoughts. I forgot you and Shamron never get tripped up over something so trivial."

"Don't lump me in with Shamron."

"Why not? Because he gives orders, and you follow them?"

"What about Tunis?" Gabriel asked. "You knew Tunis was an assassination job, but you willingly took part in it. You even volunteered to go back the night of the killing."

"That's because the target was Abu Jihad. He had the blood of hundreds of Israelis and Jews on his hands."

"This one has blood on his hands too. Don't forget that."

"He's just a boy, a boy whose family was butchered while the Israeli army looked on and did nothing."

"He's not a boy. He's a twenty-five-year-old man who helps Tariq kill people."

"And you're going to use him to get to Tariq, because of what Tariq did to you? When does it end? When there's no more blood to shed? When, Gabriel?"

He stood up and pulled on his jacket.

Jacqueline said, "I want out."

"You can't leave now."

"Yes, I can. I don't want to sleep with Yusef anymore."

"Why?"

"*Why?* You have the nerve to ask me *why?*"

"I'm sorry, Jacqueline. That didn't come out—"

"You think of me as a whore, don't you, Gabriel! You think it doesn't bother me to sleep with a man I don't care for."

"That's not true."

"Is that what I was to you in Tunis? Just a whore?"

"You know that's not true."

"Then tell me what I was."

"What are you going to do? Are you going back to France? Back to your villa in Valbonne? Back to your Parisian parties and your photo shoots and your fashion shows, where the most difficult question is deciding what shade of lipstick to wear?"

She slapped him across the left side of his face. He stared back at her, eyes cold, color rising in the skin over his cheekbone. She drew back her hand to slap him again, but he casually lifted his left hand and deflected her blow.

"Can't you hear what's going on?" Gabriel said. "He told you the story of what happened to him at Shatila for a reason. He's testing you. He wants you for something."

"I don't care."

"I thought you were someone I could depend on. Not someone who was going to fall apart in the middle of the game."

"Shut up, Gabriel!"

"I'll contact Shamron—tell him we're out of business."

He reached out for the door. She grabbed his hand. "Killing Tariq won't make it right. That's just an illusion. You think it will be like fixing a painting: you find the damage, retouch it, and everything is fine again. But it's not like that for a human being. In fact it's not even like that for a painting. If you look carefully you can always see where it's been retouched. The scars never go away. The restorer doesn't heal a painting. He just hides the wounds."

"I need to know if you're willing to continue."

"And I want to know if I was just your whore in Tunis."

Gabriel reached out and touched her cheek. "You were my lover in Tunis." His hand fell to his side. "And my family was destroyed because of it."

"I can't change the past."

"I know."

"Did you care for me?"

He hesitated a moment, then said, "Yes, very much."

"Do you care for me now?"

He closed his eyes. "I need to know whether you can go on."

# 30

## HYDE PARK, LONDON

Karp said, "Your friend picked a damned lousy place for a meeting."

They were sitting in the back of a white Ford van on the Bayswater Road a few yards from Lancaster Gate, Karp hunched over a console of audio equipment, adjusting his levels. Gabriel could scarcely hear himself think over the riotous din of cars, taxis, lorries, and double-decker buses. Overhead, the trees lining the northern edge of the park writhed in the wind. Through Karp's microphones the air rushing through the branches sounded like white water. Beyond Lancaster Gate the fountains of the Italian Gardens splashed and danced. Through the microphones it sounded like a monsoonal downpour.

Gabriel said, "How many listeners do you have out there?"

"Three," Karp said. "The guy on the bench who looks like a banker, the pretty girl tossing bread to the ducks, and the guy selling ice cream just inside the gate."

"Not bad," Gabriel said.

"Under these conditions don't expect any miracles."

Gabriel looked at his wristwatch: three minutes past two. He thought: *He's not going to show. They've spotted Karp's team, and they're aborting.* He said, "Where the fuck is he?"

"Be patient, Gabe."

A moment later Gabriel saw Yusef emerge from Westbourne Street and dart across the road in front of a charging delivery truck. Karp snapped a couple of photographs as Yusef entered the park and strolled around the fountains. During the middle of his second circuit, he was joined by a man wearing a gray woolen overcoat, face obscured by sunglasses and a felt hat. Karp switched to a longer lens, took several more photographs.

They circled the fountains once in silence, then during the second circuit began to speak softly in English. Because of the noise from the wind and the fountains, Gabriel could make out only every third or fourth word.

Karp swore softly.

They circled the fountains for a few minutes, then walked up a small rise to a playground. The girl who had been feeding the ducks walked slowly after them. After a moment the surveillance van was filled with the joyous screams of children at play.

Karp pressed his fists against his eyes and shook his head.

Karp delivered the tape to Gabriel at the listening post three hours later with the resigned air of a surgeon who had done all he could to save the patient. "I fed it through the computers, filtered out the background noise, and enhanced the good stuff. But I'm afraid we got only about ten percent, and even that sounds like shit."

Gabriel held out his hand and accepted the cassette. He slipped it into the deck, pressed PLAY, and listened while he paced the length of the room.

*". . . needs someone . . . next assignment . . ."*

A sound, like static turned up full blast, obliterated the rest of the sentence. Gabriel paused the tape and looked at Karp.

"It's the fountain," Karp said. "There's nothing I can do with it."

Gabriel restarted the tape.

*". . . check out her . . . in Paris . . . problems . . . thing's fine."*

Gabriel stopped the tape, pressed REWIND, then PLAY.

*". . . check out her . . . in Paris . . . problems . . . thing's fine."*

*". . . not sure . . . right person for . . . sort of . . ."*

*". . . be persuasive . . . if you explain the importance . . ."*

*". . . what am I . . . tell her exactly?"*

*". . . vital diplomatic mission . . . cause of true peace in the Middle East . . . routine security precaution . . ."*

*". . . it supposed to work . . ."*

The audio level dropped sharply. Karp said, "They're walking toward the playground right now. We'll get coverage in a moment when the girl moves into position."

*". . . meet him . . . de Gaulle . . . from there . . . to the final destination . . ."*

*". . . where . . . "*

An injured child cries out for its mother, obliterating the response.

*". . . do with her after . . ."*

*". . . up to him . . ."*

*". . . what if . . . says no . . ."*

*"Don't worry, Yusef. Your girlfriend won't say no to you."*

STOP. REWIND. PLAY.

*"Don't worry, Yusef. Your girlfriend won't say no to you."*

And the next thing Gabriel heard was a mother berating her son for scraping a lump of chewing gum off the bottom of the seesaw and putting it into his mouth.

That evening Jacqueline picked up curry after work and brought it to Yusef's flat. While they ate they watched an American film on television about a German terrorist on the loose in Manhattan. Gabriel watched along with them. He muted his own television and listened to Yusef's instead. When the film was over Yusef pronounced it "total crap" and shut off the television.

Then he said, "We need to talk about something, Dominique. I need to ask you something important."

Gabriel closed his eyes and listened.

Next morning Jacqueline stepped off the carriage at the Piccadilly Underground station and floated along with the crowd across the platform. As she rode up the escalator she looked around her. They had to be following her: Yusef's watchers. He wouldn't let her loose on the streets of London without a secret escort, not after what he had asked her to do last night. A black-haired man was staring at her from a parallel escalator. When he caught her eye he smiled and tried to hold her gaze. She realized he was only a lecher. She turned and looked straight ahead.

Outside, as she walked along Piccadilly, she thought she spotted Gabriel using a public telephone, but it was only a Gabriel look-alike. She thought she saw him again stepping out of a taxi, but it was only Gabriel's nonexistent younger brother. She realized there were versions of Gabriel all around her. Boys in leather jackets. Young men in stylish business suits. Artists, students, delivery boys—with minor alterations Gabriel could pass for any of them.

Isherwood had arrived early. He was seated behind his desk, speaking Italian over the telephone and looking hungover. He placed his hand over the receiver and mouthed the words "Coffee, please."

She hung up her coat and sat down at her desk. Isherwood could survive a few more minutes without his coffee. The morning mail lay on the desk, along with a manila envelope. She tore open the flap, removed the letter from inside. *I'm going to Paris. Don't set foot outside the gallery until you hear from me.* She squeezed it into a tight ball.

# 31

## PARIS

Gabriel hadn't touched his breakfast. He sat in the first-class carriage of the Eurostar train, headphones on, listening to tapes on a small portable player. The first encounters between Yusef and Jacqueline. Yusef telling Jacqueline the story of the massacre at Shatila. Yusef's conversation with Jacqueline the previous night. He removed that tape, inserted one more: Yusef's meeting with his contact in Hyde Park. He had lost track of how many times he had heard it by now. Ten times? Twenty? Each time it disturbed him more. He pressed the REWIND button and used the digital tape counter to stop at precisely the spot he wanted to hear.

"... *check out her ... in Paris ... problems ... thing's fine.*"

STOP.

He pulled off the headphones, removed a small spiral notebook from his pocket, turned to a blank page. He wrote: *check out her ... in Paris ... problems ... thing's fine.* Between the staccato phrases he left blank spaces corresponding approximately to the times of the drop-outs on the tape.

Then he wrote: *We sent a man to check out her story in Paris. There were no problems. Everything's fine.*

It was possible that's what he had said, or it could have been this: *We sent a man to check out her story in Paris. There were big problems with it. But everything's fine.*

That made no sense. Gabriel crossed it out, then slipped on the headphones and listened to the section of the tape yet again. Wait a minute, he thought. Was Yusef's contact saying *thing's fine* or *other side*.

This time he wrote: *We sent a man to check out her story in Paris. There were big problems with it. We think she may be working for the other side.*

But if that were the case, why would they ask her to accompany an operative on a mission?

Gabriel pressed the FAST-FORWARD button, then STOP, then PLAY.

*"Don't worry, Yusef. Your girlfriend won't say no to you."*

STOP. REWIND. PLAY.

*"Don't worry, Yusef. Your girlfriend won't say no to you."*

Gabriel caught a taxi at the train station and gave the driver an address on the avenue Foch. Five minutes later he announced he had changed his mind, handed the driver some francs, and got out. He found another taxi.

In the accent of an Italian, he asked to be taken to Notre-Dame. From there he walked across the river to the St-Michel Métro station. When he was confident he was not being followed, he flagged down a taxi and gave the driver an address in the Sixteenth Arrondissement, near the Bois de Boulogne. Then he walked fifteen minutes to an apartment house on a leafy street not far from the place de Colombie.

On the wall in the entranceway was a house phone and next to the phone a list of occupants. Gabriel pressed the button for 4B, which bore the name Guzman in faded blue script. When the phone rattled on the other end, he murmured a few words, replaced the receiver, waited for the door to open. He crossed the foyer, rode the lift to the fourth floor, and knocked softly on the door of the flat. He heard a chain sliding away, followed by a dead bolt snapping back. To Gabriel's ears it sounded like a gunman ejecting a spent cartridge and forcing a new round into the chamber.

The door drew back. Standing in the threshold was a man of Gabriel's height, square of head and shoulders, with steel blue eyes and strawberry blond hair. He seemed inordinately pleased with himself—like a man who had had too much success with women. He didn't shake Gabriel's hand, just drew him inside by the elbow and closed the door as if he were trying to keep out the cold.

A large flat, dark, the smell of burning coffee and Shamron's cigarettes hanging on the air. Big couches, reclining leather chairs, fat throw pillows—a place for agents to wait. On the wall opposite an entertainment center filled with Japanese components and American films. No pornography in safe flats: Shamron's rule.

Shamron came into the room. He made a vast show of looking at his watch. "Ninety minutes," he said. "Your train arrived ninety minutes ago. Where the hell have you been? I was about to send out a search party."

*And I never told you how I was getting to Paris or what time I would be arriving. . . .*

"A proper surveillance detection run takes time. You remember how to do one of those, Ari, or have you stopped teaching that course at the Academy?"

Shamron held out his parched hand. "You have the tapes?"

But Gabriel looked at the other man. "Who's this?"

"This is Uzi Navot. Uzi's our *katsa* in Paris now, one of my best men. He's been working with me on this case. Meet the great Gabriel, Uzi. Shake the hand of the great Gabriel Allon."

Gabriel could see that Navot was one of Shamron's acolytes. The Office was full of them: men who would do anything—betray, cheat, steal, even kill—in order to win Shamron's approval. Navot was young and he was brash, and there was a smugness about him that made Gabriel dislike him instantly. He shone like a newly minted coin. The instructors at the Academy had told him he was a member of the elite—a prince—and Navot had believed them.

As Gabriel handed Shamron the tapes and sank into

the leather reclining chair, he could think of only one thing: Shamron, on the Lizard in Cornwall, promising him that the operation would be a closely held secret within the halls of King Saul Boulevard. If that was the case, who the hell was Uzi Navot and what was he doing here?

Shamron crossed the room, inserted a tape into the stereo system, and pressed PLAY. Then he sat opposite Gabriel and folded his arms. As Yusef began to speak, he closed his eyes and cocked his head slightly to one side. To Gabriel he looked as though he were listening to the strains of distant music.

*"A friend of mine, a very important Palestinian, needs to make a trip abroad for a crucial meeting. Unfortunately, the Zionists and their friends would rather this man not attend this important meeting, and if they spot him during his journey they'll probably seize him and send him back home."*

*"Why would they do that?"*

*"Because he has dared to question the fairness of the so-called peace process. Because he has dared to challenge the Palestinian leadership. Because he believes the only just solution to the Palestinian problem is to allow us to go back to our homes, wherever they might be, and to establish a truly binational state in the land of Palestine. Needless to say these views have made him very unpopular—not only among the Zionists and their friends but also among some Palestinians. As a result he is an exile and lives in hiding."*

"What do you want from me?"

"Because this man is under constant threat, he finds it necessary to take certain precautions. When he travels he does so under an assumed name. He's very educated, and he speaks many languages. He can pass for several different nationalities."

"I still don't know what you want from me, Yusef."

"The passport control officers of all Western countries use what's known as profiling to single out travelers for closer scrutiny. Unfortunately, because of 'Arab terrorism,' Arab men traveling alone are subject to the harshest scrutiny of all. Therefore, this man prefers to travel under a Western passport and with another person—a woman."

"Why a woman?"

"Because a man and woman traveling together are less suspicious than two men. This man needs a traveling companion, a partner, if you will. I'd like you to go with him on this trip."

"You can't be serious."

"I wouldn't joke about something like this. The meeting this man needs to attend could change the course of history in the Middle East and for the Palestinian people. It is vital that he arrive at his destination and be allowed to attend this meeting and represent the views of a great number of Palestinians."

"Why me?"

"For one reason, your appearance. You are a very attractive, very distracting woman. But also because of your passport. This man—and I'm sorry, Dominique, but I'm *not allowed to tell you his name—prefers to travel on a French passport. You will be posing as lovers, a successful businessman and his younger girlfriend."*

*"Posing as lovers?"*

*"Yes, just posing as lovers. Nothing more, I assure you. This Palestinian leader has nothing on his mind except the welfare and the future of the Palestinian people."*

*"I'm a secretary in an art gallery, Yusef. I don't do things like this. Besides, why should I stick my neck out for you and the Palestinian people? Find a Palestinian woman to do it."*

*"We would use a Palestinian woman if we could. Unfortunately, a European woman is required."*

*"We, Yusef? What do you mean by we? I thought you were a student. I thought you were a waiter, for God's sake. When did we become involved with a man who has to travel under an assumed name to a meeting that will change the course of history in the Middle East? So much for complete honesty, eh, Yusef?"*

*"I've made no secret of my political beliefs. I've made no secret of my opposition to the peace process."*

*"Yes, but you did make a secret of the fact you were involved with people like this. What is he, Yusef? Is he some kind of terrorist?"*

*"Don't be ridiculous, Dominique! The people I'm involved with would never commit an act of violence, and they condemn any group that does. Besides, do I really strike you as some sort of terrorist?"*

*"So where is he going? How would it work?"*

"Are you saying you'll do it?"

"I'm asking you where your friend is going and how it would work—nothing more."

"I can't tell you where he's going."

"Oh, Yusef, please. This is—"

"I can't tell you where he's going because even I don't know. But I can tell you how it would work."

"I'm listening."

"You'll fly to Paris—to Charles de Gaulle Airport. You'll meet the Palestinian leader in the terminal. Only he and a few of his closest aides know where he's going. You'll accompany him to the gate and board the airplane. The destination may be the site of the meeting, or you may have to take another flight—or a train, or a ferry, or drive. I don't know. When the meeting is over, you'll return to Paris and go your separate ways. You'll never see him again, and you'll never mention this to another person."

"And what if he's arrested? What happens to me?"

"You've done nothing wrong. You'll be traveling on your own passport. You'll say that this man invited you to come on a trip with him and that you accepted. Very simple, no problems."

"How long?"

"You should plan for a week but expect less."

"I can't just leave the gallery for a week. I'm not due any time off, and Isherwood will fall to pieces."

"Tell Mr. Isherwood that you have a family emergency in Paris. Tell him it's unavoidable."

"What if he decides to fire me?"

*"He won't fire you. And if it's money you're concerned about, we can arrange something for you."*

*"I don't want money, Yusef. If I do it, it will be because you asked me to do it. I'll do it because I'm in love with you, even though I don't quite believe you're really the person you appear to be."*

*"I'm just a man who loves his country and his people, Dominique."*

*"I need to think about it."*

*"Of course you need to think about it. But while you're making your decision it is critical that you not discuss this with anyone."*

*"I understand, I suppose. When do you need an answer?"*

*"Tomorrow night."*

When the tape ended, Shamron looked up.

"Why so glum, Gabriel? Why aren't you jumping for joy?"

"Because it sounds too good to be true."

"You're not going to start this again, are you, Gabriel? If they thought she was working for us she'd already be dead, and Yusef would be going to ground."

"That's not the way Tariq plays the game."

"What are you talking about?"

"Maybe he wants more than a low-level agent like Jacqueline. You remember the way he killed Ben-Eliezer in Madrid. He set a trap, baited it, lured him there. He left nothing to chance. Then he shot him in the face and walked out as if nothing had happened. He beat us at our own game, and Ben-Eliezer paid the price."

"He beat *me*. That's what you're trying to say, isn't it, Gabriel? If I had been more cautious, I would never have let Ben-Eliezer walk into that café in the first place."

"I wasn't blaming you."

"If not me, then who, Gabriel? I was the head of operations. It happened on my watch. Ultimately, his death is my responsibility. But what would you have me do now? Run and hide, because Tariq has beaten me before? Fold up my tent and go home? No, Gabriel."

"Take Yusef. Walk away."

"I don't want Yusef! I want *Tariq*!" Shamron slammed his thick fist against the arm of the chair. "It makes perfect sense. Tariq likes to use legitimate women for cover. He always has. In Paris it was the young American girl. In Amsterdam it was the whore who liked heroin. He even used one—"

Shamron stopped himself, but Gabriel knew what he was thinking. Tariq had used a woman in Vienna, a pretty Austrian shopgirl who was found in the Danube the night of the bombing with half her throat missing.

"Let's assume you're right, Gabriel. Let's assume Tariq suspects Jacqueline is working for the Office. Let's assume he's setting a trap for us to walk into. Even if that is the case, we'll still have the upper hand. *We* decide when to force the action. *We* pick the time and place, not Tariq."

"With Jacqueline's life hanging in the balance. I'm

not prepared to take that chance. I don't want her to end up like all the others."

"She won't. She's a professional, and we'll be with her every step of the way."

"Two weeks ago she was working as a model. She hasn't been in the field in years. She may be a professional, but she's not prepared for something like this."

"Allow me to let you in on a little secret, Gabriel. *No* one is ever completely prepared for something like this. But Jacqueline can look after herself."

"I don't like their ground rules either. We're supposed to let her go to Charles de Gaulle and get on a plane, but we don't know where the plane is going. We'll be playing catch-up from the moment the game begins."

"We'll know where they're going the moment they go to the gate, and we'll be watching them the moment they step off the plane at the other end. She won't be out of our sight for a minute."

"And then?"

"When the moment presents itself, you'll take Tariq down, and it will be over."

"Let's arrest him at Charles de Gaulle."

Shamron pursed his lips and shook his head.

Gabriel said, "Why not?"

Shamron held up a thick forefinger. "Number one, because it would require involving the French, something I'm not prepared to do. Number two, no one has managed to build a case against Tariq that's going to stand up in a courtroom. Number three, if we tell the French and our friends in Langley that we know where Tariq is going to be on a certain day, they're going to want to know how we came by this information. It would also mean confessing to our brethren in London that we've been running an operation on their soil and neglected to tell them about it. They're not going to be pleased about that. Finally, the last thing we need is Tariq behind bars, a symbol for all those who would like to see the peace process destroyed. I would rather he disappear quietly."

"How about a snatch job?"

"Do you *really* think we could take Tariq from the middle of a crowded terminal at Charles de Gaulle? Of course not. If we want Tariq, we're going to have to play by his rules for a few hours."

Shamron lit a cigarette and violently waved out the match. "It's up to you, Gabriel. An operation like this requires the direct approval of the prime minister. He's in his office right now, waiting to hear whether you're prepared to go through with it. What should I tell him?"

# 32

## ST. JAMES'S, LONDON

The middle afternoon, Julian Isherwood had decided, was the cruelest part of the day. What was it exactly? The fatigue of a good lunch? The early dark of London in winter? The sleepy rhythm of the rain rattling against his windows? This nether region of the day had become Isherwood's personal purgatory, a heartless space of time wedged between the sentimental hope he felt each morning when he arrived at the gallery and the cold reality of decline he felt each evening as he made his way back home to South Kensington. Three o'clock, the hour of death: too early to close up—that would feel like complete capitulation—too many hours to fill with too little meaningful work.

So he was seated at his desk, his left hand wrapped around the comforting shape of a warm mug of tea, his right flipping morosely through a stack of papers: bills he could not pay, notices of good pictures coming onto the market he could not afford to buy.

He lifted his head and peered through the doorway separating his office from the anteroom, toward the creature seated behind the headmasterly little desk. A striking figure, this girl who called herself Dominique: a real work of art, that one. At least she had made things at the gallery more interesting, whoever she was.

In the past he had insisted on keeping the doorway separating the two offices tightly closed. He was an important man, he liked to believe—a man who had important discussions with important people—and he had wanted a rampart between himself and his secretary. Now he found he preferred to keep it open. Oh, that he were twenty years younger, at the height of his powers. He could have had her back then. He'd had a good many back then, girls just like her. It wasn't just the money, or the villa in St-Tropez, or the yacht. It was the art. The paintings were a better aphrodisiac than cocaine.

In his copious spare time, Isherwood had concocted all sorts of fantasies about her. He wondered whether she was French at all or just one of those Israelis who could pass herself off as almost anything. He had also discovered that he found her vaguely intimidating, which made it quite impossible to even contemplate the physical act of love with her. *Or is it just me?* he thought. *Is this how we cope with the decay of aging? With the dwindling of our power? The deterioration of our skills? Does the mind mercifully release us from desire so we can step aside gracefully for the younger generation and not make complete jackasses of ourselves over women like Dominique Bonard?*

But as he watched her now he knew there was something wrong. She had been on edge all day. She had refused to leave the gallery. He had invited her to lunch at Wilton's—nothing suspicious, mind you: no ulterior motives—but she had declined and ordered a sandwich delivered from the café instead. Perhaps it had something to do with that Arab boy who'd come to the gallery the other night—Yusef, she had called him. *Or perhaps it was Gabriel.* Isherwood was certain of one thing. If Gabriel ever hurt her, the way he hurt that little boy in Cornwall—God, what was his name? Pearl? Puck? No, Peel it was—*well.* . . . Unfortunately, there was not much he could do to Gabriel except never forgive him.

Outside, he heard two short bursts of an automotive horn. He stood and walked to the window. Below him, on the bricks of Mason's Yard, was a delivery van standing just outside the sealed doors of the loading bay.

Funny, there were no deliveries scheduled for today. The driver honked again, long and loud this time. *For Christ's sake,* Isherwood thought. *Who the hell are you? What do you want?*

Then he peered down through the front windshield. Because of the angle he could not see the driver's face, he could only see a pair of hands, wrapped around the steering wheel. He would have recognized those hands anywhere. Best hands in the business.

They rode the lift to the upper gallery, Jacqueline between them like a prisoner, Gabriel to her left, Shamron to her right. She tried to catch Gabriel's eye, but he was looking straight ahead. When the door opened, Shamron guided her to the viewing bench as though he were placing a witness in the dock. She sat with her legs crossed at the ankles, elbows resting on her knees, her chin resting on her hands. Gabriel stood behind her. Shamron paced the length of the gallery like a prospective buyer unimpressed with the merchandise.

He spoke for twenty minutes without pausing. As Jacqueline watched him, she thought about the night he asked her to join the Office. She felt the same sense of purpose and duty she had felt that night. Shamron's taut little body portrayed so much strength that her fears seemed to melt away. On its face what he was asking of her was outrageous—accompany the world's most dangerous terrorist on a mission—but she was able to evaluate his words without the cumbersome emotion of fear. She thought: *Shamron is not afraid; therefore I am not afraid.* She had to admit that she was enthralled by the mere idea of it. Imagine, the girl from Marseilles whose grandparents were murdered in the Holocaust, helping to destroy Tariq al-Hourani and preserve the security of Israel. It would be the perfect end to her career with the Office, the fulfillment of every desire that made her join in the first place. It would also prove to Gabriel that she could be brave too.

"You have every right to tell us no," Shamron said. "You signed up for a very different operation than this— one much shorter in duration and with considerably less physical risk. But the situation has changed. Sometimes operations are like that."

He stopped pacing and stood directly in front of her. "But I can assure you of one thing, Jacqueline. Your safety will be our first priority. You'll never be alone. We'll walk you to the airplane and be waiting at the other end when you come off. We'll go wherever you go. And the first time an opportunity presents itself, we'll move in and end things. You also have my word that if your life is in danger, we will move in at that moment, regardless of the consequences. Do you understand what I'm saying to you?"

She nodded. Shamron reached into his briefcase, withdrew a small gift box, about two inches by two inches, and handed it to Jacqueline. She opened it. A gold lighter, nestled in white cotton filler.

"It sends out a beacon with a range of thirty miles. Which means if something goes wrong—if we lose contact with you for some reason—we'll always be able to find you again."

Jacqueline removed the lighter from the box and snapped the hammer. The lighter expelled a slender tongue of flame. When she slipped the lighter into the breast pocket of her blouse, Shamron's face broke into a brief smile. "I feel obligated to inform you that your friend Gabriel has serious reservations about this whole thing." He was on the move again, this time standing before the landscape by Claude. "Gabriel is afraid you may be walking straight into a trap. Usually I trust Gabriel's opinion. We have a considerable history between us. But in this case I find myself in respectful disagreement with him."

"I understand," Jacqueline murmured, but she was thinking of the night she had brought Yusef to this very room.

*"Claude was born in France, but he lived almost his entire life in Venice, if I'm not mistaken."*

*"Actually, you're mistaken. Claude lived and worked in Rome."*

Perhaps he was testing her, even then.

Shamron continued, "I could tell you many things. I could tell you that Tariq is an animal with the blood of hundreds of Jews on his hands. I could remind you that he killed our ambassador and his wife in cold blood in Paris. I could remind you that he murdered a great friend of Israel and his wife in Amsterdam. I could tell you that he's planning to strike again. That you will be doing a great service to the State of Israel and the Jewish people. I could tell you all these things, but I can't tell you to do this."

Jacqueline looked at Gabriel, but he was standing in front of the del Vaga, craning his neck sideways, as if he was looking for flaws in the last restoration. Don't look at me, he was saying. This is your decision, yours alone.

Shamron left them alone. Gabriel crossed the room and stood where Shamron had been. Jacqueline wanted him closer, but Gabriel seemed to require a buffer zone. His face had already changed. It was the same change that had come over him in Tunis. There had been two Gabriels in Tunis. The Gabriel of the surveillance phase, when they had been lovers, and Gabriel the night of the assassination. She remembered the way he had looked during the drive from the beach to the villa: part grim determination, part dread. He looked the same way now. It was his killing face. When he spoke, he resumed where Shamron had left off. Only the quality of his voice was different. When Shamron spoke Jacqueline could almost hear drums beating. Gabriel spoke softly and quietly, as if he were telling a story to a child at bedtime.

"Your link to the Office will be the telephone in your flat here in London. The line will be routed through to headquarters in Tel Aviv on a secure link. When you arrive at your destination, tell Tariq you need to check your messages. When you call, the people in the Office will see the number you're dialing from and locate it. If you're alone you can even talk to them and pass along messages to us. It will be very secure."

"And what if he refuses to let me use the telephone?"

"Then you throw a fit. You tell him that Yusef never said you wouldn't be allowed to use the telephone. You tell him Yusef never said you were going to become a prisoner. Tell him that unless you're allowed to check your messages you're leaving. Remember, as far as you know, this man is a Palestinian dignitary of some sort. He's on a diplomatic mission. He's not someone you're supposed to fear. If he senses you're afraid of him, he'll suspect you know more than you should know."

"I understand."

"Don't be surprised if you hear messages on your machine. We'll place a few there. Remember, according to the rules laid down by Yusef, no one but Julian Isherwood is allowed to know that you've gone away. Perhaps Isherwood will call and ask when you're planning to return. Perhaps he'll have some sort of emergency at the gallery that will require your attention. Perhaps a family member or a friend will call from Paris to see how things are going for you in London. Maybe a man will call and ask you to dinner. You're an attractive woman. It would be suspicious if there weren't other men pursuing you."

She thought: *So why not you, Gabriel?*

"Tonight, before you give him your answer, I want you to express serious doubts about the whole thing one more time. To Jacqueline Delacroix the concept of traveling with a strange man might sound reasonable, but to Dominique Bonard it sounds like utter lunacy. I want you to quarrel with him. I want you to force him to make assurances about your safety. In the end, of course, you'll agree to go, but not without a fight. Do you understand me?"

Jacqueline nodded slowly, mesmerized by the serene intensity of Gabriel's voice.

"Make sure you have this conversation in his flat. I want to hear what he has to say. I want to listen to his voice one last time. After you agree to do it, don't be surprised if he refuses to allow you to leave his presence. Don't be surprised if he moves you to another location for the night. Dominique Bonard may want to complain about it—she may want to make idle threats about walking out—but Jacqueline Delacroix should not be surprised in any way. And no matter where he takes you, we'll be close by. We'll be watching. I'll be watching."

He paused for a moment and, like Shamron before him, began to pace the length of the gallery slowly. He paused in front of the Luini and gazed upon the image of Venus. Jacqueline wondered whether he was capable of appreciating the beauty in a piece of art or whether he had been condemned to search only for flaws. He turned around and sat down next to her on the bench. "I want to tell you one more thing. I want you to be prepared for how it's going to end. It may happen someplace quiet, completely out of sight, or it may happen in the middle of a busy street. The point I'm trying to make is that you'll never know when it's going to end. You may see me coming, you may not. If you do see me, you're not to look at me. You're not to flinch or call out my name. You're not to make a sound. You must do nothing that alerts him to my presence. Otherwise we both might end up dead."

He paused for a moment, then added, "He won't die right away. A twenty-two-caliber Beretta isn't that kind of weapon. It takes several shots in the right place. After

I knock him down I'll have to finish the job. There's only one way to do that."

He fashioned his hand into the shape of a pistol and placed his forefinger against the side of her temple.

"I don't want you to watch me when I do this. It's not who I am."

She reached up and took his hand away from the side of her head. She folded his forefinger into his palm, so that his hand was no longer shaped like a Beretta. Then, finally, Gabriel leaned forward and kissed her lips.

"How is she?" asked Shamron as Gabriel turned into Oxford Street and headed east.

"She's resolute."

"And you?"

"My feelings are immaterial at this point."

"You're not excited in any way? You're not thrilled by the prospect of going into battle? The chase does not make you feel completely alive?"

"I lost those feelings a long time ago."

"You and I are different, Gabriel. I'm not ashamed to admit it, but I live for this moment. I live for the moment that I can place my foot against the throat of my enemy and crush the wind out of him."

"You're right. You and I *are* very different."

"If I didn't know better, I'd say you had feelings for her."

"I've always liked her."

"You've never *liked* anyone or anything in your life. You feel love, you feel hate, or you feel nothing at all. There's no middle ground for you."

"Is this what the psychiatrists at headquarters used to say about me?"

"I didn't need a psychiatrist to tell me something so obvious."

"Can we please change the subject?"

"All right, we'll change the subject. How do you feel about *me*, Gabriel? Is it love, hate, or nothing at all?"

"Some things are better left unsaid."

Gabriel crossed Tottenham Court Road and entered Holborn. At New Square he pulled to the curb. Shamron removed a thin file from his briefcase and held it up for Gabriel. "This has every known photograph of Tariq. There aren't many, and the ones we do have are dated. Have a look at them anyway. It would be rather embarrassing if we shot the wrong man."

"Like Lillehammer," Gabriel said.

Shamron grimaced at the mere mention of Lillehammer, a Norwegian skiing village and the site of the worst operational fiasco in the history of Israeli intelligence. In July 1973, a pair of *kidons* from Shamron's team assassinated a man they believed to be Ali Hassan Salameh, Black September's chief of operations and the mastermind of the Munich massacre. It turned out to be a tragic case of mistaken identity—the man was not Salameh but a Moroccan waiter who was married to a Norwegian woman. After the murder Gabriel and Shamron escaped, but several members of the hit team fell into the hands of the Norwegian police. Shamron barely managed to salvage his career. At King Saul Boulevard the Lillehammer disaster became known as Leyl-ha-Mar, Hebrew for "the night of bitterness."

Shamron said, "Please, do you really think now is a good time to mention Leyl-ha-Mar?" He paused, then smiled with surprising warmth. "I know you think I'm a monster. I know you think I'm a man completely without morals. Perhaps you're right. But I always loved you, Gabriel. You were always my favorite. You were my prince of fire. No matter what happens, I want you to remember that."

"Where are you going, by the way?"

"We're going to need an airplane tomorrow. I thought I'd book a reservation on Air Stone."

"Ari, you're not drinking! Unfair!"

"Sorry, Benjamin, but I have a long night ahead of me."

"Work?"

Shamron inclined his head slightly to indicate the affirmative.

"So what brings you here?"

"I need a favor."

"Course you need a favor. Wouldn't be here otherwise. Hope you haven't come looking for money, because the Bank of Stone is temporarily closed, and your account is badly overdrawn. Besides, money's gone. Creditors are singing a bloody aria. They want what's rightfully theirs. Funny how creditors can be. And as for my lenders, well, let's just say they're heading for calmer waters. What I'm trying to say to you, Ari, my old stick, is that I am in *serious* fucking financial trouble."

"It's not about money."

"So what is it? Speak, Ari!"

"I need to borrow your jet. Actually, I need to borrow you *and* your jet."

"I'm listening. You have my attention now."

"Tomorrow an enemy of the State of Israel is going to board a flight at Charles de Gaulle. Unfortunately we don't know what flight or what his destination is. And we won't know until he gets on the plane. It's imperative that we follow rapidly and that we arrive with some degree of secrecy. An unscheduled El Al charter, for example, might raise eyebrows. You, however, have a reputation for impetuous travel and last-minute changes in your schedule and itinerary."

"Damn right, Ari. Come and go like the wind. Keeps people on their fucking toes. It's that business in Paris, isn't it? That's why you took my money before. I must say I'm intrigued. It sounds as though I'm going to be involved in a *real* operation. Front lines, heavy stuff. How can I possibly say no?"

Stone snatched up the telephone. "Get the plane ready. Paris, one hour, usual suite at the Ritz, usual girl. One with the diamond stud in her tongue. A dream, that one. Have her waiting in the room. *Ciao.*"

He rang off, refilled his glass of champagne, and raised it in Shamron's direction.

"I can't thank you enough, Benjamin."

"You owe me, Ari. Someday *I'm* going to need a favor. Someday, all debts come due."

# 33

## ST. JAMES'S, LONDON

Jacqueline had hoped a brief walk alone would settle her nerves. It was a mistake. She should have taken a taxi straight to Yusef's door, because now she felt like turning around and telling Shamron and Gabriel to go to hell. She had just a few seconds to pull herself together. She realized she was not used to fear, at least not the kind of fear that made it nearly impossible to breathe. She had felt fear like this only once in her life—the night of the raid in Tunis—but that night Gabriel had been at her side. Now she was alone. She thought of her grandparents and the fear they must have felt while they were waiting to die at Sobibor. *If they could face death at the hands of the Nazis, I can face this,* she thought.

But there was something else she was feeling: love. Intense, unbearable, intolerable love. Perfect love. Love that had survived twelve years, meaningless relationships with other men. It was the promise of Gabriel that finally pushed her forward toward Yusef's door. She thought of something Shamron had said to her the night he recruited her: "You must believe in what you are doing."

*Oh, yes, Ari,* she thought. *I definitely believe in what I'm doing now.*

She pressed the buzzer for Yusef's flat. A moment. Nothing. Pressed it again, waited, looked at her watch. He had told her to come at nine. She was so nervous about arriving late that she had managed to come five minutes early. *So what should I do, Gabriel? Stay? Walk around the block?* If she left she might never come back. She lit a cigarette, stamped her feet against the cold, waited.

A moment later a Ford van braked to a halt in the street in front of her. The side door slid open, and Yusef leaped onto the wet asphalt. He walked toward her, hands in the pockets of his leather jacket, head swiveling from side to side. "How long have you been standing here?"

"I don't know. Three minutes, five minutes. Where the hell have you been?"

"I told you to come at nine. I didn't say five minutes before nine. I said nine."

"So I was a few minutes early. What's the big deal?"

"Because the rules have changed."

She remembered what Gabriel had said to her: You have no reason to be afraid. If they push you, push back.

"Listen, the rules haven't changed until I say they've changed. I haven't decided whether I'm going. This is crazy, Yusef. You won't tell me where I'm going. You won't tell me when I'll be back. I love you, Yusef. I want to help you. But you have to put yourself in my shoes."

His demeanor softened immediately. "I'm sorry, Dominique. I'm just a little tense. Everything has to go right. I didn't mean to take it out on you. Come inside. We'll talk. But we don't have much time."

Gabriel had never seen the Ford van till now. He wrote down the registration number as it vanished into the darkness. Shamron joined him in the window. Together they watched Yusef and Jacqueline disappear into the lobby. A moment later lights burned in Yusef's flat. Gabriel could hear two voices. Yusef, calm and reassuring; Jacqueline, edgy, stressed. Shamron made a base camp at the end of the couch and watched the scene across the street as though it were being played out on a movie screen. Gabriel closed his eyes and listened. They were stalking each other, circling the room like prizefighters. Gabriel didn't have to watch it. He could hear it in the way the audio level rose each time one of them passed by the telephone.

"What is it, Yusef? Drugs? A bomb? Tell me, you bastard!"

So convincing was her performance that Gabriel feared Yusef would change his mind. Shamron seemed to be enjoying the show. When Jacqueline finally agreed to go, he looked up at Gabriel. "That was marvelous. A nice touch. Well done. Bravo."

Five minutes later Gabriel watched them climb into

the back of a dark blue Vauxhall. A few seconds after the Vauxhall drove away, a car passed beneath Gabriel's window: Shamron's watchers. There was nothing to do now but wait. To fill the time he rewound the tape and listened to their conversation again. *"Tell me something,"* Jacqueline had said. *"When this is over will I ever see you again?"* Gabriel stopped the tape and wondered whether she was speaking to Yusef or to him.

The Cromwell Road at midnight: the dreary corridor connecting Central London to the western suburbs had never looked so beautiful to Jacqueline. The bleak Edwardian hotels with their flickering neon vacancy signs seemed enchanting to her. She watched the changing patterns of traffic lights reflected in the wet pavement and saw an urban masterpiece. She lowered her window a few inches and smelled the air: diesel fumes, damp, cheap fried food cooking somewhere. London at night. Spectacular.

They had switched cars, the blue Vauxhall for a gray Toyota with a cracked windshield. The Vauxhall had been driven by a good-looking boy with his hair drawn back into a ponytail. Sitting behind the wheel now was an older man—at least forty, she guessed—with a narrow face and nervous black eyes. He drove slowly.

Yusef murmured a few words to him in Arabic.

Jacqueline said, "Speak French or English or nothing at all."

"We are Palestinians," Yusef said. "Arabic is our language."

"I don't give a shit! I don't speak Arabic. I can't understand what you're saying, and it's making me uncomfortable, so please speak fucking English, or you can find someone else."

"I was only telling him to slow down a little."

*Actually, Yusef, you were telling him to make certain we aren't being followed, but let's not get hung up on the details.*

On the seat between them lay a small suitcase. Yusef had taken her to her flat and helped her pack. "There won't be time to go to baggage claim," he had said. "If you need more clothing you'll be given money to buy more clothing." He had watched her pack carefully, inspecting each item she placed in the bag. "How should I dress?" she had asked sarcastically. "Warm climate or cold? Are we going to Norway or New Zealand? Sweden or Swaziland? What's the dress code? Formal or casual?"

She lit a cigarette. Yusef took one out too and held out his hand for Jacqueline's lighter. She gave it to him and watched him light his cigarette. He was about to hand it back when something made him stop and inspect the lighter more carefully.

Jacqueline felt as if she had forgotten how to breathe.

"This is very nice." He turned it over and read the inscription. " *'To Dominique, with affection and fond memories.'* Where did you get this cigarette lighter?"

"I've had it for about a hundred years."

"Answer my question."

"It was a gift from a man. A man who didn't send me off with a complete stranger."

"He must have been very kind, this man. Why have I never seen this?"

"You haven't seen a lot of things. That doesn't mean anything."

"Should I be jealous?"

"Look at the date, you idiot."

" *'June nineteen ninety-five,'* " he recited. "Is this man still in the picture?"

"If he was, I wouldn't be with you."

"When was the last time you saw him?"

"June nineteen ninety-five, *with affection and fond memories.*"

"He must have been very important to you. Otherwise, you wouldn't have kept his lighter."

"It's not his lighter—it's my lighter. And I kept it because it's a good lighter."

She thought: *Gabriel was right. He suspects something. I'm going to die. He's going to kill me tonight.* She looked out her window and wondered whether the Cromwell Road on a wet winter's night was going to be her last snapshot of the world. She should have written a letter to her mother and locked it in a safety deposit box. She wondered how Shamron would break it to her. Would he explain that she had been working for the Office? Or would they cover up her death in some other way? Would she have to read about it in the newspapers? *Jacqueline*

*Delacroix, the Marseilles schoolgirl who rose to the peak of European modeling before a precipitous decline, died under mysterious circumstances. . . .* She wondered if the journalists she had treated with such contempt while she was alive would rise up en masse and savage her in death. At least Rémy would write well of her. They had always been cordial. Maybe she could get something nice out of Jacques. Perhaps even Gilles—*No, wait. Remember the party in Milan, the argument over the coke.* Christ, Gilles was going to rip her to shreds.

Yusef handed her the lighter. She dropped it back into her purse. The silence was appalling. She wanted to keep him talking; somehow talking made her feel safe, even if it was lies. "You never answered my question," she said.

"Which question is that? You've had so many tonight."

"When this is all over, am I going to see you again?"

"That's entirely up to you."

"And you're still not answering my question."

"I always answer your questions."

"Do you? If you'd told me the truth in the beginning, I doubt I'd be flying off with a complete stranger in the morning."

"I had to keep some things from you. And what about you, Dominique? Have you been completely honest with me? Have you told me everything about yourself?"

"Everything of consequence."

"That's a very convenient answer. You use it very effectively when you want to avoid talking anymore."

"It also happens to be the truth. Answer my question. Am I ever going to see you again?"

"I certainly hope so."

"You're full of shit, Yusef."

"And you're very tired. Close your eyes. Get some rest."

She leaned her head against the window. "Where are we going?"

"Someplace safe."

"Yes, you've told me that, but how about telling me where?"

"You'll see it when we arrive."

"Why would we need someplace safe? What's wrong with your flat? What's wrong with my flat?"

"This place belongs to a friend of mine. It's close to Heathrow."

"Is your friend going to be there?"

"No."

"Are you going to stay the night?"

"Of course. And in the morning I'll fly with you to Paris."

"And after that?"

"After that you'll be in the company of our Palestinian official, and your journey will begin. I wish I could be in your shoes. It would be such an honor to be with this man on this trip. You have no idea how lucky you are, Dominique."

"What's his name, this great man? Maybe I know him."

"I doubt you know him, but I still can't tell you his name. You will refer to him only by his cover name."

"And that is?"

"Lucien. Lucien Daveau."

"Lucien," she said softly. "I've always liked the name Lucien. Where are we going, Yusef?"

"Close your eyes. It won't be long now."

Shamron answered the telephone in the listening post before it could ring a second time. He listened without speaking, then gently replaced the receiver as if he had just been informed of the death of an old adversary. "It looks as though they've settled for the night," he said.

"Where?"

"A council estate in Hounslow near the airport."

"And the team?"

"In place, well hidden. They'll spend the night with her."

"I'd feel better if I were there."

"You have a long day ahead of you tomorrow. I suggest you get a few hours' sleep."

But Gabriel went into the bedroom and returned a moment later, jacket on, nylon rucksack over his shoulder.

Shamron said, "Where are you going?"

"I need to take care of something personal."

"Where are you going? When will you be back?"

But Gabriel walked out without another word and followed the stairs down to the street. As he walked past the front of the building, he thought he saw Shamron eyeing him through a slit in the blinds. And as he moved closer to the Edgware Road, he had the uncomfortable feeling that Shamron had one of his teams watching him too.

# 34

## HOUNSLOW, ENGLAND

The Toyota dropped them and then sped away. A car park bathed in yellow sodium light, a colony of stout redbrick council flats that looked like an industrial complex fallen on hard times. Jacqueline offered to carry her own bag, but Yusef wouldn't hear of it. He took her hand and led her across the car park, then across a common strewn with crushed beer cans and bits of broken toys. A red wagon with no front wheels. A headless baby with no clothing. A plastic pistol. *Gabriel's pistol,* thought Jacqueline, remembering the night in the hills of Provence, when he had tested her ability to shoot. Seemed like ages ago. A lifetime ago. A cat spit at them from the shadows. Jacqueline grabbed Yusef's elbow and nearly screamed. Then a dog began to bark, and the cat scampered along the sidewalk and slithered beneath a fence.

"This is lovely, Yusef. Why didn't you tell me you kept a place in the country?"

"Please don't talk until we're inside."

He led her into a stairwell. Dead leaves and old newspaper in the corners, lime green walls, yellow light fixture overhead. The collision of color made them both look nauseated. They climbed two flights, then passed through a connecting door and walked the length of a long corridor. A cacophony of disharmonious sounds greeted them. A child screaming for its mother. A couple quarreling in Caribbean-accented English. A crackling radio blaring a play on the BBC, Tom Stoppard's *The Real Thing.* Yusef stopped in front of a doorway with the number 27 mounted below a security peephole. He unlocked the door, led her inside, switched on a small parchment-shaded lamp.

The living room was empty except for one molting armchair and a television set. Its cord wound across the linoleum like a dead garden snake. Through a half-open door she could see a bedroom with a mattress on the floor. Through another doorway a small kitchen, a bag of groceries resting on the counter. Despite the absence of furnishings, the flat was impeccably clean and smelled of lemon air deodorizer.

She opened the window; cold air poured in. Below the window ran a fence, and beyond the fence lay a football pitch. A half-dozen young men, dressed in colorful warm-up suits and woolen caps, kicked a ball about in the headlights of a car parked along the sideline. Their long shadows played over brick walls below Jacqueline's window. In the distance she could hear the soggy grumble of the motorway. An empty train rattled past on an elevated track. A jetliner screamed overhead.

"I like what your friend's done with the place, Yusef,

but it's not really my style. Why don't we check into one of the hotels at the airport? Someplace with room service and a decent bar."

Yusef was in the kitchen, unpacking the bag of groceries. "If you're hungry I can make you something. There's some bread, cheese, eggs, a bottle of wine, and coffee and milk for the morning."

Jacqueline walked into the kitchen. There was barely enough room for the two of them in the cramped space. "Don't be so literal. But this *is* a shithole. Why is it empty?"

"My friend just got the place. He hasn't had a chance to move his things. He's been living with his parents."

"He must be very happy, but I still don't know why we have to stay here tonight."

"I told you, Dominique. We came here for reasons of security."

"Security from who? Security from what?"

"Perhaps you've heard of the British security service, better known as MI5. They make it their business to infiltrate exile and dissident communities. They watch people like us."

"Like *us*?"

"Like *me*. And then there are the guys from Tel Aviv."

"You lost me there, Yusef. Who are the guys from Tel Aviv?"

Yusef looked up and stared at her incredulously. "Who are the guys from Tel Aviv? The most ruthless, murderous intelligence service in the world. A gang of hired killers might be a more appropriate description."

"And why would the Israelis be a threat here in Britain?"

"The Israelis are everywhere that we are. National boundaries are of no concern to them."

Yusef emptied the bag and used it to line the wastebasket. "Are you hungry?" he asked.

"No, just extremely tired. It's late."

"Go to bed. I have some business to take care of."

"You're not leaving me here alone, are you?"

He held up a mobile phone. "I just have to make a couple of calls."

Jacqueline put her arms around his waist. Yusef drew her forehead to his lips and kissed her softly.

"I wish you wouldn't make me do this."

"It'll just be for a few days. And when you come back, we can be together."

"I wish I could believe you, but I don't know what to believe anymore."

He kissed her again, then placed a finger beneath her chin and lifted her face so he could look into her eyes. "I wouldn't say it if I didn't mean it. Go to bed. Try to get some sleep."

She entered the bedroom. She didn't bother to turn on the light; it would feel less depressing if she had only a vague sense of her surroundings. She reached down, grabbed a handful of the bedding, and sniffed. Newly laundered. Still, she decided to sleep in her clothing. She lay down and carefully placed her head on the pillow so that it touched no portion of her face or neck. She left on her shoes. She smoked a last cigarette to cover up the overpowering smell of the disinfectant. She thought of Gabriel, her dance school in Valbonne. She listened to the jetliners and the trains and the resounding thump of a foot making solid contact with a leather ball out on the football pitch. She watched the shadows of high-stepping athletes dancing on her wall like marionettes.

Then she heard Yusef, speaking in a low murmur over his mobile phone. She couldn't quite make out what he was saying. She didn't care. Indeed, her last thought before drifting into a feverish sleep was that Yusef, her Palestinian lover, probably did not have long to live.

Isherwood opened the door of his home in Onslow Gardens a few inches and eyed Gabriel malevolently through the security chain. "Do you have any idea what time it is?" He unchained the door. "Come inside before we both get pneumonia."

Isherwood wore pajamas, leather slippers, a silk dressing gown. He led Gabriel into the drawing room, then disappeared into the kitchen. He returned a moment later with a pot of coffee and a couple of mugs. "I hope you take your coffee black, because I'm afraid the milk in the fridge was purchased during the Thatcher government."

"Black is fine."

"So, Gabriel, my love. What brings you here at"—he

paused to look at his watch and grimaced—"Christ, at two forty-five in the morning?"

"You're going to lose Dominique."

"I guessed that when Ari Shamron rolled into my gallery like a poisonous cloud. Where's she off to? Lebanon? Libya? Iran? What was her real name, by the way?"

Gabriel just sipped his coffee and said nothing.

"Hate to see her go, actually. An angel, that one. And not a bad secretary once she got the hang of things."

"She won't be coming back."

"They never do. I have a way of driving away women. Always have."

"I hear you're in final negotiations with Oliver Dimbleby to sell the gallery."

"One doesn't really negotiate when one is tied to the railroad tracks, Gabriel. One grovels. One begs."

"Don't do it."

"How dare you sit there and tell me how to run my affairs? I wouldn't be in this mess if it weren't for you and your friend Herr *Heller.*"

"The operation may be over sooner than we expected."

"And?"

"And I can get back to work on the Vecellio."

"There's no way you can finish it in time to save my neck. I am now officially insolvent, which is why I'm *negotiating* with Oliver Dimbleby."

"Dimbleby's a hack. He'll ruin the gallery."

"Frankly, Gabriel, I'm too tired to give a shit at this point. I need something stronger than coffee. You?"

Gabriel shook his head. Isherwood shuffled over to the sideboard and dumped an inch of gin into a tumbler. "What's in the bag?"

"An insurance policy."

"Insurance on what?"

"Against the possibility that I'm unable to complete work on the Vecellio in time." Gabriel handed the bag to Isherwood. "Open it."

Isherwood set down his drink and unzipped the bag. "My God, Gabriel. How much is it?"

"A hundred thousand."

"I can't take your money."

"It's not mine. It's Shamron's, via Benjamin Stone."

"*The* Benjamin Stone?"

"In all his glory."

"What the hell are you doing with a hundred thousand pounds of Benjamin Stone's money?"

"Just take it and don't ask any more questions."

"If it's really Benjamin Stone's, I think I will." Isherwood raised his glass of gin. "Cheers, Gabriel. I'm sorry for all the miserable things I've thought about you during the past few weeks."

"I deserved it. I should have never run out on you."

"All is forgiven." Isherwood stared into his drink for a long moment. "So where is she? Gone for good?"

"The operation has moved into its final stages."

"You've not put that poor girl in any danger, have you?"

"I hope not."

"So do I, for her sake and yours."

"What are you talking about?"

"You know, I've been in this lousy racket for almost forty years, and in all that time, no one's ever managed to sell me a forgery. Dimbleby's had his fingers burned. Even the great Giles Pittaway has managed to buy a fake or two in his time. But not me. I have the gift, you see. I may be a lousy businessman, but I can always tell a fraud from the real thing."

"Are you coming to the point of this?"

"She's the real thing, Gabriel. She's golden. You may never get another chance like this. Hang on to her, because if you don't, it will be the biggest mistake of your life."

# PART THREE

# RESTORATION

# 35

*Before the Catastrophe, Daoud al-Hourani lived in the Upper Galilee. He was a* muktar *and the richest man in the village. He owned livestock—several head of cattle, many goats, and a large flock of sheep—as well as a grove of lemon, orange, and olive trees. When it was time to pick the fruit, he and the other village elders organized a communal harvest. The family lived in a whitewashed house with cool tile floors and fine rugs and cushions. His wife bore him five daughters but only one son, Mahmoud.*

*Daoud al-Hourani kept up good relations with the Jews who had settled on land near the village. When the Jews' well became fouled, he drafted men from the village to help them dig a new one. When several Arabs in the village fell sick with malaria, Jews from the settlement came and drained a nearby swamp. Daoud al-Hourani learned to speak Hebrew. When one of his daughters fell in love with a Jewish man from the settlement, he permitted them to marry.*

*Then came the war, and then the Catastrophe. The al-Hourani clan, along with most of the Arabs of the Upper Galilee, fled across the border into Lebanon and settled in a refugee camp near Sidon. The camp itself was organized much like the villages of the Upper Galilee, and Daoud al-Hourani retained his status as an elder and a respected man, even though his land had been taken and his animals lost. His large whitewashed home was replaced by a cramped tent, broiling in the heat of summer, freezing and porous in the cold rains of winter. In the evenings, the men sat outside the tents and told stories of Palestine. Daoud al-Hourani assured his people that the exile would only be temporary—that the Arab armies would gather themselves and hurl the Jews into the sea.*

*But the Arab armies didn't gather themselves, and they didn't try to hurl the Jews into the sea. At the camp in Sidon, the tents turned to tattered rags, only to be replaced by crude huts, with open sewers. Slowly, as the years passed, Daoud al-Hourani began to lose influence over his villagers. He had told them to be patient, but their patience had gone unrewarded. Indeed, the plight of the Palestinians seemed only to worsen.*

*During those first awful years in the camp, there was only one piece of joyous news. Daoud al-Hourani's wife became pregnant, even though she had reached the age when most women can no longer bear children. In the spring of that year, five years to the day after the al-Hourani clan fled its home in the Upper Galilee, she gave birth to a son in the infirmary of the camp. Daoud al-Hourani called the boy Tariq.*

*Branches of the al-Hourani clan were scattered throughout the diaspora. Some were across the border in Syria, some in camps in Jordan. A few, including al-Hourani's brother, had managed to make it to Cairo. A few years after the birth of Tariq, Daoud al-Hourani's brother died. He wished to attend his brother's funeral, so he traveled to Beirut and obtained the necessary visas and permits to make the journey. Because he was a Palestinian, he had no passport. The following day he boarded a flight for Cairo but was turned back at the airport by a customs official who declared his papers were not in order. He returned to Beirut, but an immigration official denied him permission to reenter Lebanon. He was locked in a detention room at the airport, with no food or water.*

*A few hours later a dog was placed in the room. It had arrived unaccompanied on a flight from London, and, like Daoud al-Hourani, its papers had been challenged by Lebanese immigration officials. But one hour later a senior customs officer appeared and led the dog away. The animal had been granted special dispensation to enter the country.*

*Finally, after a week, Daoud al-Hourani was allowed to leave the airport and return to the camp at Sidon. That night, as the men sat around the fires, he gathered his sons to his side and told them of his ordeal.*

*"I asked our people to be patient. I promised them that the Arabs would come to our rescue, but here we are, many years later, and we are still in the camps. The Arabs treat us worse than the Jews. The Arabs treat us worse than dogs. The time for patience has ended. It is time to fight."*

*Tariq was too young to fight; he was still just a boy. But Mahmoud was nearly twenty now, and he was ready to take up arms against the Jews. That night he joined the fedayeen. It was the last time Tariq would see him alive.*

## CHARLES DE GAULLE AIRPORT, PARIS

Yusef slipped his hand into Jacqueline's and guided her through the crowded terminal. She was exhausted. She had slept miserably and shortly before dawn had been awakened by a nightmare in which Gabriel assassinated Yusef while Yusef was making love to her. Her ears were ringing, and there was a flickering in the periphery of her vision, like flashbulbs popping on a runway. They passed through the transit lounge, cleared a security check, and entered the departure terminal. Yusef released her hand, then kissed her cheek and placed his lips close to her ear. When he spoke, it reminded her of the way Gabriel had spoken to her the previous night in the gallery—softly, as if he were telling her a bedtime story.

"You're to wait in that café. You're to order a cup of coffee and read the newspaper that I've slipped into the flap of your bag. You're not to leave the café for any reason. He'll come for you unless he thinks there's a problem. If he doesn't appear within an hour—"

"—Get on the next available flight for London, and don't try to contact you when I arrive," Jacqueline said, finishing his sentence for him. "I remember everything you've told me."

Another kiss, this time on her other cheek. "You have a spy's memory, Dominique."

"Actually, I have my mother's memory."

"Remember, you have nothing to fear from this man and nothing to fear from the authorities. You're doing nothing wrong. He's a kind man. I think you're going to enjoy his company. Have a safe trip, and I'll see you when you get back."

He kissed her forehead and gave her a gentle nudge in the direction of the café, as if she were a toy boat adrift on a pond. She walked a few steps, then stopped and turned to have one last look at him, but he had already melted into the crowd.

It was a small airport restaurant, a few wrought-iron tables spilling into the terminal to create the illusion of a Parisian café. Jacqueline sat down and ordered a café au lait from the waiter. She was suddenly conscious of her appearance and felt an absurd desire to make a good first impression. She wore black jeans and an ash-colored cashmere pullover. Her face had no makeup, and she had done nothing with her hair except pull it back. When the waiter brought her coffee, Jacqueline lifted the spoon and looked at the distorted reflection of her eyes. They were red-rimmed and raw.

She stirred sugar into her coffee and looked around her. At the table behind her a young American couple were quietly quarreling. At the next table were a pair of German businessmen studying a performance chart on the screen of a laptop computer.

Jacqueline suddenly remembered she was supposed to be reading the newspaper. She removed the *Times* that Yusef had left in her bag and unfolded it. A British Airways cocktail napkin fell out onto the table. Jacqueline picked it up and turned it over. On the back was a note, penned in Yusef's chaotic hand: *I'll miss you. With love and fond memories, Yusef.*

She crumpled it and left it next to her coffee. *Sounds like a farewell note.* She picked up the newspaper and leafed through the front section. She paused to scan the news from the Middle East: U.S. PRESIDENT APPLAUDS INTERIM AGREEMENT REACHED BETWEEN ISRAEL AND THE PALESTINIANS . . . SIGNING CEREMONY NEXT WEEK AT UNITED NATIONS. She licked the tip of her finger and turned another page.

Boarding announcements blared from the public address system. She had a terrible headache. She reached into her purse, removed a bottle of aspirin, washed down two tablets with the coffee. She looked for Gabriel. Nothing. *Damn it, where the hell are you, Gabriel Allon? Tell me you haven't left me here alone with them. . . .* She placed the cup carefully in the saucer and returned the aspirin bottle to her purse.

She was about to resume reading when a stunningly attractive woman with lustrous black hair and wide brown eyes appeared at the table. "Do you mind if I join you?" the woman said in French.

"Actually, I'm meeting someone."

"You're meeting Lucien Daveau. I'm Lucien's friend." She pulled out the chair and sat down. "Lucien asked me to collect you and take you to your flight."

"I was told that *Lucien* himself would meet me here."

"I understand, but I'm afraid there's been a slight

change in plan." She smiled a radiant, seductive smile. "You have nothing to be afraid of. Lucien asked me to take good care of you."

Jacqueline had no idea what to do. They had violated the terms of the agreement. She had every right to stand up and walk off and be done with it. *But then what?* Tariq would slip away and continue his campaign of terror. More innocent Jews would die. The peace process would be placed in jeopardy. And Gabriel would go on blaming himself for what had happened to Leah and his son in Vienna.

"I don't like this, but I'll do it."

"Good, because they've just called our flight."

Jacqueline stood up, picked up her bag, and followed the woman out of the café. "*Our* flight?" she asked.

"That's right. I'm going to be traveling with you for the first leg of your journey. Lucien will join you later."

"Where are we going?"

"You'll find out in a moment."

"Since we're going to be traveling together, do you think you could tell me your name?"

The girl smiled again. "If you feel you must call me something, you may call me Leila."

Gabriel stood in a duty-free shop one hundred feet away, pretending to look at cologne, while he watched Jacqueline at the café. Shamron was aboard Benjamin Stone's private plane. All they needed was Tariq.

Suddenly, he realized that he was excited by the prospect of finally seeing Tariq. The photographs in Shamron's file were useless—too old, too grainy. Three of them were only *presumed* to be pictures of Tariq. The truth was no one inside the Office really knew what he looked like. Gabriel was about to get the first good look at him in years. Was he tall or short? Was he handsome or ordinary-looking? Did he look like a ruthless killer? *Of course not,* Gabriel thought. *He'll be someone who blends naturally into his surroundings.*

*He'll be like me.* Then he thought: *Or am I like him?*

When the attractive, raven-haired girl sat down at Jacqueline's table, he thought for a moment that it was just one of those horrid accidents that sometimes sends operations into a tailspin—girl needs a seat, girl assumes Jacqueline's alone, girl helps herself to the empty chair. Then he realized it was part of Tariq's game. He had survived all these years because he was unpredictable. He made plans and changed plans constantly—told different stories to different members of his organization. Never let the left hand know what the right was doing.

The two women stood up and started walking. Gabriel waited for a moment, then trailed them from a safe distance. He felt dejected. The game had barely begun and already Tariq had bested him. He wondered whether he was really ready to do battle with a man like Tariq. He had been out of the game too long. Perhaps his reactions had slowed, his instincts for survival waned. He thought of the night he'd planted the bugs in Yusef's flat, how he had nearly been caught because he had lost his concentration for a few seconds.

He felt the sickening rush of adrenaline all over again. For a moment he considered rushing forward and pulling her out. He forced himself to calm down and think clearly. She was just getting on an airplane. She would be safe while they were in the air, and Shamron would have a team waiting at the other end. Tariq had won the first round, but Gabriel decided to let the game continue.

The girl led Jacqueline into a glass-enclosed gate area. Gabriel watched as they passed through a final security check and handed over their tickets to a gate attendant. Then they headed into the Jetway and were gone. Gabriel glanced up at the monitor one last time to make certain he had seen it right: Air France flight 382, destination Montreal.

A few moments after takeoff Shamron hung up the secure telephone in the office of Benjamin Stone's private jet and joined Gabriel in the luxuriously appointed salon. "I just notified Ottawa station."

"Who's in Ottawa these days?"

"Your old friend Zvi Yadin. He's on his way to Montreal now with a small team. They'll meet the plane and put Jacqueline and her new friend under watch."

"Why Montreal?"

"Haven't you read the papers?"

"I'm sorry, Ari, but I've been a bit busy."

On the table next to Shamron's chair was a stack

of newspapers, neatly arranged so the mastheads were visible. He snatched the top paper and flipped it into Gabriel's lap. "There's going to be a signing ceremony at the UN in three days. Everyone's going to be there. The American president, the prime minister, Arafat and all his deputies. It looks as though Tariq's going to try to spoil the party."

Gabriel glanced at the newspaper and tossed it back onto the table.

"Montreal is a natural staging point for a man like Tariq. He speaks fluent French and has the capability to secure false passports. He flies to Montreal as a Frenchman and enters Quebec without a visa. Once he's in Canada he's almost home. There are tens of thousands of Arabs living in Montreal. He'll have plenty of places to hide. Security along the U.S.-Canadian border is lax or nonexistent. On some roads there are no border posts at all. In Montreal he can switch passports—American or Canadian—and simply drive into the States. Or, if he's feeling adventurous, he can walk across the border."

"Tariq never struck me as an outdoorsman."

"He'll do whatever is necessary to get his target. And if that means walking ten miles through the snow, he'll walk through the snow."

"I don't like the fact that they changed the rules in Paris," Gabriel said. "I don't like the fact that Yusef lied to Jacqueline about how this was going to work."

"All it means is that for reasons of security Tariq finds it necessary to deceive his own people. That's standard procedure for a man like him. Arafat did it for years. That's the reason he's alive today. His enemies within the Palestinian movement couldn't get to him."

"And neither could you."

"Point well taken."

The door connecting the salon to the office opened, and Stone entered the room.

Shamron said, "There's a stateroom in the back of the plane. Go get some sleep. You look terrible."

Gabriel stood up without a word and left the salon. Stone lowered his mammoth body into a chair and scooped up a handful of Brazil nuts. "He has passion," he said, popping a pair of nuts into his mouth. "An assassin with a conscience. I like that. The rest of the world is going to like him even better."

"Benjamin, what on earth are you talking about?"

"He's the meal ticket. Don't you understand, Ari? He's the way you repay your debts to me. All of them, wiped out in a single neat payment."

"I didn't realize you were keeping a ledger. I thought you helped us because you believed in us. I thought you helped us because you wanted to help protect the State."

"Let me finish, Ari. Hear me out. I don't want your money. I want *him*. I want you to let me tell his story. I'll assign it to my best reporter. Let me publish the story of the Israeli who restores old master paintings by day and kills Palestinian terrorists by night."

"Are you out of your mind?"

"On the contrary, Ari. I'm quite serious. I'll serial-ize it. I'll sell the film rights to Hollywood. Give me an exclusive on this manhunt. The view from the inside. It will send a message to my troops that we still have what it takes to shake up Fleet Street. *And*—this is the best part, Ari—*and* it will send a strong signal to my backers in the City that I'm still a force to be reckoned with."

Shamron made an elaborate show of lighting his next cigarette. He studied Stone through a cloud of smoke, nodding slowly while he considered the gravity of his proposition. Stone was a drowning man, and unless Shamron did something to cut him away, he would take them both straight to the bottom.

Gabriel tried to sleep, but it was no use. Each time he closed his eyes, images of the case appeared in his mind. Instinctively he saw them rendered as motionless repro-ductions captured in oil on canvas. Shamron on the Liz-ard, calling him back to service. Jacqueline making love to Yusef. Leah in her greenhouse prison in Surrey. Yusef meeting his contact in Hyde Park. . . . *Don't worry, Yusef. Your girlfriend won't say no to you.*

Then he thought of the scene he had just witnessed at Charles de Gaulle. Restoration had taught Gabriel a valuable lesson. Sometimes what appears on the surface is quite different from what is taking place just below. Three years earlier he had been hired to restore a Van Dyck, a piece the artist had painted for a private chapel in Genoa depicting the Assumption of Mary. When Gabriel performed his initial analysis of the painting's surface, he thought he saw something beneath the Virgin's face. Over time the light-toned paints Van Dyck had used to render her skin had faded, and it seemed an image below was beginning to rise. Gabriel performed an extensive X-ray examination of the picture to view what was taking place beneath the surface. He discovered a completely finished work, a portrait of a rather fleshy woman clad in a white gown. The black-and-white film of the X ray made her appear specterlike. Even so, Gabriel recognized the shimmering quality of Van Dyck's silks and the expressive hands that characterized the paintings he produced while living in Italy. He later learned that the work had been commissioned by a Genoese aristocrat whose wife had hated it so much that she refused to accept it. When Van Dyck was commissioned to paint the chapel piece, he simply covered up the old portrait in white paint and re-used the canvas. By the time the canvas reached Gabriel's hands, more than three and a half centuries later, the wife of the Genoese aristocrat had taken her revenge on the artist by rising to the surface of his painting.

He closed his eyes again and this time drifted into a restless sleep. The last image he saw before slipping into unconsciousness was Jacqueline and the woman seated in the airport café, rendered as an Impressionist street scene, and standing in the background was the ghostly, translucent figure of Tariq, beckoning Gabriel forward with an exquisite Van Dyck hand.

# 36

## PARIS

Yusef took a taxi from the airport to the center of the city. For two hours he moved steadily about Paris—by Métro, by taxi, and on foot. When he was confident he was alone, he walked to an apartment house in the Sixteenth Arrondissement not far from the Bois de Boulogne. On the wall in the entranceway was a house phone and next to the phone a list of occupants. Yusef pressed the button for 4B, which bore the name Guzman in faded blue script. When the door opened he stepped quickly inside, crossed the foyer, and rode the lift up to the fourth floor. He knocked on the door. It was opened instantly by a stout man with steel blue eyes and strawberry blond hair. He pulled Yusef inside and quietly closed the door.

It was early evening in Tel Aviv when Mordecai stepped out of his office in the top-floor executive suite and made his way down the corridor toward Operations. As he entered the room a pair of Lev's black-eyed desk officers stared at him contemptuously over their computer terminals.

"Is he still in?"

One of the officers pointed toward Lev's office with the tip of a chewed pencil. Mordecai turned and walked down the corridor. He felt like a stranger in a besieged village. Outsiders were not welcome in Lev's realm, even if the outsider happened to be the second-most-senior officer in the service.

He found Lev seated in his cheerless office, hunched forward, elbows resting on the desk, long hands folded at the last knuckle and pressed against his temples. With his bald head, protruding eyes, and tentacle-like fingers, he looked very much like a praying mantis. As Mordecai moved closer, he could see that it was not a case file or field report that held Lev's attention but a large volume on the beetles of the Amazon Basin. Lev closed the book deliberately and pushed it aside.

"Is there something going on in Canada I should know about?" Mordecai asked.

"What are you talking about?"

"I was reviewing the expense reports from Ottawa station, and there was a minor discrepancy in the payouts for the support staff. I thought I'd save a few minutes and deal with it by telephone rather than cable. It really is just a minor thing. I thought that Zvi and I could clear it up in a moment or two."

Lev drummed his fingers impatiently on the desk. "What does this have to do with Operations?"

"I couldn't find Zvi. In fact I couldn't find anyone. It seems your entire Ottawa station is missing."

"What do you mean *missing*?"

"I mean nowhere to be found. Gone without explanation."

"Who did you speak to?"

"A girl from the code room."

"What did she say?"

"That Zvi and all his field personnel took off in a hurry a few hours ago."

"Where's the old man?"

"Somewhere in Europe."

"He just came *back* from Europe. Why did he go this time?"

Mordecai frowned. "You think the old man tells me anything? That old bastard is so secretive that half the time I don't think *he* even knows where he's going."

"Find him," Lev said.

# 37

## MONTREAL

Leila rented a car at the airport. She drove very fast along an elevated motorway. To their right lay an icy river; to their left freezing fog drifted over a vast rail yard like the smoke of battle. The lights of downtown Montreal floated in front of them, obscured by a veil of low cloud and falling snow. Leila drove as if she knew the way.

"You've been here before?" Leila asked. It was the first time she had spoken to Jacqueline since the café at Charles de Gaulle in Paris.

"No, never. How about you?"

"No."

Jacqueline folded her arms against her body and shivered. The heater was roaring, but it was still so cold in the car she could see her breath. "I don't have clothes for this kind of cold," she said.

"Lucien will buy you whatever you need."

So, *Lucien* was meeting her here in Montreal. Jacqueline blew on her hands. "It's too cold to go shopping."

"All the best boutiques in Montreal are underground. You'll never have to set foot outside."

"I thought you said you've never been here."

"I haven't."

Jacqueline leaned her head against the window and briefly closed her eyes. They had sat in business class, Leila across the aisle and one row behind. An hour before landing, Leila had gone to the lavatory. On the way back to her seat she'd handed Jacqueline a note: *Go through immigration and customs alone and meet me at the Hertz counter.*

Leila turned off the motorway and turned onto the boulevard René Lévesque. Wind howled through the canyons of high-rise office buildings and hotels. The snowbound sidewalks seemed to have been depopulated. She drove a few blocks, stopped in front of a large hotel. A porter rushed out and opened Jacqueline's door. "Welcome to the Queen Elizabeth. Checking in?"

"Yes," said Leila. "We can manage the bags, thank you."

The porter gave her a claim check for the car and climbed behind the wheel. Leila led Jacqueline into the large, noisy lobby. It was filled with Japanese tourists. Jacqueline wondered what on earth could bring them to Montreal in the dead of winter. Leila deliberately switched her bag from her right hand to her left. Jacqueline forced herself to look the other way. She had been trained in the art of impersonal communication; she knew a good piece of body talk when she saw it. The next act was about to begin.

\*　　\*　　\*

Tariq watched them from the hotel bar. His appearance had changed since Lisbon: charcoal-gray wool trousers, a cream-colored pullover, Italian blazer. He was neatly shaved and wore small gold-rimmed eyeglasses with clear lenses. He had added a touch of gray to his hair.

He had seen the photograph of the woman called Dominique Bonard, but he was still taken aback by her appearance. He wondered how Shamron and Gabriel Allon could justify putting a woman like that into such danger.

He glanced around the lobby. He knew that they were here, somewhere, hidden among the tourists and the businessmen and the hotel employees: Shamron's watchers. Tariq had stretched their resources by taking the woman from London to Paris and then Montreal. But surely they had regrouped and moved their assets into place. He knew that the moment he approached the woman he would be revealing himself to his enemies for the first time.

He found that he was actually looking forward to it. Finally, after all these years in the shadows, he was about to step into the light. He wanted to shout: *Here I am. See, I'm a man like you, flesh and blood, not a monster.* He was not ashamed of his life's work. Quite the opposite. He was proud of it. He wondered if Allon could say the same thing.

Tariq knew that he had one major advantage over Allon. He knew he was about to die. His life was over. He had survived on the knife edge of danger to be betrayed in the end not by his enemies but by his own body. He would use the knowledge of his impending death like a weapon, the most powerful he had ever possessed.

Tariq stood up, smoothed the front of his blazer, and crossed the lobby.

They rode an elevator to the fourteenth floor, walked along a quiet corridor, stopped at room 1417. He opened the door with an electronic card key, then slipped the card into his pocket. When Jacqueline entered the room, Shamron's awareness and memory drills took over: small suite, separate bedroom and sitting room. On the coffee table was a room service tray with a half-eaten salad. A garment bag lay on the floor, open, still packed.

He held out his hand. "Lucien Daveau."

"Dominique Bonard."

He smiled: warm, confident. "I was told by my associates that you were a very beautiful woman, but I'm afraid their descriptions did not do you justice."

His mannerisms and speech were all very French. If she had not known he was a Palestinian, she would have assumed he was a well-to-do Parisian.

"You're not what I expected," she said truthfully.

"Oh, really? What did you expect?" He was already testing her—she could sense it.

"Yusef said you were an intellectual. I suppose I was

expecting someone with long hair and blue jeans and a sweater with holes in it."

"Someone more professorial?"

"Yes, that's the word." She managed a smile. "You don't look terribly *professorial*."

"That's because I'm not a professor."

"I'd ask what you are, but Yusef told me not to ask too many questions, so I suppose we'll just have to make pleasant small talk."

"It's been a long time since I made pleasant small talk with a beautiful woman. I think I'm going to enjoy the next few days immensely."

"Have you been in Montreal long?"

"You just asked me a question, Dominique."

"I'm sorry. I just—"

"Don't apologize. I was just joking. I arrived this morning. As you can see, I haven't had a chance to unpack."

She walked from the sitting room into the bedroom.

He said, "Don't worry. I intend to sleep on the couch tonight."

"I thought we were supposed to be posing as lovers."

"We are."

"What if the hotel staff notices that you slept on the couch?"

"They might assume we're quarreling. Or they might assume that I was working late and didn't want to disturb you and that I fell asleep on the couch."

"They might."

"Yusef said you were intelligent, but he neglected to say that you also possess a conspiratorial mind."

It had played out long enough. Jacqueline was proud of the fact that *she* was guiding the conversation and not he. It gave her the sense that at least she was in control of *something*.

"Do you mind if I smoke?"

"Not at all."

She placed a cigarette between her lips and struck the lighter Shamron had given her. She could almost imagine the radio waves flying out, searching for a receiver.

"I didn't bring clothing for this kind of weather. Leila said you would take me out shopping for something warmer."

"I'd be happy to. I apologize for the way we had to keep you in the dark about where you were going. I assure you it was quite necessary."

"I understand." A pause. "I suppose."

"Answer one question for me, Dominique. Why did you agree to come on this mission with me? Do you believe in what you are doing? Or are you doing it simply for love?"

The coincidence of his question was almost too vulgar to contemplate. She calmly placed the lighter back into her handbag and said, "I'm doing it because I believe in love. Do you believe in love?"

"I believe in the right of my people to have a homeland of our own choosing. I've never had the luxury of love."

"I'm sorry—" She was about to call him Lucien, but for some reason she stopped herself.

"You don't want to say my name, Dominique? Why won't you call me Lucien?"

"Because I know it isn't your real name."

"How do you know that?"

"Yusef told me."

"Do you know my real name?"

"No, Yusef wouldn't tell me."

"Yusef is a good man."

"I'm very fond of him."

"Is Dominique really your name?"

She was caught off guard. "What are you talking about?"

"It's a simple question, really. I want to know if your name is really Dominique."

"You've seen my passport."

"Passports can easily be forged."

"Maybe for people like you!" she snapped. "Listen, Lucien, or whatever the fuck your name is, I don't like your question. It's making me uncomfortable."

He sat down and rubbed his temples. "I'm sorry, you're right. Please accept my apology. The politics of the Middle East tend to make one paranoid after a while. I hope you'll forgive me."

"I need to check my machine in London."

"Of course." He reached out and pressed the speaker button on the telephone. "Tell me the number, and I'll dial it for you."

She recited the number, and his fingers worked over the keypad. A few seconds later she heard the phone ringing—the two-beat moan of a British phone—followed by the sound of her own voice on the message tape. She pictured a technician, seated behind a computer console in Tel Aviv, reading the words *Hotel Queen Elizabeth, Montreal, Room 1417*. She reached out for the receiver, but he covered it with his hand and looked up at her. "I'd like to listen, if you don't mind. Paranoia is creeping up on me again."

She had three messages. The first was from a woman who identified herself as Dominique's mother. The second was from Julian Isherwood—he had misplaced a file and was wondering if she could give him a ring at some point to help him locate it. The third was from a man who didn't identify himself. She instantly recognized the sound of Gabriel's voice. *"I just wanted you to know that I was thinking of you. If you need anything I'm here for you. See you soon, I hope. Cheers."*

"You can hang up now."

He punched the speaker button and severed the connection. "That didn't sound much like Yusef."

"It wasn't Yusef. It was a man I knew before Yusef."

"It sounds to me as though this man still cares for you."

"No, he never really cared for me."

"But it's obvious to me you cared for him. Perhaps you still do."

"I'm in love with Yusef."

"Ah, yes, I forgot." He stood abruptly. "Let's go shopping."

# 38

## MONTREAL

Zvi Yadin met Gabriel and Shamron at the airport and drove them into Montreal. He had thick, curly hair, a rather shaggy full beard, and the body of a rugby player. Because he was large, people tended to think he was stupid, which he was not. Gabriel had spent time at the Academy with him. They had been paired for the physical combat course, despite the vast difference in their size. On the final day Yadin had broken two of Gabriel's ribs. Gabriel had retaliated with an elbow to Yadin's chin that dislocated his jaw. Later, when they were being patched up in the infirmary, Yadin had admitted that Shamron had put him up to it—that he had wanted to test Gabriel's capacity for pain. Gabriel wished he had broken Shamron's jaw instead.

"They say it's going to be thirty below tonight," Yadin said as he sped along the motorway toward downtown. "I brought you some parkas and gloves. And I brought this for you, Gabriel."

He handed Gabriel a stainless steel combat case. Inside was a .22 Beretta target pistol. Gabriel stroked the barrel and the walnut grip. The gun felt cold. He closed the lid and placed the case beneath the seat.

Shamron said, "Thanks for the weather update, Zvi, but where the hell is Jacqueline?"

Yadin brought them quickly up-to-date. The flight from Paris had arrived twenty minutes late. Yadin's team had picked them up after they cleared immigration and customs. The girl had rented a car from Hertz and driven downtown to the Hotel Queen Elizabeth. She'd handed Jacqueline to a man: forties, well dressed, decent-looking. They went upstairs to a room. Yadin had a *sayan* on the hotel staff: a senior concierge. He said the fellow in question had checked into the hotel earlier that day under the name Lucien Daveau. Room 1417.

"Pictures?" Shamron asked hopefully.

"No way, boss. Not possible under the circumstances."

"Was it Tariq?"

"Could have been. Hard to say."

"What happened to the girl?"

"After the handoff she left the hotel. She was picked up by another car outside on the boulevard René Lévesque. I didn't try to follow her. I didn't think we could spare the personnel."

"How many people do you have?"

"Three experienced men and that new girl you sent me from the Academy."

"How are they deployed?"

"Two members of the team are in the hotel lobby

pretending to be shopping. The other two are outside in the car."

Gabriel said, "Can our friend on the concierge desk get us inside the room?"

"Sure."

"I want to put a glass on his telephone."

"No problem. I brought a kit from Ottawa. We can get another room at the hotel to set up a listening post. It will tie down one member of the team, though."

"Getting his phone is well worth one member of your team."

"I'll use the new girl."

"No, I may need the girl for street work."

Yadin glanced at Shamron. "Now for the problems, boss."

"What problems?"

"Lev."

"What about Lev?"

"While I was waiting for you to arrive, I checked in with the station."

"And?"

"Mordecai called on a routine housekeeping matter after we'd left. Obviously he told Lev the entire station was missing, because Lev fired off a cable from the operations center about a half hour later, wondering what the fuck was going on."

"What was Lev told?" Shamron said wearily.

"I left a cover story in place with our secretary. She told Lev that we received a tip from a friend in the Canadian service that a member of Islamic Jihad might be living in Quebec City and that we had run up to QC to have a look at him. Lev sends another rocket: *On whose authority? Please supply the name of IJ Activist.* So on and so forth. You get the picture, boss."

Shamron swore softly. "Send him a message when you get home. Tell him it was a false alarm."

"Listen, boss, we go back a long way. But you're going to retire again soon, and Lev may be running this place. He could make my life miserable. He enjoys that sort of thing. He's a bastard."

"Let me worry about Lev. You were just doing what I told you to do."

"Just following orders—right, boss?"

Yadin's cell phone chirped softly. He flipped open the mouthpiece and brought it to his ear. "Yes?"

A pause.

"When?"

Another pause.

"Where?"

Another pause, slightly longer.

"Stay with them. But remember who you're dealing with. Keep a safe distance."

He severed the connection and tossed the phone onto the dash.

"What is it?" asked Shamron.

"He's on the move."

"What about Jacqueline?"

"They're together."

"Where?"

"Look's like they've gone shopping."

"Get me a picture, Zvi. I need to make sure it's him."

There are two Montreals. There is the Montreal of the surface. In winter it becomes a snowbound tundra. Icy Arctic winds roar between the skyscrapers and prowl the winding alleyways of the Old City down by the river. Then there is underground Montreal: a labyrinth of gleaming shops, cafés, bars, markets, and designer clothing stores that snakes its way beneath much of downtown, making it possible to travel for blocks without ever setting foot outside.

A fitting spot for it to end, thought Jacqueline; two worlds, two layers, two realities. *I'm Jacqueline Delacroix, the model. I'm Dominique Bonard, the secretary from Isherwood Fine Arts in London. I'm Sarah Halévy, the Jewish girl from Marseilles, the agent from the Office.* She had more layers than Montreal.

She was walking at his side. His hand was resting lightly on her shoulder, and he was using it to guide her through the crowds of evening shoppers. Jacqueline studied the kaleidoscope of faces streaming past her: pretty French boys and girls, Arabs, Africans, Jews—the ethnic patchwork quilt that is Montreal. She might have forgotten she had ever left Paris except for the blunt edge of their French accents.

He was checking to see if they were being followed—

Jacqueline could see that. Pausing in storefronts, making abrupt changes in direction, inventing excuses to double back. She hoped Shamron's team was good. If they weren't, Tariq was going to spot them.

They walked through the exclusive shops beneath the rue St-Catherine. In one she picked out a full-length down-lined coat. In another a fur hat. In a third two pairs of jeans and several pairs of long underwear. Finally, in a shop specializing in outdoor goods, she picked out a pair of insulated boots. He hung at her side the entire time. When she went into a changing room to try on the jeans he waited just outside the door and smiled pleasantly at the salesgirls. He paid for everything with a credit card in the name of Lucien Daveau.

When they were finished they walked back toward the hotel. She thought: *What are you waiting for? Do it now. Take him down.* But they couldn't do it here—not in underground Montreal. The entire network of shopping malls could be sealed off in a matter of minutes. Gabriel and the rest of the team would be trapped inside. They would be arrested and questioned. The police would establish a link to the Office, and the whole thing would blow up in Shamron's face.

He suggested a coffee before dinner, so they stopped in an espresso bar a short distance from the hotel. Jacqueline flipped idly through a tourist guide while he sipped his drink. At one point he removed a prescription bottle from his pocket and swallowed two tablets. Five minutes later—she knew the exact time because she had been playing Shamron's awareness games throughout the excursion—a man in a gray business suit sat down at the next table. He placed his briefcase on the ground: black leather, soft sides, gold combination latches. The man stayed for a few minutes, then stood and walked away, leaving the bag behind. When Tariq had finished his coffee, he nonchalantly picked up the bag along with Jacqueline's parcels.

Two Montreals, two realities, thought Jacqueline as they walked back to the hotel. In one reality they had just gone shopping. In the other Tariq had spent an hour checking to see if he was being followed, and Tariq had taken possession of his gun.

Gabriel appeared at the concierge desk and asked directions to a good restaurant. The concierge was called Jean—small and neat, with the thin mustache and frozen smile of an accomplished hotelier. Gabriel spoke rapid French. The concierge answered him in the same language. He told Gabriel about an excellent Parisian-style bistro called the Alexandre; then he handed him a folded tourist map and told him the address. Gabriel tucked the map into the inside breast pocket of his jacket, thanked the concierge, and walked away. But instead of heading toward the street entrance, he strode across the lobby, boarded an elevator, and rode it to the fourteenth floor.

He walked quickly along the corridor. In his right hand was a plastic shopping bag from one of the boutiques in the lobby, and inside the bag was a hotel telephone, wrapped in tissue paper. As he approached the door he removed the map from his breast pocket and unfolded it. Inside was the credit card–style key to Tariq's room. A Do Not Disturb sign hung from the latch. Gabriel slipped the card key in and out of the door slot, then stepped into the room and quietly closed the door.

For their command post Yadin had taken a suite at the Sheraton, a few blocks up the boulevard René Lévesque from the Queen Elizabeth. When Gabriel entered the suite, Shamron was there, along with Yadin and a black-haired girl whom Yadin introduced as Deborah. She reminded Gabriel a great deal of Leah, more than he might have wished at that moment. A large-scale street map of Montreal was spread over the bed. Shamron had shoved his glasses onto his forehead and was rubbing the bridge of his nose as he paced. Gabriel poured himself a cup of coffee and held it tightly to warm his hands.

Yadin said, "They're back in the room. The glass is picking up their conversation perfectly. Nice work, Gabriel."

"What are they saying?"

"Small talk, mostly. I'll send a man over to collect the tapes. If there's anything urgent, the boy in the room will call."

"Where'd they go while they were out?"

"Shopping, mainly, but we think Tariq may have a gun."

Gabriel lowered his coffee cup and looked up sharply.

"Deborah was following them at the time," Yadin said. "She saw the whole thing."

She quickly described the scene at the coffee bar. She spoke English with an American accent.

"How's Jacqueline holding up?"

"She looked good. A little tired but fine."

The telephone rang. Yadin picked it up before it could ring a second time. He listened for a moment without speaking, then set down the receiver and looked up at Shamron. "He just booked a table at a restaurant on the rue St-Denis."

"What's the area like?"

"Cafés, shops, bars, discos, that sort of thing," said Yadin. "Very busy, very bohemian."

"The kind of place we could mount a surveillance operation?"

"Absolutely."

"The kind of place where a *kidon* might be able to get close to a target?"

"No problem."

Gabriel said, "What about escape routes?"

"We'd have several," Yadin said. "You could head north into Outremont or Mont-Royal or go south, straight to the expressway. The rest of the team could melt into the Old City."

There was a soft knock outside. Yadin murmured a few words through the closed door, then opened it. A boyish-looking man with fair hair and blue eyes entered the room.

"I've got them on videotape."

Shamron said, "Let's see it."

The young man connected the handheld recorder to the television set and played the tape: Jacqueline and the man called Lucien Daveau, moving through the underground mall. It had been shot from a balustrade one level up.

Shamron smiled. "It's him. No question."

Gabriel said, "How can you tell from that angle?"

"Look at him. Look at the photographs. It's the same man."

"You're certain?"

"Yes, I'm certain!" Shamron shut off the television. "What's wrong with you, Gabriel?"

"I just don't want to kill the wrong man."

"It's Tariq. Trust me." Shamron looked down at the street map of Montreal. "Zvi, show me the rue St-Denis. I want to end this thing tonight and go home."

# 39

MONTREAL

They left the hotel room at eight o'clock, rode the elevator down to the lobby. The evening check-in rush had ended. A Japanese couple was having their picture taken by a stranger. Tariq paused, turned around, and theatrically beat his pockets as if he were missing something important. When the photo session ended he resumed walking. A roar rose from the hotel bar: Americans watching a football game on television. They rode an escalator down to underground Montreal, then walked a short distance to a Metro station. He made a point of keeping her to his right. She remembered he was left-handed—obviously he didn't want her in a position to grab his arm if he had to go for his gun. She tried to remember what kind of gun he preferred. A Makarov; that was it. Tariq liked the Makarov.

He moved through the station as if he knew the way. They boarded a train and rode east to the rue St-Denis. When they stepped outside on the crowded boulevard, the bitter cold nearly took her breath away.

*It may happen someplace quiet, completely out of sight, or it may happen in the middle of a busy street. . . .*

She kept her eyes down and resisted the impulse to look for him.

*You may see me coming, you may not. If you do see me, you're not to look at me. You're not to flinch or call out my name. You're not to make a sound.* . . . .

"Is something wrong?" He spoke without looking at her.

"I'm just freezing to death."

"The restaurant isn't far."

They walked past a row of bars. The ragged sound of a blues band spilled from a cellar tavern. A used-record store. A vegetarian restaurant. A tattoo parlor. A gang of skinhead boys walked past them. One of them said something crude to Jacqueline. Tariq eyed him coldly; the boy shut his mouth and walked away.

They arrived at the restaurant. It was in an old Victorian house, set slightly back from the street. He guided her up the steps. The maître d' helped them off with their coats and showed them upstairs to a table by the window. Tariq sat facing out. She could see his eyes scanning the street below. When the waiter appeared, Jacqueline ordered a glass of Bordeaux.

"Monsieur Daveau?"

"Just some sparkling water, please," he said. "I'm afraid I have a bit of a headache tonight."

The Italian restaurant was a half block to the north, on the opposite side of the rue St-Denis. To reach it Gabriel and Deborah had to descend a short flight of icy steps.

The tables next to the window were all filled, but they were seated close enough so that Gabriel could see Jacqueline's long black hair in the window across the street. Shamron and Zvi Yadin were outside in a rented van. At the southern end of the block, closer to the edge of the Old City, one of Yadin's men sat behind the wheel of the getaway car. Another man waited in a car one block to the west on the rue Sanguinet. Tariq was in a box.

Gabriel ordered wine but drank none of it. He ordered a salad and a bowl of pasta, but the odor of food nauseated him. The girl was well schooled in Office doctrine. She was carrying him. She flirted with the waiter. She talked to a couple at another table. She devoured her food and part of Gabriel's. She held his hand. Once again Gabriel found uncomfortable comparisons with Leah. Her scent. The flecks of gold in her nearly black eyes. The way her long hands floated when she spoke. Gabriel looked out the window at the pavement of the rue St-Denis, but in his mind he was back in Vienna, sitting with Leah and Dani in the trattoria in the Jewish Quarter.

He was sweating. He could feel cold water running down the groove at the center of his back, sweat running over his ribs. The Beretta was in the front pocket of his parka, the parka hanging over the back of his chair, so that Gabriel could feel the comforting weight of the gun pressing against his thigh. The girl was talking—"Maybe we should get away," she was saying. "The Caribbean, St. Bart's, someplace warm with good food and wine." Gabriel was listening to her with one corner of his mind—he was nodding at appropriate times and even managed a few words now and again—but for the most part he was visualizing how he would kill Tariq. He took no pleasure from these thoughts. He engaged in them not out of rage or a desire to inflict punishment but in the same way he might plot a tacking maneuver through a particularly difficult stretch of wind and water; or the way he might mend a bare spot in a five-hundred-year-old canvas.

He visualized what would happen after Tariq was down. Deborah would look after herself. Gabriel was responsible for Jacqueline. He would grab her and move away from the body as quickly as possible. One of Yadin's men would pick them up on the rue St-Denis in a rental car, a green Ford, and they would head toward the airport. They would switch cars once along the way. At the airport they would go directly to the private aviation terminal and board Benjamin Stone's jet. If things went according to plan, he would be back in Israel by the following afternoon.

If they didn't . . .

Gabriel pushed the image of failure from his mind.

Just then his cell phone chirped softly. He brought it to his ear, listened without speaking. He severed the connection, handed the telephone to the girl, stood up, pulled on his coat. The Beretta banged against his hip. He reached into the pocket of the parka, held the gun by its grip.

He had paid the check ahead of time so he wouldn't cause a scene when the time came to leave. The girl led the way through the restaurant. Gabriel was burning. Outside, he slipped and nearly fell climbing the stairs. The girl caught his arm and steadied him. When they reached the sidewalk there was no sign of Tariq and Jacqueline. Gabriel turned and faced the girl. He kissed her on the cheek, then brought his mouth close to her ear. "Tell me when you see them."

He buried his face against the side of the girl's neck. Her hair covered his face. She smelled shockingly of Leah. He held her with his left hand. His right was still in his coat pocket, wrapped around the grip of the Beretta.

He rehearsed it one last time. It played out in his head like an Academy lecture. Turn around, walk directly toward him. Don't hesitate or loiter, just walk. Get close, draw the gun with your right hand, start shooting. Don't think about the bystanders, think only of the target. Become the terrorist. Cease being the terrorist only when he is dead. The spare clip is in your left pocket if you need it. Don't get caught. You are a prince. You are more valuable than anyone else. Do anything to avoid capture. If a policeman challenges you, kill the policeman. Under no circumstances are you to allow yourself to be arrested.

"There they are."

She gave him a slight push to separate their bodies. Gabriel turned and started across the street, taking his eyes off Tariq just long enough to make certain he wasn't walking into the path of a car. His hand was making the gun wet. He could hear nothing except his own breathing and the hiss of blood rushing through his inner ears. Jacqueline looked up. Their eyes met for a fraction of a second; then she abruptly looked away. Tariq took her by the elbow.

As Gabriel pulled the Beretta from his pocket, a car careened around the corner and accelerated toward him. He had no choice but to quickly step out of the way. Then the car skidded to a halt, with Gabriel on one side and Tariq and Jacqueline on the other.

The rear door facing Tariq flew open. He pulled Jacqueline forward and forced her into the car. Her handbag fell from her shoulder and tumbled into the street. Tariq smiled wolfishly at Gabriel and climbed into the backseat next to Jacqueline.

The car sped away. Gabriel crossed the street and picked up Jacqueline's purse. Then he went back to the restaurant and collected the girl. Together they walked up the rue St-Denis. Gabriel opened Jacqueline's purse and thumbed through the contents. Inside was her wallet, her passport, some makeup, and the gold lighter Shamron had given her at the gallery.

"You should have taken the shot, Gabriel!"

"I didn't have a shot!"

"You had a shot over the roof of that car!"

"Bullshit!"

"You had a shot, but you hesitated!"

"I *hesitated* because if I had missed that shot over the roof of the car, the bullet would have ended up in the restaurant across the street, and you might have a dead bystander on your hands."

"You never used to consider the possibility of missing."

The van accelerated away from the curb. Gabriel was seated on the floor of the rear cargo bay, the girl opposite him, knees beneath her chin, eyeing him intently. Gabriel closed his eyes and tried to think calmly for a moment. It was a complete disaster. Jacqueline was gone. She had no passport, no identification, and, more important, no tracking beacon. They'd had one major advantage over Tariq: the ability to know where she was all the time. Now that advantage had vanished.

He pictured the sequence of events: Tariq and Jacqueline leaving the restaurant; the car appearing out of nowhere; Tariq pushing Jacqueline into the backseat; Tariq's wolfish smile.

Gabriel closed his eyes and saw the ghostly image of Tariq beckoning him forward with a Van Dyck hand. *He knew all along,* thought Gabriel. *He knew it was me coming for him on the rue St-Denis. He led me there.*

Shamron was talking again. "Your first responsibility was to Jacqueline. Not to someone in a bistro behind her. You should have taken the shot, regardless of the consequences!"

"Even if I'd managed to hit him, Jacqueline still would be gone. She was in the car, the engine was running. They were going to take her, and there was nothing I could have done to stop it."

"You should have fired at the car. We might have been able to trap them on that street."

"Is that what you wanted? A gunfight in the middle of Montreal? A shoot-out? You would have had another Lillehammer on your hands. Another Amman. Another disaster for the Office."

Shamron turned around, glared at Gabriel, then stared straight ahead.

Gabriel said, "What now, Ari?"

"We find them."

"How?"

"We have a very good idea where they're going."

"We can't find Tariq in the States alone."

"What are you suggesting, Gabriel?"

"We need to alert the Americans that he's probably coming their way. We need to tell the Canadians too. Maybe they can prevent him from taking her across the border. If we get lucky they might be able to stop them before they reach the border."

"Tell the Americans and the Canadians? Tell them what, exactly? Tell them that we intended to assassinate a Palestinian on Canadian soil? Tell them that we botched the job, and now we'd like their help cleaning up the mess? I don't think that would go over very well in Ottawa or Washington."

"So what do we do? Sit on our hands and wait?"

"No, we go to America, and we tighten security around the prime minister. Tariq didn't come all this way for nothing. Eventually he has to make his move."

"And what if his target isn't the prime minister?"

"The security of the prime minister is my only concern at this point."

"I'm sure Jacqueline would be pleased to know this."

"You know what I mean, Gabriel. Don't play word games with me."

"You've forgotten one thing, Ari. She doesn't have a passport any longer." Gabriel held up her handbag. "It's here. How are they going to get her across the border without a passport?"

"Obviously, Tariq's made other arrangements."

"Or maybe he doesn't intend to take her across the border. Maybe he's going to kill her first."

"That's why you should have taken the shot, Gabriel."

# 40

## SABREVOIS, QUEBEC

Jacqueline had tried to follow the road signs. Route 40 through Montreal. Route 10 across the river. Route 35 into the countryside. Now this: Route 133, a two-lane provincial road stretching across the tabletop of southern Quebec. Strange how quickly cosmopolitan Montreal had given way to this vast empty space. A brittle moon floated above the horizon, ringed by a halo of ice. Wind-driven snow swirled across the asphalt like a sandstorm. Occasionally an object floated out of the gloom. A grain silo poking above the snow cover. A dimly lit farmhouse. A blacked-out agricultural supply store. Ahead she saw neon lights. As they drew closer she could see that the lights formed the outlines of women with enormous breasts: a strip joint in the middle of nowhere. She wondered where they got the girls. Maybe they enjoyed watching their sisters and girlfriends dance topless. *Desolation,* she thought. *This is why the word was created.*

After an hour of driving they were just a few miles from the U.S. border. She thought: *How's he going to take me across when my passport and the rest of my things are lying back on the rue St-Denis in Montreal?*

*My passport and the cigarette lighter with the beacon . . .*

It had all happened so quickly. After spotting Gabriel she had looked away and prepared herself for what she thought would happen next. Then the car appeared, and he pushed her inside so roughly that her handbag fell from her grasp. As the car sped away she yelled at him to go back and let her get her bag, but he ignored her and told the driver to go faster. It was then that Jacqueline noticed the woman she knew as Leila was driving the car. A few blocks away they switched cars. The driver was the same man who had left his briefcase for Tariq in the underground coffee bar. This time they drove several blocks to the part of Montreal known as Ou-tremont. There they switched cars one last time. Now Tariq was driving.

He was sweating. Jacqueline could see the shine on his skin in the lime-colored glow of the dashboard lights. His face had turned deathly white, dark circles beneath his eyes, right hand shaking.

"Would you like to explain to me what happened back there in Montreal?"

"It was a routine security precaution."

"You call that routine? If it was so routine, why didn't you let me go back and get my purse?"

"From time to time I find myself under surveillance by Israeli intelligence and by their friends in the West.

I'm also monitored by my enemies within the Palestinian movement. My instincts told me that *someone* was watching us in Montreal."

"That charade cost me my handbag and everything in it."

"Don't worry, Dominique. I'll replace your things."

"Some things can't be replaced."

"Like your gold cigarette lighter?"

Jacqueline felt a stab of pain in her abdomen. She remembered Yusef toying with the lighter on the way to the council flat in Hounslow. *Christ, he knows.* She changed the subject. "Actually, I was thinking about my passport."

"Your passport can be replaced too. I'll take you to the French consulate in Montreal. You'll tell them that it was lost or stolen, and they'll issue a new one."

*No, they'll discover it was forged, and I'll end up in a Canadian jail.*

"Why do these people watch you?"

"Because they want to know where I'm going and who I am meeting with."

"Why?"

"Because they don't want me to succeed."

"What are you trying to accomplish that would make them so concerned?"

"I'm just trying to bring a little justice to the so-called peace process. I don't want my people to accept a sliver of our ancestral land just because the Americans and a handful of Israelis are willing to let us have it now. They offer us crumbs that fall from their table. I don't want the crumbs, Dominique. I want the entire loaf."

"Half a loaf is better than nothing."

"I respectfully disagree."

A highway sign floated out of the swirling snow. The border was three miles ahead.

Jacqueline said, "Where are you taking me?"

"To the other side."

"So how do you intend to get me across the border without a passport?"

"We've made other arrangements."

"*Other* arrangements? What kind of other arrangements?"

"I have another passport for you. A Canadian passport."

"How did you get a Canadian passport?"

Another sign: the border was now two miles ahead.

"It's not yours, of course."

"Hold on a minute! Yusef promised you wouldn't ask me to do anything illegal."

"You're not doing anything illegal. It's an open border, and the passport is perfectly valid."

"It might be valid, but it's not mine!"

"It doesn't matter if it's not yours. No one's going to question you."

"I'm not going to enter the United States on a false passport! Stop the car! I want out!"

"If I let you out here you'll freeze to death before you ever reach safety."

"Then drop me somewhere! Just let me out!"

"Dominique, this is why we brought you from London: to help me get across this border."

"You lied to me! You and Yusef!"

"Yes, we found it necessary to mislead you slightly."

"Slightly!"

"But none of that matters now. What matters is that I need to get across this border, and I need your help."

The border was now a mile away. Ahead she could see the bright white lights of the crossing. She wondered what to do. She supposed she could simply tell him no. Then what would he do? Turn around, kill her, dump her body into the snow, and cross the border on his own. She considered deceiving him: saying yes and then alerting the officer at the crossing point. But Tariq would just kill her *and* the border patrolman. There would be an investigation, the Office's role in the affair would come to light. It would be an embarrassing fiasco for Ari Shamron. She had only one option. Play the game a little longer and find some way to alert Gabriel.

She said, "Let me see the passport."

He handed it to her.

She opened it and looked at the name: Hélène Sarrault. Then she looked at the photograph: Leila. The likeness was vague but convincing.

"You'll do it?"

Jacqueline said, "Keep driving."

He entered the plaza at the border crossing and braked to a halt. A border patrolman stepped out of his booth and said, "Good evening. Where are you headed this evening?"

Tariq said, "Burlington."

"Business or pleasure?"

"My sister is ill, I'm afraid."

"Sorry to hear that. How long are you planning to stay?"

"One day, two at the most."

"Passports, please."

Tariq handed them across. The officer opened them and examined the photographs and the names. Then he looked into the car and glanced at each of their faces.

He closed the passports and handed them back. "Have a pleasant stay. And drive carefully. Weather report says there's a big storm coming in later tonight."

Tariq took the passports, dropped the car into gear, and drove slowly across the border into Vermont. He placed the passports in his pocket and a moment later, when they were well clear of the border, he removed a Makarov pistol and placed the barrel against the side of her head.

# 41

## WASHINGTON, D.C.

Yasir Arafat sat behind the desk in the presidential suite at the Madison Hotel, making his way through a stack of paperwork, listening to the late-evening traffic hissing along the damp pavement of Fifteenth Street. He paused for a moment, popped a Tunisian date into his mouth, then swallowed a few spoonfuls of yogurt. He was fastidious about his diet, did not smoke or consume alcohol, and never drank coffee. It had helped him survive a demanding revolutionary lifestyle that might have destroyed other men.

Because he was expecting no more visitors that evening, he had changed out of his uniform into a blue tracksuit. His bald head was bare, and as usual he had several days' growth on his pouchy face. He wore reading glasses, which magnified his froglike eyes. His thick lower lip jutted out, giving him the appearance of a child on the verge of tears.

He possessed a near-photographic memory for written material and faces, which allowed him to work through the stack of documents quickly, pausing now and then to scribble notes in the margins of memoranda or sign his name. He was now in charge of the Gaza Strip and a large portion of the West Bank, a development that had seemed impossible only a few years earlier. His Palestinian Authority was responsible for the mundane details of ordinary governance, like trash collection and schools. It was a far cry from the old days, when he had been the world's most famous guerrilla.

He set aside the remainder of his work and opened a document bound in a leather cover. It was a copy of the interim agreement he was to sign the following day at the United Nations in New York. The agreement was yet another incremental step toward the fulfillment of his life's work: the establishment of a Palestinian state. It was much less than he had wanted when he set out on this path—back then he had dreamed of the destruction of Israel—but it was the best he was going to get. There were some within the movement who wished him failure, some who even wished him death. The rejectionists, the dreamers. If they'd had their way, the Palestinians would be forever condemned to the refugee camps of the diaspora.

An aide knocked on the door. Arafat looked up as he entered the room. "Sorry to disturb you, Abu Amar, but the president is on the phone."

Arafat smiled. This too would have been impossible only a few years earlier. "What does he want so late at night?"

"He says his wife is out of town and he's bored. He

wants to know whether you would be willing to come to the White House and keep him company."

"Now?"

"Yes, now."

"To do what?"

The aide shrugged. "Talk, I suppose."

"Tell him I'll be there in ten minutes."

Arafat stood up, removed his tracksuit, and dressed in his usual plain khaki uniform and traditional Palestinian headdress. He wore the black-and-white kaffiyeh of the peasant with the front shaped to a point to symbolize the map of Palestine. The aide reappeared with an overcoat and draped it over Arafat's shoulders. Together they stepped into the hall and were immediately surrounded by a group of security men. Some were members of his personal bodyguard, the rest were officers of the U.S. Diplomatic Security Service. They moved down the corridor, Arafat in the center of the party, and stepped into a private elevator, which whisked them downward to the garage. There Arafat slipped into the back of a limousine. A moment later his motorcade was speeding south on Fifteenth Street toward the White House.

Arafat looked out his window. A bit like the old days, this late-night dash through wet streets—like the days when he never spent two nights in a row in the same bed. Sometimes he even switched residences in the middle of the night when his well-tuned instincts sensed trouble. He avoided public places—never ate in restaurants, never went to the cinema or the theater. His skin turned blotchy from lack of sun. His survival skills had thwarted hundreds of attempts on his life by the Israelis and his enemies within the movement. Some had not been so lucky. He thought of his old friend and second in command, Abu Jihad. He had led the war effort in the Occupied Territories; helped to organize the *intifada*. And for that the Israelis had murdered him in his villa in Tunis. Arafat knew that without Abu Jihad he would not be where he was today: driving across Washington for a secret meeting with the American president. It was a shame his old friend was not here to see this.

The motorcade passed through the barricade on Pennsylvania Avenue and entered the White House grounds. A moment later Arafat's car stopped beneath the shelter of the North Portico.

A Marine guard stepped forward and opened the door. "Good evening, Mr. Arafat. Right this way, please."

President James Beckwith was waiting in the drawing room of the residence in the Executive Mansion. He looked as though he had just stepped off the deck of his sailboat. He wore a pair of wrinkled khaki trousers and a crewneck pullover sweater. He was a tall man with a full head of silver hair and a genteel manner. His permanently tanned face projected youth and exuberance, despite the fact that he was nearly seventy years old.

They sat in front of the fire, Beckwith nursing a glass of whiskey, Arafat sipping tea sweetened with honey. When Beckwith had been in the Senate he had been one of Israel's staunchest allies and led the opposition to U.S. recognition of the PLO—indeed, he had regularly referred to Arafat and the PLO as "bloodthirsty terrorists." Now the two men were close allies in the quest for peace in the Middle East. Each needed the help of the other to succeed. Arafat needed Beckwith to press the Israelis to make concessions at the negotiating table. Beckwith needed Arafat to keep the radicals and fundamentalists in line so the talks could continue.

After an hour Beckwith raised the murders of Ambassador Eliyahu and David Morgenthau. "My CIA director tells me your old friend Tariq was probably behind both attacks, but they have no proof."

Arafat smiled. "I've never doubted for a moment that it was Tariq. But if your CIA thinks they're going to find *proof* of this, I'm afraid they're sadly mistaken. Tariq doesn't operate that way."

"If he continues to kill Jews, it's going to make it more difficult to keep moving toward a final settlement."

"Forgive my bluntness, Mr. President, but Tariq is only a factor if you and the Israelis allow him to be a factor. He does not act on my behalf. He does not operate from territory controlled by the Palestinian Authority. He does not speak for those Palestinians who want peace."

"All true, but isn't there anything you can do to dissuade him?"

"Tariq?" Arafat shook his head slowly. "We *were* close friends once. He was one of my finest intelligence officers. But he left me over the decision to renounce terrorism and begin peace talks. We haven't spoken in years."

"Perhaps he might listen to you now."

"I'm afraid Tariq listens to no voice but his own. He's a man haunted by demons."

"All of us are, especially when you reach my age."

"*And* mine," said Arafat. "But I'm afraid Tariq is haunted by a different kind of demon. You see, he's a young man who's dying, and he wants to settle accounts before he leaves."

Beckwith raised his eyebrows in surprise. "Dying?"

"According to my sources he has a severe brain tumor."

"Do the Israelis know this?"

"Yes," Arafat said. "I've told them myself."

"Who?"

"Their chief of intelligence, Ari Shamron."

"I wonder why their chief of intelligence neglected to share this piece of information with the Central Intelligence Agency."

Arafat laughed. "I suppose you've never met Ari Shamron. He's crafty and a warrior from the old school. Shamron makes a habit of never letting the left hand know what the right is doing. Do you know the motto of the Israeli secret service?"

"I'm afraid I don't."

" 'By way of deception, thou shalt do war.' Ari Shamron lives by those words."

"You think Shamron might be playing some game?"

"Anything's possible when it comes to Shamron. You see, there are some people inside the Israeli secret service who want Tariq dead, whatever the political costs. But there are others, I'm afraid, who would like to see him succeed."

"Into which category does Shamron fall?"

Arafat frowned. "I wish I knew."

Shortly before midnight the president walked Arafat down to his waiting car. They were a mismatched pair, the tall, patrician president and the little revolutionary in his olive drab and flowing kaffiyeh.

Beckwith said, "I understand you're attending a reception at the home of Douglas Cannon after the signing ceremony tomorrow. Douglas and I are good friends."

"He and I are friends as well. He saw the justness of the Palestinian cause long before most American politicians. It took a great amount of courage, considering the fact that he was a senator from New York, where the Jewish lobby is so powerful."

"Douglas always stood his ground and let the political chips fall where they might. That's what set him apart from most of the politicians in this damned town. Please give him my warmest regards when you see him."

"I will indeed."

They shook hands formally beneath the North Portico; then Arafat turned and walked toward his limousine.

"And do me one other favor, Mr. Arafat."

The Palestinian turned around and raised one eye-brow. "What's that?"

"Watch your back."

"Always," said Arafat. Then he climbed into the back of his car and disappeared from sight.

# 42

## BURLINGTON, VERMONT

"Your name is not Dominique Bonard, and you don't work for an art gallery in London. You work for Israeli intelligence. And we left Montreal the way we did because your friend Gabriel Allon was coming to kill me."

Jacqueline's mouth went dry. She felt as though her throat might close up. She remembered what Gabriel had told her in London: Dominique Bonard has nothing to fear from this man. If he pushes, push back.

"What the hell are you talking about? I don't know anyone named Gabriel Allon! Stop this fucking car! Where the fuck do you think you're taking me! What's wrong with you?"

He hit her in the side of the head with the gun: a short, brutal blow that instantly brought tears to her eyes. She reached up, touched her scalp, found blood. "You bastard!"

He ignored her. "Your name is not Dominique Bonard, and you don't work for an art gallery in London. You work for Ari Shamron. You're an Israeli agent. You're working with Gabriel Allon. That was Gabriel Allon who was crossing the street toward us in Montreal. He was coming to kill me."

"I wish you would just shut up about all this shit! I don't know what you're talking about! I don't know anyone named Gabriel, and I don't know anyone named Ari Shamron."

He hit her again, another blow that seemed to come out of nowhere. It landed in precisely the same spot. The pain was so intense that in spite of every effort she began to cry. "I'm telling you the truth!"

Another blow: harder.

"My name is Dominique Bonard! I work for—"

Another blow: harder still. She felt as though she was going to lose consciousness.

"You bastard," she said, weeping. She pressed her fingers against the wound. "Where are you taking me? What are you going to do to me?"

Once again he ignored her. If he was trying to drive her mad, it was working. When he spoke there was an edge of pity to his voice, as if he felt sorry for her. She knew what he was trying to do. He was trying to tear down the last of her resistance, to make her believe she had been betrayed and was completely alone.

"You went to Tunis with Gabriel Allon and posed as his lover while he planned the murder of Abu Jihad."

"I've never been to Tunis in my life, let alone with someone named Gabriel Allon!"

He lifted the gun to hit her again, but this time she

saw the blow coming and raised her hands in defense. "Please," she cried. "Don't hit me again."

He lowered the gun. Even he seemed to have no stomach for it.

"He's aged a bit since I saw him last. I suppose he has a right, considering everything he's been through."

Jacqueline felt her will to resist crumble. The reality of intelligence work set in. Before, it had been an adventure, something she did to make herself feel that she was more than just a face and a body. But this was the true nature of Ari Shamron's secret war. It was dirty and violent, and now she was caught in the middle of it. She had to think of some way to gain control of the situation. Perhaps she could discover his plans. Maybe she could find some way to warn Gabriel and Shamron. *Maybe I can find some way to survive.*

"They'll come for you," she said. "Half the police in Canada and America are probably looking for us right now. You'll never get to New York."

"Actually, I doubt anyone's looking for us but your friends Gabriel Allon and Shamron. I suspect they can't ask the Canadians for help, because the Canadians and Americans probably don't know they're here. If they found out now, it could prove very embarrassing to your service."

He reached into his pocket and handed her a handkerchief for her head. "By the way, we knew you were working for the Office the moment you walked into Yusef's life."

"How?"

"Do you really want to know this?"

"Yes."

"All right, but first you have to answer a few questions for me. Are you really French?"

*So,* she thought, *he doesn't know everything.* She said, "Yes, I'm French."

"Are you also Jewish?"

"Yes."

"Is Dominique Bonard your true name?"

"No."

"What is your real name?"

She thought: *What is my real name? Am I really Jacqueline Delacroix? No, that was just the name Marcel Lambert gave to a pretty young girl from Marseilles. If I'm going to die, I'm going to die with the name I was born with.*

"My name is Sarah," she said. "Sarah Halévy."

"Such a beautiful name. Well, Sarah Halévy, I suppose you're entitled to know how you ended up in a mess like this." He looked at her to see her reaction, but she stared back at him with icy hostility. "By the way, if you wish, you may call me Tariq."

He spoke for nearly an hour without stopping. He was clearly enjoying himself. After all, he had outmaneuvered one of the most feared intelligence services in the world. He told her how they had learned Gabriel had been brought back to the Office to find him. He told her

about the security alert they had issued to all their operatives in the field. He told her how Yusef had immediately
informed his control officer about the contact with the
attractive French woman.

"We told Yusef to continue seeing you while we
checked out your cover story in Paris. We discovered
a flaw; a minor flaw, but a flaw nonetheless. We made
photographs of you in London and compared them with
photographs of a woman who worked with Gabriel Allon
in Tunis. We told Yusef to deepen his relationship with
this Dominique Bonard. We told him to develop an emotional bond with her: a bond of trust."

She thought of their long conversations. His lectures
about the suffering of the Palestinian people. His confession about the scars on his back and the horrible night
in Shatila. All the while she had believed that she was
controlling the game—that she was the deceiver and the
manipulator—when in reality it was Yusef.

"When we felt your relationship had progressed to
that point, we told Yusef to ask a very special favor of
you: Would you be willing to accompany a Palestinian
dignitary on an important secret mission? You put up a
very convincing argument, but in the end you said yes,
of course, because you're not Dominique Bonard, a secretary from a London art gallery, but Sarah Halévy, an
agent of Israeli intelligence. Ari Shamron and Gabriel
Allon assumed correctly that this Palestinian dignitary
was in reality me, since I have a history of using unsus-
pecting women in my operations. They placed you in this

extremely dangerous situation because they wanted me. But now I'm going to turn the game against them. I'm going to use *you* to bring Allon to me."

"Leave him," she said. "He's suffered enough because of you."

"Allon has suffered? Gabriel Allon murdered my brother. His suffering is nothing compared to the suffering he inflicted on my family."

"Your brother was a terrorist! Your brother deserved to die!"

"My brother fought for his people. He didn't deserve to be shot like a dog as he lay in bed."

"It was a long time ago. It's over now. Take me instead of Gabriel."

"That's very noble of you, Sarah, but your friend Gabriel is not going to lose another woman to me without a fight. Close your eyes and get some rest. We have a long way to go tonight."

It was nearly dawn as Tariq sped across the Whitestone Bridge and entered Queens. The traffic began to thicken as he passed La Guardia Airport. To the east the sky had turned light gray with the coming dawn. He switched on the radio, listened to a traffic report, then turned down the volume and concentrated on his driving. After a few minutes the East River appeared. Jacqueline could see the first rays of sunlight reflected on the skyscrapers of Lower Manhattan.

He exited the expressway and drove along the surface streets of Brooklyn. Now that it was light she could see him clearly for the first time since the previous afternoon. The long night of driving had taken its toll. He was pale, his eyes bloodshot and strained. He drove with his right hand. His left hand lay in his lap, clutching the Makarov.

She looked at the street signs: Coney Island Avenue. The neighborhood had turned markedly Middle Eastern and Asian. Colorful Pakistani markets with fruit stands spilling onto the sidewalk. Lebanese and Afghan restaurants. Middle East travel companies. A carpet and tile store. A mosque with a false green-and-white marble facade mounted on the brick exterior of an old commercial property.

He turned into a quiet residential street called Parkville Avenue and drove slowly for one block, stopping outside a square three-story brick building on the corner of East Eighth Street. On the ground floor was a boarded-up delicatessen. He shut off the engine, gave two short beeps of the horn. A light flared briefly in the second-floor apartment.

"Wait for me to walk around the car," he said calmly. "Don't open the door. If you open the door, I'll kill you. When we get out of the car, walk straight inside and up the stairs. If you make a sound, if you try to run, I'll kill you. Do you understand?"

She nodded. He slipped the Makarov into the front of his coat and climbed out. Then he walked around the back of the car, opened her door, and pulled her out by the hand. He closed the door, and together they walked quickly across the street. The ground-floor door was slightly ajar. They stepped inside and crossed a small foyer littered with flyers. The frame of a rusting bicycle with no tires leaned against the flaking woodwork.

Tariq mounted the stairs, still clutching her hand; his skin was hot and damp. The stairwell smelled of curry and turpentine. A door opened, and a face briefly appeared in the darkness, a bearded man wearing a white gown. He glanced at Tariq, then slipped back into his apartment and softly closed the door.

They came to a doorway marked 2A. Tariq knocked softly twice.

Leila opened the door and pulled Jacqueline inside.

# 43

## NEW YORK CITY

One hour later Ari Shamron arrived at the Israeli diplomatic mission to the United Nations on Second Avenue and Forty-third Street. He slipped through a knot of protesters, head bowed slightly, and stepped inside. A member of the mission security staff was waiting for him in the lobby and escorted him upstairs to the secure room. The prime minister was there, surrounded by a trio of nervous-looking aides, drumming his fingers on the tabletop. Shamron sat down and looked at the prime minister's chief of staff. "Give me a copy of his schedule and leave the room."

As the aides filed out of the room, the prime minister said, "What happened in Montreal?"

Shamron gave him a detailed account. When he finished, the prime minister closed his eyes and pressed his fingers against the bridge of his nose. "I brought you out of retirement to restore the reputation of the Office, Ari—not to create yet another disaster! Do we have any reason to believe the Canadians were aware of our presence in Montreal?"

"No, Prime Minister."

"Do you think your agent is still alive?"

"It's hard to say, but the situation appears to be rather bleak. The women who have encountered Tariq in the past have not fared terribly well."

"The press is going to have a field day with this one. I can see the headlines now: Beautiful French Fashion Model Secret Agent for Israel! Fuck, Ari!"

"There's no way she can be formally linked to the Office."

"Someone's going to get the story, Ari. *Someone* always does."

"If they do, we'll use our friends like Benjamin Stone to knock it down. I can assure you complete deniability of all aspects of this affair."

"I don't want *deniability*! You promised me Tariq's head on a platter with no fuckups and no fingerprints! I still want Tariq's head on a platter, and I want Jacqueline Delacroix alive."

"We want the same things, Prime Minister. But at this moment your security is our first priority." Shamron picked up the schedule and began to read.

"After the ceremony at the United Nations, it's down to the financial district for a meeting with investors, followed by an appearance at the New York Stock Exchange. After that you go to the Waldorf for a luncheon hosted by the Friends of Zion." Shamron looked up briefly. "And that's the first half of the day. After lunch you go to Brooklyn to visit a Jewish community center and discuss the peace process. Then it's back to Manhattan for a round of cocktail parties and receptions."

Shamron lowered the paper and looked at the prime minister. "This is a security nightmare. I want Allon assigned to your personal detail for the day."

"Why Allon?"

"Because he got a good look at Tariq in Montreal. If Tariq's out there, Gabriel will see him."

"Tell him he has to wear a suit."

"I don't think he owns one."

"Get one."

It was a tiny apartment: a sparsely furnished living room, a kitchen with a two-burner stove and cracked porcelain sink, a single bedroom, a bathroom that smelled of damp. The windows were hung with thick woolen blankets, which blocked out all light. Tariq opened the closet door. Inside was a large, hard-sided suitcase. He carried the suitcase into the living room, placed it on the floor, opened it. Black gabardine trousers, neatly pressed and folded, white dinner jacket, white shirt, and bow tie. In the zippered compartment, a wallet. Tariq opened it and studied the contents: a New York driver's license in the name of Emilio Gonzales, a Visa credit card, a video store rental card, an assortment of receipts, a clip-on identification badge. Kemel had done his work well.

Tariq looked at the photograph. Emilio Gonzales was a balding man with salt and pepper hair and a thick mustache. His cheeks were fuller than Tariq's; nothing a few balls of cotton wouldn't take care of. He removed the clothing from the suitcase and laid it carefully over the back of a chair. Then he removed the final item from the suitcase—a small leather toiletry kit—and went into the bathroom.

He placed the toiletry kit on the basin and propped the photograph of Emilio Gonzales on the shelf below the mirror, Tariq looked at his reflection in the glass. He barely recognized his own face: deep black circles beneath his eyes, hollow cheeks, pale skin, bloodless lips. Part of it was lack of sleep—he couldn't remember when he had slept last—but the illness was to blame for most of it. The tumor was stalking him now: numbness in his extremities, ringing in his ears, unbearable headaches, fatigue. He did not have much longer to live. He had arrived at this place, this moment in history, with little time to spare.

He opened the toiletry kit, removed a pair of scissors and a razor, and began cutting his hair. It took nearly an hour to complete the job.

The transformation was remarkable. With the silver hair coloring, mustache, and thicker cheeks, he bore a striking resemblance to the man in the photograph. But Tariq understood that the subtleties of his performance were just as important as the actual likeness. If he behaved like Emilio Gonzales, no security guard or policeman would question him. If he acted like a terrorist on a suicide mission, he would die in an American prison.

He went into the living room, removed his clothing,

changed into the waiter's uniform. Then he walked back to the bathroom for one final look in the mirror. He combed his thinned-out hair over his new bald spot and felt vaguely depressed. To die in a strange land, with another man's name and another man's face. He supposed it was the logical conclusion to the life he had led. Only one thing to do now: make certain his life had not been wasted on a lost cause.

He walked into the bedroom.

As he entered, Leila stood, face alarmed, and raised her gun.

"It's only me," he said softly in Arabic. "Put the gun down before it goes off and you hurt somebody."

She did as he said, then shook her head in wonderment. "It's remarkable. I would never have recognized you."

"That's the point."

"You obviously missed your true calling. You should have been an actor."

"So, everything is in place. All we need now is Gabriel Allon."

Tariq looked at Jacqueline. She lay spread-eagled on the small bed, wrists and ankles secured by four sets of handcuffs, mouth gagged by heavy electrical tape.

"I found it interesting that within minutes of arriving at the hotel room in Montreal you checked your telephone messages at your *flat* in London. When I was working for the PLO, we discovered that the Israelis had the ability to take virtually any telephone in the world and route it directly to their headquarters in Tel Aviv on a secure link. Obviously that was done to your telephone in London. When you called that number, it must have alerted headquarters that you were in the Hotel Queen Elizabeth in Montreal."

Tariq sat down on the edge of the bed, gently pushed Jacqueline's hair out of her face. She closed her eyes and tried to draw away from his touch.

"I'm going to use that device one more time to deceive Ari Shamron and Gabriel Allon. Leila is not a bad actress herself. When I'm ready to move against the target, Leila will telephone your number in London and impersonate you. She will tell headquarters where I am and what I'm about to do. Headquarters will tell Shamron, and Shamron will quickly dispatch Gabriel Allon to the scene. Obviously, I will know that Allon is coming. Therefore, I will hold a significant advantage."

He removed the Makarov, placed the barrel beneath her chin. "If you are a good girl, if you behave yourself, you will be allowed to live. Once Leila makes that telephone call, she will have to leave this place. It's up to her whether Ari Shamron finds a dead body chained to this bed. Do you understand me?"

Jacqueline stared back at him with a cold insolence. He pressed the barrel of the gun into the soft flesh of her throat until she groaned through the gag.

"Do you understand me?"

She nodded.

He stood up, slipped the Makarov into the waistband

of his trousers. Then he walked into the living room, pulled on an overcoat and a pair of gloves, and went out.

A clear, cold afternoon, the sun shining brightly. Tariq slipped on a pair of sunglasses, turned up the collar of his overcoat. He walked to Coney Island Avenue, strolled along a row of shops until he found a grocer specializing in Middle Eastern goods. He entered the cramped market, accompanied by the tinkle of a small bell on the door, and was immediately overwhelmed by the scents of home. Coffee and spices, roasting lamb, honey and tobacco.

A teenage boy stood behind the counter. He wore a Yankees sweatshirt and was speaking rapid, Moroccan-accented Arabic on a cordless telephone.

"Dates," Tariq said in English. "I'm looking for dried dates."

The boy paused for a moment. "Back row on the left."

Tariq picked his way through the narrow aisles until he arrived at the back of the store. The dates were on the top shelf. As Tariq reached up to grasp them, he could feel the Makarov digging into the small of his back. He pulled down the dates and looked at the label. Tunisia. Perfect.

He paid and went out. From Coney Island Avenue he walked east through quieter residential streets, past small apartment houses and tiny brick homes, until he arrived at the Newkirk Avenue subway stop. He purchased a token, then walked down the stairs to the small exposed platform. Two minutes later he boarded a train bound for Manhattan.

Gabriel was beginning to think he would never find Tariq. At that moment he was speeding up Park Avenue in the front seat of a black minivan, surrounded by the rest of the prime minister's security detail. A few feet ahead of them was the prime minister's limousine. To their right, a motorcycle outrider. Gabriel wore a gray suit he had borrowed from one of the other bodyguards. The jacket was too big, the pants too short. He felt like a damned fool—like someone who comes to an expensive restaurant without proper attire and has to borrow the house blazer. It was no matter; he had more important things to worry about.

So far the day had gone off without a problem. The prime minister had had coffee with a group of high-powered investment bankers to discuss business opportunities in Israel. Then he had toured the floor of the New York Stock Exchange. Gabriel had been at his side the entire time. He left nothing to chance. He stared at every face—the bankers, the traders, the janitors, people on the street—looking for Tariq. He remembered Tariq's face from the rue St-Denis in Montreal: the mocking smile as he pushed Jacqueline into the car and drove away.

He wondered whether she was even still alive. He thought about the string of dead women Tariq had left in his wake: the American in Paris, the hooker in Amsterdam, the shopgirl in Vienna.

He borrowed a cell phone from one of the other security officers and checked in with Shamron at the mission. Shamron had heard nothing. Gabriel severed the connection, swore softly. It was beginning to feel hopeless. It seemed Tariq had beaten them again.

The motorcade pulled into the parking garage at the Waldorf-Astoria Hotel. The prime minister bounded out of his limousine and shook a few hands before he was escorted to the grand ballroom. Gabriel followed a few paces behind him. As the prime minister entered the ballroom, a thousand people stood up and began to applaud. The noise was thunderous. It could easily cover the sound of a gunshot. The prime minister walked to the podium, basked in the warm reception. Gabriel slowly circled the ballroom, looking for Tariq.

Tariq left the Q train at the Broadway–Lafayette Street station and boarded an uptown Number 5 train. He got off at East Eighty-sixth Street and strolled from Lexington Avenue across town to Fifth Avenue, taking in the grand old apartment houses and brownstones. Then he walked uptown two blocks to Eighty-eighth Street. He stopped in front of an apartment house overlooking the park. An Elite Catering truck was double-parked on Eighty-eighth Street; white-jacketed waiters were carrying trays and food and cases of liquor through the service entrance. He looked at his watch. It wouldn't be long now. He crossed Fifth Avenue, sat down on a bench in a patch of sunlight, and waited.

Jacqueline closed her eyes, tried to think. Tariq was going to use the resources and technology of the Office to lure Gabriel into a trap. She pictured him in his new disguise; even *she* barely recognized him, and they had been together every minute for the past eighteen hours. It would be difficult, if not impossible, for Gabriel to spot him. Tariq was right: he would hold every advantage. Gabriel would never see him coming.

The girl came into the room, a mug of tea in her hands, gun shoved down the front of her jeans. She paced slowly, looking at Jacqueline, drinking the tea. Then she sat on the edge of the bed. "Tell me something, *Dominique*. Did you make love to Tariq while you were in Montreal?"

Jacqueline stared back at the girl, wondering what possible relevance this question could have now. The girl lifted the bottom of Jacqueline's blouse, exposing her abdomen, and poured the scalding tea over her skin.

The gag muffled Jacqueline's scream. The girl tenderly blew air over the burned skin and covered it with Jacqueline's blouse. Even the sensation of the light cotton lying on her flesh caused pain. She closed her eyes and felt hot tears running over her cheeks.

Leila said, "Let's try again. Did you ever make love to Tariq?"

Jacqueline shook her head, eyes still closed.

"Too bad for you," she said. "I hear he's a wonderful lover. The girl in Paris told me everything in explicit detail. In a way I suppose she's lucky Tariq killed her in the end. No man would have ever made love to her the way he did. Her love life would have been a series of disappointments."

Jacqueline realized that she was never going to set foot outside this room alive. Leila was a psychopath who had no intention of allowing her to live. Indeed, she would probably take pleasure in Jacqueline's death. No, she thought, if she were going to die, she would die on her own terms. She would die trying to save Gabriel.

*But how?*

She had to create an opportunity to get away. To do that she had to convince Leila to let her out of the bed.

Through her gag Jacqueline managed to mumble, "I have to go to the bathroom."

"What did you say?"

Jacqueline repeated her words, more forcefully.

Leila said, "If you have to go, go."

"Please," said Jacqueline.

Leila set the empty mug on the floor and removed the gun from the waistband of her trousers. "Remember, we don't need you for anything. If you try to get away I'll shoot you in that beautiful face of yours. Do you understand me?"

Jacqueline nodded.

Leila unlocked the cuffs, starting with Jacqueline's hands and ending with her feet.

"Stand up," said Leila. "*Slowly*. And walk, *slowly,* into the bathroom with your hands behind your head."

Jacqueline did as she was told. She entered the bathroom, turned around, started to close the door. Leila put her hand on it and aimed the gun at Jacqueline's face. "What do you think you're doing?"

"Please," said Jacqueline.

Leila looked around. The bathroom was windowless, no way out except the door. "Knock on the door when you're finished, *Dominique*. Stay inside until I tell you to come out."

Jacqueline lowered her jeans and sat down on the toilet. Now what? To have any chance of getting away she needed a weapon of some sort. Maybe she could hit her with the lid to the toilet tank. No, too big, too heavy. She looked around the bathroom: a shampoo bottle, a bar of soap, a can of shaving cream, a disposable razor, a nail file.

*A nail file.*

It was resting on the shelf above the sink, below the mirror: a metal nail file, rounded at one end, sharp at the other. Jacqueline remembered her self-defense course at the Academy. The simplest device could be turned into a lethal weapon if the attacker struck in the right place: the eyes, the ears, the throat. Carefully, she picked up the nail file and gripped it across her palm, so that about an inch of the blade protruded from the heel of her hand.

*But can I really do this?*

Jacqueline thought of what Tariq was going to do to

Gabriel. She thought about what Leila was going to do to her. She raised her blouse and looked at the burned skin of her abdomen.

She stood up and knocked on the door.

"Open the door slowly and step out with your hands behind your head."

Jacqueline concealed the nail file in the palm of her right hand, opened the door, and placed her hands behind her head. Then she walked out into the living room. Leila was there, pointing the gun at Jacqueline's chest. "Back to the bedroom," she said, motioning with the gun.

Jacqueline turned and walked to the bedroom, Leila trailing a pace behind her, the gun in her outstretched hands. Jacqueline stopped at the edge of the bed.

Leila said, "Lie down and attach the handcuff to your right wrist."

Jacqueline hesitated.

Leila shouted, "Do it!"

Jacqueline whirled around. As she turned she used her thumb to press the blade of the nail file into view. Leila was caught completely off guard. Instead of shooting she instinctively raised her hands. Jacqueline was aiming for her ear canal, but Leila moved just enough so that the tip of the file tore into the flesh of her cheekbone.

It was a deep wound, and blood immediately began to spout from it. Leila howled in pain, the gun tumbling from her grasp.

Jacqueline resisted the natural impulse to grab for the

gun and forced herself to stab the girl again. She drew back her arm and swung it in a wide arc. This time the blade struck Leila in the side of the neck.

Warm blood spurted onto Jacqueline's hand.

She let go of the file. It was protruding from the side of Leila's neck. Leila looked at Jacqueline, her gaze a peculiar mixture of pain, horror, and utter surprise, her hands clutching at the metal object in her neck.

Jacqueline reached down and picked up the fallen gun.

Leila pulled the nail file from the side of her neck and lunged toward Jacqueline with a killing rage in her eyes.

Jacqueline raised the gun and shot her through the heart.

# 44

## NEW YORK CITY

Tariq stood up and crossed Fifth Avenue. He walked to the service entrance of the apartment house and picked up a case of champagne that was standing just inside the doorway. A man with an apron and heavily oiled black hair looked up. "What the hell do you think you're doing?"

Tariq shrugged, still holding the case of champagne. "My name is Emilio Gonzales."

"So?"

"I was told to come here. I work for Elite Catering."

"So how come I don't know you?"

"This is my first job for them. I got a call this morning. Guy told me to get my ass over here right away—big party, needed some extra help. So here I am."

"Well, it *is* a big party, and I could use a pair of extra hands. Someone important too. Helluva lot of security up there."

"So?"

"So what the fuck are you standing there for? Take that upstairs and get your ass back down here."

"Yes, sir."

*　　*　　*

In the small apartment the gunshot sounded like a cannon blast. Surely someone had heard it. Jacqueline had to get away quickly. But she had to do one thing first. She had to warn Gabriel about Tariq's plan.

She stepped over Leila's dead body, snatched up the receiver, dialed the number in London. When she heard the recording of her own voice, she pressed three more numbers. There was a series of clicks, followed by a humming tone, then the voice of a young woman.

"Yes."

"I need Ari Shamron, priority one. It's an emergency."

"Security word."

"Jericho. Please, *hurry!*"

"Stand by, please."

The calmness in the woman's voice was maddening. There was another series of clicks and buzzes, but this time it was the voice of Shamron on the line.

"Jacqueline? Is that really you? Where are you?"

"I'm not sure. Somewhere in Brooklyn, I think."

"Hold on. I'll get your exact address from headquarters."

"Don't leave me alone!"

"I'm not. I'm right here."

She began to cry.

"What happened?"

"Tariq's out there somewhere! He's disguised as a waiter. He looks totally different from Montreal. He was going to use the secure link to lure Gabriel into a trap, but I killed Leila with a nail file and her gun."

She realized she probably sounded like a hysteric.

"Is the girl there now?"

"Yes, right next to me, on the floor. Oh, Ari, it's horrible."

"You have to get out of there. Just tell me one thing: Do you know where Tariq is going?"

"No."

Just then she heard heavy footfalls in the stairwell.

*Shit!*

She whispered, "Someone's coming!"

"Get out of there!"

"There's only one way out."

She heard knocking at the door: two crisp blows that seemed to shake the entire apartment.

"Ari, I don't know what to do."

"Be quiet and wait."

Three more knocks, harder still. No more footsteps. Whoever was out there hadn't left yet.

She was unprepared for the next sound: a violent thud, followed by the crackle of splintering wood. The noise was so loud that Jacqueline expected to see several people charge into the room, but it was only one man— the man who had appeared in the doorway that morning when Tariq brought her into the building.

He held a baseball bat in his clenched fists.

Jacqueline dropped the receiver. The man looked down at Leila's body, then at Jacqueline. Then he raised the bat and started running toward her. Jacqueline leveled the gun and squeezed off two shots. The first struck him high in the shoulder, spinning him around. The second tore into the center of his back, severing his spinal cord. She moved forward and fired two more shots.

The room was filled with gun smoke and the smell of powder, the walls and floor spattered with blood. Jacqueline bent down and picked up the telephone.

"Ari?"

"Thank God it's you. Listen carefully, Jacqueline. You have to get out of there now."

"No shit, Ari! Where do I go?"

"Apparently, you're at the corner of Parkville Avenue and East Eighth Street in Brooklyn."

"That doesn't mean *shit* to me."

"Leave the building and walk to Parkville Avenue. Make a left turn onto Parkville and walk to Coney Island Avenue. At Coney Island Avenue make a right turn. Do *not* cross Coney Island. Stay on that side of the street. Keep walking. Someone will pick you up."

"Who?"

"Just do as I say, and get out of there now!"

The line went dead.

She dropped the receiver onto the floor and picked up her coat, which was lying on the floor next to the bed. She pulled on the coat, slipped the gun into the front pocket, and walked quickly out. She followed Shamron's instructions and a moment later was walking past the storefronts of Coney Island Avenue.

\*     \*     \*

One mile away, in the auditorium of a Jewish community center on Ocean Avenue, Gabriel stood a few feet from the prime minister as he read the story of Masada to a group of schoolchildren. Another member of the prime minister's security detail tapped Gabriel on the shoulder lightly and whispered, "You have a phone call. Sounds urgent."

Gabriel stepped into the lobby. Another bodyguard handed him a cell phone.

"Yes?"

Shamron said, "She's alive."

"What! Where is she?"

"Heading your way on Coney Island Avenue. She's walking on the west side of the street. She's alone. Go get her. I'll let her tell you the rest."

Gabriel severed the connection and looked up. "I need a car. Now!"

Two minutes later Gabriel was speeding north along Coney Island Avenue, his eyes scanning the pedestrians on the sidewalks for any sign of Jacqueline. Shamron had said she would be on the west side of the street, but Gabriel looked on both sides in case she had become confused or frightened by something else. He read the passing street signs: Avenue L, Avenue K, Avenue J. . . .

*Damn! Where the hell is she?*

He spotted her at the intersection of Coney Island and Avenue H. Her hair was mussed, her face swollen.

She had the air of the hunted about her. Still, she was composed and cool. Gabriel could see her eyes scanning slowly back and forth.

He quickly made a U-turn, pulled to the curb, and reached across the front seat to open the passenger-side door. Reflexively, she backed away a few steps and reached into her pocket. Then she saw it was him, and her composure dissolved. "Gabriel," she whispered. "Thank God."

"Get in," he said calmly.

She climbed in and closed the door.

Gabriel pulled into traffic, accelerating rapidly.

After a few blocks she said, "Pull over."

Gabriel turned into a side street and parked, engine running. "Are you all right, Jacqueline? What happened? Tell me everything."

She started to weep, softly at first; then her entire body began to convulse with wrenching sobs. Gabriel pulled her to him and held her tightly. "It's over," he said softly. "It's all over."

"Please don't ever leave me again, Gabriel. Be with me, Gabriel. Please, be with me."

# 45

## NEW YORK CITY

Tariq circulated through the magnificent rooms overlooking Central Park while the guests carelessly dropped items on his oval-shaped tray: empty glasses, half-eaten plates of food, crumpled napkins, cigarette butts. He glanced at his watch. Leila would have made the call by now. Allon was probably on his way. It would be over soon.

He walked through the library. A pair of French doors led onto the terrace. In spite of the cold, a handful of guests stood outside admiring the view. As Tariq stepped onto the balcony, the wail of distant sirens filled the air. He walked to the balustrade and looked up Fifth Avenue: a motorcade, complete with police escort and motorcycle outriders.

The guest of honor was about to arrive.

*But where the hell is Allon?*

"Excuse me? Hello?"

Tariq looked up. A woman with a fur coat was waving at him. He had been so absorbed by the sight of the approaching motorcade that he had forgotten he was posing as a busboy.

The woman held up a half-empty glass of red wine. "Can you take this, please?"

"Certainly, madam."

Tariq walked across the terrace and stood next to the woman, who was now talking to a friend. Without looking she reached out and tried to place the glass on Tariq's tray, but it teetered on its small base and tipped over, splashing red wine over Tariq's white jacket.

"Oh, heavens," the woman said. "I'm so sorry." Then she turned away as if nothing had happened and resumed her conversation.

Tariq carried his tray back to the kitchen.

"What the fuck happened to you?" It was the man with the apron and the oiled black hair: Rodney, the boss.

"A woman spilled wine on me."

Tariq placed his full tray on the counter next to the sink. Just then he heard a round of applause sweep through the apartment. The guest of honor had entered the room. Tariq picked up an empty tray and started to leave the kitchen.

Rodney said, "Where do you think you're going?"

"Back out to do my job."

"Not looking like that, you're not. You're on kitchen duty now. Get over there and help with the dishes."

"I can clean the jacket."

"It's red wine, pal. The jacket's ruined."

"But—"

"Just get over there and start on those dishes."

*     *     *

Douglas Cannon said, "President Arafat, so good to see you again."

Arafat smiled. "Same to you, Senator. Or should I say *Ambassador* Cannon now?"

"*Douglas* will do you just fine."

Cannon took Arafat's small hand in his own bearish paws and shook it vigorously. Cannon was a tall man, with broad shoulders and a mane of unruly gray hair. His middle had thickened with age, though his paunch was concealed nicely by an impeccably tailored blue blazer. *The New Yorker* magazine had once called him "a modern-day Pericles"—a brilliant scholar and philanthropist who rose from the world of academia to become one of the most powerful Democrats in the Senate. Two years earlier he had been called out of retirement to serve as the American ambassador to the Court of St. James's in London. His ambassadorship had been cut short, however, when he was gravely wounded in a terrorist attack. He showed no sign of it now as he took Arafat by the hand and propelled him into the party.

"I was so saddened by the attempt on your life, Douglas. It's good to see you looking so fit again. Did you receive the flowers that Suhla and I sent for you?"

"Yes, indeed. They were the most beautiful in the hospital room. Thank you so much. But enough about me. Come, this way. There are a lot of people here who are interested in meeting you."

"I don't doubt it," said Arafat, smiling. "Lead on."

*   *   *

Gabriel sped over the Brooklyn Bridge into Manhattan. Jacqueline had regained her composure and was giving him a thorough account of the last forty-eight hours, beginning with the night in the council flat near Heathrow, ending with the gruesome sequence of events in Brooklyn. Gabriel forced himself to listen dispassionately, to set aside momentarily his rage over what Tariq had done to her so he could search for clues to his intentions.

One detail caught his attention. Why did Tariq feel it was necessary to bring Gabriel to *him* by having Leila impersonate Jacqueline over the secure phone link?

The answer was probably quite simple: because he did not believe Gabriel would be at the place where he intended to strike. But why not? If he had come to New York to assassinate the prime minister of Israel, the great peacemaker, then surely he would assume that Gabriel would be at the prime minister's side. After all, Gabriel had just seen Tariq in Montreal.

Gabriel thought of the painting by Van Dyck: a religious scene on the surface, a rather ugly woman beneath. One painting, two realities. The entire operation had been like that painting, and Tariq had beaten him at every turn.

*Damn it, Gabriel. Don't be afraid to trust your instincts!*

He picked up the cell phone and dialed the number for Shamron at the diplomatic mission. When Shamron came on the line, Gabriel said tersely, "Where's Arafat?"

He listened for a moment, then said: "*Shit!* I think Tariq is there disguised as a waiter. Tell his people I'm coming."

He severed the connection and looked at Jacqueline. "You still have the girl's gun?"

She nodded.

"Anything left?"

Jacqueline released the magazine and counted the remaining rounds. "Five," she said.

Gabriel turned north onto the FDR Drive and put the accelerator to the floor.

Tariq walked to the entrance of the kitchen and peered through the passageway into the party. Flashbulbs popped as guests posed for photographs with Arafat. Tariq shook his head. Ten years ago these same people had written Arafat off as a ruthless terrorist. Now they were treating him like a rock star in a kaffiyeh.

Tariq looked around the room for Allon. Something must have gone wrong. Perhaps Leila had been unable to get through on the telephone. Perhaps Allon was playing some sort of game. Whatever the case, Tariq knew he could not wait long to act. He knew Arafat better than anyone. The old man was prone to last-minute changes in plans. That's how he had survived all these years. He could walk out of the party at any time, and Tariq would lose his opportunity to kill him.

He had wanted to kill them both at the same time— Allon and Arafat, one final act of vengeance—but it looked as though that was not to be. Once he killed Arafat, the bodyguards would swarm him. He would fight back and leave them no choice but to kill him. *Anything is better than letting the tumor kill me.* Allon would miss everything, and therefore his life would be spared. Arafat the traitorous coward would not be so lucky.

Rodney tapped Tariq on the shoulder. "Start washing dishes, my friend, or this will be the last party you ever work."

Rodney walked away. Tariq went into the pantry and switched on the light. He reached up to the top shelf and removed the bag of Tunisian dates he had hidden there an hour earlier. He carried the dates into the kitchen, arranged them on a white china plate. Then he started picking his way through the crowd.

Arafat was standing in the center of the main drawing room, surrounded by a half-dozen aides and security men and a crowd of well-wishers. Ambassador Cannon stood at his side. Tariq moved forward, the butt of the Makarov pressing into the flesh of his abdomen. Arafat was now ten feet away, but there were five people between him and Tariq, including a bodyguard. Arafat was so short that Tariq could barely see him through the crowd—only the black-and-white of his checkered kaffiyeh. If he drew the Makarov now, surely one of the bodyguards would spot it and open fire. Tariq had to get closer before he drew the gun. He had to play out the ruse with the dates.

But now Tariq had another problem. The crowd around Arafat was so tightly packed that he could move no closer. Standing directly in front of him was a tall man in a charcoal-gray suit. When Tariq tapped him on the shoulder, the man turned briefly and, spotting the tray and Tariq's white jacket, said, "No thank you."

"They're for President Arafat," Tariq said, and the man reluctantly stepped aside.

Next Tariq was confronted with a woman. Once again, he tapped the woman on the shoulder, waited for her to step aside, and moved another three feet closer to the target. But now he was standing beside one of Arafat's aides. He was about to tap the man on the shoulder when he heard a cell phone chirp. The aide reached into the breast pocket of his suit jacket and brought the telephone quickly to his ear. He listened intently for a moment, then slipped the phone into his pocket, leaned forward, and whispered into Arafat's ear. Arafat then turned to Cannon and said, "I'm afraid I have an urgent matter to attend to."

Tariq thought: *Damn it, but the man has the luck of the devil!*

Arafat said, "I need to conduct a telephone conversation in private."

"I think you'll find my study to your liking. Please, come right this way."

Arafat disengaged himself from the crowd and, together with Cannon and his bevy of aides, moved along a corridor toward the back of the apartment. A moment later they disappeared into a room. One of Arafat's bodyguards immediately took up a post outside the door. Cannon and the aides emerged a moment later and rejoined the party.

Tariq knew he had to strike now or he would lose his chance. He sliced his way through the crowded living room, and walked down the hallway, stopping in front of the bodyguard. Tariq could see he was a member of Arafat's personal security unit, a man who would know that the Palestinian leader loved nothing more than a good Tunisian date.

"One of Mr. Arafat's assistants asked me to bring these to him."

The guard looked at the plate of dates, then at Tariq.

Tariq thought: *We can do this one of two ways. You can let me pass peacefully, or I can take out my gun and shoot you in the face and then go inside.*

The guard snatched one of the dates and popped it in his mouth. Then he opened the door and said, "Leave the plate and come right out again."

Tariq nodded and stepped into the room.

Gabriel double-parked the minivan on Eighty-eighth Street. He climbed out, ignoring the shouts of a foot patrolman, and ran to the entrance of the building on Fifth Avenue, Jacqueline a few strides behind him. When they entered the lobby, three people were waiting for them: a member of Arafat's personal security unit, an American Diplomatic Security Service agent, and a New York City policeman.

A doorman was holding one of the elevators. He pressed the button for the seventeenth floor as the five people piled into the car.

The DSS agent said, "I hope to hell you're sure about this, my friend."

Gabriel removed his Beretta, chambered the first round, and slipped it back beneath his coat.

The doorman said, "Jesus Christ."

It was a small study: a carved antique desk with leather inlay, recessed lighting high in the molded ceiling, bookshelves filled with volumes of history and biography, a wood fire burning slowly in a marble fireplace. Arafat was on the telephone, listening intently. Then he murmured a few words in Arabic, replaced the receiver, and looked at Tariq. When he saw the plate of dates, his face broke into a warm, childlike smile.

Tariq said in Arabic: "Peace be with you, President Arafat. One of your aides asked me to bring these to you."

"Dates! How marvelous." He took one, inspected it briefly, and bit into it. "This date is from Tunisia, I'm sure of it."

"I believe you're right, President Arafat."

"You speak Arabic with the accent of a Palestinian."

"That's because I am from Palestine."

"What part of Palestine?"

"My family lived in the Upper Galilee before *al-Nakba*. I grew up in the camps of Lebanon."

Tariq placed the plate of dates on the desk and un-buttoned his jacket so that he could get at his Makarov. Arafat cocked his head slightly and touched his lower lip. "You are not well, my brother?"

"I'm just a bit tired. I've been working very hard lately."

"I know what fatigue looks like, my brother. I've seen what lack of sleep has done to me over the years. I've seen what it's done to the men around me. But you are not suffering only from fatigue. You're sick, my brother. I can see it. I have a very powerful instinct for these things."

"You're correct, President Arafat. I am not well these days."

"What is the nature of your illness, my brother?"

"Please, President Arafat—you are far too busy, and too important, to worry about the problems of a common man like me."

"That's where you are wrong, my brother. I've al-ways thought of myself as the father of *all* the Palestinian people. When one of my people suffers, I suffer."

"Your concern means the world to me, President Arafat."

"It is a tumor, isn't it, my brother? You are sick from a cancer of some sort?"

Tariq said nothing. Arafat abruptly changed the di-rection of the conversation. "Tell me something, my friend. Which one of my aides asked you to bring me those dates?"

Tariq thought, *So, his survival instincts are still as*

*strong as ever.* He thought of a night in Tunis a long time ago. An interminable meeting, a typical Arafat session, beginning at midnight and stretching till dawn. At some point a package arrived, addressed to Arafat himself, from an Iraqi diplomat in Amman. It sat on his desk for some time, unopened, until finally Arafat stood up and said, "There is a bomb in that package, Tariq! I can smell it! Take it away!" Tariq removed the package and gave it to a Fatah engineer to inspect. The old man had been right. The Israelis had managed to place a bomb in a senior PLO staff meeting. If Arafat had opened the package, all the top leadership would have been liquidated.

Tariq said, "He didn't tell me his name. He just told me to bring the dates."

Arafat reached out and took another date from Tariq's tray. "It's strange, but you seem very familiar. Have we met before?"

"Unfortunately, no."

"Are you sure about that? You see, I never forget a face."

"I'm certain, President Arafat."

"You remind me of an old comrade—a man who served at my side during the good times and the bad."

"I'm afraid I'm just a laborer."

"I owe my life to this man. He protected me from my enemies. He saved my life more times than I care to remember." Arafat lifted his face toward the ceiling and closed his eyes for a moment. "I remember one night in

particular. I had been summoned to Damascus for a meeting with the brother of President Assad. This friend of
mine begged me not to go. It was in the old days, when
Assad and his secret police wanted me dead. The meeting
went off fine, but as we were about to board our motorcade for the drive back to Beirut, this friend of mine tells
me it is not safe. You see, he had learned that the Syrians
intended to ambush the motorcade and assassinate me.
We sent the motorcade on its way as a decoy, and this man
managed to hide me in Damascus, right under the noses of
the Syrians. Late that night we received word that Syrian
special forces had attacked the motorcade outside Damascus and that several of my men were killed. It was a very
sad night, but I was still alive, thanks to this man."

"A very interesting story, President Arafat."

"Will you allow me to indulge in another?"

"I should probably be going," Tariq said, reaching
for the Makarov.

"Please, it will only take a moment."

Tariq hesitated and said, "Of course, President Arafat.
I'd love to hear the story."

"Sit down, my friend. You must be tired."

"It would not be appropriate."

"As you wish," Arafat replied. "It was during the siege
of Beirut. The Israelis were trying to finish off the PLO
once and for all. They wanted me dead, too. Everywhere
I went Israeli bombs and rockets fell. It was as if they
knew where I was all the time. So this friend of mine
starts investigating. He discovers that Israeli intelligence

has recruited several spies among my staff. He discovers that the Israelis have given the spies radio beacons, so they know where I am all the time. He detains the spies and convinces them to confess their crimes. He wants to send a message to other potential spies that this sort of betrayal will not be tolerated. He asks me to sign death warrants so the spies can be executed."

"And did you?"

"I did not. I told this man that if I executed the traitors, I would be making enemies of their brothers and cousins. I told this man that they would be punished in a different way—that they would be cut off from the revolution. Banished. Exiled. For me, this would be a punishment worse than death. But I told him one other thing. I told him that no matter how serious their crimes, we Palestinians cannot be killing each other. We have too many enemies as it is."

"And how did this man react?"

"He was angry with me. He told me I was a fool. He was the only one of my senior staff who had the courage to speak to me that way. He had the heart of a lion, this man." Arafat paused, then said, "I have not seen him in many years. I hear he's very sick. I hear he does not have long to live."

"I'm sorry to hear that."

"When we have our own state, I will repay him for all the great things he did for the movement. When we have our own state, and our own schools, the children of Palestine will learn about all his heroic deeds. In the villages they will tell stories about this man around the fires at night. He will be a great hero of the Palestinian people." Arafat lowered his voice. "But not if he does something foolish now. Then he will be remembered as just another fanatic."

Arafat looked into Tariq's eyes and said calmly, "If you must do this thing, my brother, then do it and get it over with. If you have no stomach for it, then I suggest you leave here, and quickly, and find some way to end your life with dignity."

Arafat lifted his chin slightly. Tariq lowered his gaze, smiled slightly, and slowly buttoned his coat. "I believe you've mistaken me for another man. Peace be with you, my brother."

Tariq turned and walked out of the room.

Arafat looked at the bodyguard and said, "Come in here and close the door, you idiot." Then he let out a long breath and tried to quiet his trembling hands.

They entered the apartment, Gabriel and Jacqueline side by side, surrounded by the group of security men. The sudden appearance of five very agitated people sent a shock wave through the guests, and the party immediately fell silent. Gabriel had his hand inside his jacket, fingers wrapped around the butt of the Beretta. He looked quickly around the room; there were at least a half-dozen white-jacketed waiters moving through the crowd. He looked at Jacqueline. She shook her head.

Douglas Cannon joined the group as they moved from the entrance hall to the large living room overlooking Fifth Avenue and the park. Three waiters were moving through the guests, passing out hors d'oeuvres and glasses of champagne. Two of the waiters were women. Jacqueline looked at the man. "Not him."

At that moment she spotted a white-jacketed man disappear into the kitchen. She had seen him for just an instant, but she was certain of it. "Gabriel! There he is!"

Gabriel looked at Cannon. "Where's Arafat?"

"In my study using the telephone."

"Where's the study?"

"At the end of that hall!"

Gabriel pushed his way past the guests and ran down the hallway. When he burst through the door, he found himself confronted by a bodyguard pointing a pistol directly at his chest. Arafat was seated calmly behind the desk. "I'm afraid he's come and gone," Arafat said. "I'm still here, however—no thanks to you."

Gabriel turned and ran out of the room.

Tariq walked quickly through the kitchen. There was a back door, leading onto a set of service stairs. He stepped out the door and quickly closed it. Several cases of champagne stood on the landing. He pushed the cases against the door. They were not heavy enough to block it completely, just heavy enough to slow down whoever was trying to get through, which was his intention. He walked down to the next landing, removed his Makarov, and waited.

Gabriel charged into the kitchen, Beretta drawn, as the back door was closing. He sprinted across the room and tried to open it. The knob turned, but the door itself wouldn't move.

Jacqueline came into the room on the run.

Gabriel took a step back and then drove his shoulder into the door. It opened a few inches, and on the other side he could hear a loud thud, followed by the sound of shattering glass.

He pushed the door again. This time it gave way, though there was still some resistance.

He pushed again, and the door opened completely. Gabriel stepped onto the landing and looked down.

Tariq stood on the landing below, feet apart, the Makarov in his outstretched hands.

Gabriel saw the muzzle flashes in the dim light, felt the first bullet tearing into his chest. He thought how fitting it was that it should end like this. He had killed his first man in the stairwell of an apartment house, and now he would die the same way. There was a circular quality about it, like a good piece of music. He wondered if Tariq had planned it this way all along.

He could hear Tariq running down the stairs. Then he saw Jacqueline's face leaning over him—Jacqueline's beautiful face. Then her face turned to water, only to be replaced by the face of the woman in the lost Van Dyck. And then he blacked out.

As Gabriel slipped into unconsciousness, Jacqueline screamed, "Call an ambulance!" Then she stood and started running down the stairs.

Above her she heard one of the security officers scream, "Stop!" She ignored him.

She could hear the pounding of Tariq's feet echoing up the stairwell toward her. She reached into her pocket and removed the gun she had taken from the apartment in Brooklyn. She thought: *I've done this twice today. I can do it again.*

She ran. The stairs seemed to go on forever. She tried to remember what floor the apartment had been on. Seventeen—yes, that was it; she was sure of it. She passed a door that said eighth floor.

She thought: *Keep going, Jacqueline. Don't slow down. He's sick. He's dying. You can catch him. Move!*

She thought of Gabriel, his life draining out of him on the landing above her. She forced herself to run even faster. She propelled herself down the stairs so quickly that her feet struggled to stay beneath her body. She imagined that by catching up with Tariq and killing him she might save Gabriel's life.

She thought of the day Gabriel had come for her, remembered the bicycle ride she had taken through the hills around Valbonne, the fire in her thighs as she had pushed herself to a new record.

*Do it again!*

She reached the bottom of the stairwell. There was a metal fire door, and it was slowly closing.

Tariq was right in front of her!

She ripped open the door and sprinted through it. Ahead of her stretched a corridor about fifty feet long, with another door at the opposite end. Halfway down the corridor was Tariq.

He was clearly exhausted. His pace was beginning to flag, his strides short and uncoordinated. He turned and looked over his shoulder, his face a mask of pain from the run down the stairs. Jacqueline raised the gun and fired two shots in quick succession. The first appeared to sail harmlessly over his head, but the second struck him high in the left shoulder, knocking him from his feet. As he landed on the ground, his gun fell from his grasp and slid along the corridor until it rattled against the door at the other end. Jacqueline moved forward and fired again, and again, and again, until the gun contained no more bullets and she was quite certain Tariq al-Hourani was dead.

Then the door at the end of the corridor opened. She leveled the gun at the man coming through, but it was only Ari Shamron. He stepped forward, loosened her grip on the gun, and slipped it into his coat pocket.

"Where's Gabriel?"

"Upstairs."

"Is it bad?"

"I think so."

"Take me to him."

Jacqueline looked at the body of Tariq. "What about him?"

"Let him lie there," said Shamron. "Let the dogs lap up his blood. Take me to Gabriel. I want to see Gabriel."

# 46

Gabriel awakened. He looked at the luminous face of his watch, closed his eyes: five-fifteen. He lay there trying to calculate how long he had slept. Trying to remember when he had lifted himself from the couch and dragged himself into bed—how long after that had it taken to slip into unconsciousness? Had he *really* slept? His mind had been so alive with dreams it felt as though he hadn't.

He lay very still, waiting to see if sleep would take him again, but it was no good. Then came the sounds: the cry of a muezzin, drifting over the Hinnom Valley from Silwan. A church bell tolling in the Armenian Quarter. The faithful had awakened. The faithless and the damaged had little choice but to join them.

He probed his chest with his fingertips, testing for pain. Not as bad as yesterday. Each day was a little better. He rolled gingerly out of bed, walked into the kitchen, brewed coffee, toasted some bread. He was a prisoner, and like any prisoner he took comfort in the ritual of routine.

His cell was not a cell at all, but a pleasant safe flat

overlooking Zion Gate: cool tile floors, white throw rugs, white furniture. It reminded Gabriel of a hospital, which in many respects it was. He pulled on a sweater, a gray cotton pullover with a stretched neck, and carried his breakfast through the French doors to the small table on the balcony.

As he waited for daybreak he sifted through the individual scents that combine to create the unique fragrance of Jerusalem: sage and jasmine, honey and coffee, leather and tobacco, cypress and eucalyptus. Then dawn came. In the absence of his restoration work, Jerusalem at sunrise had become Gabriel's art. The last stars melted, the sun peeked over the backbone of mountain separating Jerusalem from the desert of the West Bank. The first light seeped down the chalk-colored slope of the Mount of Olives, then ignited a golden fire on the Dome of the Rock. Then the rays fell upon the Church of the Dormition, turning the east-facing surfaces of the church to scarlet and leaving the rest deep in shadow.

Gabriel finished his breakfast, carried the dishes into the kitchen, washed them fastidiously in the sink, placed them on the basin to dry. What now? Some mornings he stayed indoors and read. Lately he had taken to walking, a little farther on each occasion. Yesterday he'd walked all the way up the slope of Mount Scopus. He found it helped him to think, to sort through the wreckage of the case.

He showered, dressed, and walked downstairs. As he stepped out of the apartment building and entered the street, he heard a series of sounds: a hoarse stage whisper, a car door closing, a motor turning over. Shamron's watchers. Gabriel ignored them, zipped his coat against the morning chill, started walking.

He moved along the Khativat Yerushalayim, entered the Old City through the Jaffa Gate. He wandered through the hectic markets of El Bazaar: piles of chickpeas and lentils, stacks of flatbread, sacks overflowing with aromatic spices and roasted coffee beans, boys hawking silver trinkets and coffeepots. An Arab boy pressed an olive wood statue of Jesus into Gabriel's hand and named an exorbitant price. He had Tariq's sharp brown eyes. Gabriel gave the statue back to the boy and in flawless Arabic told him it was too much.

Once free of the noisy market, he meandered through the quiet, twisting alleyways, making his way gradually eastward, toward the Temple Mount. The air warmed slowly. It was nearly spring. Overhead was a sky of cloudless azure, but the sun was still too low to penetrate the labyrinth of the Old City. Gabriel floated among the shadows, a skeptic among the believers in this place where devotion and hatred collided. He supposed like everyone else he was looking for answers. Different answers, but answers nonetheless.

He wandered for a long time, thinking. He followed the dark, cool passageways wherever they led him. Sometimes he would find himself at a locked gate or an impenetrable wall of Herodian stone. Sometimes he would come upon a courtyard bathed in warm sunlight. For an instant things would seem clear to him. Then he would embark down another twisting passage, the shadows would close in, and he would realize he was still no closer to the truth.

He came to an alley leading to the Via Dolorosa. A few feet ahead of him a shaft of light fell upon the stones of the path. He watched as two men, a Hasid in a black *shtreimel* and an Arab in a flowing white kaffiyeh, approached each other. They passed sightlessly, without a nod or glance, and continued their separate ways. Gabriel walked to the Beit ha-Bad and left the Old City through the Damascus Gate.

Shamron summoned Gabriel to Tiberias that evening for supper. They ate on the terrace beneath a pair of hissing gas heaters. Gabriel didn't want to be there, but he played the role of gracious guest—listened to the old man's stories, told a few of his own.

"Lev gave me his resignation today. He said he can no longer serve in an organization in which the director of Operations is kept in the dark about a major operation."

"He has a point. Did you accept it?"

"I had no choice." Shamron smiled. "Poor little Lev's position had become untenable. We had crushed the serpent. We had beheaded Tariq's organization and rounded up his foot soldiers. Yet Lev was completely out of the loop. I explained my reasons for running the operation the way I did. I told him the prime minister needed iron-clad deniability and, unfortunately, that required deceiving my own deputy. Lev wasn't mollified."

"And the rest of your problem children?"

"They'll be gone soon." Shamron set down his fork and looked up at Gabriel. "There'll be several vacancies in the executive suite at King Saul Boulevard. Can I tempt you back? How does chief of Operations sound?"

"Not interested. Besides, I was never much of a headquarters man."

"I didn't think so, but I'd never forgive myself if I didn't try."

"What about the Americans? Have you managed to get back into their good graces?"

"Slowly but surely. They seem to have accepted our version of the story: That we'd run an agent into Tariq's organization and that the agent had been exposed. That we had no choice but to take appropriate steps to safeguard the agent's life. They're still furious that we didn't bring them into the picture earlier."

"That's quite understandable, considering the way it ended. What did you tell them?"

"I told them we had no idea Tariq was in New York until Jacqueline freed herself and alerted us."

"And they believed this?"

"Even I believe it now."

"My name ever come up?"

"From time to time. Adrian Carter would like another go at you."

"Oh, God."

"Don't worry. I'm not going to let him talk to you again."

Before Gabriel had been allowed to leave the United States, he was forced to endure eight hours of questioning: CIA, FBI, New York City police. Shamron had been at his side, like a good defense attorney at a deposition—objecting, stonewalling, impeding every step of the way. In the end it disintegrated into a shouting match. A full account of the operation against Tariq, based on anonymous "Western and Middle Eastern intelligence sources," appeared in *The New York Times* two days later. Gabriel's name made it into print. So did Jacqueline's.

"I'm convinced it was Carter who leaked everything to the *Times*." Gabriel detected a hint of admiration in the old man's voice. He'd used the press to eviscerate an enemy once or twice himself over the years. "I suppose he had a right to be angry with me. I lied to his face about our knowledge of Tariq's involvement in Paris."

"Lev must have talked too."

"Of course he did. Carter's beyond my reach. Little Lev will pay dearly." Shamron pushed his plate away a few inches, rested his stubby elbows on the table, and covered his mouth with his fist. "At least our reputation as a bold action service has been restored. After all, we *did* take down Tariq in the middle of Manhattan and save Arafat's life."

"No thanks to me."

"What are you talking about?"

"Tariq nearly killed me. And he could have killed Arafat if he hadn't gotten cold feet at the last minute. Why *did* he let him live?"

"Arafat is being very tight-lipped about what transpired in that room. Obviously, he said something that made Tariq change his mind."

"Any sign of Yusef?"

Shamron shook his head. "We'll keep looking for him, of course, but I doubt we'll ever find him again. He's probably deep in the mountains of Afghanistan by now."

"And Benjamin Stone?"

"Relaxing in the Caribbean aboard his yacht." Shamron abruptly changed course. "I stopped in on Jacqueline today."

"How is she?"

"Why don't you ask her yourself? She wants to see you."

"I have to get back to Jerusalem."

"Why, Gabriel? So you can waste more time wandering the Old City with the crazies? Go see the girl. Spend some time with her. Who knows? You might actually enjoy yourself."

"When do I get to leave?"

"In my professional opinion it will never be safe for you to leave Israel."

"I want to go home."

"*This* is your home, Gabriel!"

But Gabriel just shook his head slowly.

"What have I done to you, Gabriel? Why do you hate your people and your country so?"

"I don't hate anyone. I just have no peace here."

"So you want to run back to Europe? Back to your paintings? Do me a favor. Get out of Jerusalem for a few days. Take a car and travel this country of yours. Get to know her again. You might like what you see."

"I'm not up to it. I'd rather stay in Jerusalem until you set me free."

"Damn you, Gabriel!" Shamron slammed his fist onto the table, rattling dishes. "You've spent the last years of your life fixing everything and everyone but yourself. You restore paintings and old sailboats. You restored the Office. You restored Jacqueline and Julian Isherwood. You *even* managed to restore Tariq in a strange way—you made certain we buried him in the Upper Galilee. But now it's time to restore yourself. Get out of that flat. Live life, before you wake up one day and discover you're an old man. Like me."

"What about your watchers?"

"I put them there for your own good."

"Get rid of them."

Shamron stuck out his jaw. "Fine, you're on your own."

As Gabriel rode back to Jerusalem that night, he thought how well things had worked out for the old man. Lev and the others were gone, Tariq was dead, and the reputation of the Office had been restored. Not bad for a few weeks' work, Ari. Not bad at all.

Gabriel went south first, down through the barren escarpments and craters of the Negev to Eilat and the Red

Sea. He spent a day sunning himself on the beach but soon grew restless and set out toward the north, taking the fast road up the western Negev to Beersheba, then the black ribbon of highway through the Wilderness of Judea and the West Bank.

Something made him scale the punishing Snake Path up the eastern face of Masada and roam the ruins of the ancient fortress. He avoided the tourist kitsch of the Dead Sea, spent an afternoon wandering the Arab markets of Hebron and Jenin. He wished he could have seen Shamron's face, watching him as he haggled with the merchants in their white kaffiyehs under the steady gaze of dark-eyed veterans of the *intifada*.

He drove through the Jezreel Valley and paused beyond the gates of the farming settlement, just outside Afula on the road to Nazareth, where he had lived as a boy. He considered going in. *To do what? To see what?* His parents were long dead, and if by some miracle he actually came across someone he knew, he could only lie.

He kept driving, kept moving north. Wildflowers burned on the hillsides as he headed into the Galilee. He drove around the shores of the lake. Then up to the ancient hill city of Safed. Then into the Golan. He parked beside the road near a Druse shepherd tending his flock, watched the sunset over the Finger of Galilee. For the first time in many years he felt something like contentment. Something like peace.

He got back into the car, drove down the Golan to a kibbutz outside Qiryat Shemona. It was a Friday night.

He went to the dining hall for Shabbat meal, sat with a group of adults from the kibbutz: farmworkers with sunburned faces and callused hands. They ignored him for a time. Then one of them, an older man, asked his name and where he was from. He told them he was Gabriel. That he was from the Jezreel Valley but had been away for a long time.

In the morning he crossed the fertile flatlands of the coastal plain and drove south along the Mediterranean— through Akko, Haifa, Caesarea, and Netanya—until finally he found himself on the beach at Herzliya.

She was leaning against the balustrade, arms folded, looking out to sea at the setting sun, wind pushing strands of hair across her face. She wore a loose-fitting white blouse and the sunglasses of a woman in hiding.

Gabriel waited for her to notice him. Eventually she would. She had been trained by Ari Shamron, and no pupil of the great Shamron would ever fail to take notice of a man standing below her terrace. When she finally saw him a smile flared, then faded. She lifted her hand, the reluctant wave of someone who had been burned by the secret fire. Gabriel lowered his head and started walking.

They drank icy white wine on her terrace and made small talk, avoiding the operation or Shamron or Gabriel's wounds. Gabriel told her about his journey. Jacqueline said she would have liked to come. Then she apologized for saying such a thing—she had no right.

"So why did you come here after all these weeks, Gabriel? You never do anything without a reason."

He wanted to hear it one more time: Tariq's version of the story. The way he had told it to her that night during the drive from the border to New York. He looked out to sea as she spoke, watching the wind tossing the sand about, the moonlight on the waves, but he was listening fiercely. When she was done, he still couldn't put the final pieces into place. It was like an unfinished painting or a series of musical notes with no resolution. She invited him to stay for dinner. He lied and said he had pressing matters in Jerusalem.

"Ari tells me you want to leave. What are your plans?"

"I have a man named Vecellio waiting for me in England."

"Are you sure it's safe to go back?"

"I'll be fine. What about you?"

"My story has been splashed across newspapers and television screens around the world. I'll never be able to return to my old life. I have no choice but to stay here."

"I'm sorry I got you mixed up in this business, Jacqueline. I hope you can forgive me."

"*Forgive* you? No, Gabriel—quite the opposite, actually. I thank you. I got exactly what I wanted." A second's hesitation. "Well, almost everything."

She walked him down to the beach. He kissed her softly on the mouth, touched her hair. Then he turned and walked to his car. He paused once to look over his shoulder at her, but she had already gone.

He was hungry, so instead of going straight to Jerusalem he stopped in Tel Aviv for dinner. He parked in Balfour Street, walked to Sheinkin, wandered past trendy cafés and avant-garde shops, thinking of the rue St-Denis in Montreal. He had the sense he was being followed. Nothing specific, just the flash of a familiar face too many times—a color, a hat.

He purchased a newspaper from a kiosk, sat down in a restaurant with small round tables spilling onto the sidewalk. It was a warm evening, sidewalks filled with people. He ordered falafel and beer, then opened the newspaper and read the lead article on the front page: "Benjamin Stone, the maverick publisher and entrepreneur, is missing and feared drowned off St. Martin in the Caribbean. Authorities believe Stone fell overboard from his luxury yacht sometime during the night."

Gabriel closed the newspaper.

*"How's Benjamin Stone?"*

*"Relaxing in the Caribbean aboard his yacht."*

When the food arrived he folded his newspaper and dropped it onto the extra chair. He looked up and spotted a man outside on the sidewalk: slender, good-looking, black curly hair, blond Israeli girl on his arm. Gabriel laid down his fork, stared directly at him, throwing all discretion and tradecraft to the wind.

There was no doubt about it: Yusef al-Tawfiki.

*       *       *

Gabriel left money on the table and walked out. For thirty minutes he followed him. Along Sheinkin, then Allenby, then down to the Promenade. A face can be deceiving, but sometimes a man's walk is as unique as his fingerprints. Gabriel had followed Yusef for weeks in London. His walk was imprinted on Gabriel's memory. The flow of his hips. The line of his back. The way he always seemed to be on the balls of his feet, ready to pounce.

Gabriel tried to remember whether he was left-handed or right-. He pictured him standing in his window, wearing nothing but his briefs, a thick silver watch on his left wrist. *He's right-handed*. If he was trained by the Office, he'd wear his gun on his left hip.

Gabriel increased his pace, closing the distance between them, and drew his Beretta. He pressed the barrel of the gun against Yusef's lower back, then in one quick movement reached beneath his jacket and snatched the gun from the holster on his hip.

Yusef started to swivel.

Gabriel shoved the gun into his back even harder. "Don't move again, or I'll leave a bullet in your spine. And keep walking." Gabriel spoke Hebrew. Yusef stood very still. "Tell your girlfriend to take a walk."

Yusef nodded to the girl; she walked quickly away.

"Move," Gabriel said.

"Where?"

"Down to the beach."

They crossed the Promenade, Yusef leading, Gabriel

behind him, gun pressed against Yusef's kidney. They descended a flight of steps and walked across the beach until the lights of the Promenade grew faint.

"Who are you?"

"Fuck you! Who do you think you are, grabbing me like that?"

"You're lucky I didn't kill you. For all I know you're a member of Tariq's organization. You might have come to Israel to plant a bomb or shoot up a market. I still might kill you unless you tell me who you are."

"You have no right to talk to me like that!"

"Who ran you?"

"Who do you think?"

"Shamron?"

"Very good. Everyone always said you were smart."

"Why?"

"You want to know why, you talk to Shamron. I just did what I was told. But let me tell you one thing. If you ever come near me again, I'll kill you. I don't care who you used to be."

He held out his hand, palm up. Gabriel gave him the gun. He slipped it back into his holster. Then he turned and walked across the darkened beach toward the bright lights of the Promenade.

Lightning flickered over the hills of the Upper Galilee as Gabriel drove along the shore of the lake toward Shamron's villa. Rami waited at the gate. When Gabriel lowered the window, Rami poked his head inside and looked quickly around the interior. "He's on the terrace. Park here. Walk up to the house."

Rami held out his hand.

"You don't actually believe I'd shoot the bastard?"

"Just give me your fucking gun, Allon, or you can't go up to the house."

Gabriel handed over his Beretta and walked up the drive. Lightning exploded over the hills, illuminating the swirling clouds, wind tossing up whitecaps on the surface of the lake. The screams of waterbirds filled the air. He looked up toward the terrace and saw Shamron, lit by the swirling gas lamps.

When Gabriel reached the terrace, he found Shamron in the same position, but instead of looking down at the drive his gaze was fixed on the storm over the mountains. Just then the lightning ceased and the wind died. The lake went still and the birds stopped their screaming. There was not a sound. Only the hiss of Shamron's gas lamps, burning brightly.

Yes, Shamron began, there *was* a real Yusef al-Tawfiki, but he was dead—killed in Shatila, the night of the Phalangist massacre, along with the rest of his family. One of Shamron's agents went into the house after the killing and cleaned out the family's personal papers. The al-Tawfikis had no other relatives in Lebanon. Only an uncle in London—a maternal uncle who had never seen his young nephew. A few days later a boy turns up in a hospital in West Beirut. Gravely wounded, no identification. The doctors ask his name. He tells them his name is Yusef al-Tawfiki.

"How did he get the wound on his back?" Gabriel wondered.

"It was put there by a doctor connected to the Office. The boy was treated at the hospital in West Beirut, and the UN started looking for this mysterious uncle in London. It took them a week to find him. They told him what had happened to the boy. The uncle made arrangements to bring him to England."

He was a child, thought Gabriel: thirteen, fourteen maybe. Where had Shamron found him? How had he trained him? It was too monstrous to contemplate.

Shamron snapped his powerful fingers so loudly that Rami, standing in the drive outside the guardhouse, looked up suddenly.

"Just like that we have an agent in the enemy's camp, a boy whose life has been torn by unimaginable brutality. A boy with fire in his belly, who loathes the Israelis. A boy who will one day become a fighter and take his revenge on the people who butchered his family."

"Remarkable," said Gabriel.

"When he was old enough, Yusef began moving with London's radical Palestinian set. He came to the attention of a talent spotter for Tariq's organization. They vetted him. Clean, or so they thought. They put him to work in their intelligence and planning section. The Office now had an agent inside one of the most dangerous terrorist organizations on earth. He was so valuable his material had the shortest distribution list in the history of the Office: one person, me."

Shamron sat down and gestured toward the empty chair. Gabriel remained standing.

"A few months ago Yusef sent us a fascinating report. There was a rumor sweeping the organization: Tariq had a brain tumor. Tariq was dying. The succession fight was on. Tariq's colonels were jockeying for position. And one other thing: Tariq didn't intend to go quietly. He intended to raise a little hell on earth before he floated off to Paradise. Kill an ambassador or two. Bomb a few airline offices. Maybe shoot down a jetliner."

"So you come to me after Paris. You tell me this sad tale about how the Office can't shoot straight anymore. How the Office couldn't find the Office without a map. Like a fool I agree. And at the same time you whisper into Tariq's ear that I'm back and looking for him. And the game has begun."

"His organization was rigidly compartmentalized. Even with a man on the inside, I knew he was going to be hard to take down. I had to help him make a mistake. I thought if I waved Gabriel Allon in front of him, I could make him angry. I thought I could make him charge, leave himself exposed just long enough for me to plunge a sword into his heart."

"So you send me after Yusef, your own agent. You tell me he's vulnerable to an approach by a woman. It was in his file. I watch him for two days, he's with two different women. Were they Office too?"

"They were Yusef's girls. Yusef never had much trouble finding women on his own."

"I ask Jacqueline to help me. It's supposed to be a quick job. But Yusef takes an interest in her. Yusef wants to keep seeing her. I tell you to pull her out. But you force me to keep her in."

Shamron folded his arms, set his jaw. Clearly he wanted to see how much of it Gabriel had figured out on his own.

"Yusef tells his people he thinks he's being watched. He also tells them about a French girl he's been seeing. He tells them he thinks she might be an Israeli agent. Tariq is ecstatic. Tariq has been waiting for this. He tells Yusef to recruit the girl under false pretenses for a mission. They know Jacqueline will bite, because they know she's Office."

"Bravo, Gabriel."

"Did she know?"

"Jacqueline?"

"Yes, Jacqueline! Did she know the truth?"

"Of course not. She's in love with you. She would never have agreed to deceive you."

"Why didn't you just tell me the truth?"

"Tell me something, Gabriel. If I had come to Cornwall and asked you to come out of retirement to serve as bait for Tariq, would you actually have done it? Of course not."

"So you put my life on the line. And Jacqueline's!"

"I'm sorry about what happened in New York. It went much further than I ever anticipated."

"But he was already dying. Why didn't you just let the tumor kill Tariq?"

"Because his organization would have carried on without him. It would have been more dangerous and unpredictable than before. And because *my* organization was in shambles. The Office needed a coup to restore the confidence of the government and the people of Israel."

"What if the government and the people found out exactly how you pulled off this great coup?"

"The prime minister knows everything."

"And the people?"

"Don't get any ideas about running to the newspapers."

"Why? Because I might end up like Benjamin Stone?"

Shamron said nothing.

Gabriel shook his head. "You'd do it, wouldn't you? You'd kill me too if I got in your way. And you wonder why you can't sleep at night."

"Someone has to do these things, Gabriel! If not me, who? If our enemies think the Office is weak, then our enemies will test us. They might kill a few Jews whenever they felt like it. The Syrians might come rolling out of those hills again and try to drive us into the sea. Another Hitler might get the idea that he can exterminate my people while the world stands by and does nothing. I may embarrass you from time to time. I may use methods that you find distasteful, but secretly you're glad I'm here. It helps *you* sleep at night."

"Why?" said Gabriel. "Why lie to me after all these years? Why not play it straight? Why engage in such an elaborate deception?"

Shamron managed a weak smile. "Did I ever tell you about the night we kidnapped Eichmann?"

"I've heard the story a hundred times."

"Never the whole story, though." Shamron closed his eyes and winced slightly, as if the memory were painful. "We knew the bastard rode the same bus home every night. All we had to do was grab him as he stepped off. We'd practiced it a hundred times. During the drills I was able to perform the snatch in twelve seconds. But that night, as I climbed out of the car, I tripped. Eichmann nearly got away from us because I tripped. Do you know why I tripped, Gabriel? I tripped because I had forgotten to tie my shoelaces. I got him of course. But I learned a valuable lesson that night. Leave absolutely nothing to chance."

"So it was no accident Yusef walked past my table to-night in Tel Aviv?" Gabriel asked. "You sent him there so I would see him. You wanted me to know the truth."

Shamron inclined his head a fraction of an inch. Indeed.

It was four o'clock in the morning by the time Gabriel returned to the flat in Jerusalem. On the table was a large Office envelope. Inside were three smaller packets: one containing an airline ticket for the morning flight to London, another containing three passports of different nationalities, and a third filled with American dollars and British pounds. Gabriel placed the smaller envelopes in the larger one and carried it into the bedroom, where he packed his remaining possessions into his rucksack. The flight wasn't for another five hours. He thought about sleeping, knew he couldn't. He thought about driving up to Herzliya. *Jacqueline.* None of it had been real. Only Jacqueline. He went into the kitchen and made coffee. Then he stepped out onto the balcony and waited for dawn.

# Epilogue

Something made Peel wake up. He rolled onto his side, snatched the torch from his bedside table, and shone it at his watch: 3:15 A.M. He switched off the light and lay awake in the darkness, listening to the wind moaning in the eaves and his mother and Derek quietly quarreling in the room next door.

He could hear only snatches of their conversation, so he closed his eyes, remembering something about the blind hearing better than the sighted. "Having trouble with the new play," Derek was saying. "Can't seem to find my way into the first act . . . hard with a child in the house . . . back to London to be with his father . . . time alone together . . . lovers again . . ." Peel squeezed his eyes tightly, refusing to permit the tears to escape onto his cheeks.

He was about to cover his ears with his pillow when he heard a sound outside on the quay: a small car, rattling like an oxcart with a broken wheel. He sat, threw off his blankets, placed his feet on the cold wood floor. He carried his torch to the window and looked out: a single red taillight, floating along the quay toward the oyster farm.

The car vanished into the trees, then appeared a moment later, only now Peel was staring directly into the headlights. It was an MG, and it was stopping in front of the old foreman's cottage. Peel raised his torch, aimed it at the car, and flashed the light twice. The lights of the MG winked back. Then the engine died, and the lights went dark.

Peel climbed back into bed and pulled his blankets beneath his chin. Derek and his mother were still quarreling, but he didn't really care. The stranger was back in Port Navas. Peel closed his eyes and soon was asleep.

# ACKNOWLEDGMENTS

This book could not have been written without the generous assistance of David Bull. He truly is one of the world's finest art restorers, and I was privileged to spend many enjoyable hours in his company. He gave freely of his time and expertise, and allowed me to wander through his studio and through his memories as well. For that I am eternally grateful. A special thanks to David's talented wife, Teresa Longyear; to Lucy Bisognano, formerly of the National Gallery conservation staff, who tried to teach me the basics of X-ray analysis; and to Maxwell Anderson, director of the Whitney Museum of American Art, for his friendship and assistance. It goes without saying that they bear no responsibility for errors, omissions, or dramatic license.

Wolf Blitzer, a friend and colleague from my days at CNN, generously helped fill in some blanks in my research on the Israeli intelligence community. Louis Toscano, author of *Triple Cross,* a groundbreaking book on the Vanunu affair, read my manuscript and offered his keen insights. Glenn Whidden answered all my questions on the art of audio surveillance, as did a former head of the CIA's Office of Technical Services.

Ion Trewin, the managing director of Weidenfeld & Nicolson in London, read my manuscript and, as always, offered wise counsel. Andrew Neil opened his home to us and shared some of his remarkable experiences in the world of London newspaper publishing. Ernie Lyles answered all my questions on semi-automatic hand-guns and made me a decent shot with a Glock and a Browning.

A special thanks to Peter and Paula White for an enchanting week in West Cornwall and a memorable boat trip up Helford Passage. Also, to the staffs of the venerable London art supplies shop L. Cornelissen & Son and the Hotel Queen Elizabeth in Montreal. And to Phyllis and Bernard Jacob, for their love, support, and a day roaming the streets of Brooklyn that I will never forget.

Among the dozens of nonfiction books I consulted while preparing this manuscript, several proved particularly helpful: *Every Spy a Prince*, by Dan Raviv and Yossi Melman; *Gideon's Spies*, by Gordon Thomas; *Israel: A History* and *The Holocaust: A History of the Jews of Europe During the Second World War*, by Martin Gilbert; *The Gun and the Olive Branch*, by David Hirst; *By Way of Deception*, by Victor Ostrovsky and Clair Hoy; *The Hit Team*, by David B. Tinnin with Dag Christensen; *My Home, My Land*, by Abu Iyad; *The Quest for the Red Prince*, by Michael Bar-Zohar and Eitan Haber; *The Palestinians*, by Jonathan Dimbleby; *Arafat*, by Alan Hart;

and *The Holocaust and the Jews of Marseille*, by Donna
F. Ryan.

Finally, to the talented group of professionals at Random House and Penguin-Putnam. And of course none of this would have been possible without my wife, Jamie Gangel, and my children, Lily and Nicholas.

Please read on for an excerpt from
Daniel Silva's exciting novel

# THE
# SECRET SERVANT

Available from Signet

# AMSTERDAM

It was Professor Solomon Rosner who sounded the first alarm, though his name would never be linked to the affair except in the secure rooms of a drab office building in downtown Tel Aviv. Gabriel Allon, the legendary but wayward son of Israeli Intelligence, would later observe that Rosner was the first asset in the annals of Office history to have proven more useful to them dead than alive. Those who overheard the remark found it uncharacteristically callous but in keeping with the bleak mood that by then had settled over them all.

The backdrop for Rosner's demise was not Israel, where violent death occurs all too frequently, but the normally tranquil quarter of Amsterdam known as the Old Side. The date was the first Friday in December, and the weather was more suited to early spring than to the last days of autumn. It was a day to engage in what the Dutch so fondly refer to as *gezelligheid*, the pursuit of small pleasures: an aimless stroll through the flower stalls of the Bloemenmarkt, a lager or two in a good bar in the Rembrandtplein, or, for those so inclined, a bit of fine cannabis in the brown coffeehouses of the Haarlemmerstraat. Leave the fretting and the fighting to the hated Americans, stately old Amsterdam murmured that golden late-autumn afternoon. Today we give thanks for having been born blameless and Dutch.

Solomon Rosner did not share the sentiments of his countrymen, but then he seldom did. Though he earned a living as a professor of sociology at the University of Amsterdam, it was Rosner's Center for European Security Studies that occupied the lion's share of his time. His legion of detractors saw evidence of deception in the name, for Rosner served not only as the center's director but was its only scholar in residence. Despite those obvious shortcomings, the center had managed to produce a steady stream of authoritative reports and articles detailing the threat posed to the Netherlands by the rise of militant Islam within its borders. Rosner's last book, *The Islamic Conquest of the West*, had argued that Holland was now under a sustained and systematic assault by jihadist Islam. The goal of this assault, he maintained, was to colonize the Netherlands and turn it into a majority Muslim state, where, in the not too distant future, Islamic law, or *sharia*, would reign supreme. The terrorists and the colonizers were two sides of the same coin, he warned, and unless the government took immediate and drastic action, everything the free-thinking Dutch held dear would soon be swept away.

The Dutch literary press had been predictably appalled. Hysteria, said one reviewer. Racist claptrap, said another. More than one took pains to note that the views expressed in the book were all the more odious given the fact that Rosner's grandparents had been rounded up with a hundred thousand other Dutch Jews and sent off to the gas chambers at Auschwitz. All agreed that what the situation required was not hateful rhetoric like Rosner's but tolerance and dialogue. Rosner stood steadfast in the face of the withering criticism, adopting what one commentator described as the posture of a man with his finger wedged firmly in the dike. Tolerance and dialogue by all means, Rosner responded, but not capitulation. "We Dutch need to put down our Heinekens and hash pipes and wake up," he snapped during an interview on Dutch television. "Otherwise we're going to lose our country."

The book and surrounding controversy had made Rosner the most vilified and, in some quarters, celebrated man in the country. It had also placed him squarely in the sights of Holland's homegrown Islamic extremists. Jihadist Web sites, which Rosner monitored more closely than even the Dutch police did, burned with sacred rage over the book, and more than one forecast his imminent execution. An imam in the neighborhood known as the Oud West instructed his flock that "Rosner the Jew must be dealt with harshly" and pleaded for a martyr to step forward and do the job. The feckless Dutch interior minister had responded by proposing that Rosner go into hiding, an idea Rosner vigorously refused. He then supplied the minister with a list of ten radicals he regarded as potential assassins. The minister accepted the list without question, for he knew that Rosner's sources inside Holland's extremist fringe were in most cases far better than those of the Dutch security services.

At noon on that Friday in December, Rosner was hunched over his computer in the second-floor office of his canal house at Groenburgwal 2A. The house, like Rosner himself, was stubby and wide, and it tilted forward at a precarious angle, which some of the neighbors saw as fitting, given the political views of its occupant. Its one serious drawback was location, for it stood not fifty yards from the bell tower of the Zuiderkirk church. The bells tolled mercilessly each day, beginning at the stroke of noon and ending forty-five minutes later. Rosner, sensitive to interruptions and unwanted noise, had been waging a personal jihad against them for years. Classical music, white-noise machines, soundproof headphones—all had proven useless in the face of the onslaught. Sometimes he wondered why the bells were rung at all. The old church had long ago been turned into a government housing office—a fact that Rosner, a man of considerable faith, saw as a fitting symbol of the Dutch morass. Confronted by an enemy of infinite religious zeal, the secular Dutch had turned their churches into bureaus of the welfare state. *A church without faithful*, thought Rosner, *in a city without God*.

At ten minutes past twelve, he heard a faint knock

and looked up to find Sophie Vanderhaus leaning against the doorjamb with a batch of files clutched to her breast. A former student of Rosner's, she had come to work for him after completing a graduate degree on the impact of the Holocaust on postwar Dutch society. She was part secretary and research assistant, part nursemaid and surrogate daughter. She kept his office in order and typed the final drafts of all his reports and articles. The minder of his impossible schedule, she tended to his appalling personal finances. She even saw to his laundry and made certain he remembered to eat. Earlier that morning, she had informed him that she was planning to spend a week in Saint-Maarten over the New Year. Rosner, upon hearing the news, had fallen into a profound depression.

"You have an interview with *De Telegraaf* in an hour," she said. "Maybe you should have something to eat and focus your thoughts."

"Are you suggesting my thoughts lack focus, Sophie?"

"I'm suggesting nothing of the sort. It's just that you've been working on that article since five thirty this morning. You need something more than coffee in your stomach."

"It's not that dreadful reporter who called me a Nazi last year?"

"Do you really think I'd let her near you again?" She entered the office and started straightening his desk. "After the interview with *De Telegraaf*, you go to the NOS studios for an appearance on Radio One. It's a call-in program, so it's sure to be lively. Do try not to make any more enemies, Professor Rosner. It's getting harder and harder to keep track of them all."

"I'll try to behave myself, but I'm afraid my forbearance is now gone forever."

She peered into his coffee cup and pulled a sour face. "Why do you insist on putting out your cigarettes in your coffee?"

"My ashtray was full."

"Try emptying it from time to time." She poured the contents of the ashtray into his rubbish bin and removed the plastic liner. "And don't forget you have the forum this evening at the university."

Rosner frowned. He was not looking forward to the forum. One of the other panelists was the leader of the European Muslim Association, a group that campaigned openly for the imposition of *sharia* in Europe and the destruction of the State of Israel. It promised to be a deeply unpleasant evening.

"I'm afraid I'm coming down with a sudden case of leprosy," he said.

"They'll insist that you come anyway. You're the star of the show."

He stood and stretched his back. "I think I'll go to Café de Doelen for a coffee and something to eat. Why don't you have the reporter from *De Telegraaf* meet me there?"

"Do you really think that's wise, Professor?"

It was common knowledge in Amsterdam that the famous café on the Staalstraat was his favorite haunt.

And Rosner was hardly inconspicuous. Indeed, with his shock of white hair and rumpled tweed wardrobe, he was one of the most recognizable figures in Holland. The geniuses in the Dutch police had once suggested he utilize some crude disguise while in public—an idea Rosner had likened to putting a hat and a false mustache on a hippopotamus and calling it a Dutchman.

"I haven't been to the Doelen in months."

"That doesn't mean it's any safer."

"I can't live my life as a prisoner forever, Sophie"—he gestured toward the window—"especially on a day like today. Wait until the last possible minute before you tell the reporter from *De Telegraaf* where I am. That will give me a jump on the jihadists."

"That isn't funny, Professor." She could see there was no talking him out of it. She handed him his mobile phone. "At least take this so you can call me in an emergency."

Rosner slipped the phone into his pocket and headed downstairs. In the entry hall, he pulled on his coat and trademark silk scarf and stepped outside. To his left rose the spire of the Zuiderkirk; to his right, fifty yards along a narrow canal lined with small craft, stood a wooden double drawbridge. The Groenburgwal was a quiet street for the Old Side: no bars or cafés, only a single small hotel that never seemed to have more than a handful of guests. Directly opposite Rosner's house was the street's only eyesore: a modern tenement block with a lavender-and-lime-pastel exterior. A trio of housepainters dressed in smudged white coveralls was squatting outside the building in a patch of sunlight.

Rosner glanced at the three faces, committing each to memory, before setting off in the direction of the drawbridge. When a sudden gust of wind stirred the bare tree limbs along the embankment, he paused for a moment to bind his scarf more tightly around his neck and watch a plump Vermeer cloud drift slowly overhead. It was then that he noticed one of the painters walking parallel to him along the opposite side of the canal. Short dark hair, a high flat forehead, a heavy brow over small eyes. Rosner, connoisseur of immigrant faces, judged him to be a Moroccan from the Rif Mountains. They arrived at the drawbridge simultaneously. Rosner paused again, this time to light a cigarette he did not want, and watched with relief as the man turned to the left. When the man disappeared round the next corner, Rosner headed in the opposite direction toward the Doelen.

He took his time making his way down the Staalstraat, now dawdling at the window of his favorite pastry shop to gaze at that day's offerings, now sidestepping to avoid being run down by a pretty girl on a bicycle, now pausing to accept a few words of encouragement from a ruddy-faced admirer. He was about to step through the entrance of the café when he felt a tug at his coat sleeve. In the few remaining seconds he had left to live, he would be tormented by the absurd thought that he might have prevented his own murder had he resisted the impulse to turn around. But he did turn around, because that is what one does on a glorious December afternoon in Amsterdam, when one is summoned in the street by a stranger.

He saw the gun only in the abstract. In the narrow street the shots reverberated like cannon fire. He collapsed onto the cobblestones and watched helplessly as his killer drew a long knife from inside his coveralls. The slaughter was ritual, just as the imams had decreed it should be. No one intervened—hardly surprising, thought Rosner, for intervention would have been intolerant—and no one thought to comfort him as he lay dying. Only the bells spoke to him. *A church without faithful*, they seemed to be saying, *in a city without God*.

From #1 *New York Times*
bestselling author
# DANIEL SILVA

## The Gabriel Allon series

*The Kill Artist*
*The English Assassin*
*The Confessor*
*A Death in Vienna*
*Prince of Fire*
*The Messenger*
*The Secret Servant*
*Moscow Rules*
*The Defector*
*The Rembrandt Affair*

"Allon is Israel's Jack Bauer…
Thrill factor: Five stars."
—*USA Today*

s0051